*Beloved authors
Cait London and Anne McAllister
cordially invite you
to the Western weddings
of two commitment-shy cowboys
and the women who teach them
a thing or two about true love....*

Guest
"A new love story
from Cait London guarantees
hours of reading pleasure."
—*Romantic Times Magazine*

Table 1
The Loving Season

Guest
"Anne McAllister
sets our hearts beating faster..."
—*Romantic Times Magazine*

Table 2
Cowboys Don't Cry

CAIT LONDON,

whom *Affaire de Coeur* hails as a "tremendous Western romance writer," is an award-winning and national bestselling author with millions of copies of her books in print worldwide. The winner of *Romantic Times Magazine*'s Career Achievement and Reviewer's Choice awards, Cait also writes historical romance. She's written nearly thirty contemporary romance novels for Silhouette Books.

The mother of three daughters, Cait lives in the Missouri Ozarks.

ANNE McALLISTER

RITA-Award-winning author Anne McAllister has written forty-five books for Silhouette Desire and Special Edition, Harlequin Presents and American Romance in the past fifteen years. She likes lone-wolf heroes—and heroines who can make them reconsider just how alone they really want to be. Drop Anne a line at P.O. Box 3904, Bozeman, Montana 59772 (SASE appreciated). She'd love to hear from you.

CAIT LONDON
ANNE McALLISTER

DO YOU TAKE THIS COWBOY?

Published by Silhouette Books
America's Publisher of Contemporary Romance

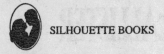

SILHOUETTE BOOKS

Recycled Paper · Recycled Paper

ISBN 0-373-21708-0

by Request

DO YOU TAKE THIS COWBOY?

Copyright © 2000 by Harlequin Books S.A.

The publisher acknowledges the copyright holders of the individual works as follows:

THE LOVING SEASON
Copyright © 1989 by Lois Kleinsasser

COWBOYS DON'T CRY
Copyright © 1995 by Barbara Schenck

Visit Silhouette at www.eHarlequin.com

Printed in U.S.A.

CONTENTS

Dear Reader,

The Loving Season, my first book for Silhouette, in 1989, remains a favorite; it represents a valued benchmark in my career and life. I'd already written other books for another publisher, and my first single-title historical under another pseudonym was about to be launched. *The Loving Season* marks a time in my life when I wrote for two publishers, worked a day job and was the single mother of three daughters. I continued on that schedule for many years, and *The Loving Season* spun off into *Angel vs. MacLean* and then *The Daddy Candidate,* which remains ever popular with readers for its humor and warmth. In *The Loving Season,* neither protagonist is expecting love, and it was sheer delight to have them find it amid chili-making, bagpipe playing, helicopter flying and dog sledding.

I hope you enjoy Diana and Mac's story, *The Loving Season,* and that we have many more years together.

Enjoy!

Cait London

THE LOVING SEASON
Cait London

For all the good guys,
with their tender hearts,
and especially for Donna

One

The whine of bagpipes floated on the frigid night wind as Diana walked toward the lights of a farmhouse. Located just off the deserted Colorado highway, the large two-story house loomed amid sprawling pastures. At eleven o'clock on Halloween night, the house looked as eerie and foreboding as Count Dracula's castle. The surrounding buildings looked capable of holding a crowd of zombies each, and the weathered barn seemed the perfect hiding place for a mummy.

"A mix-up in reservation," she muttered. She glanced back at her station wagon parked at the gate to the MacLean ranch. Nestled in the shadows of a tall aspen, the car looked safer than she felt.

The Rayfield Inn clerk had thoroughly apologized for mistakenly placing her reservation for December. "Sure am sorry, lady. We're booked up solid this week. But let me make a call—Old Mac puts up our leftovers once in a while. It's miles to the next town, and chances are they're booked up, too. It's hunting season, you know.''

Diana glanced at the rugged San Juan mountains, silhouetted against the clear night sky. A gust of icy wind swept up her neck, whipping her short hair about her face. The cold air penetrated her green sweater and blue jeans, and she shivered. Stuffing her freezing hands into the pockets of her denim jacket, she wondered who slept in her nice warm room in the inn.

Diana had wanted quiet and time to weigh her life and her future, and the travel brochure for Benevolence's only bed-and-breakfast inn had made the tiny town seem ideal. Situated up in the mountains and overlooking the upper Rio Grande river, Benevolence had been deserted by miners at the turn of the century and now catered to those who craved fresh air and majestic scenery.

I'm a forty-two-year-old orphan, she thought darkly. Twenty years as a housewife and supportive mate had ended with the crushing discovery of her husband, Alex's, frequent infidelity. She had scrambled out of the marriage with as much sanity and dignity as she could manage. When the divorce was final, her fears had eased a little. With careful managing, she could save enough of the child support allotments to provide for her two sons' future college expenses.

Having no employable skills had left her confidence shaken and her financial survival questionable. But she'd snagged a job that offered a small paycheck *and* a training period. Teaching clients how to run several different software programs began as part-time work, then bloomed into a well-paying learning experience. Taking a deep breath, Diana had waded through selling the huge family house, giving Alex his half and buying a modest, more practical home.

Diana had run on nothing but the will to survive, each day testing her mental and physical abilities. Finally the day came when she realized how utterly dry she felt inside. She'd taken a hard look at her modest savings, and with the instincts of a bird let out of a cage, she'd decided to fly.

Quitting her job had been difficult, but the manager was also a divorcée, and she had understood. With Rick and Blaine both away at college, Diana leased her home for a year and packed the bare necessities into her car. For the first time, she was going to find what she really wanted out of her life. Reserving a room for a week was her first step. She'd worry about the second step after resting; she'd earned that privilege, after all.

Now, two years after the divorce, Diana—out on her own at last—was a bed-and-breakfast "leftover."

"Okay, Diana, admit it," she coached herself as she had in the recent past. "You're tired and you're cold and you're peeved about some blasted hunter snoring in your room. Part of being an independent woman is recognizing what you feel."

Her mouth tightened as a wave of bitterness swept over her. But then, divorce did that to a person, she decided. It left sharp edges.

As she neared the white farmhouse, she heard the sound of a dog howling to the music of the bagpipes. Hereford cattle stirred in the barn lot, lowing as she passed. A bulky shadow swayed beside the fence, and Diana stopped to stare at a large buffalo.

Taking a deep breath, she hurried to the house, marched up the wooden steps and across the wide porch to the front door. "Whoever is playing that…instrument, needs lessons," she muttered as she jabbed at the doorbell.

The shrill sound of the ancient buzzer caused her to jump back. Instantly the bagpipes stilled and a dog began barking excitedly. Oh, great, Diana thought, reminded of the sharp teeth of the Hound of the Baskervilles.

The porch light snapped on, and she blinked, surprised. The door opened, and the fiercest man she had ever seen stepped out, thrusting an overflowing bowl of candy at her. Dressed in an open flannel shirt and worn jeans, he glared down at her from his six-foot-plus height. The wind whipped his slightly long dark hair around his face. Bagpipes were tucked under his arm, wheezing their last throes. "A little old for trick-or-treating, aren't you?" he asked in a voice that made her think of a grizzly bear disturbed while hibernating.

She tilted her head back to stare at his very dark eyes. She didn't like his imperious tone, not a bit. Alex had used it too many times—whenever he'd told her what to do. Right now, she felt bone-tired and was in no mood for a dominating male. "I am not trick-or-treating."

Before she could continue, a massive husky ran out of the house and stopped before her. Legs wide apart and hackles raised, it regarded her closely. Diana decided it was male when it growled at her, baring huge teeth. His protectiveness seemed to her to be unnecessary, considering how tall and muscular his master was.

They were a matched set, Diana thought. Two males disturbed in their castle, defending their territory from an encroaching female.

"Quiet, Red," the man ordered roughly. The dog calmed instantly. "Car trouble, then," the man snapped, turning to look at the road that led to his ranch. "Women. They should stay home where they belong."

He glanced down at the husky, who was padding around Diana's legs, sniffing her curiously. "Red isn't used to perfume," he explained. "Get back, Red."

Diana could feel the cords in her neck tighten with anger at the man's arrogance. She hadn't driven practically nonstop from Missouri just to be at the mercy of someone who shared her ex-husband's chauvinistic views!

"What's the problem? Radiator? Run out of gas?" he rattled off as he placed the candy dish back inside the house.

Diana took a deep breath, trying to rein in the temper she'd discovered she had during the divorce. "The Rayfield Inn sent me," she stated through gritted teeth. "The clerk called?"

He answered with a nod. His eyes ran down her petite body, lingering on the curves. "I didn't know Ray would send me a woman." He took a deep weary breath, as though he'd baby-sat every woman from Colorado to Wyoming and was deeply tired of the entire female race.

His jaw, too square for him to be handsome, jutted out pugnaciously. "I'm fixing chili for a cook-off tomorrow. I don't have time to make you comfortable. You'll have to do that yourself. Get in here.''

Diana's temper began to send out big red warning flares. Caveman-style hospitality, she thought. ''I wouldn't think of disturbing you,'' she stated icily. ''After meeting you, I really don't think this is a very good idea, after all.''

The man's bushy brows rose. ''Well now, spitfire, don't go getting snooty. If you're looking for a bed, it's my house or Wyoming.''

She glared up at him, all six-foot-plus of male superiority. She'd rather freeze to death on the Colorado mesas than ask him for help. ''I'm so sorry I interrupted your symphony. Thank you for the invitation, but no thanks.''

''If you're thinking about sleeping in your car, forget it. It's damned cold and dangerous for a little thing like you.''

Diana took a deep breath, counting silently to ten to steady her rising anger. ''I am quite able to take care of myself, Mr. MacLean.''

She pivoted, took one step and felt his big hand latch on to her belt. He pulled her into his house as easily as if she were a child.

Diana's carefully checked temper erupted. The door clicked shut just as her open hand met his hard cheek. ''How dare you?'' she exclaimed, stepping back. Her anger swept over her like a Colorado forest fire fanned by a high wind.

He tossed the bagpipes to a battered couch. His eyes blazed. ''Lady, I dare plenty when some half-grown female thinks she can take me on.''

His mouth tightened into a grim line, and he looked at her from head to toe. His hard gaze seemed to penetrate her thick winter clothes and note her thinness underneath. "You barely outweigh Red. You don't look like you've got enough fight left in you to start anything."

Pride kept Diana from rubbing her burning palm. She still felt the pain of contact right up to her shoulder. Stunned, she realized she'd never hit another person in her life. She felt her knees go weak and her skin prickle. Why in heaven's name had she slapped him? He was so big, she barely reached his shoulder. "Keep your hands off me," she warned, spacing the words carefully.

"You're nothing but skin and bone. When I put my hands on a woman, I like something soft and warm."

Diana glared at the hardest face she had ever seen. Lines crossed his forehead, creasing the deeply tanned skin. His hair was as black as midnight but shot by streaks of white at the temples. His deep-set eyes glittered menacingly above prominent cheekbones. But when he scratched his muscular chest, which was covered by dark hair, she felt something within her stir.

He pointed at the telephone, almost buried under a stack of sportsmen's magazines. "There's the phone. Find someplace else, if you can. Good luck."

He turned and walked off, presenting Diana with a view of his broad back. She allowed her eyes to wander down to his lean hips and long legs, then to his feet. He wore a red sock and a green sock. Both heels were worn through.

Diana took a deep breath and hugged herself. Uneasy, she glanced away from the tattered hole on his jeans, which revealed the back of his muscular thigh. Maybe he needed money.

The husky stared up at her. "Shoo!" Diana whispered. "Go away."

He growled ominously just as a large white cat strolled into the room. While the cat twisted around and rubbed against Diana's ankles, the massive dog seemed to wither. He stared warily at the feline as he backed away a foot.

When the cat began to walk, tail held high, toward the dog, the beast fled after his master as though his life were in danger.

"Nice kitty. Stay here, kitty," Diana cooed. "I bet you're female." She drew the inn's telephone number from her pocket and dialed. After five rings, a sleepy voice answered, "Rayfield Inn."

When Diana explained that "Old Mac" wasn't exactly hospitable and asked for other recommendations, the clerk chuckled. "Nope. None. You'll have to make do."

"'Mac is a good old boy,'" she intoned, repeating the clerk's description as she hung up.

"I can't imagine staying a night, let alone a week," Diana muttered, glancing around at the battered furniture. Huge hunting bows and quivers of arrows hung on the oak paneling. A cabinet of assorted rifles stood in a disheveled corner. A variety of tattered scatter rugs covered the worn carpeting. Beneath a curtainless window, a sheet covered an angular object.

She picked up a magazine designed for cattlemen and read the address label: Mac MacLean, Rural Route, Benevolence, Colorado. She closed her eyes, thinking of her modest home in southwest Missouri—

her safe home, free from black-eyed giants and bag-pipes.

But Missouri also held painful memories and friends torn between Alex and herself. She had launched this trip with a desperate determination to slug it out with her past and find her future, to meet herself as a woman. She had to survive. *She had to.*

A ripple of sheer fatigue almost sent her to the overstuffed couch. Oh, how she'd love to crawl under that crocheted afghan and sleep.

The toe of her left sneaker touched something, and she glanced down. Mac MacLean's work-worn boots reminded her of the man's ungroomed appearance.

Tossing the magazine onto the cluttered coffee table, she glanced longingly at the huge black wood-burning stove placed against one wall. A blazing fire crackled and lured her a step nearer. "I'd be safer in the station wagon, freezing. No telling what type of person this MacLean is."

Mac didn't need any half-pint female making him feel like a heel, he decided as he stalked back into the living room. He jammed his fists on his waist and faced her, not bothering to temper his belligerence. "This chili cook-off is important to me. Last year Fred Donaldson won, but this year I want the trophy. Got it?" He scowled at her. "It takes all night to make my chili recipe. Can't leave it for a minute. Did you find a place to stay?"

Looking at her big brown eyes, Mac felt himself go all weak. Who would she call? She had a stranded look about her, and there was something so soft about her pale face that touched him.

She'd slapped him hard, but Mac had seen the undeniable fear widen her eyes…as though she had expected him to return the blow. He'd seen enough of the wounded to recognize this woman as a refugee from pain.

"What's your name?" he asked roughly, to cover the emotions churning within him. The woman looked as though she were glued together by sheer determination and not much else, but he had to admit she had plenty of spirit. Right now, she stood ramrod straight, her eyes meeting his defiantly.

"Diana Phillips," she answered.

Mac liked the low wispy sound of her voice. It reminded him of the mountain wind sweeping through pine needles. He stared at her curiously. She had a classy look, he decided, wondering suddenly how many women would look as good without makeup. Her short dark brown hair glistened beneath the overhead light. Her lips, although pressed together firmly, still showed their soft full shape. But it was her eyes that tore at him. They were so wary beneath layers of long straight black lashes.

She looked like a stray, Mac decided finally. And he had always taken care of strays.

"Diana," he repeated gently, watching her small teeth tug at her bottom lip. "Di."

For just a second, her brown eyes turned almost black. "I detest that name, Mr. MacLean," she declared passionately. "I'm a little old for nicknames."

"Diana," he said carefully, meeting her on her own territory. "You're wearing a big chip on that little shoulder."

She glared at him for just a second, then turned her head to look out at the cold night. She's skittery as a colt, Mac thought. The urge to pick her up and hold her was so strong he took a step toward her. He saw her small body tense. "I'll take care of you," he whispered huskily. He was glad then that he ran his ranch with the help of neighbors and highschool boys. With no one else around, he was the only one available to help her.

He'd ached for a woman's pain before, had held her as her life slipped away... He swallowed hard, forcing the past behind him.

Diana looked up at him. "I don't need your help, Mr. MacLean."

What the hell, Mac decided instantly. He had the extra room; it wouldn't matter if he took a few minutes to make her comfortable. The chili cook-off was important to him, but he'd lost to Donaldson before. Diana needed him now, and he wasn't letting her escape into the cold night.

Appointing himself her protector, Mac crossed his arms in front of his chest. Every woman deserved her white knight, and he decided to be Diana's.

"I must be going, Mr. MacLean. Thank you for the telephone."

She'd walk out his door if he didn't act soon. "Call me Mac, but skip the MacLean," he ordered gently. "Look, I've been thinking. If you'll follow my directions *exactly*, I'll let you finish browning the meat for my chili. While you're doing that, I'll clear out the spare room and get your things from the car."

She hesitated. "I'm not a cook, Mr.—"

"Mac—most people call me Mac." He could feel her trying to get away from him. And he couldn't allow that. Strays often hurt themselves, and he was certain that would happen to her; she looked as if she bore the weight of the world on her shoulders.

"Listen. I've cut my own prime beefsteak just right for chili. It's browning in the skillet now. All you have to do is stir it up once in a while."

"No," she repeated sharply, buttoning up her jacket to the neck. "I need a room, not sympathy. But thank you for the offer."

Then he knew. She was damned independent and wouldn't give an inch unless she could give him something substantial back.

Frustrated, he pushed his fingers through his hair. "Okay, then what about cleaning up the kitchen and the spare room…when you're rested?"

When he caught the flicker of interest in her eyes, he continued, "What I said about clearing the room out, I meant. I've been using it for storage. You can change the sheets and whatnot."

"What about your chili?"

"It'll keep." Mac didn't hesitate; he had snared her, and he intended to keep her safe, if only for the night.

He sat and put on his boots. Standing up, he saw Diana taking in the length of him. He'd never seen such wounded eyes on a grown woman. How old was she? Twenty? Thirty-five?

"That's right. I'm a big hombre—it runs in the family," he murmured gently. He reached out his hand slowly, taking care not to alarm her. "I'll need your keys. You can hold my house for ransom."

"I can bring my bags in myself…if I decide to stay."

"I've got the room, and I could use some help cleaning up." Testing her, he held his hand steady, palm up. Come on, he coaxed her silently. You have to trust someone.

She stared at him, trying to read his expression, then carefully extracted her keys from her jeans. She dropped them into his palm, and he noted the slender pale hands with their perfect nails. Soft hands, he thought....

Shoot. He always was a pushover where strays were concerned.

He grabbed his shearling coat and called for Red. Walking out the door, he said, "See you in a little bit." He needed the brisk walk in the cold air to think.

Outside, the frigid wind chilled his nostrils and throat as he remembered her tense face. He scowled. Was she married?

He decided then to keep her—if he could.

"Keep her," he murmured, slightly surprised at his thoughts. He chuckled. It was ridiculous. This woman couldn't be added to his menagerie. Diana didn't fit in with the owls with broken wings and the motherless fawn. True, he wanted to hold her and protect her, as he did with the hurt animals he'd found. Then he remembered the curves beneath her clothes....

He shook his head to clear it. "Oh hell, she needs help, that's all."

He drove her white station wagon, coated with road dirt, to the house and brought her luggage in. Tucking Diana beneath his wing might take some doing because of her independent streak. But she'd trusted him with her keys, and that was a first step.

He had to keep her, somehow.

Diana took a deep breath and walked into Mac's kitchen. She would not owe him...or any man, ever.

She rubbed her palm against her thigh, remembering the hard slap. She closed her eyes. She'd never raised her hand in anger to anyone. Yet tonight, she'd let her buried fury explode against a stranger? Her reaction had been savage, impulsive. But then, Mac MacLean had the look of the untamed.

She took off her jacket and tossed it over an aged wooden chair. Rolling up her sweater sleeves, she surveyed the disaster. The old enamel sink had seen better days and was filled with an assortment of battered pots and dishes. An apartment-size electric stove, heaped with another stack of pans, stood in one corner. An ancient wood stove dominated the small kitchen. Shiny and black, trimmed with white enamel, the antique held a blazing fire.

On the table, Mac had carefully lined up his spices and cans of tomatoes. Diced onions and garlic were scattered across a wooden block. A scrubbed stockpot, filled with cooked red beans, stood next to a huge black skillet. Apparently, between blowing his bagpipe at odd hours and handing out candy, Mac had been carefully cooking his prizewinning chili.

Diana glanced at the iron skillet and knew that only a man the size of Mac could possibly lift it with one hand. She thought of his size, of the dark hair swirling over his broad chest, and shivered.

There was something about Mac that she responded to, and that frightened her deeply. She'd lost twenty years. What were the rules of the man-woman game now?

Diana stared into the night beyond the kitchen window. Wide-eyed and innocent at twenty, she had married Alex with all the bright hopes of a bride. Painful memories now wrapped around her, and Diana heard an anguished sob that was her own.

She had to survive—to place the pain behind her and seek the flow of the rest of her life.

The cat rubbed against her legs, and Diana reached down to scratch her ears. "I like you, kid. Stay by me when that monster of a dog comes back, will you?"

The animal purred and rubbed harder, then jumped onto a chair and looked at her with unblinking yellow eyes.

Taking a deep breath, Diana began searching for the dishwashing detergent, plugged the sink with the rubber stopper and turned on the faucets. Great, she thought, testing the water—cold water.

Knowing about old stoves, Diana lifted a lid and discovered the hot water reserve. She dipped a clean pot into it, filled the sink and began washing the dishes.

She heard the car door slam, then Mac's movements as he went about preparing the spare room for her. There was something companionable about the sounds, she decided, scraping the burnt film from a pan.

Diana knew how to clean with a fury. She'd done it endless times.

She grimaced, scrubbing a battered pot with a scouring pad. She'd read an article once about the compulsive need to clean. The endless urge, according to the author, was fueled by the need to fill an emotional void.

Why hadn't she been enough?

Diana worked harder, feeling an almost frantic energy beat through her. She heard a slight noise and turned to see Mac watching her intently, his arms filled with chopped wood.

Something sizzled when their eyes met, and Diana
felt an unwelcome flutter in her pulse. She lowered
her gaze and scrubbed the pot harder. "I'm almost
finished."

"I didn't ask you to wash the whole house. The
cleaning up could have waited until you were rested,"
Mac murmured softly, dropping the wood into a box
by the stove. He glanced at the pot in her shaking
hands. "If you don't stop worrying that, you'll scrub
a hole clean through it."

Realizing he was right, Diana stopped and rinsed
and dried the remaining dishes, instead, stacking them
carefully on the cabinet shelves.

Mac stripped off his coat, tossed it onto a wooden
chair and sat. He began drawing off his boots. "I
changed the sheets on the bed. Your keys and bags
are on it."

"Thank you. I'll leave in the morning."

His bushy brows met in a scowl. "Why? I thought
you needed a room for a week."

Diana's defenses rose. She felt her plans were being threatened by this man, felt him challenging her
right to make her own decisions. "I can't stay."

"Like hell," he stated tersely. "We'll talk about
this when you've had some rest."

"That sounds patronizing. As though I'm a sleepy
grumpy child who can't think straight." Meek Diana
Phillips, who never challenged anyone, suddenly
wanted to tear into the arrogant Mac and read him
her Bill of Rights. He might be a Colorado cattle
baron, but he wasn't her lord and master.

While she simmered in her own juices, Mac
thoughtfully rubbed his bearded jaw with his hand.
The scraping sound caused her backbone to tingle.

"Can we talk about this some other time?" he asked in a reasonable tone. "I'm going to be busy with my chili all night."

"I don't see how that would change things. I wanted a vacation in a bed-and-breakfast and—"

"Stay here. What's the difference? I've got plenty of room." Mac shifted his large frame uneasily on the creaky wooden chair, glancing away from her like a boy caught in an act of mischief.

Diana watched the changing expression on his face and noted the fatigue deepening the lines around his eyes and mouth. "Why?"

He swallowed, stretching his long legs out to examine the mismatched socks on his feet. "I could say, nothing's open in Benevolence. But the truth is, I just want you here." Where you're safe, he added silently.

The simple statement jolted Diana to her fingertips, almost causing her to drop the chipped plate in her hands.

Mac glanced at her, scowling. "Be straight with a woman and you scare the wind out of her. Shoot. I've never been good at playing games.... Okay, I need the money. How about that one?"

She thought about the well-fed cattle and the sprawling land, and she knew that money was something that Mac did *not* need. Why did he want her to stay? "Try again, Mac," she said quietly, watching him. "I'm not buying that one."

"Don't look so damned scared—you're white as a sheet."

"I can't stay," she managed to say shakily, trying unsuccessfully to get her legs to walk toward the door. Everything south of her brain had apparently stopped functioning. Except for her heart, which was beating wildly.

At forty-two, Diana had never been alone in a house with any man other than her sons or her ex-husband. *She didn't know the rules of the game.*

"I can't," she repeated, fighting to draw air into her lungs.

"Why not?" Mac asked curiously as he stood, moving closer to her, causing her throat to dry. "Why are you so scared?" he asked in a low tone that raised goose bumps all over her flesh. "What have I done, Diana?"

The heat of his body penetrated her clothing, and Diana sidled a few inches away from him. Her hips met the kitchen counter, and she looked up at Mac's heavy frown.

He moved too quickly for her to escape the light sweep of his finger down her cheek. His eyes held hers with their gentleness. "Since there isn't anyone else here to tell you this, I have to. I've never hurt a woman in my entire life. I like kids and I pay my bills. All in all, most women like me and trust me. You're the only one to slap me since I was a teenager."

With a crooked grin, he added, "Maybe I'm just lonesome tonight. You can move on in the morning if you want. But tonight, would you stay with me? Help me stir the chili, maybe have a cup of coffee? Or maybe we could play a game of cards and shoot some pool."

The low wistful tone of his voice soothed Diana's worn nerves. She felt the taut wires within her loosen, the trembling of her fingers against the counter ease. His body heated hers and she felt herself almost lean toward him. Alex had never considered her as a companion, not for a moment.

Mac looked safe. Maybe, just for tonight. "People would talk—your neighbors..."

His grin widened and Diana felt a wave of femininity wash over her.

"Shoot. I'm a big boy. Do you like poker or rummy?"

Diana smiled, realizing she'd just broken one of the chains to her past. She'd been cautious all her life. What would people think? had been her guideline for years. "I would really like a cup of tea, Mac," she said softly, watching his eyes widen with surprise. "If you have any tea, I'll make a pot."

"Tea?" he repeated blankly.

"Dried, crushed leaves," she explained, astonished at the teasing tone in her voice. "You pour hot water over them and let them steep."

"Uh-huh," he murmured, looking thoughtfully at the cupboards. He began jerking open doors and rummaging through the stuffed shelves. "I used to like the stuff. Drank gallons while I was waiting—"

"Waiting for what, Mac?" Diana asked when he didn't finish.

He pulled out a tin, lifting it like a prize. His eyes met hers, and she saw the ache there. "Waiting for my wife to die."

Just then, just for an instant, Diana wanted to move into his arms. The emotion was so strong that she took a step forward. To stop herself, she wrapped her arms around her chest and stared at the worn linoleum floor.

She was just tired and susceptible, she decided, watching Mac search the cupboards again to extract a delicate China teapot. He placed it on the table like a trophy, pushing aside his chili condiments. "There. I knew there was one around here somewhere," he stated proudly. He shoved the tin at her. "You'd better make it. When I make coffee, it tastes like mud. No telling what my tea would taste like now."

In the next hour, Diana experienced her first taste of a man's companionship.

She liked Mac and his concerned questions. "Do you think the tea is too old? Don't drink it if you don't like it."

The man needed company, and maybe she did, too. Just for one night....

Sometime between his "Are you cold? I'll stoke up the stove," and watching him brown the meat for his chili, Diana's lids began to droop.

"Hey, Diana, do you know anything about chili?" Mac turned just as Diana fought to open her lids.

She smiled at him drowsily. "Mmm?"

Mac crouched in front of her, looking at her almost tenderly. "You're tired. Go on, the bedroom is just off the living room."

Diana yawned and stretched.

"Think about it after you've rested," Mac said, gently placing his hand on her knee. The vibrant warmth of his touch startled her, and a warning stirred within her. She moved her leg away.

How long had it been since she really trusted a man? What did Mac really want from her? Her head hurt with the questions racing through her brain. "I think I will go on to bed, if you don't mind."

"I'm not the kind to offer and not mean it," he snapped, offended. His broad shoulders tensed beneath the flannel shirt. "The bathroom isn't much, but there's clean towels."

Feeling Mac's curious gaze on her back, Diana left the kitchen and went into the small neat bedroom. He had turned back the patchwork quilt on the single bed; the tiny pink rosebuds decorating the sheets and pillows seemed to invite her...

Suddenly, Diana felt the weight of every mile from Missouri to Colorado in her bones and muscles. Without a second thought, she eased her bags to the floor, kicked off her shoes, then curled up in bed.

A moment later, she heard Mac's off-key singing. It soothed her torn nerves somehow, and she drifted off to sleep.

TWO

"Shhh, honey," Mac murmured, drawing the woolen afghan higher on Diana's shoulders.

Mac had opened the bedroom door to let the heat from the living room penetrate the cold room. Unable to keep himself from entering the room to make sure she was all right, he had stepped up to the bed and had become intrigued by how vulnerable she looked sleeping.

Honey. He'd used the word to comfort his wife, Eleanor. He'd grieved long and hard, and he didn't intend to open himself to that pain again.

With a fleeting sense of panic, he realized that Diana just might reopen his old wounds. He remembered the slender knee beneath his hand before she moved away.... He released the afghan, as though it burned his fingers.

He didn't need any stirring up at his age. He'd dealt

with the pain, and he intended to keep his troubled waters smooth. Diana was hurting, and he just wanted to help, that's all, he rationalized.

"If there's one thing I know about myself, Red," he whispered to the dog, who had padded into the room, "I'm a sucker for anything that looks as though it needs tucking under my wing."

Diana slept heavily, oblivious to Mattie, the cat, who'd jumped up on the bed. Diana snuggled to the animal, and Mac decided to let Mattie stay there.

Mac had spent hours sitting at his wife's bedside, and now it seemed natural for him to settle into the old cherry rocker by the bed. Eleanor couldn't be healed, and he'd watched her seep into death, a part of him dying with her.

He realized he'd been thinking of Diana as "his stray" and quietly discussed her with Red. "She looked like a shivering kitten standing on the porch, cold but too proud to ask for a warm saucer of milk. Whether Ms. Diana Phillips will admit it or not, Red, she's hurting bad."

Diana shifted slowly, sighing tiredly.

He hadn't turned on the shortwave radio in his living room, not needing the chatter to fill his loneliness tonight—he had Diana. She looked small and just about the most feminine woman Mac had ever seen.

He picked up one of her shoes. It almost fit into the palm of his hand. Barely worn, the shoe was as new as her jeans and jacket. "Our Ms. Diana is on the run, Red," Mac murmured, leaning forward to lift a strand of red-brown hair back from her cheek. "She's scared of men."

Her skin enticed him. Smooth and pale, its fragrance wafted out to him, tantalizing him. Mac held his body rigid. How he wanted to hold her against him, just to comfort her.

All strays needed comforting, didn't they?

He wrapped his fingers around his knee to steady their trembling. Closing his eyes, he saw Eleanor's perfumes and powders discarded into the trash after her death. He shuddered, feeling a fresh streak of pain.

He smiled grimly, opening his lids. "Watch it, old man, you're having an off night. And an attack of the middle-age lonelies."

Patting Red's shaggy head, Mac continued his quiet monologue. "Halloween night and she strolls right in here. She's hunting something.... What is it?"

He studied Diana's face, the long lashes and the dark circles beneath her eyes. "She's exhausted, on the run and needing to hole up for a time. We can give her some peace, Red. If just for a short time."

Would she stay?

Diana's lashes fluttered and her eyes, glazed with sleep opened suddenly. She watched him warily. "Are you frightened of me, Diana?" he asked gently.

Her lids drifted down drowsily as she turned her back to him, drawing the afghan over her shoulder. "No."

Mac leaned forward, bracing his forearms over his knees. "Diana?"

"Mmm?"

"Diana, you're safe here. I'll take care of you."

"Mmm. That's good," she answered sleepily.

Mac settled back in the rocker to search out all the ways he could keep her near. By dawn he'd decided that sometimes strays needed to be lassoed and placed in a nice safe corral. Sometimes a cowboy had to move in quick and close the gate.

"Hey, sleepyhead, wake up," a masculine voice rumbled in Diana's ear. "Come on, wake up. Your breakfast is ready."

Keeping her lids closed, Diana relished the warmth that enveloped her. Then she heard a purr and felt a movement against her side. She also felt something heavy weighing down her legs. She quickly opened her eyes and found herself looking down at Red's dark brown eyes. She turned her head and saw the cat sleeping beside her.

"It's nine o'clock," the male voice continued softly. She felt a gentle hand stroking back the strand of hair clinging to her cheek. "You've slept almost nine hours."

Diana summoned her courage and looked into Mac's smiling eyes. He was sitting in the battered old rocker in front of the window. His jaw had grown a heavy beard during the night, and his hair was damp, clinging to his forehead. He'd obviously just showered. His deeply tanned chest was bare, and her fingers itched to play with the thick dark hair covering the muscular planes. She could almost feel the rough texture beneath her fingertips.

She swallowed and looked away, embarrassed by the flow of her thoughts. She blamed the early morning hours for her weakness. It still came hard—the sleeping alone.

Sensuality had never been a big part of her life with Alex, but for some reason, Mac made her feel conscious of herself as a woman.

She looked back at him when he chuckled. "I must be an unholy sight for a lady like you, Diana."

Gazing at her closely, he stopped smiling. "You're pretty first thing in the morning," he whispered huskily.

When Diana flushed, Mac stood to his full awesome height. "I'm not used to women waking up in the house. I'll shave and put on a shirt. Otherwise, you might slap me again for poor manners," he said, then turned and walked toward the kitchen.

She yawned and stretched, staring at Mac's back. It was a nice back, power evident in the muscles beneath the dark skin. By the rigid way he moved, she knew she'd hurt him. Mac couldn't understand how terrified she was of her emotions.

She sat up and dislodged the cat. Reluctantly leaving her warm nest, she moved to the windows, looking out at the heavy fog that covered the ranch. The cat rubbed against her legs, and she picked it up, taking it into the kitchen with her.

Mac had thrown on a green wool shirt, and standing in his bare feet before a mirror on the wall, was lathering his jaw with a foaming brush. He picked up an old-fashioned straightedge razor and saw her. "Sit down and eat. My coffee may not be any good, but I make the best pancakes in the country. Then we're going to the cook-off. Donaldson's chili hasn't got a chance this year."

Diana took a deep breath and hugged the purring cat, gathering her courage. "Mac, I'm not going with you. I'll freshen up, then be on my way."

He grinned. "Cranky little cuss in the morning, aren't you, Diana?"

She felt the slightest twinge of anger. Mac was trying to make her smile, but she didn't feel like smiling just yet. "I don't like being treated like a child, with you deciding where I'm going or what I'll be doing. A chili contest is not on my agenda."

He shifted on those incredibly long legs, turning toward her. His stance indicated that he would discuss the situation with her until she agreed. One of his heavy eyebrows rose. "No reason to balk, Diana. The cook-off is one of the kickoff festivities for the annual Benevolence Fall Hunt. The tourists like it. So do the hunters. Just part of the local color."

Diana put the cat on the floor and straightened up, uncomfortable with his friendly tone. Actually, she would like playing tourist, for a change of pace. But she could do so on her own.

Watching her mutinous expression, Mac's eyes narrowed. He moved his mouth to one side and took a clean swipe with the flashing blade. "Lady, I've got a hunch you could be trouble—real trouble," he mumbled, then took another swipe down his jaw. "You're too edgy and you've got a nasty right hook."

She glared at him, wanting to forget the slap. What right had he to go probing at her psyche, tearing at her privacy and taunting her? "You're just plain nasty," she flung back. "Bagpipes in the middle of the night," she scolded, feeling herself gear up. "You probably scare the poor bears out of their caves."

Mac's prominent chin jutted out beneath the shaving foam; a tiny white fleck clung to his ear. "Huh! Well, little lady, people around here ask me to play the bagpipes."

He pinched his nose, raising it to safety as he took another swipe with the razor. "Women," he muttered to the mirror. "You take 'em in, get 'em warm, and they turn on you the first chance they get."

"What did you say, Mac?" Diana asked. She watched his hand swish the razor in a small enamel basin. He dried the blade on a towel.

He pivoted, meeting her stare with his own. The opened shirt revealed that intriguing mass of hair covering his chest. "I said, it's a small thing, but it's important to me. I want you to go to the cook-off with me. Be my date, sort of. So far as I can see, there's no reason you can't come. Unless some jealous husband is going to come after my scalp."

"You don't need to worry—I'm divorced." His accusation had come quickly and too sharply, but somehow she thought he already knew about her.

Mac continued to look at her, and Diana could feel his challenge wrap around her. Long ago she'd stopped thinking of herself as a desirable woman, but now this rough-hewn cowboy was raising those emotions she had sheltered for an eternity. "I can't," she said weakly.

"Why in Sam Hill can't you?" he demanded, walking over to her. "Look, I checked back with Ray. You did have reservations for a full week. So you had plans to stay in Benevolence, anyway. Your room is gone, Diana. Ray rented it out to hunters from Missouri. There's snow coming down in the passes, and that little wagon of yours needs some fine-tuning. So what's your big excuse?"

Feeling flustered and feminine and utterly vulnerable, Diana shivered. In a gesture of self-protection, she wrapped her arms around herself. "I don't owe you any explanation."

"Huh!" Mac snorted as he padded back to the mirror to complete his shaving. "You don't have any reason not to spend the day with me, do you?"

"Maybe I just don't want to," Diana ventured softly, resenting how easily Mac had reduced her to sounding obstinate. "You are a pushy man, Mac."

"Pushy?" he growled, taking out a pair of socks from his shirt pocket. She noted that one was navy blue and the other was black with red stripes. "Nobody ever called me that before."

"Then maybe it's time someone did." Diana badly needed the coffee he had offered. She reached for the battered tin pot on the stove.

"Use a pot holder," he warned behind her. "I don't want you burning your hands."

Taking a deep breath, Diana swiped a rag from the table and reached for a mug. "I have been taking care of myself for quite a while now," she said through her teeth.

"I'll have a cup, please," Mac murmured near her. "Maybe after we eat, both our temperaments will have improved."

She glared at him, certain that nothing would improve her mood at the moment.

The poacher on her right grinned at her boyishly as he sat at the table. "Okay, maybe I didn't ask you right, but I'd really like you to come with me to the cook-off. I am a little rough around the edges when it comes to women."

When she sat, watching him put on his unmatched socks, he shot her a grin of undiluted satisfaction. There was excitement dancing around him like hundred-volt electricity.

Diana sipped her coffee slowly, while Mac drank his quickly. He motioned to the stack of buckwheat pancakes in the center of the table. "Help yourself—you're too thin."

That statement rankled. Who was he to criticize her? "By whose standards?"

"Mine," he stated flatly. "You look like a good wind would blow you up the canyon."

"You're the wrong sex for a nanny," she shot back hotly. "And I don't need a Dutch uncle, either."

Suddenly, she panicked. She blinked, horrified at her tumbled emotions. Mac had a knack for knocking her off her isolated perch. Since she'd met him just last night, he'd managed to disrupt her plans for a restful solitary vacation. And he had succeeded in making her explode with anger—and respond to his blatant masculinity.

He leaned back in his chair, eyeing her speculatively. "Look, if we knew each other well enough, I'd give you that fight you're spoiling for," he began reasonably. "But as it is, it may have to wait until later; then, when I know what's got you so riled, I'll tangle with you. To your heart's content. Whatever makes you happy. But right now, all I can promise you is Benevolence's Fall Hunt Festival. What do you say?"

She eyed him, feeling slightly guilty about snapping at him. Holding grudges did not sit comfortably with her. "I'll think about it."

"You do that," he murmured almost smugly. "I'll pack up my chili while you freshen up. By the way—" he looked at her rumpled jeans and wrinkled sweater "—wear some dancing shoes."

"I haven't agreed to anything, Mac."

He shrugged, grinning down at her. "Neither have I. But folks around here like to think of me as an old widower. Just once I'd like to knock them on their backsides by turning up with a pretty woman like you."

Diana never strayed out of her path for an escapade in her life. For some reason, today she felt like doing just that. Mac might have the wrong approach, but the adventure had a certain lure....

Mac winked with the air of a conspirator. "What do you say, kid?"

She frowned, turning the matter over carefully within her.

A warm finger touched her between her brows and trailed down her nose. She looked up to see Mac's gentle expression. "Frowning causes wrinkles. Haven't you heard? Give it a rest, Diana—for today?"

"Maybe I can't," she answered honestly.

"Maybe you can," he said evenly. "Try."

Diana stared into his dark eyes and decided that maybe she did need a breather, after all. She'd been on a fun-restricted diet, and the opportunity to fudge was enormously appealing. "Count me in," she agreed.

In Mac's four-wheel-drive pickup an hour later, Diana was forced to sit right up against him. She held his Stetson on her lap, protecting it from the musket rifles, which leaned precariously on the passenger door. The notorious bagpipes, on the seat beside her, poked her ribs. She glared up at Mac. "You're taking advantage of the situation."

"Oh, sure. Accuse me of ulterior motives—that's just like a woman." He glanced down at her, then back at the winding highway. "Be reasonable, Diana. I had to put the chili cooker on the floor, and the only place my musket rifles will fit is up against the door like that—by the way, you'll like the black powder shoot—so, the only place left for you to sit was right next to me.''

Mac drove leisurely, allowing Diana to view the scenery—tumbling creeks, heavily bordered by white aspens and red pines. Mac tugged her closer.

"See that peak?" he asked, nodding his head toward a rugged mountain. "There are bighorns up there, above the timberline. Deer and elk are coming down from the mountains now, headed for warmer fields. And old Mr. Black Bear is fat from berries, getting ready for his winter nap.''

Diana stiffened, pulling her shoulder away from him. Mac seemed to like fitting her to his side, but she wasn't certain just how to handle this much of him at close range. Is this how it begins with men and women? she wondered frantically, trying to place inches between their bodies.

The close confines of the pickup were filled with his scent—wood smoke, soap and tangy after-shave. Mac moved, bringing his side against her. He was like a fresh wind sweeping out the stale air. It had been years since she'd felt feminine…and excited.

But she didn't want to feel any of that. She just wanted strength to plot out her life.

"See that creek, Diana? One of the miners back in 1858 first spotted gold nuggets in that creek. Benevolence was named after a gold mine, back in the mining boom. There was a Ute uprising that scared off most of the homesteaders before the turn of the century. Benevolence was a ghost town until the tourist trade discovered us.''

Diana shifted again but still felt his hard thigh move when he braked, then accelerated the pickup.

"You're quiet—no one could accuse you of being a magpie. What are you thinking?" he asked.

The honest answer frightened her. She'd been thinking about the way his body moved against her, the way his heat was seeping through her clothes. Instead, Diana ducked her head, feeling suddenly shy. "It's beautiful here, Mac."

"Uh-huh. I grew up here with my brothers, J.D. and Rafe. Rafe's playing at being semi-retired near here. And J.D. is a Denver businessman. Denver may suit J.D., but I wouldn't live anywhere but here." He took a deep breath, a man obviously pleased with his life.

He scanned the fields surrounding the highway. His fingers tightened on her shoulder. "Deer grazing over there. See them?"

"They're so graceful," she said as the deer raised their heads to watch them. "Do you hunt them with those big bows on your wall?"

"Compound bows with more pound power than you must weigh. Yes, I used to hunt. I was a guide and a pretty good tracker. Guess it's the Ute blood in me."

"Where did you learn to play the bagpipes?" she asked, suddenly wanting to know more.

He shrugged. "My grandfather was a Scotsman— the bagpipes were his. The Ute and Spanish blood come from my mother's side. The Spanish explored this country, you know."

He looked down at her, his eyes narrowing. "I'm part hot-blooded Spanish lover. What do you think about that?'' he asked suggestively, raising his eyebrows.

His cocky leer caused her to giggle for the first time in years. She felt giddy. ''I think you're as windy as your bagpipes, MacLean,'' she shot back, grinning.

''Whoops! You smiled,'' he teased, tugging her hair. ''I was wondering if you had one locked inside you.''

Despite herself, Diana smiled again and looked away.

Catching the scent of his chili, Mac also caught an appealing idea. With Diana on his arm, Ms. Simpson just might take a second taste of his deserving chili. The elderly judge was a romantic right down to her lace pantalets. The first thing he'd do would be to talk to Ray. Ray had badgered him about buying an expensive compound bow he owned; bribing him to play along would be easy.

Immediately upon their arrival at the town hall, Mac installed his electric slow cooker—filled with chili—in the enormous kitchen. Other pots bubbled and steamed, all in a row. Mac lovingly stirred his concoction with a wooden spoon but he took the time out to speak privately with Ray. Then he began introducing Diana to his friends as his ''lady.'' Diana was stunned. ''What are you doing, MacLean?'' she had asked between her teeth when they were alone.

''Huh?'' He glanced at Ms. Simpson, who stared at them over the top of her glasses. He took Diana's hand and kissed the back of it before she could withdraw it.

''Mac! What are you doing?'' she repeated, rubbing the lingering warmth of his mouth away.

''Don't look now. See Ms. Simpson over there?

The gray-haired lady with the bun? She's the judge of the contest."

Diana tilted her head, feeling as though she had stepped into the Twilight Zone. "What does she have to do with the fact that you just kissed my hand?"

"She's a romantic, Diana," he explained flatly, as though she would instantly understand. "With you next to me, I could win the contest."

Diana stared up at him, taken aback by his tender loverlike smile. She felt a little flutter around her heart. Mac's obvious loneliness had touched her last night. To be Mac's lady for a day wouldn't cost her an ounce of pride. After all, her visit was temporary, and she could manage a little kindness along the way. If he wanted to win the chili contest so badly he'd stay up all night making it, she could manage to play along. *If* he didn't go to extremes.

"Okay, I'll pretend to be your girlfriend," she whispered as he slid his hand to the back of her neck. The possessive gesture caused her skin to tingle. "Just don't overdo it, will you?"

He glanced appraisingly at Ms. Simpson again. "She's a real tough cookie, Diana. Do you think you could help a little?" he asked, pulling her up against him.

Tucked under his arm, his fingers at her waist, Diana had to remind herself that Mac really did need her help. His chili needed her help, she corrected. "I'm here, aren't I?" she asked, trying to wedge space between their bodies.

"Yes, you are. And you just don't know how thankful I am for whatever help you can give me." He scowled at another rancher. "Donaldson, over there, has been walking off with the trophy for years. I'd give a lot to set him on his ear—"

Ray wandered by, smiling widely. "Howdy, Mac. Howdy, Ms. Phillips. Everything okay?"

Mac took a deep breath. "Dandy."

Ray's smile grew. "I'd like my bow as soon as possible, son. Put a ribbon on it, a red one."

"Right. Talk to you later, Ray. Now leave my lady and me alone, okay?"

"Sure, just don't forget our bargain."

Ray moved off into the crowd, and Mac turned to his chili. He glanced at Diana. "You might as well know. I had to bribe him not to tell everyone why you're staying with me."

"Mac..." she began, beginning to question her own sanity. Why on earth had she agreed to this conspiracy?

"I do want that trophy. I've wanted it for years," Mac said softly, slowly. "Now is my one chance."

His tone was just wistful enough to sink her resistance. Diana paused in midbreath and changed her refusal to a simple, "I know. You owe me, though. Just how are you going to explain my getaway?"

"Simple. We'll have a doozy of a fight. You get mad and leave." Mac saw Ms. Simpson easing her way to them through the crowd. "Could we, ah, talk about this later? I really need to talk to Ms. Simpson. Something about a secret spice."

When he returned a few minutes later, Diana found him watching her intently. He had a thoughtful expression that totally unsettled her. "Exactly why are you looking at me like that, Mac?" she asked carefully.

He took her plate from her and placed it on the

bench beside him. Taking both her hands, he held them between his own. "Diana, I made sure Ms. Simpson knew that you were my girlfriend."

Mac had the same look her boys did just before they admitted their guilt about something. "And?"

He shook his head. "It didn't seem to affect her. Being my girlfriend isn't enough. I have to come up with something else fast to turn the contest my way."

Diana took a deep breath, trying to withdraw her hands. She didn't like her sinking premonition. Not a bit. "And?"

His fingers tightened as he frowned. "We need to show her we're really serious about each other. We need to be believable. Do you think you could manage a great big kiss?"

"A kiss? Mac!"

"Shh! Don't get excited. It's just the edge I need—"

"You need a straitjacket."

"Haven't you ever wanted anything bad?" he asked urgently, scanning the crowd.

She shook her head. "Let go of my hands so I can—"

A cluster of giggling teenagers passed, keeping Diana from telling Mac just what he could kiss. "You're single-minded, Mac," she finally said. "You can take your contest and—"

Ray walked up to them, munching on a carrot stick. "Problems, Mac?"

Mac glared at the clerk. "Not a one. Everything is smooth as good bourbon. Go away."

While Diana was still trying to plan her escape, Mac turned back to her and whispered, "We really need one big kiss to put this whole thing over."

"You're not getting one, Mac. You just back off," Diana firmly asserted just before the black powder shoot-out was announced.

Mac stared at her, lifting one eyebrow. "You're not afraid, are you?" he asked mildly. "I didn't think you could last out the day."

His challenge hit Diana broadside. Feeling a full tide of fury wash over her, she announced too quietly, "I can take anything you can dish out, cowboy."

"Huh," he said simply as he led her outside to the target range. "A good kiss would—"

"Oh, shut up," Diana ordered curtly. She wondered how she could steal his pickup and drive back to the ranch, get her bags and drive away in her car.

Everyone in Benevolence seemed to have a match-making twinkle in his eyes, Diana noticed. It seemed that the woman occupying Mac MacLean's strong arm was more of a curiosity than a two-headed calf. She felt as though she were being mobbed, with a smiling Ms. Simpson leading the crowd.

On the target range, Mac held out a seven-foot musket to her, his eyes daring her. Because she was angry, Diana jerked it from his hands, then struggled to aim the heavy barrel at the target. Mac's arms moved around her to support the musket.

The intimate position implied a blazing love affair, firing Diana's temper. She pulled the trigger impatiently; the blast knocked her back into his waiting arms.

Mac cursed. Then his hands trembling, he embraced her tightly. "Damn, I should have known. Are you hurt, Diana?" he demanded fiercely, pressing his lean cheek against her soft one.

Diana pulled away from him, feeling the sensual

warmth begin to flow through her. "Let me go, Mac," she said huskily, wondering if her legs could carry her to the nearby benches. The tantalizing ripples sweeping inside her intensified.

Through taut lips, he whispered, "Now, Diana. Don't go making mountains out of molehills. You're getting all worked up when all I want is a kiss."

"You deliberately maneuvered me into this." A flush traveled from her face downward. Her nipples hardened in response to his staring at her mouth.

"Since you're mad anyway..." He gathered her into his arms as if he had the right to have her locked against him. He ignored the thrust of her palms against his stomach, and his lips touched hers tenderly.

For a moment, she stared into his eyes, felt the warmth of his face on hers, the gentle hand supporting her head. Diana's anger wavered, then vanished as his mouth began to move over hers. Her lids closed and her senses ached with unfulfilled hunger. It plagued her, causing her finger to coil around his belt. She forgot everything but his searing touch.

His hand slid down her back, urging her nearer.

She thought she heard a sigh and recognized it as her own. When Mac reluctantly ended the kiss, he gazed at her with undisguised need. His eyes darkened as a dull flush rose in his lean cheeks. "I didn't mean for that to happen. At least not that way, Diana," he admitted slowly.

Diana's knees threatened to buckle; her breath was coming unevenly. She forced a swallow and moistened her dry lips. Never in her entire life had any man looked as longingly at her as Mac did just then. He was like a starving man viewing a banquet.

The musket shots rang out, and the pungent scent of sulfur floated by on the cold mountain air. Mac's gaze wandered down her slight body appraisingly, and she found she could no more stop her eyes from blazing the same trail down his body than she could stop the winter snows. Diana felt the world slip away; everything around them was blocked out by Mac's broad shoulders looming nearer.

Carefully, Mac drew her to him once more. Through the layers of their clothing, she felt his tense anticipation. "Now you've done it," he murmured huskily, lowering his mouth to hers.

Something new and utterly delicious quivered within her as he tasted her delicately. When his hand slid beneath her denim jacket to caress her back, she moved deeper into his arms.

His breath was warm, fanning her cheek. The kiss went gently on, destroying her defenses, taking away the pain…and replacing it with hunger.

His taut body was trembling when he released her reluctantly. His sultry gaze traveled over her upturned face, lingering on her swollen lips.

When the cheer went up, the two looked around and saw they were surrounded by spectators.

"Just what you wanted." Diana was frightened suddenly and unable to move back from his light embrace. New emotions hit her like a blast of hot dry desert wind. She'd forgotten the power of a man's sensuality, the needs stirring within her. She'd kept them wrapped up for too long, and now this Colorado cowboy had reached right into the tender bruised heart of her.

"I didn't intend it to turn out that way," he said cautiously.

Mac drew her behind a weathered aspen tree. His forefinger lightly trailed down her cheek, tracing the fullness of her bottom lip. "What's wrong? Was it so awful?" he murmured intimately.

She shivered when he caressed her nape. Mac seemed to know where to touch her. "You're shaking," he whispered gently.

"We're standing in front of a lot of people, Mac. Making out in front of a crowd," she said unevenly, glancing away. "Like teenagers."

He smiled. "Be glad they're here. It's the best protection you could have."

Unable to meet his tender stare, Diana watched the crowd move toward the town hall. "They're leaving, Mac."

"Uh-huh. It's judging time for the cook-off."

"Aren't you entering your chili, Mac?"

His eyes widened in surprise. "Shoot. I'd forgotten. Come on."

Mac insisted Diana stay near him as Ms. Simpson tasted the enormous selection of chili. The contest was finally narrowed to Donaldson and Mac.

Donaldson, a big man with a round stomach, elbowed Mac. "I've got it sewed up this year, Mac. Had some green chilies imported from Texas and added my special spice." He grinned. "It's called edge, son. Of course, I'm not sporting that little piece on my arm."

Mac glared at him. "Cut it, Donaldson. Diana and I are getting married. And I imported some Idaho sweet onions the size of footballs especially for this—"

"Married?" The rancher and Diana interrupted jointly.

"Why, sure." Mac drew Diana closer to his side. "Did everybody hear that?" he called out to everybody. "Diana and I have just gotten engaged. We're getting married. We'll put together a shindig this town has never seen for a wedding."

A cheer went from up the crowd.

"Mac, can we talk?" Diana said weakly.

"Later, honey. They're judging the cook-off right now. And I want to be here to get *my* trophy."

"Oh, that's the edge, Mac. Not the onions," Donaldson growled. The two tall men pressed Diana between them as they glared at each other. "You know you'll get old Ms. Simpson's vote once she finds out you're finally getting hitched. She's a sucker for romance. And she's been trying for years to find somebody who would have your cantankerous self. Who could resist a hermit in love?" he scoffed. "Of all the low, conniving—"

The angry rancher's cheeks puffed out, his short beard standing out like porcupine quills. "This is worse than the time you sabotaged my chili with that bottle of cheap hot sauce and added vinegar to boot," Donaldson accused.

"It was so weak, it needed something for body," Mac returned. "What about the time you dumped a bag of chili mix—"

"*Married?*" Diana repeated, feeling as if she'd been dropped into never-never land.

Mac glanced down at her as though he'd just remembered something—her. "That's right, honey. We are engaged, you know. As soon as we can, we'll go up to Creede and get a ring."

Diana felt numb. A full-fledged Colorado wild man wanted to marry her. A rancher who played bagpipes on Halloween and stayed up brewing his chili all night. She stared up at Mac's clean-shaved jaw. Hard-nosed determination lodged in every bone in his tall lean body. *Mac wanted that trophy.*

Donaldson threw another verbal jab. "That time you rappelled down the face of that canyon wall, Mac, I should have cut the rope."

"I was after your ewe, Donaldson. That bighorn sheep would have splattered her all over the face of that rock," Mac growled back. "What about those poachers hunting on your spread last year? I helped locate them, didn't I?"

"'Help'? Is that what you call it? Boy, your copter scared my Herefords into a stampede. Ran fifty pounds of good fat off of each one. I could have han-dled those lamebrain trophy hunters by myself." Donaldson's massive jowls shook as Ms. Simpson tasted Mac's chili and slowly smiled.

When Ms. Simpson took another delicate spoonful, Donaldson's three-hundred-pound frame seemed to vibrate. "You play those damned bagpipes this year, and I won't donate a cent to the city's old-time board-walk."

"Mac?" Diana called softly.

Mac snorted, slipping his big hand around Diana's numb fingers. "Huh. Big deal. I already donated the money."

When Ms. Simpson sampled Donaldson's chili, Mac stopped growling and raised Diana's fingers to his mouth. He frowned, rubbing his lips across the smooth back of her hand. "What's wrong, honey? Your fingers are like ice. Aren't you warm enough?" He touched her forehead with his palm. "No fever. Diana, what's wrong?"

Diana felt the real world spinning away from her. "Married?" she finally managed to say just as Ms. Simpson raised the trophy.

A guilty expression crossed Mac's face. His black eyes shifted away from Diana's accusing ones. "I was stuck," he whispered. "The marriage was a stroke of genius—Donaldson was right, I needed an edge to win. He's got some secret spice grown by his Mexican housekeeper. All I had was you," he said desperately. "You've got to help me."

For a moment Diana wondered if she could reach high enough to dump Mac's chili over his head. "You—"

"That's it! That's good, Diana. Let all those hostilities come out," he said, looking around anxiously. "But not here."

Ms. Simpson's voice crackled over the microphone. "We have this year's winner—Mac MacLean!"

Donaldson cursed and the crowd cheered.

Locking his fingers with Diana's, Mac dragged her to the waiting judges. Scooping her against him and lifting her feet from the wooden floor, Mac raised his trophy in his free hand. He kissed her on the cheek, then grinned boyishly at the crowd. "Thanks to my good luck charm, my future wife, Diana."

He kissed her full on the lips, then whispered softly, "Don't worry about anything, Diana. I've got everything under control."

Three

"It's about time, Mac," Ms. Simpson cooed. She turned to Diana. "Congratulations, young lady, I didn't think Mac would ever get around to proposing to another woman. We've all been afraid that he'd live alone forever, waste away up there on that ranch."

The old woman peered up at Mac, who was accepting hearty congratulations from his friends. She confided to Diana, "He's a nice boy. Took care of his ailing parents and tended his wife until the day she died. Poor Eleanor, she just wasn't suited to that rough ranch life. I couldn't be happier for you both. Now, if we could just marry those other brothers, Rafe and J.D. Heartbreakers, all three of them. When the MacLean boys were about, you could always count on some poor girl losing her heart."

Smiling with a happiness she did not feel, Diana managed to reply, "Mac hasn't exactly asked—"

Donaldson gave her a bear hug, almost lifting her off her feet. He grinned at Mac's outraged expression. "The poor thing looks confused, Mac. Of course, after smelling your chili all night, she probably needs detoxification. Maybe she'll keep you from running that damned copter all across the county at all hours of the night. Good luck, boy."

Once freed from Donaldson, Diana fought for breath as she secretly checked her ribs. She looked up at Mac, keeping her lips pasted in a smile. "I'd like to talk to you privately, please, Mac."

His thick eyebrows went up, showing his surprise. "But, Diana, they just asked me to play the bagpipes to start the dancing."

Diana controlled her rising need to scream. The muscles of her face hurt with tension as she valiantly maintained the smile. "I feel like blowing up, Mac," she enunciated slowly. "And I may. Right here in front of your chili-eating friends. You could lose the trophy by default."

Mac stooped a little to examine her closely. He frowned. "Is something wrong, Diana?"

She nodded, still smiling.

"Uh-huh. Well, they're all waiting for the dancing to begin."

Through her teeth, Diana asked, "Could they possibly begin without you, Mac?"

He rubbed his jaw, studying her. "I don't know. The Hunter's Bash has never opened without me before. Not since I got back from Nam."

Donaldson's beefy shoulder nudged Mac's arm. "We'll struggle along without you this year, Mac. Go on, the little lady obviously has something to say. Maybe she'd like to skip the bagpipes, too.''

Mac found an empty office, and he and Diana went inside. He closed the door behind them. Standing in a corner, Diana wrapped her arms around her chest and glared up at him. ''Just where do you get off, big man?'' she asked tightly.

Mac slipped his hands in his back pockets, then leaned against a wall. ''You're upset.''

''That's an understatement.'' Diana felt her temper begin to flare. The ''house mouse,'' as Alex had named her, was turning into a lion. ''I'm on vacation, Mac. I didn't come to make a fool of an entire town.''

He shrugged, his expression wary. ''I know that.''

She tapped the toe of one small jogger. ''Tell me what else you know. Just so I won't waste time repeating the facts to you.''

''I know that you're scared, Diana, on the run from yourself.... I know that I want to help.''

Stunned by his admission, Diana shook her head, trying to clear it. She fought confusion. She looked at Mac's face, his high cheekbones, that sensuous mouth and hard jaw. ''You don't know me, Mac, and I don't know a thing about you,'' she said, unable to glance away from him. ''I'm not shopping for good Samaritans.''

''I know everything I need to know about you, Diana Phillips. I lost a lot of buddies in Nam, and I learned that you'd better grab friendships when you can.''

She cleared her dry throat, wondering if she was dreaming. Who was crazy here? Had she missed something? ''Lying to everyone inside this town hall is not the way to keep friendships. And I know what being lied to is like.''

"Maybe I did put my foot in it." Mac took a step toward her, keeping his hands in his jeans pockets. His eyes blazed down at her. "Blame it on my wanting to win the chili trophy. I'm high on a well-deserved victory.''

"You're playing games, while I'm..." She struggled for the right words to make him understand. "Mac, I'm trying to stand on my own feet. I'm trying to fit all the pieces together. I need peace."

Floundering in a jumble of emotions, Diana flung out her hand, and somehow it grazed his flat stomach. She jerked her fingers away, as though they had been burned.

The heat of his body reached out to her as Mac took another step nearer. She tilted her head back. "Mac," she began to protest as his head lowered. "I'm not up to this. Games aren't for me."

"I wouldn't hurt you for the world." Mac's lips touched hers lightly in a brief kiss.

When he straightened, Diana forced herself to gaze at the first button of his shirt. She wanted to place her arms around him and snuggle against his broad chest. She swallowed the lump of need drying her throat.

"Your husband really did a job on you, didn't he?"

Diana began to shake, desperately fighting to keep her distance. She was raw and bleeding, and knowing instinctively that Mac could soothe her made it that much harder to stay away.

"Diana Phillips, stay with me for a time. Let me be your friend?" Mac asked gently. "Why don't you wrap your arms around me and hold on tight."

She shook her head, and Mac sighed deeply. "My

hands are in my pockets. Come on, trust me enough to tell me about it.''

Diana looked up at him. She had to keep all her secrets locked inside. Just until she had turned them around, studied them and put them in order. ''Not now, Mac.''

''I'll be here when you want to talk. That's what friends are for.'' Mac's lips lifted in a wry smile.

Suddenly, Diana felt young and shy and uncertain. Her lashes fluttered, and she felt her hands move.

Beside her ear, Mac whispered, ''Put them on my face. Touch me. You've been looking at my mouth for a time now, so kiss me, too. If you like.''

When she looked up at him warily, Mac added, ''So far as I know, no one ever died from a kiss. In fact, it was a kiss that awoke Sleeping Beauty.''

Diana couldn't resist sneaking a look at Mac's firm lips. She'd walked in the cold loneliness for an eternity. Now the gentleness in Mac's face offered her solace.

Taking a step, Diana placed her body against him lightly. She eased her cheek to that safe, warm chest and heard the rapid beating of his heart.

''That's it,'' he murmured, his jaw nuzzling the top of her head. ''Rest awhile.''

Diana slid her arms around his waist. For just this moment, Mac was her harbor in the storm.

His arms closed around her slowly, lightly. Broad palms stroked her back and shoulders, soothing her as he rocked her in his arms.

Then the tears came, the ones she'd fought for so long. They trailed down her cheeks and fell on his skin. She rubbed his chest with her cheek, trying to dry the tears. ''I'm sorry.''

She heard a rough sound and felt Mac's chest lifting and falling unevenly beneath her head. "Oh, honey," he said, the husky timbre telling her he understood her pain and loneliness, as though her aching heart were his own. She looked up through her veil of tears, her fingers seeking his face. Mac stood absolutely still as she touched his damp cheeks.

"Why?" she asked, then remembered how he'd lost his wife.

He tilted his head and kissed her fingers. "I'm a softy," he whispered raggedly. "Lord, honey, there's enough pain in you to last a lifetime."

"I'm afraid," she returned, tracing his lips, entranced by the hard yet sensitive line.

Mac cradled her cheek in the palm of his hand. She felt the rough skin and calluses. "Please don't be afraid."

Her mouth met his, and she felt his breath on her cheek. This time, Mac's lips moved firmly across hers. Leaning back in his arms, Diana savored his kisses, waited for the sweet calming glow...

Her hands swept slowly across his back, and she felt the hard muscles ripple beneath her touch. Mac shuddered, pulling her hips nearer his thighs, fitting her into his long body.

Diana's breath caught when her breasts pressed against his chest. Then Mac groaned, a ragged masculine sound that spoke of his need. His lips parted and his tongue darted hungrily into her mouth, as though he needed her essence.

Diana moved against his hard form. Mac cradled her, sliding one big hand low on her back.

Incredible heat began to throb inside her, burning through the clothes separating them. She groaned, aching, and he murmured something roughly, his fingers sliding between them.

Gently, his hand cupped her breast. Mac sighed and trailed tiny kisses from the corners of her lips to her ear. He was breathing heavily as his fingers moved across the delicate slopes of her breasts.

Trembling with the effort, Diana pulled back and gazed up at his face. "No," she said simply, and Mac responded with a nod. She touched his hair, felt the silky strands glide through her fingers as she eased them back from his temple.

Mac's hand slid to her cheek. "You're shaking. This is all new to me, too." She blushed and tucked her head beneath his chin.

"Don't worry," he murmured gently. "We'll work everything out."

He gave her a playful smacking kiss that made her tingle all over. "Friends?"

Friends. Not once in her lifetime had a man asked friendship of her. Possession was the main rule in her relationship with Alex. What were Mac's rules?

"Back to this marriage thing," he was saying. "It has a certain appeal to a man in my condition."

Diana jumped out of his arms like a scalded cat. "But it's out of the question. We don't know each other." Diana felt her knees begin to weaken as his darkened gaze traveled down her body, resting on her breasts.

"You're afraid to stay the week you'd planned."

"You are hardheaded, Mac," she said, wondering vaguely how this one man could stir her passions so quickly.

"A week-long engagement with a wham-bang fight at the end. We can fight over squeezing the toothpaste tube at the wrong end, or something. You can fly off free as a bird. If you still want to, then.''

Diana closed her eyes, suddenly weary to her bones. She leaned against the wall for support.

Mac took her hand and led her to the couch. ''Rest awhile with me. Let me take care of you.''

She searched his gentle expression and found only concern. ''Mac, this is unreal. It must be the elevation.''

''Nope. The only thing that's unreal is your past.'' He winked with the air of a conspirator. ''What do you say? Want to go along with my plan, or do you want to spoil my big day? Just a week?''

How could this stranger know her so well? she wondered. ''Does Donaldson really have a secret spice?''

''Hell, yes! I've tried to find out what it is for years. But now I've got you,'' he announced cheerfully. ''Are you game?''

''You've already got the trophy. Why—''

''I'd just like to set this town on its collective ear, that's all. They've been calling me a hermit for years.'' A shadow crossed his face. ''Ever since my wife died.''

In an abrupt change of mood, he grinned widely, placing his hand over his chest dramatically. ''I'll be heartbroken when you leave in a snit. Of course, every single woman in the valley will probably come calling with fresh-baked pies.''

Diana giggled, drawn by his comic appeal. ''You are a con man, Mac.''

Staring at her intently, Mac whispered huskily, ''I could use a friend, too, Diana. How about it?''

Their eyes met and held. "Maybe," she agreed softly. "For a week."

The band began playing, and music floated into the office. Diana leaned on Mac's shoulder, content for a moment. "They started without your bagpipes."

He kissed her forehead. "So they did. I'll play the songs for you later at the house."

She smiled softly, wondering if Mac could really be her friend. "I can't wait."

He grinned. "Ready to get back in there and dance? I'm pretty rusty, but I'll try."

"I haven't danced in years, Mac. I'm not sure I know how."

"Trust me. You'll remember."

Diana ran her palm along his cheek. *Her friend?* "You ask a lot, Mac."

At one o'clock in the morning, Mac turned the pickup into his driveway, the frozen landscape no longer seeming lonely to him. Diana's head rested against his shoulder, her breath tickling the hair at the base of his neck. She had snuggled to him so easily— he liked that.

He'd studied her all night, watching her dance and laugh. When she thought he wasn't looking, Diana had sneaked wary curious glances at him.

She'd been on a nervous high for hours, and the instant they began to drive home, her head settled peacefully onto his shoulder and she quickly fell asleep.

His mouth turned down. Mac's gut instinct had told him to make the announcement, using it to snare the chili trophy. He'd almost scared her to death, he should have known better.

He liked her soft mouth moving beneath his....

Mac eased Diana's sleeping body into his arms and carried her into the house.

Wanting attention, Red whined and nuzzled Mac's legs as Mac placed Diana on the bed. He looked at her pale face on the pillow. She belonged here, he decided, tugging off her shoes and socks.

He eased off her jacket and slid her under the blankets. Diana slept heavily throughout.

Mac had to force himself to leave her. He stoked the woodstove in the kitchen, making it warmer than usual for her. Then he sat looking out the windows as he rubbed Red's shaggy head. "It wouldn't be too bad, old dog. Having her around for a while."

Diana coming into his arms was one of the sweetest things to happen in his life....

Mac settled deeper in his chair, remembering his anger at the man who had hurt Diana. Shaking his head, he looked down at Red. "I intend to keep her for a time. After all, it does a man good to shake people up once in a while."

Finally, when he could resist no longer, Mac went into the bedroom to watch his lady sleep. Red whined and followed.

Mac watched Diana in the dim light coming from the hallway. Her face turned toward him. She sighed, stirring restlessly. Would she wake in the night and leave him? Panic rippled inside him. His heart seemed to stop beating. He had to keep her, somehow.

Without a second thought, Mac eased himself on the bed on top of the blankets and drew the quilt over him. Taking care in the small space, he laid an arm and a leg over Diana. There, he thought, now she wouldn't be able to get away without waking him. He closed his eyes, praying she would choose to stay.

Her hair clung to his cheek, its scent fresh and feminine. He savored the softness within his arms, realizing the depth of his own loneliness. In the dreamy realm between reality and sleep, he wondered how it would feel to hold her every night.

He dozed, but when she stirred, Mac jumped out of bed, feeling a jolt of pure panic race through him. Would she stay? There wasn't a thing he could do if she decided to leave.

Diana's brown eyes opened slowly. She stared at him blankly for a moment. "Hi, Mac," she murmured drowsily. "You're here again."

He adjusted the covers around her, his hands trembling. "I hope you're not cold. You shouldn't be. You've got two blankets wrapped around you."

She lifted her arms, stretching and yawning. The vulnerable line of her throat caused Mac's mouth to dry. Diana in the morning was very sensuous. To wake up to her every morning would be an adventure in itself.

"Why are you so nice, Mac?" she asked.

"Because you're mine to take care of. I found you on my front porch. It's that simple," he answered honestly. "Do you want to talk now?"

She stared at him for a long moment, with sleepy eyes. "About what?"

He shivered. "I'm cold. Do you think you can spare a little warmth for a freezing man?"

She looked away from him, her black lashes sheltering her expression. "I'm not up to any of that, you know."

He took her chin in his hand. "I haven't asked a

thing but a blanket on a cold November morning. That, and helping me put one over on Benevolence.''

Diana sat up and stared out of the window, her expression that of pain. ''There have been too many people asking too many things of me, Mac,'' she whispered slowly. ''Who am I, really? I don't know anymore.''

The aching tone cut at Mac, and he wanted to hold her. Instead, taking care not to alarm her, he sat down on a chair. ''We'll find out, honey. But I can tell you this—you've got an independent streak in you a mile wide.''

''Not now. It's gone—I'm too tired.'' They were both quiet for a while. Then she smiled at him and handed him the quilt, which he wrapped around him. ''You know, I haven't slept with my clothes on since I was a little girl.''

He chuckled. ''It's been some time since I lay in bed with all my clothes on, too. I think it was when I was about ten and had sneaked out for some moonlight dogsledding with Red's grandfather. My brothers and I had to be up early for chores, and we didn't want the folks to know, so we slept in our clothes. That was one long day.''

He talked easily, knowing that the sound of his voice soothed her. That was all that mattered as daylight slipped into the bedroom. ''Old Red's grandfather was a purebred McKenzie River husky. His grandmother was a Coppermine husky, and both of them knew how to pull better than any dog team around. There's an old Yukon-type sled in the barn— about seven feet long. As boys, my brothers and I used to hitch up the dogs and let them run. We had five dogs then, all in working weight in the winter.

That was for rescue on the mountains, before snow-mobiles.''

Diana shifted and sighed. Mac's heart skipped a beat when he realized that if the engagement was real, he could hold her every day, every night. It was a thought that slid over him like dark sweet honey; it lingered and tantalized. He had to fight to keep from taking her in his arms. ''Boring, huh?''

''No,'' she answered sleepily. She sighed again, her lashes drifting down. ''Please, Mac, continue.''

The scent of her hair was exotic and irresistible. Mac wanted to slide his fingers through it, taste the silky skin of her neck. Instead, he forced himself to talk. ''Each dog can pull about two hundred pounds. There's a small birch sleigh in the barn, too. When you want, honey, we'll harness Red and take you out for a run. There's nothing like it—the sun hitting the snow, the cold freezing on your face. It's like catching a dream. You forget everything but the sleigh gliding over the snow, the dogs running, pulling the sled.''

Diana dozed and Mac felt sleep overcoming him, too. Yawning, he wrapped the warmth of her nearness around him and drifted off into the first peaceful sleep he'd had in years.

Mac awoke in a panic, feeling the empty bed. He scrambled to his feet and raced to the front door, his heart slamming against his chest. Red barked excitedly, leaping around his legs as Mac jerked open the door and ran out onto the porch. ''Damn! She's gone, isn't she?'' Mac scanned the road, looking for Diana and knowing she'd left him.

He felt a movement behind him and pivoted, almost closing the door on Diana's surprised face. He stepped back into the house. "Where have you been?" he demanded roughly, placing his hands on his hips.

Her dark delicate eyebrows lifted; her expression was indignant. "Who wants to know?" she shot back. "It would serve you right if I drove out today and made you the laughing stock of Benevolence. How would you explain that one, big guy?"

Because she'd scared him so badly, Mac felt raw. He frowned, breathing heavily. "You weren't this mad last night. Why are you now?"

She looked him up and down, her gaze meeting his evenly. "Why am I mad, he asks? You knew I was tired, and you wore me down with your talk of concern. Like a brainwasher, or something. But that was yesterday. Now I've had some rest, and I'm furious. You used me. You took advantage of me. If you ever—repeat, ever—put me in a position like you did yesterday, I just don't know what I'll do. But it won't be pleasant!"

Something within him sang. He liked the cocky tilt of her head, the flashing dark brown eyes and temper staining her cheeks. She was so alive, every ounce of her held fire. "Now, Diana," he began, taking a step toward her.

Diana jabbed his chest with her finger, tilting her head back to glare at him. "You snore," she accused firmly. "Big dragging snores. Like a walrus on land. I had to move to the couch."

Mac blinked. For a moment she had him off balance. In his lifetime, few women had come at him like a cornered bobcat. "Are we in a snit?" he asked carefully, examining the sleek lines of her legs beneath her cotton-knit skirt.

"That's putting it delicately. You're sneaky—you creep up on people when they're bone tired."

"Maybe you're right," he returned. Watching Diana lay down the law with the morning sun outlining her slender legs was sheer pleasure. "Wait until I have my morning coffee, and I'll argue with you about anything you want."

"I'm not comfortable about this week-long farce at all. Even though I can walk out at any time and leave you to play the fool. My honor is at stake." She breathed heavily, pushing back her overlong sleeves impatiently. She stalked around him, gauging him from head to toe. Mac held perfectly still, knowing that Diana needed to turn over everything in her mind.

When she had come full circle, Diana said, "Okay, you want to be friends—I can understand that coming from a hermit. Maybe no one but a stranger would have you for a friend. *You* need me. But I want to know more about you. There's more to life than playing jokes on whole towns, you know. Do you have a job, Mac?"

"Not right now. Unless you count running this ranch."

Her small hand slashed the air impatiently. "Fine. So what is the drawing board and all the whachamacallits doing beneath that sheet in the living room? And the computer?"

Mac took a deep breath and answered her question. "I'm an engineer."

She frowned, digesting his answer. "Why aren't you working in an office? Surely you can't have many clients out here."

"A consulting free-lance engineer. There's a helicopter out back. It's just a hop and a skip to the airport. Some people enjoy concrete mazes and asphalt—I don't.''

Diana's dark eyes lighted up. "A helicopter?"

"I flew one in Nam. I have a license."

"You must be good. You probably transmit data with a telephone modem, don't you?"

"Straight from my computer to theirs," he agreed quietly.

"One of the capable ones—a man who can do anything. A chili-cooking, bagpipe-playing, helicopter-flying rancher/engineer. You know just who you are and what you can do, don't you? Just what I need." She began backing toward the kitchen, her face taut with anger.

He took a step, wanting to hold her. "Now, Diana, don't get all worked up."

She threw up her hands, and he noticed flour dusting her wrists. "'Worked up'? Why would I do that? You had the advantage all the time, didn't you? You know what you want and how to get it. I just walked into your neat little plans to make fools of a whole town. You wanted to use me—I never had a chance."

"I've never taken advantage of a woman in my life, Diana," he stated, feeling the tension in his body. Would she run now? Helpless before her rising temper, Mac decided to keep quiet. He scratched his newly grown beard, contemplating the spitfire before him.

"I'm baking bread. I always bake bread when I'm angry," she said ominously. "Stay out of my way."

"Smells good…" he began gently, then stopped when he saw Diana's hips sway as she walked away from him.

He thrust his hands into his pockets, wanting to cup

that gentle softness. Damn, he cursed. She needed to bring out all that long-suppressed anger, and he needed—what? To play her big brother, her friend, her lover? Mac closed his eyes, remembering the feel of her breasts against him.

Then he settled himself on the couch and watched Diana warily over the top of his newspaper. She worked feverishly.

Coming out of the kitchen, Diana studied him. Then she marched straight into the living room and stood squarely in front of him. "I don't owe you a thing but bed and board, mister. You need me, got that? You're lonesome and you've gotten us both into a corner. And I'm the only one who can get you out. Ha!"

She thrust a mug of coffee at him. "I want every last sock you own on the kitchen table in five minutes. My fiancé isn't going to go anywhere wearing those." She pointed to his feet.

Mac wriggled his toes and stared at his socks. "What's wrong with them?"

Diana took a deep breath, exhaling slowly. Mac forced his eyes away from her breasts, which were thrusting at the thin cloth of her shirt. "Other than the left stocking is navy blue and the right one is black with red stripes, nothing is wrong with your socks."

"Are you staying, then, Diana?" he asked quietly, waiting.

"A week. I need to show myself—and you—that I can handle the situation." She looked shyly away from him, the color slowly creeping up her cheeks. He could see her heartbeat pulsing in the hollow in her throat, and he knew that she was thinking of their kisses. How long had it been since she'd been kissed so hungrily? How long had it been since she'd felt wanted as a woman? Somehow he felt it was years.

Meeting his gaze, she added firmly, "Besides, I liked those nice people at the cook-off. They may need protecting from you."

"It will be my pleasure to extend the hospitality of my kingdom to you, ma'am. For as long as it's needed," he answered truthfully and felt the emptiness begin to slide away.

Four

Diana breathed the crisp morning air as she picked her way through the blue spruce and aspen trees in the small canyon. In the two days since Mac's announcement of their engagement, she'd taken several long walks with Red. The quiet solitude was restful, and she found her pain easing.

Pulling her jacket collar higher against the cold wind, she thought of her marriage and family. The white picket fence and the all-American dream. She'd given herself to that dream, heart and soul, and now it was gone. She'd pasted her life together, survived by sheer willpower, but now there were odd pieces missing from her life. Somehow, she had to find the strength to make herself whole again.

She stared at the ranch and spotted Mac instantly. "I knew Mac would be outside, Red. Trying to look as though he's checking on the cows, when he's really watching us from beneath that Stetson of his. Spying on us, that's what he does. He acts like a rumpled old badger when we don't invite him on our walks,'' she noted to the husky, who walked close to her heels.

Diana scowled as she approached the barn's feed-lot. The small herd of Herefords looked up at her while Mac turned his back. ''See that; Red? Oh, now he's trying to play the innocent.''

There was something about Mac that caused her to want to confront him. She liked catching Mac off guard; he got such a sheepish boyish look on his face. ''I wouldn't steal your dog, Mac. He's probably your only friend.''

Beneath the brim of the Stetson, his heavy brows lifted. He was the picture of innocence. ''Who said you would?''

The buffalo bull lumbered toward her and nudged her knee. When she stepped back, frightened by the shaggy mountain of animal, Mac looked up. ''That's Old Bob. He's harmless.''

''Why on earth—''

Mac shrugged, rubbing the buffalo's large hump roughly. The bull swayed and almost seemed to purr with delight. ''I couldn't stand to see him made into buffalo burgers, so I bought him from Donaldson. Pet him—Old Bob likes that.''

Tentatively, she stroked the buffalo's head. Mac nodded approvingly, then easily lifted a fifty-pound sack of grain to pour into a feed trough. He looked as though he wanted to say something, but just somehow couldn't.

''Do you have a problem, Mac?'' Diana asked quietly, knowing that Mac would answer truthfully. He didn't have a dram of deceit in his large well-muscled body, and Diana had repeatedly tested her new skill of attacking problems face-to-face on him.

"Okay, you asked for it," he said slowly. "You just don't realize what could happen on those precious walks of yours. I know you're working out some pretty serious burrs in your life and need to be alone, but if you fell down a rocky slope or if a wounded bear decided to have you for his supper—"

"Red is always with me, Mac."

"Huh! And what about that jacket?" He reached out and tugged at the denim. "It doesn't even have a flannel lining."

Mac playing mother hen was a sight that warmed Diana's bruised heart. In the few days since she'd arrived, she'd noted his excellent care of the livestock and assorted strays that seemed to head unerringly for his ranch.

But she couldn't allow him to rule her life. Mac sometimes made her feel like a child. But then there were other times when he made her feel... Diana shivered. She felt restless and torn apart. She looked at a tree, comparing the stark leafless limbs to her life.

"You're working at it, aren't you?" he asked softly, running a warm fingertip along her jaw. "Getting all stewed up, working at what's eating you."

"Maybe I am," she answered, stepping away from his disturbing touch.

"Why don't you do something just for the sheer hell of it?" he asked lightly, his eyes glittering.

She laughed, knowing it to be a nervous reaction. "You mean staying with you and playing a game with the innocent people of Benevolence isn't enough?"

"Hell, no," he began. He reached out and ruffled her short hair playfully. "What do you say about running into town and stirring things up?"

Diana smiled. "You realize that after this week, you're going to have a lot of explaining to do?"

When he simply looked at her, she added, "Mac, I'm not a dropout with a million dollars in my pocket. I need to begin looking for work here or somewhere else. Maybe in Denver—"

"My future wife?" Mac felt a cold wave of panic. He couldn't let her out of his grasp now. She'd dropped into his dreary life like a bright tropical flower. "Now, look, Diana. I can provide—"

Diana raised one slender but firm finger. "Don't hallucinate, Mr. MacLean."

"Hell, I'm thinking about our game plan—for appearance's sake," he snapped, knowing she'd reached inside him to touch a live nerve. He'd spent part of the previous night holding her, absorbing the warmth of her body. Now he could feel Diana sliding away. Desperately, he thought of future nights.... "You can't look for work within days of arriving—"

"So you have it, too?" she asked quietly, frowning. "The macho-big guy syndrome—keep the little wife at home and under your thumb. Is that what happened to Eleanor?"

Because Diana was hurting, Mac let the accusation slide off. His marriage with Eleanor had been pure gold. But now she was gone. The horror of her dying had stunned him, and he had slipped into a mechanical life without her.

Then a half-pint stray had come drifting into his empty world and swept the loneliness out of his heart. He wanted Diana in his home, in his life and in his bed permanently, Mac realized sharply. She'd come to him a stray, but that had all changed. Holding a woman in his arms all night gave a man certain rights, he decided firmly. Kissing the sweetness on her lips and feeling like starting all over again really gave a man ideas about living.

Especially when he started worrying about her leaving. Especially since he'd begun to think of waking up to her every morning like a real husband.

He closed his eyes a moment, allowing the tantalizing fantasy to enfold him. Marriage to Diana would be a spicy delight, a daily confection—

Diana jabbed Mac's flannel-covered chest with her finger. Her mouth pursed but before she could speak, he grabbed her wrist, trapping it securely but gently against his warm body. "Is that what happened to you?" he said.

Diana stepped back from him, her back meeting the weathered boards of the old barn. She stiffened, trying to fight her jumbled emotions. She could feel the heat start to smolder between them.

His fingers stroked the smooth flesh of her inner wrist as he wrapped his other hand around the nape of her neck, drawing her face nearer. Mac gave her a long soul-searching stare that tangled all her emotions. "You can tell me about it, you know. That's the good part about ships passing in the night— strangers make good listeners," he said gently, sheltering her against the chilly wind.

"I can't stay here forever."

"Why in the Sam Hill can't you? Whose rules are you taking into account now? Look, take a job if you need to, but I'm asking you to stay."

Diana put her hand on his chest to place some distance between them, and felt the hard beat of his heart beneath her palm. She had to fight to keep herself from responding to his scent, his warmth and those probing eyes.

The wind blew through her hair, causing one strand to brush his lips. His mouth, held in a firm line, softened sensuously as his fingers began to caress the back of her neck. "You're fighting the past," he whispered, his head lowering. "Why don't you let it go?"

Entranced by his slow deep drawl, Diana tilted back her head. His knuckles brushed her breasts, and she felt his lean body grow taut, saw the almost savage flaring of his nostrils.

"Alex called while you were walking." Mac's voice now had a clipped edge to it, as though he didn't want to relay any messages for Alex. "It seems you left the bed-and-breakfast number with your sons. Alex traced you here. He's hot on your trail, isn't he?"

Mac placed both hands on the barn, effectively trapping her. Anger flickered in his eyes.

Diana took a deep steadying breath, feeling Mac's very solid frame warm her. Closing her eyes she inhaled his scent and willed new life into her. She wanted to be rid of her insecurities.

Mac's raw and caring voice whispered urgently into her ear. "Let it go, Diana."

She trembled, fighting the futile desperation that still surfaced in her quiet moments. "Oh, Mac, you don't know—"

"Maybe I do." Placing one finger beneath her chin, he raised her face to his. His mouth brushed hers lightly. "Loving and losing are hard things to do. You're a strong woman, Diana. You wouldn't be here slugging it out with yourself if you weren't."

When she remained silent, he added, "Alex wants you to call him back."

Diana studied Mac's tanned face, trying to see beyond his steady gaze. "Is it about the boys? Are they hurt?"

Mac gently stroked her cheek. "I don't think that's exactly why Alex wanted you to call." He held her tightly for a moment, and then he stepped back, crossing his arms over his chest. "He wants you back, doesn't he?"

"He's not going to get me," Diana answered firmly.

Mac smiled lightly. "Atta girl. I didn't like his remark about us shacking up together very well myself."

Diana's eyes widened. "Did he say that?" Fierce anger was suddenly coursing hotly through her.

Mac pushed the Stetson back from his face, and a strand of black hair fell across his dark forehead. "Not exactly in those terms."

"Oh, I see. The famous 'man talk' that can't be repeated in front of females," she snapped.

Mac's lean cheeks darkened with a flush. "Something like that. Are you going to call him back? He's worried about your reputation. Nettled as hell about you staying with me. Seems that Ray put in a word or two about us getting married. We had quite a conversation. He wanted me to tuck you in your station wagon and send you home."

"What did you say?"

Mac's head tilted, the brim of the Stetson shadowing his eyes. "I invited him to drop by and do it himself."

"And?"

"He said he just might do that."

Diana felt anger slicing through her like a hot knife. Alex deserved to get back a little of his own, and she suddenly found advantages to Mac's game.

Without pressing her, Mac had given her back her self-esteem as a woman. He had gently reawakened her femininity, and she'd needed that to feel complete.

She could feel her heels dig deeper in the mud, as though she were settled in for a good fight. She knew she could support herself financially, but there were other areas where the wounds still hadn't completely healed. If Alex needed to see her surviving, so be it. She'd spread her newfound confidence all over his leering face. Because she *knew* what she was: a desirable woman.

Desirable. The word lingered as she thought of Mac's large hand sweeping gently down her body, his fingers trembling. His rough cheeks had heated and colored, and his black eyes had flickered with need for her kiss.

She slyly glanced at Mac's broad shoulders and height. He was as virile as a man could be, and he had wanted her. Mac was absolute proof that she had all the appeal a woman needed.

Alex needed to be taught a lesson. If he had to have the complete picture drawn for him, Diana knew that Mac would comply. Alex would have to look hard and long at the new Diana to find his "house mouse."

On the other hand, Alex wasn't really worth it.

But when Mac added softly, "Seems he can't see

you forging out a life in the wilderness—without the Cadillac and his credit cards," Diana felt defiance blazing anew within her.

"Revenge can be sweet. I'm game, how about you?" Mac asked, grinning widely.

"Uh-huh," she responded. She felt like cutting all her restrictive ties to the past. With her home leased for one year and her two sons spending Thanksgiving with Alex, there was absolutely no reason she couldn't stay longer. "I've been thinking that I may stay more than a week, Mac. You wouldn't mind having a Rayfield Inn leftover for some extra days, would you?"

He shook his head. "Just for the hell of it?"

"For the sheer hell of it," she corrected. "I didn't have a thing planned past this week in Benevolence."

"Ah, there's nothing like a woman who's steamed up," Mac teased. "Suits me. I'm enjoying myself."

"Oh, so am I," she stated, knowing it was true.

They began walking toward the house. "If we're going to set up…housekeeping, we'd better buy a few things to get tongues wagging, don't you think?" Diana asked.

When Mac didn't answer, she turned sharply, catching his gaze on her hips. Diana's confidence fluttered and soared. It was really nice to have Mac around; he did wonders for her spirit. She was having a really good time now.

Mac leaned against the counter, feeling embarrassed at being in the women's lingerie section of the dry goods store. He glanced at the hunting supply section and caught Neil Wingman smirking behind aluminum tent poles. Deciding that the store owner could go to blazes, Mac gazed back at Diana.

Her slender back was up, it seemed. She'd latched on to Mac's arm the minute she'd stepped out of the pickup in downtown Benevolence. Every beaming smile was focused so brightly on him that he'd begun to sweat beneath his shearling coat. She'd tossed so many "honeys" and "sweethearts" and adoring looks at him that he was starting to feel like a real fiancé.

He was also starting to feel as possessive as a real fiancé, he realized slowly. If they were really going to get married… Mac stopped in midthought as Diana's delicate hands smoothed out a lacy black confection.

When she said, "Oh, look, Mac. Isn't it nice?" Wingman let out a snicker.

Mac, incensed that two customers were leering at Diana, tightened his fists. In another minute he'd have to politely ask all three men outside to preserve Diana's honor. "Diana, this section is for the—" he paused, his face heating "—the party set. It's a joke in a store like this. That thing is X-rated. Put it down."

Wingman laughed out loud, and Mac took just one threatening step toward the man before Diana's hand on his belly stopped him. He glanced down and found her looking at him through her lashes so seductively, so sensually promising, that he felt as though his boots were stuck to the wooden floor. His breath caught in his dry throat, and his male impulses told him to sweep her into his arms and taste that sweet petal-soft mouth. If they were married, he'd take her on home…

"What is wrong with you?" she demanded sharply through gritted teeth, still smiling. "You look as though someone snatched a piece of pie away from you. Stop it. We're creating an image, remember?"

She held the black teddy against her body, modeling the skimpy garment for him. "Mac?" she persisted, the sensuous look deepening. "You could act as though you like it. There's more to this game than just living together, you know. Even I know that."

Mac's gaze drifted over the teddy and her curves behind it. Mac could feel the wild throbbing within him, the primitive need to claim her and have her body beneath him.

He groaned inwardly, thrusting his fists into his jeans pockets. Diana needed time to sort out her problems; she didn't need him acting like a bull elk at mating season. To cover his desire, he spoke roughly. "Looks fine. Put it on my bill."

Diana's fine eyebrows lifted. "I will not. I'm quite capable of paying my own bills."

"Men are supposed to buy their ladies things like—that." He nodded at the wispy garment, hearing Wingman snicker again.

"Times have changed, Mac," Diana stated tightly.

"Better back up, boy," the storekeeper offered, moving toward them.

Mac shot him a look that could have melted lead and turned back to Diana, his jaw taut. "Get used to it, Diana. As long as you're in Benevolence, I'm footing the bill."

Her slender fingers crushed the teddy; her eyes darkened. "Says who?"

"Lovers' tiff?" Wingman teased, approaching

them. "Say, I heard you two were getting married. Short notice, isn't it? How did you meet?"

"My brother Rafe introduced us last year. I've been expecting her," Mac said. She was his to take care of, wasn't she? That meant paying her bills.

"Rafe can pick 'em. So she's staying with you?" Wingman's gaze narrowed on Diana's petite body, appraising her slender build right down to her shoes. Mac took a deep breath, held it to the count of ten and slowly wrapped his arm around her shoulders, drawing her next to him.

Acting like Diana's possessive future husband wasn't difficult, he discovered. "She's getting the place in shape. You know, measuring things," Mac explained while pressing a kiss to her temple.

The sweet scent of her hair intoxicated him, and he found himself closing his eyes, barely breathing, wishing that they were alone on the mesa. She looked as pretty as a cluster of snow buttercups breaking the winter snow.

Diana shifted away, her face averted. "Mac's right. We're getting the house ready before I look for work."

"Hmm. Work." Wingman scratched his jaw. "I'll be needing someone to help me with the paperwork after a week. My clerk, Andrea, is quitting to stay home with her kids. What do you think? Just part-time, enough to keep the receipts straight for the accountant. Some ordering stuff."

"I'd like that—" Diana began.

"Diana has enough to do at the house," Mac said firmly, determined to keep her close to him as much as possible. He didn't know how long she was staying, and he couldn't stop her from leaving when she felt it was time to go. So for now while she was here, he would make sure she stayed beside him.

"Huh!" Wingman snorted. "I've known you for a long time, Mac. Never figured you to stop a woman from working if she wanted to. Funny, you hermits have weird ideas about women—once you finally trap one."

Wingman winked at Diana, who boldly returned the gesture. "She's got that soft look, Mac," he observed thoughtfully. "Like Eleanor, but different, you know? Diana looks like she might like taking a wilderness survival trip up on old Smokey."

He laughed, watching Mac begin to simmer. "Boy, you MacLean boys are slow to get riled, but now we've got you."

Diana's arm slipped around Mac's waist. She pinched him just once, but hard enough to make him wince. "We can have the place in shape in two weeks, Mac. Besides, he said only part-time."

Standing on tiptoe, she reached up and kissed his cheek. "Shut up or you'll never get another loaf of homemade bread," she whispered urgently. "Or berry pie."

Still leaning against Mac, Diana smiled at Wingman. "We'll talk it over, and I'll give you a call. I don't see anything wrong with part-time work, at least through the holidays. Would that be okay, for now?"

"I'll take whatever hours you can give me and appreciate 'em," Wingman answered heartily. "When things settle down for you two, we might work out something else."

Later, Mac followed Diana through the grocery store, pushing the laden cart. Actually he enjoyed shopping with her, watching her study the different brands intently before choosing one and placing it in the cart. He missed shopping with a woman.

Diana struggled with a twenty-five-pound sack of flour. He lifted it into the cart for her. "Are you sure you need this much?"

Her eyes blazed; she looked furious. "Are you always going to question my needs? I'm good and mad, Mac. And when I'm mad, I bake," she stated, placing a bottle of vanilla in the cart.

"What's wrong?"

"Let's just say I had different plans for my little sabbatical from reality. I hadn't planned to be a prisoner in your house when I agreed to this farce. I didn't like your domineering noises at the store. *I* want to work at Wingman's."

Mac studied his hands on the handle of the cart. "The outfitter's is a man's hangout, Diana. For hunting guides and their customers," he said carefully, uncertain as to her reaction. "The language gets rough in there sometimes. Ah, colorful, you know."

"I raised two sons, Mac. I haven't been all that sheltered." Then she looked at him carefully. "Are you blushing?"

"Hell, no. I'm just saying that Wingman's is okay, but—"

"I can handle myself, Mac. You can't do it for me," Diana stated softly, placing a hand on his cheek. "You're hot. You *are* blushing," she asserted.

"I haven't had a lot of practice at this," Mac said. "Anything could happen to you. What I mean is, you're just getting your bearings. Don't dive in headfirst."

"You said I was strong, Mac." Diana's fingers explored the crease between his thick brows. "Don't you see? While we're playing at this—'' she lowered her voice ''—engagement, I have some very serious thinking to do. I'm questioning my past, building foundations for the future. Do you understand? Didn't you go through that when you lost your wife?''

''I went through a lot,'' Mac said, looking at the huge gunnysack of potatoes to avoid Diana's searching gaze. ''Eleanor shouldn't have been out in that blizzard, helping me feed cattle. She never fully recovered from pneumonia.''

''I know. And you're hurting just like me, right?''

Her gentle tone made him look up, and he saw her concerned expression. ''I did hurt plenty. Then I shut the door. It was that or go crazy.'' Mac felt his heart miss a beat when her hand rested on the side of his neck.

Mac swallowed as she caressed his cheek. He didn't want the pain of loving and losing again, the happiness now, then the ripping of heart and soul later....

''And you play bagpipes at midnight. Oh, Mac,'' Diana murmured. ''You look so sad.''

He thought he heard her sigh, and his gaze strayed down to her lips and lingered there. When he saw her tongue flick moisture on them, it was all he could do to reach out and pull her into his arms.

It had been so long....

Her dark eyes shone brightly beneath her lashes. ''I'll be your friend, Mac,'' she stated unevenly.

After a moment, he smiled. ''Friend. That's nice.''

The next morning, Diana was shaping bread dough just as Mac padded into the kitchen.

He mumbled a halfhearted greeting, his stockinged

feet locked on a path to the coffeepot. In the light of dawn passing through the windows, Diana could see the line of dark hair trailing down from his bare chest to below that open first snap of his jeans. A pale strip of flesh showed above the waistband. Totally entranced, she stopped working on the dough.

Mac turned his back—a rippling, intriguing back—to pour coffee into a mug. He had such a nice physique—broad shoulders, lean waist and narrow hips. The worn jeans clung to his firm buttocks, the back pocket faded from his wallet.

Cup of coffee in hand, he made his way toward the table. He sat, staring at the dark liquid as though it could solve the world's problems. Sleepy and rumpled, Mac had a totally lovable look about him, and Diana found her thoughts returning to the woman he had loved. Wingman had said Eleanor had a "soft" look.

Mac needed a soft woman, she decided.

"Good morning, sleepyhead." She placed the dough in the pans, oiled the top of the loaves and put them aside to rise. "You're up early."

"It's hard to sleep with pots and pans clanging in the middle of the night," he grumbled. He surveyed the kitchen counter, covered with platters of brownies and cookies. "You've been busy. We can't eat all that."

"I thought you could take some over to that nice Mr. Clancy. He's promised to teach me how to mush."

Mac glared up at her. "That old codger isn't getting all of it."

"I have cookie dough in the refrigerator. There will be plenty." Diana wiped her hands on the towel serv-

ing as her apron. She'd had a bad night, the cold small
bed plaguing her sleep. Eventually, she'd wrapped the
blanket around her and spent the night on the couch,
snuggling against the back.

In the twilight hours, she seemed to be defenseless
against the nagging emptiness. Was that the reason
people took lovers—to fill the empty nights? At her
age, how could a second love be as exciting and demanding as the first passion?

She couldn't spend her life baking and cleaning
nooks and crannies. At the moment, she could only
think of baiting Mac—a sport she had come to enjoy.
"Someone tried to play bagpipes out in the barn last
night."

Over the rim of his cup, his eyes widened almost
comically. "Tried? Those cows like my midnight ser-
enades. I'll have you know…" He paused as she slid
a platter of bacon, eggs and hash brown potatoes in
front of him. His eyes lighted up, and he grinned up
at her. "Mmm."

After a moment he turned serious, rubbing the stubble covering his jaw. "I didn't sleep well," he said,
looking intently at her. "I came down at two o'clock
and found you on the couch."

"You worked on your plans." She could feel
Mac's gaze stripping her, probing her emotions. Uncomfortable at his scrutiny, she turned to the window
to watch the pink dawn rise over the sawtooth-shaped
mountaintops. In the stillness of the night, the sounds
he'd made—the rustling of paper, the creaking of his
chair, his talking quietly on the radio—had made her
feel safe. They'd wrapped around her like a down
comforter, and gradually she had slipped into a deep
sleep.

She looked back at him. "What are you doing to-day?" she asked, trying to change the flow of her thoughts.

"I'm going out in the copter the first thing this morning," he said. "There's sign of poachers up on the Ewing Mesa. They've butchered five or six deer for bait."

She glanced outside and saw clouds hovering low on the mountains. "I want to go." Diana smiled to herself, slightly surprised by her demand.

"You can't." He put a forkful of potatoes into his mouth. "This is really good."

Diana grabbed his plate from him and held it aloft. "I want to go, Mac," she insisted.

His jaw jutted out pugnaciously. His hand ran through his sleek black hair, mussing it up in a way that made him look lovable. "No way. We'll go joy-riding some other time. I promised the game warden I'd look for signs of poachers today and bring back any information."

Diana walked to Red's food bowl and lowered Mac's plate near it, threatening him silently.

"Okay, you can go," he agreed reluctantly, eyeing Red's alert stance. "But at the first sign of trouble, I'm bringing you home."

"Why?" she demanded sharply.

"You could get hurt," he replied between his teeth as he rose to walk toward her. "Poachers don't like to get caught, you know. Once in a while they take a potshot at the copters...." His eyes narrowed. "For some reason, you get feisty in the morning, while I'm still trying to wake up."

"If you wouldn't spend all night hunched over a drawing board, you'd feel better in the mornings."

"Look who's talking." For a moment his dark eyes searched hers. A lock of hair fell across his forehead. "You sleep better when you're lying up against something…someone, Diana," he murmured. "You're the kind of woman who needs cuddling."

Diana could feel the heat from his body, almost feel the springy hair covering his chest. She backed up against the counter, still holding the plate. Mac placed his hands on her hips, looming over her. Elemental heat waves surged between them as he asked, "When are we getting married, friend?"

He took the plate from her and placed it on the counter, then inched closer to her. Mac stared at her mouth like a starved man, his chest nearing her hot cheek. "Just to answer the town's questions. You know, if we were really getting married, last night could have been better for both of us."

His low husky drawl sent tingly sparks up her spine. "We could…" Mac's lips brushed her temple.

Unsteadily, Diana placed her palms against his chest and felt his muscles tighten in response to her touch. "I've been in that Mother Goose fairy tale— it didn't work. Let me go."

His jaw hardened, his eyes flashed. "Lady, someday you'll trust me. You'll jump off that high wall and find yourself in one piece, not broken up like Humpty Dumpty."

She forced a small space between them. How could he be so sure when she was so scared? *All the king's horses and all the king's men, couldn't put Humpty together again.* "You're pushing, Mac."

He toyed with a curl just behind her ear, studying the reddish tint in the light of dawn. "Could be. I've been out of practice so long, I'm not certain. I just know that I like your perfume, the way the bathroom feels all rosy when you step out of it. A man misses those things, you know. The little things like a dainty lace bra drying over the shower rod, that sort of thing.''

"That's not enough.'' She could have told him about the emptiness then, but somehow she thought he knew. Involuntarily, her hands slid over the smooth planes of his shoulders, exploring, feeling...

"You're afraid of me, aren't you, Mac?'' The men she'd known had always seemed so sure of themselves, demanding and taking.

"I'd be a fool not to be. I've been to hell and back, and I wouldn't care to repeat the experience. You're the first one to hear that.''

He shifted slightly, the movement bringing his hips against hers. "God, you're soft.'' He nuzzled her neck. "Mmm, you smell like bread dough.''

She giggled, trusting him enough to let him touch her. It had been so long since she'd trusted a man that much. Mac's mouth slid along her jawline, his breath swirling around her hot cheek.

Diana barely breathed, enjoying the light scrape of his beard. Allowing her hands to drift to his waist, she looped her fingers through his belt. "Mr. Mac-Lean, do you know what you're doing?''

"Stirring things up?'' he asked huskily against her lips, teasing them with tiny kisses.

She trembled, wanting to run her palms over the smoothness of his back. The need to open her mouth to his became so strong that she gasped. Closing her eyes, Diana wondered about the intense emotions racing through her. "Too much, Mac,'' she murmured, moving away.

He stared at her, his eyes heavy lidded with desire. "Mmm?"

"Friends don't act like this, Mac," she began, fretting with her needs and her denials, looking away.

His warm knuckles grazed her soft cheek. "Of course they do," he returned gently, pulling her into his arms.

For a long moment, he just held her. "Yesterday is gone, Diana."

Five

Yesterday is gone. A week later, Diana repeated the words, liking the sound of them.

Seated next to Mac in the soaring helicopter, she surveyed the snow-covered buttes and the pine forests below. She adjusted the headphones he had insisted she wear. Above the valley a golden eagle soared, his huge brown wings glistening in the sun. Her eyes following him, Diana felt a kinship with the bird in his lonely flight.

The craggy panorama contrasted with Missouri's rounded hills and oaks as much as her sons' temperaments differed. Rick, a college freshmen, was dependable and even tempered, while Blaine lived for the moment.

Diana felt a pain sweep through her, and she closed her eyes. The breach between her sons and herself—caused by the divorce—remained despite her efforts.

And this "vacation" was only deepening it. She remembered how upset her sons were when she'd told them about it. They hadn't said it, but she'd known they felt she was abandoning them. When she'd called Rick at his college dorm to give him Mac's phone number, she'd suffered at the coldness in his voice. He hadn't even asked how she was.

Maybe Mac's "game" wasn't so harmless. Maybe she should pack up her things, drive to Missouri and try to patch up her marriage.... Go back to being a "house mouse"? Go back to Alex? Never! She'd find some other way of winning back her sons.

Mac broke into her thoughts by pointing out a mountain goat, who was watching them from a mountain ledge. With agile certainty, the goat leaped down and disappeared into a stand of blue spruce trees. "Slumgullion Pass is over that way, and Wagon Wheel Gap is over there."

Mac tilted the helicopter to follow a high mountain trail. Scanning a creek, he frowned. "Four-wheelers tearing up the ground," he noted. "Looks like they had a private party out here sometime this week. See that bonfire?"

"How do you know it was this week?"

"I've been prowling this mountain every few days since the poaching started. Those tracks weren't there last week."

A black bear lumbered out into a small clearing, saw the helicopter and returned to the forest. "Look over there," Mac ordered briskly. "See where they crossed that gravel bar? They're running traps, baiting for wolf and cat. Looks like they've been cutting some federal timber, too. Probably selling it for firewood—the government won't like that."

They scanned the gorges and mesas for the next hour, Mac speaking briefly to point out old mines and logging camps. He pointed to a ski lift strung between two peaks and chuckled. "I had to rescue some young lovers stranded between stations once. They never even noticed the blizzard until it was too late. Named their first child after me."

Diana nodded, enjoying the scenic beauty, aware of Mac's deep love for the rugged country.

He nodded toward an awesome sheer rock bluff that faced a rugged pine-studded mountain. A narrow passage separated the two. The helicopter swooped to the right, then dived straight for the passage.

"Mac!" Holding her breath, Diana closed her eyes and reached out to grip Mac's arm. Immediately the helicopter paused.

Diana opened one eye and saw Mac's wide grin. She looked around and realized they were hovering in the passage. "I want to live," she enunciated carefully. "That trick could have cost our lives."

He nodded, unconcerned. "True. But I've flown this spot for years." Then he pointed to his lips. "Don't I get one right here for my expertise and keeping you alive?"

Her eyes widened, the beat of her heart pounding in her ears. "What?"

He winked, his face lighting up with laughter. "I want a smooch from my best girl."

"Mac," she protested hotly, staring down the several hundred feet to the earth. "This is dangerous."

"Only if I don't get my kiss." The helicopter dipped abruptly, causing Diana to inhale sharply. Mac stared at her pale face, his grin drying. "Okay, then. I'll settle for a whopper on the ground."

The helicopter flew through the passage and headed home.

After landing, Mac unbuckled Diana's safety belt and eased her shaking legs to the solid safe earth. Her eyes were closed. When her knees buckled, he gripped her jacket collar with both his hands and leaned her against him, supporting her weight easily.

"Hey, I didn't mean to scare you that bad," he murmured. She kept her lids firmly closed. "Knock, knock. Is anyone in there?"

"I'm really mad, Mac." Though she tried, she couldn't unwrap her fingers from his strong secure wrists.

"No sense of humor," he accused. "You weren't in any danger."

Diana forced open one eye, comforted to see the pine branches above her head now. A cold mist tingled on her face. "I could kill you," she managed to say quietly, despite the anger churning within her. She was a volcano about to erupt.

"There's nothing like good honest emotion," Mac assured her. "You've been taking out your anger on that damned dough and by cleaning everything in sight. I've had to hang out wash just to get to talk to you," he said quietly, watching the color slowly return to her face. "I'll bet you've had plenty of practice hiding your emotions. In fact, you probably just waltzed around any unpleasantries, right?"

When she glared at him, he continued, "You've been brooding about your family. You've picked up the phone and put it down too many times. You've written, but no one is returning the letters. Come on, admit it. Let it out," he urged harshly. "I'm here— try it all out on me." He held on to her hips.

He'd run his scalpel too close to her emotional marrow, exposing her frustrations. He had no right to probe and push and enter her private arena of pain. She didn't owe him anything. It was he who owed her for agreeing to play along with his game.

She breathed hard, fighting back the tears. "Let me go. I'm leaving."

Mac pressed his face against hers. "That's right, run off. Find someplace else to lick your wounds. Clean the whole mountainside, for all I care. Dust the barn. Dust the pines. Reality is right here and now, Diana. I thought you had decided to fight for it. But the first time I come too close, you're ready to turn tail."

"You can't possibly know my problems. That's unfair," she insisted, throwing back her head. The wind whipped her hair around her face.

"Of course, it is. Who said life was fair?" Mac wanted to rip her free from her past and help her put together a new life. "You've still got a whole life left. How are you going to live it?" he demanded, wondering about his life and the emptiness surrounding him before Diana's arrival.

She dashed a hand across her cheek, wiping away a tear.

He hated himself for hurting her. "Call your sons, Diana," he murmured, kissing her damp lashes and feeling the tenseness of her body. "Invite them here, if you want. We've got plenty of room."

We, he repeated silently to himself. Somehow in less than two weeks, he had come to think of his house as Diana's home. He'd frightened her when he'd asked her to marry him. Hell, he'd frightened himself. He didn't mean it—or did he?

Ordinarily, he wasn't a pushy man. He'd always let a stray choose its own way. Only this stray had big velvety eyes in a pale face, sweet vulnerable lips and caused him to start feeling he was a kid again.

Or a man about to fall off a very safe, very lonely mountain. She wasn't exactly thrilled about the idea, either.

He took a deep breath, trying to get his bearings. While he held Diana's body close, his thumbs rubbing her hips, everything inside him seemed to heat up. Pressed against his chest, her soft breasts were so enticing. He shuddered with the need to hold them in his hands.

Mac began to breathe heavily. "I never got my kiss," he whispered unsteadily.

"You're deliberately keeping me off balance." Diana lowered her gaze.

Enchanted by the tiny vein throbbing beneath the satin skin of her neck, Mac bent to place his lips on that exact spot. He liked tasting Diana, feeling her slender body tense in his arms, hearing her slight gasp.

Her head turned, her parted lips brushing his somehow. An explosion of ecstasy inside him caused Mac to forget everything but the woman in his arms.

Her fingers slowly tangled in his hair. She tilted her head, looking directly into his eyes. "Do you know what you're doing?"

"I think so," he whispered, marveling at her beauty.

"We shouldn't be doing this." Her fingers slid across his brows, smoothing them. The caress trailed down his nose, causing Mac's breath to halt. He exhaled slowly as her cheek rubbed his.

"What else are friends for?" He caught the delicate lobe of her ear between his teeth, tugging it gently. *Friends?* Who was he kidding?

Diana's touch trailed down his jaw to his throat, her eyes following the glide of her slender fingers over his dark skin. Slowly, she unbuttoned his shirt, exposing his chest. "You have a...nice chest," she said, staring at it solemnly.

"Thank you. So do you." Lord, he loved those small inquisitive fingers caressing his flesh.

A flush rose from her neck, and suddenly Mac realized how very innocent she was, despite her marriage.

"How do you know?" she asked breathlessly. She lowered her cheek to rub it against the hair at the base of his neck.

"I guessed." Mac closed his eyes, fighting the throbbing need that had begun to course through him. She trailed kisses across his left shoulder, her fingers tugging his shirt aside. One fingertip prowled around his left nipple, raising a helpless groan from Mac. "You're not being fair, Diana."

His hands cupped her derriere. He tried to read her thoughtful expression. "Are we using good old Mac as an experiment, Diana?" he asked, giving in to the urge to kiss that delicious bottom lip.

She mulled the thought over, looking out into the fields. "It's the middle of the day, Mac. Someone could drive past."

"So? I thought that was the image you wanted to spread around Benevolence." He closed his eyes, envisioning holding her without the barrier of clothing.

"You're aroused," she whispered huskily, her fingers splayed across his chest, toying with the hair.

"Mmm, slightly." Mac wanted to rip off their clothes and unleash his passion. But he also wanted to be tender and take away all her pain....

She shifted her hips and he groaned, aware that his blood had begun to throb hotly. Taking a deep shuddering breath, he pressed his face into her collar, finding the delicate curve of her throat. Her satin-smooth flesh was so warm beneath his open lips.

Diana's arms locked around his neck. "Mac."

He opened the top buttons on her shirt to reveal the gentle slopes of her breasts. He stared hungrily. He could almost feel their weight—

"Mac," she protested more sharply, drawing her shirt closed with one hand. She squirmed, pushing him until his arms were empty. "Don't."

Gazing up at him solemnly, Diana whispered something, her face hot.

Dazed, wanting to pull her back into his arms, Mac found the strength to ask, "What?"

She looked at Old Bob rubbing his shoulder against the feedlot fence. "I'm sorry. You've been so kind...."

Mac felt confused. Where had they been? Where were they going? "I don't get it."

Diana's sad eyes looked away from his piercing ones. "You wouldn't. I know you're trying your best to help me over this rough spot...."

Mac swallowed, feeling the warm moment crumble. Standing guiltily before him, Diana clumsily tried to button her shirt. She looked as though she'd been found out.

"I'm all tangled up inside," she said quietly, her slender fingers twitching, as though seeking a lifeline to hold on to. Mac remained silent, knowing that she needed time to form her thoughts into words.

There was so much aching in her eyes when she looked up at him—those wounded eyes. "We were married for twenty years—a lifetime, Mac. It's difficult to explain."

Mac felt the chill of the November wind right down to his bones. "Don't you think you should stop mourning?" he asked softly as he brushed a strand of hair back from her cheek.

"I couldn't just jump into the dating arena, Mac. I'm not built that way." Her eyes darkened, meeting his. "Have you stopped hurting?" she questioned in return, the husky whisper almost knocking him against the fence.

Mac framed her delicate jaw with his hands. He felt his reluctant wistful smile right down to his boots. "Lately, it's been easier."

Sleeping wasn't easy, Mac finally admitted to himself at one o'clock the next morning. In fact, with Diana tossing and turning on her creaky bed, he couldn't sleep at all. So he'd come out to the living room to work but found he couldn't concentrate, either. He leaned back in his chair, staring at the blueprints for the electrical panels, which he'd been doing for an hour.

He scratched his bare chest, remembering once more the sight of her breasts. He groaned. A strong feeling of restlessness was pulsing in his body. It was a tightening, a sensual energy that he hadn't known for years.

He caught her scent, heard her clothing rustle before her hand rested lightly on his shoulder. The sleeve of her robe brushed his jaw. "Mac?" She leaned closer, her eyes huge and luminous and showing incredible tenderness. "What are you doing, Mac?" she asked.

He couldn't say, "Fighting to keep away from you." He couldn't say, "I need you, Diana."

"Mac?" she persisted, massaging his shoulders. "You're tired. Go on to bed."

Diana's touch soothed his aching muscles and Mac closed his eyes. Without thinking, he allowed his hand to settle on her waist, as though it had that right. She tensed as his hand followed the rounded curve of her hip in a slow caress. "Will you tuck me in?"

She laughed. "You're hardly Rick or Blaine."

The moment of intimacy lingered and grew as she stood still beneath his hand, trusting him. Mac wondered if she knew her breast almost brushed his cheek. He closed his eyes and rested his head upon the slight mound. The feeling of rightness settled around Mac like a cozy comforter on a cold, cold night.

Diana tensed, breathing lightly. Her hand stilled upon his shoulder. Her fingers touched his hair for just a fraction of a second, then lifted. "I can't stay, Mac," she stated huskily.

Mac couldn't think of anything that would take Diana from him. He turned slightly to see her face better. The movement pushed her robe aside and brought his rough cheek sliding against her bare softness.

Neither moved, the room suddenly washed with emotions.

"Mac," she protested on a soft, soft whisper. "Don't."

His lips brushed the fragrant bare flesh, the softness

luring him. She gasped when his mouth touched the sensitive crest of her breast.

"Oh, Mac," she moaned, her fingers tightening on his hair. "I'm not too sure about this."

The old house creaked, protesting the rising winter wind. Outside it was cold, but here inside the house, Mac could feel the fiery blaze within him. His senses were filled with Diana, and he trembled when he felt her heart thumping wildly beneath his cheek.

Mac wanted her. He fought the desire to carry her to his bed and claim her. But that pleasure would only be fleeting. With Diana, he wanted more.

Wrapping both arms around Diana's small waist, Mac pulled her between his knees. She was holding her robe closed now, her eyes glistening with tears, her cheeks flushed.

Diana had her ghosts and he had his, he decided, pulling her down to his lap. "Midnight is a good time to talk, Diana," he murmured, easing her head onto his shoulder.

She caught his wrist and pressed his palm to her cheek. Cradling the delicate bones of her face, Mac waited. He sensed Diana had to take her own time.

Still holding his wrist, Diana guided his hand to the softness beneath her robe. "What are you doing now, Diana?" he asked carefully, feeling the soft flesh quiver beneath his palm.

She leaned against his shoulder, her eyes guarded by the shadows of her lashes. "I...wanted to see how it would feel...again."

Mac traced the full vulnerable line of her parted lips and kissed her lightly. "And?"

She looked up at him. "I think you're a gentle man, Mac."

With his hand resting on her flesh, Mac didn't feel gentle. He felt like a leashed wild man. Her fingers caressed his brows and cheekbones, and he closed his lids, savoring her butterfly-light touch. "Well, there comes a point for any man, honey…"

"Not you," Diana returned firmly, smoothing his fierce brows with her thumb. She shifted on Mac's lap, needing his arms wrapped around her. She'd run so fast and so hard, protecting her emotions and trying to begin her new life, that there had been no time. "It gets lonely, doesn't it, Mac?"

"Sure does, honey," he agreed roughly. She felt the trembling of his hand as his fingers splayed across her chest. He wouldn't hurt her.

Diana studied the tense craggy face with the evening's growth of beard. "I feel as though I'm in a time warp, and I'm back where I was twenty years ago."

Would he laugh? Somehow, she knew he understood.

"The rules changed, didn't they?"

She nodded slowly, enjoying the feel of his hard chest beneath her palm. She loved to touch Mac.

His warm hand slid to her other breast, cradling it tenderly. "We are friends, aren't we?"

His thumb slid across the very tip of her breast, the touch striking unfamiliar cords within Diana's body. "We're the best of friends."

Diana rested her fingertips on his throat and felt his pulse beating heavily there. He swallowed, then gasped, making her look up at his tense features. "Mac?"

He shifted her and stretched his long legs out from

under the desk. He smiled tightly. "Just getting comfortable."

Diana noted the flush on his dark cheeks. "I'm not a girl any longer, Mac," she said carefully, trying out her new emotions, ones that she'd kept locked inside her.

"No, you definitely aren't." He breathed deeply, shifting her on his lap once more. Closing his eyes and leaning his head back against the wall, he placed a hand on her exposed thigh. She found the heavy warmth comforting.

Diana finally felt at peace.

Mac began caressing her thigh, and she watched his tanned hand moving over her pale skin. She noticed that the back of his broad hand bore a sprinkling of black hair, and she pictured his entire body, comparing it to her own.

"I have stretch marks, Mac," she admitted baldly before realizing she had spoken. Would he find her body ugly?

His hand stopped momentarily before continuing the caress. "I have a scar or two myself."

What would Mac expect from her as a lover? Should she touch him first? Diana shivered, surprised by her own questions. She hadn't consciously thought about her needs as a woman for years. Now she realized she'd hidden those innermost emotions, protected her vulnerability. "I have no idea what happens now, Mac," she blurted out.

He tensed and opened his eyes. "You know, neither do I. And somehow, I don't think we should worry about it, at least not tonight."

Diana sat upright, watching him intently. Mac met her gaze steadily, and she sensed the strong currents running between them. "You worry too much, woman," he said finally, brushing her lips with his.

Tracing his bottom lip with her fingertip, Diana trembled. "I don't think I can ever give myself to another man, Mac," she confessed, thinking how very familiar Mac had become to her.

The thought of his lean naked body pressing against hers, demanding, sent off warning rockets in her mind. She couldn't possibly use poor Mac for her guinea pig! To see if she could wipe away her inhibitions and fly with him? Impossible! Mac deserved better.

"I'm too old to start anything now," she murmured to herself as she stood up from his lap. With trembling fingers, she straightened her robe.

"That's what you think," he said softly, his eyes flickering beneath his lashes.

Diana's knees went weak at his hot look. She could feel his desire wrap around her and her own answering need. Abruptly she turned around and almost fled to her room. She ordered herself to close the door without looking back.

Her hand slid to her throat, covering the rapid pulse beating there. Mac deserved nothing but a whole woman in his bed to love him. She was still trying to fit the pieces of her life together. And she'd already had her chance for happiness.

Hadn't she?

Six

Mac turned over on his rumpled bed for the fiftieth time and glanced at his bedside clock. "Three o'clock," he muttered disbelievingly. It was almost two hours since Diana had walked away from him, and he had yet to fall asleep.

Mac punched the pillow beneath his head, then stretched, trying to take the knots out of his tense muscles. He felt the weight of the blanket over his naked body and ached for Diana. But she was scared of a man-woman relationship, he'd read that right enough.

He closed his eyes, listening to the creaky sounds of the house. She wouldn't hurt him, not knowingly. He didn't want the tenderness she evoked, the vulnerable exposure of his heart. But his feelings for Diana were just like the snow buttercups—pushing through the cold and blooming despite the forbidding elements. He ran his fingers through the hair covering his chest, remembering the touch of Diana's slender, trembling hands.

The floor boards outside his bedroom creaked slightly, and his door swung open gently. Mac eased higher on his pillow, leaning against the headboard. "Come in, Red. I can't sleep, either."

"You put Red out in the barn," Diana answered, her voice trembling. It flowed across the darkened room to shatter his tenuous peace into oblivion. "You said he gets restless this time of year—because of his ancestry."

He watched, spellbound, as Diana moved hesitantly toward him into a small patch of moonlight coming from the window. "Can't you sleep?" His voice sounded strangled, foreign to his ears.

Diana's hands tightened on her heavy robe as she shook her head. "I have to know, Mac. And I'm afraid—"

Mac's chest ached. His heart throbbed heavily as he watched her move stiffly to the edge of his bed. Studying his face, she slipped her hand into his. Her other hand tugged apart the robe, then placed his hand over her softness. "I have to know," she repeated, her tone raw with aching.

Mac knew she needed him then and fell helplessly before his own needs.

The robe slipped from her shoulders, exposing her flesh. Mac forced a swallow down his dry throat as his gaze flowed over her small shoulders, the large span of his hand on one delicate breast, then down to the gentle curves of her waist and stomach. He breathed heavily, fighting the rising urgency within him. He traced the fragile bones of her ribs and caressed her rounded hips. He had to reassure her, to say the words she needed to hear. Would he fail?

But he found there were no adequate words. Taking care, he shifted, making room for her slender body. She lifted his blankets and slipped in beside him.

For a moment he held his breath. Her body molded to his. She touched his chest, and he forced himself to relax. Her fingers stoked his corded shoulders before running through the hair on his chest.

Her breath fanned his chest as she kissed him there. "Mac?"

"Mmm?" His voice was raw with yearning. She lay her head upon his shoulder, and he could feel the very softness of her right down to his bones. He was afraid to touch her, afraid to unleash his passion. She needed time and tender caring.

Diana's thigh brushed his, and he tensed, restraining himself.

Diana breathed in Mac's masculine scent. She'd needed to know that as a woman she could satisfy a man. Now, she realized, she wanted to satisfy not just any man but only Mac. She needed Mac. To taste and enjoy. But there was more than just sensual pleasure to how she felt about him. She actually, really enjoyed being with him.

Her palm swept over his flat stomach, and she felt the quick intake of his breath. She'd never seduced a man and hadn't been sure how to go about it. She'd been bone-marrow nervous earlier. But Mac, lying willingly beneath her touch, made it so simple for her to play Cleopatra. She giggled at the thought: shy Diana, playing the wanton; meek Diana, playing the huntress.

"What's so funny?" Mac asked, kissing her temple.

"I've just realized that I've never done this before."

"You haven't done anything yet." There was just that touch of belligerence that she liked about Mac.

"I'm going to seduce you, Mac. What do you think about that?"

He hesitated, then carefully turned her in his arms until they lay breast to chest, thigh to thigh. "Then you should get serious," he agreed with solemn dignity.

She nuzzled his nose, slipping her arms around him. Mac felt so right, she thought as he claimed her mouth in a gentle kiss. When she parted her lips, the tip of his tongue entered her to engage her in tender play.

The old bed creaked as Mac's trembling hands caressed the length of her, cherishing her. "Oh, sweetheart," he exclaimed rawly when she accepted him into her waiting body. He stilled, and she savored the feeling of him inside her. Then began the taking and the giving, the sweet passion she had yearned for.

Beneath Mac, flowing with him, seeking his mouth for a drugging kiss, Diana felt the first ripple of ecstasy and gasped.

She breathed rapidly, aware that Mac had stopped and was watching her with a frown. "Did I hurt you?"

"I feel wonderful," she whispered against his lips. She closed her eyes, feeling Mac down the length of her body, feeling his weight rest lightly upon her. She ran her hands across his shoulders, savoring his intensity, tracing the muscles beneath his heated skin.

Mac groaned when her roaming hands slid over his taut buttocks. Her hips moved restlessly. "You'd better stop that," he threatened lightly.

For the first time in her adult life, Diana felt utterly free. Against his lips, she challenged, "Make me, big guy."

Mac's mouth devoured hers. And then there was no stopping as the throbbing heat drove them on. The final burst of passion came, leaving her surprised in its wake.

Mac breathed heavily, resting upon her, his heart racing. Diana moved beneath him, treasuring Mac's utter vulnerability. Rubbing his bulky calf with her insole, she delighted in his hair-roughened texture, so different from her own.

When she caressed his shoulders, his lips parted and prowled along her throat. His unsteady breath swept across the dampened flesh over her collarbones. "You purr," he whispered against her skin as his hands lowered to stroke her breasts. "Deep little sounds that drive me crazy. I hadn't intended to let you have your way with me so quickly."

Mac shifted, keeping her breast in his palm. His fingers teased her delicate softness into a sensitive bud. Lowering his head, he kissed the satin flesh of her neck, trailing down to her breasts. "You make me hungry," he said, flicking his tongue over her aching nipples.

It was his initiation, he realized clearly. The bonding of their flesh and emotions.

Diana's body arched, and she accepted his growing passion within her. "Mac?"

"I want you," he said. "You smell so sweet, like newly cut hay. Like meadow flowers."

All softness and hungry eyes waiting, she trembled beneath him. "I could get used to a diet of you, woman. You just could be habit-forming."

Diana shifted for more space on the bed, the immovable object at her back making huge growling noises. Like a grizzly bear. Like a sawmill. She turned to look at the noisemaker. It was Mac snoring.

She tried to untangle her legs from his, but his arm looped out to hold her nearer. She rested in his light grasp, feeling the slow beat of his heart beneath her cheek.

Mac the gentle man. She nuzzled his warm hairy chest, luxuriating in the male scent. She smiled softly. There was nothing like being in Mac's arms.

"I suppose you're pretty pleased with yourself," he rumbled against her ear, his hand caressing the smoothness of her bottom. He kissed her mouth. "'Morning."

"'Morning," she returned.

He ran his thumb across her sensitive lips, his eyes darkening. "You look all soft and drowsy, lady. Like you've been making love all night."

The tender tone in his voice caused something inside her to flutter. She could have been eighteen again, and on her first date.

Mac's lips brushed hers lightly. "Nothing ever felt so much like heaven. I couldn't ask for anything sweeter than to have you in my arms."

She rubbed his cheek with her palm playfully, very much aware of their friendship changing lanes. "You're scratchy."

Mac gazed at her as though he were memorizing her face for an eternity. "You're blushing, honey," he teased, brushing the back of his hand across her cheek. "Looks good."

He'd said that as though he knew he'd caused the flush himself and was proud of it. Mac smiled slowly, his teeth shining whitely within his stubble-covered jaw. "Diana, you are a surprise," he said softly.

Her fingers trembled as they raked through his rumpled hair. She wanted him again. Wanted the raging hunger that blazed white-hot between them. And the gentleness after, the feather-soft touches and sweet murmurs that made her feel so absolutely feminine.

Mac lifted her fingers to his mouth and started suckling them, one by one. He studied her expression. "You keep looking at me like that, lady, and you'll be late for work."

Diana gasped. She traced his hard thigh, the bulky lines so different from her own.

"If…you don't stop," Mac threatened "you'll destroy all my good intentions.…"

She giggled, feeling very young and very desired as she slipped from his bed. "Poor Mac."

Looking like the supremely satisfied male, Mac placed his hands behind his head and watched her slip on the worn robe. His intense gaze did nothing to calm the tempest within her.

Diana's fingers trembled as she tightened the sash around her waist. Good heavens, she'd been married and had two grown sons! How could the sight of a man—rumpled and unshaved—lying on a very disheveled bed, cause her heart to race?

She turned, feeling the tug of desire weaken her legs. Diana took a deep breath and forced herself to walk to the door.

"Nice fanny," she heard him murmur in a low, totally sexy tone. "Has a neat little sway to it."

That afternoon, Mac waited for Diana to get off work. He felt as tense as a cougar on the high mesas, while Diana had a definite cat-that-got-the-cream look. He felt that he'd given her just about as much rein as he could...especially with Terry Blakely hanging around like a mangy old wolf.

Mac leaned against a wall, cradling a cup of hot coffee in his hands as he watched Diana concentrate on the computer. Seated beneath a trophy rack of elk horns, she looked like a flower in a junk pile of cans and papers.

Dressed in a yellow turtleneck sweater and jeans, Diana glanced up and caught him staring at her. Even though a rack of fishing rods and a counter separated them, he saw the glow that lighted up her face.

Something special happened now when Diana looked at him. She was filled by a special kind of warmth that hadn't been there before their lovemaking.

The stare held and heated, and Mac gripped his cup tighter to keep from walking straight for her.

She turned away from him at last to concentrate on her work, and Mac studied the slender length of her neck rising above the yellow wool.

Diana frowned, rose and pushed a stock ladder against the shelves. She climbed up the four steps to the salmon-egg shelf and began counting the brightly colored jars.

Mac savored the neatly turned curve of her backside. Diana had gained just enough weight to enhance her curves, and her face had lost that tight pinched look of when they'd first met.

His visual appreciation stopped abruptly when he saw Blakely appraising those same feminine curves.

Sidestepping the how-to-catch-kokanee-salmon display, Mac headed for Diana. Blakely had no right to all that softness, not a bit, he decided darkly as Diana climbed down the ladder and bent to lift a heavy box.

"I'll do it," he said tightly, moving behind the counter. "It's too heavy for you, Diana."

She stared up at him, frowning. "I'm just fine, Mac. I've lifted heavier boxes."

"You'll hurt yourself," he stated, noting her darkening expression at his sharp tone. "Let Wingman or someone else do it. Or wait for me."

Diana's head tilted ever so slightly. The toe of her jogging shoe tapped the worn board flooring. "Now, Mac..." she began too softly.

"I mean it." He glared down at her, feeling as though he'd like to plant one on Blakely's amused jaw. Because he felt raw, uncertain as to her feelings or his emotions, he came down hard.

Her eyes widened. "Oh, is that an order from his royal highness?"

Blakely snickered and leaned his elbow against the counter. "Sounds like a regular brawl starting over here, Neil. Come on. The lovebirds are about to have it out."

Mac turned slowly, facing Blakely. "You stay the hell out of this, Terry."

Blakely straightened away from the counter, crossing his arms across his chest. "You've been aching to take me for years, old man. Maybe now is the

time. You've got an ugly streak in you, and maybe
the little woman has just discovered it. Maybe she'd
like to go out once in a while and have a little fun,
instead of being holed up with an old skunk like you.
Is that right, Diana?''

Blakely had hit Mac's tender spot. He'd been
brooding all day, wondering if he should court Diana
properly. She needed more from a man than just his
passionate hunger. Taking her out to the town dinner
and dance tonight seemed like just the thing.

But he didn't like Blakely pointing out his rough
spots. The hunting guide had chaffed his backside for
years and today, Mac decided he'd had enough.

"Where's the ring, Mac?" Blakely prodded.
"There's something phony about this whole deal."

Just as Mac took one threatening step toward
Blakely, Diana placed a hand on his chest, stopping
him. Immediately, his own rose to cover it. "Mac's
flying us to Creede the first chance we have, aren't
you, Mac?" she asked, her eyes sending him be-good
messages.

He nodded, his eyes not leaving Blakely's. For
years, he'd suspected the younger man of taking out
rich hunters on illegal trophy trips. Diana wasn't a
trophy, and Blakely wasn't coming near her.

"She's not like Eleanor, Mac." Blakely's eyes narrowed as the two big men gauged each other. "You
can't stick her up there in that deserted house. Diana's
the type who's used to socializing—"

"Mac is taking me to the town dinner and dance
tonight," Diana put in smoothly. "Aren't you, honey-
bear?"

Blakely's brows rose high. "Honey-bear? Old hermit Mac?" He laughed, doubling over and holding

his ribs. "Tell me, what are the mating habits of a hermit?"

Mac tensed. "I don't suppose you know anything about Old Bob. Do you, Terry?" Mac asked quietly, aware that Diana had looped her arm around his waist almost protectively.

Without shifting his body or taking his eyes off Blakely's dying grin, Mac felt his insides turn into melted butter. Diana's face, full of concern, turned up at him; her wide brown eyes questioned him silently. A worried frown puckered her brows. She'd moved into his house, and now it seemed she wanted to keep him safe.

"Old Bob took a high-caliber bullet in his brisket last night. He's dead," Mac said gently, feeling her shoulder shake beneath his hand.

Diana's expressive face turned hot as he knew she would. They'd both been too wrapped in their love-making to hear a rifle shot just a few yards from the house.

"What happens now?" she asked.

"Could have been a warning," Blakely said, his expression bland. "You've been upsetting people with that chopper flying at all hours of the night."

"Could have been a warning," Mac repeated, smoothing Diana's tense shoulders. He didn't want her to have any part of the ugliness that was poaching. "The sheriff made plaster casts of footprints I'd found by that stand of aspen trees just off the meadow. He's got a few clues."

He kissed Diana's soft lips lightly, savoring the taste of her. He needed her alone and away from Blakely's narrowed eyes.

"Let's go home," she whispered, easing from him

to turn off the computer. "I want to bake a pie for the dance."

"I'll be there, Diana," Blakely stated, watching her. "See you later."

Mac felt the emptiness where Diana had stood with her arms around him. Could he let her go when she decided it was time for her to leave?

The hell with letting her go.

That evening, Diana glanced at Mac's profile, at the taut jaw and furrowed brow. In the light of the pickup's dashboard, she could see his smooth-shaved jaw slide, as though he were gritting his teeth. Despite his black mood, he looked…quite handsome.

Mac's groomed attire contrasted with the older man's, seated on the other side of Diana. Clancy exuded the flavor of a rough cowboy down to his boots and his chewing tobacco.

Diana's gaze drifted back to Mac. His carefully combed hair just touched the collar of his gray Western-style suit. The cut emphasized his broad shoulders, and his woodsy after-shave added to his country-boy image. He turned, his gaze warming as it strolled down her formfitting green sweater-dress. Her breasts tingled as his stare lingered there. He was remembering, she knew, aware that his hand had moved to cup her knee. His thumb rubbed the inside of her leg slowly.

"You know, when I said, 'Let's skip the doings and have a night out at Creede,' I didn't mean bring Clancy along, too," he whispered.

"Shh." She nudged him with her shoulder. "He just wanted a ride."

Mac scowled at the craggy musher, who seemed

oblivious to their conversation, though he sat next to Diana. "We're stuck with him. My plans didn't call for a threesome."

Diana placed her hand over his on the steering wheel—she loved touching Mac—feeling just a twinge of remorse. When Clancy had asked for a ride, she'd actually been relieved. She'd felt as nervous about tonight as though it were her first date, and she knew Clancy's presence would ease the tension.

She was right. Clancy had an absolutely marvelous time at Howard's Cantina, noisily devouring a full rack of barbecued ribs and preventing intimate conversation. As Mac glowered at him for an ill-disguised burp, Clancy sat back to blow the suds off his beer. "Hey, why don't you two kids cut a rug? The music sounds good. May dance with Diana myself, later maybe, after a few more brews. Reminds me of good times up the Yukon, mushing. We'd sit around, enjoy the company of a good woman. There was a woman up there who could warm your—"

"Oh, hell, Clancy, you've never been up the Yukon," Mac said in a tone that reminded Diana of Red's low growl.

"Sure was, entered dogsledding races all the time. But it was awful cold in the winter. Ran a lot of dogs in my time, though. Been meaning to ask you if I could use Red to break in a new team of sled dogs. Think I could borrow him?"

Mac leaned back in his chair, contemplating the old-timer darkly. His long dark fingers laced with Diana's slender ones, his thumb stroking her palm. "Clancy, if you'll manage to lose yourself for a few hours, I'll let you borrow Red."

The older man grinned widely and rose. "Okay by

me. Thought my plan would work. Sorry about Old Bob, Mac. Call for me over at Charlie's back room just before you decide to light out. They got a good poker game going, I hear."

Then bending gallantly, he took Diana's hand and kissed the back of it before walking off.

"Blackmail," Mac accused, muttering as Clancy wove between the restaurant's round tables. "That old man can be a real nuisance. He's not teaching you dog-pushing. It's too dangerous."

Diana fought the smile playing about her mouth. Since the evening was so special, she decided not to tell Mac that she had already had her first run. Clancy had even praised her.

The country quartet played a two-step, and Mac grinned at her. "Want to try out the floor?"

He had such an expectant air about him that she couldn't bear to start an argument. Freed from Clancy, Mac was all smiles and sexy promising looks.

Once on the dance floor, Mac wrapped his arms around her waist. She leaned back, startled by the unconventional stance. "People dance like this now, honey. Trust me," he said.

They danced slowly, barely swaying with the music as his strong thighs moved against hers. With her head tucked beneath his chin and her cheek resting over his slow-beating heart, she let herself imagine they were in love.

There it was again, she thought. That feeling of being feminine and desirable, as though she were with her first beau. The years didn't exist when Mac held her close, and she let her barriers slip a little more.

Mac nuzzled her temple, kissing it. "You're awfully quiet, Diana."

When she leaned back to look up at him, Mac's tender gaze changed into a dark smoldering look. Reminded of how devastatingly attractive Mac had looked that morning—stretched out on the rumpled bed, his hair disheveled by her fingers—Diana closed her eyes and snuggled to Mac's warm secure chest.

Swaying in his arms, Diana lost herself to the music and Mac. He just felt so…right. She looked up and studied the endearing familiar lines of his face. How could a man's mouth be so firm and yet so tender?

While staring at the sensuous line, Diana felt ripples of excitement coursing through her body. The hot ripples of excitement that belonged to a young woman with her first love. "Oh, Mac," she whispered helplessly, confused by her emotions.

"'Oh, Mac,'" he repeated teasingly. "I like that—you gasping my name with that sexy little tone." He moved her into a dark corner of the room, his tall body hiding her from others. He watched her waiting expression intently, then raised his hand to her face. He touched her eyebrows, then trailed his fingers down to her cheeks.

His touch was so like him—gentle with a raspy texture that excited. His thumb stroked her bottom lip, and his gaze darkened. His breath was coming more quickly. His face was all intense, as if nothing else mattered but this moment in time. Then Mac lowered his head, taking her mouth.

He rubbed his lips across her parted ones, savoring their softness. With a slight movement of her head, she rested her cheek against his palm.

Framing her small face within his hand, Mac barely breathed. When the tip of her tongue slid over his lips, then dipped inside, he trembled. In her warm moistness, he tasted the heady desire of a woman.

Placing his forehead against hers, Mac whispered, "It's been a long day."

She rubbed his nose with hers. "Has it? Shall we go home?" She saw the excitement in his eyes.

"We've still got to pick up that damned Clancy," he said.

Mac paid their bill, then eased her into her winter coat. He adjusted the collar carefully, then kept his arm around her as they walked into the night. Diana leaned against him, savoring the hard strength of his lean body. He held her to him, as though she were a necessary part of him, of his life.

She felt a tiny ripple of uneasiness. Mac's love-making took her to the heights, but he had a tendency to want his own way, which sometimes rankled her. This darker side of his passion intrigued her, too. She just had to prod it a little, explore....

She also wanted to flirt outrageously with him. The thought shocked her at first, then enticed her.

Passing through the darkened alley to the pickup, Diana couldn't resist putting her arm around his waist, then slipping it lower until it reached Mac's firm buttocks. After all, he'd surprised her once or twice.

He paused, glancing down at her. "You're playing with fire," he murmured in a provocative tone that sent excitement down to her toes. "You'd better keep your distance."

For a moment Diana hesitated, waylaid by the novelty of the situation—forty-two was an odd time to start feeling her sensual oats. But Mac had this aura about him of masterful self-control that just begged for a mussing. Feeling the challenge course through her, Diana stopped to lock her arms around him. She was surprised to hear herself asking, "What if I don't want to?"

She could feel him tense, as though he was struggling to keep piercing emotions leashed. Something within her wanted to lift the lid to those feelings, to taste the raw male desire he tempered so well.

Deliberately she stood on tiptoe to trace the line of his mouth with the tip of her tongue. Just to give her that special edge, she tugged his face nearer to blow in his ear.

When Mac went taut as his bow strings, Diana felt a jolt of sheer feminine satisfaction. She just had to taste the tempting whorl of his ear with her tongue.

"Now you've done it." Mac gathered her to him like a man who had waited years for the taste of her. Diana trembled, fighting the demanding ache within her, then yielded to her immediate need to touch Mac.

As she eased his coat open, he groaned and said, "Unbutton my shirt, let me feel you touch me."

His trembling hands pulled her sweater up as her fingers fumbled at exposing his enticing chest.

"You aren't wearing a bra, lady," he exclaimed, staring at the hardened tips of her breasts. He was breathing hard, his eyes widened in shock. "You mean every man in there could have brushed against you, danced with you and felt this?"

Just this once Diana forgave him for dishing out his macho talk. Teasing Mac was absolutely delightful. Pressing her breasts against his bare chest, she grinned up at him. In this mood, he made her feel as though life were just beginning. "But Mac, isn't this nice?"

"Mmm, nice. I could make a meal of you," he whispered huskily, his fingers caressing her.

She kissed the hard line of his lips, softened by previous kisses. "I like your mouth on me," she admitted shyly, watching his eyes darken and the deep red color flag his cheeks. She watched his reaction, knowing that this was the very first time she had encouraged a man's blatant hunger. Mac didn't need encouragement as he lifted her on tiptoe for a soul-shattering kiss.

"You don't know what you do to me," he admitted unevenly.

Diana's ego soared outrageously, and she couldn't resist a pleased smile.

"You'd better worry about your effect on me, woman," he continued, a sensuous smile lurking around his mouth. "I can't take much more. I feel like I'm a kid making out in the back seat."

She traced the enticing curve of his lips. "Mac, don't you think we're...a little old for making out in dimly lit alleys?"

"A man can only stand so much temptation, woman. I hadn't counted on this, either. Somehow, when you get near me, all my good intentions are blown to smithereens."

For his ego-bolstering admission, Diana decided to give Mac the most seductive kiss she could ever hope to give in her life. When she was finished, she nibbled on his lobe, enjoying the unsteady way he breathed. She smiled, nuzzling against his throat. "Don't fight me. I intend to have my way with you again."

"Diana." He gasped as her tongue gently traced his ear. "There's more to this than... I mean, we're friends, aren't we? I wouldn't take advantage of the situation.... Hell, you deserve champagne and roses.''

Diana whispered, "I know, but for now there's this...."

Seven

At two o'clock in the morning, after dropping Clancy off at his house, Mac let Red outside, then pulled Diana to him. "Come here, you."

Once his mouth fitted to hers, fireworks started exploding. Hungry and demanding, his body radiated a hard male need. Diana couldn't wait to touch him, to feel the steely planes of his chest. She gasped as he swung her up in his arms and started to carry her toward the bedroom.

Diana couldn't get enough of his kisses, his taste. The groans coming from deep in his throat ignited her.

When they were halfway across the living room, Red began barking, and Mac shuddered, his arms tightening around her as though he never wanted to let her go. "Someone is here," he whispered against the side of her neck. His left hand gently rubbed the small of her back. "Red's got that special bark."

He kissed her lips, the wild heat of his cheeks warming her own. Slowly, very reluctantly, Mac lowered her to her feet. "Don't move one step."

When Mac finally released her, Diana wondered if her knees could support her. She closed her eyes, listening to the sound of his voice outside. She wanted to hear him whisper those sweet things to her in the blackness of the night. Impatient to have him against her, she gripped a pillow from the couch and hugged it to ease the aching.

Gradually, Diana realized that another man was talking to Mac. She listened intently. The man's voice was familiar. Mac swung the door open, and beneath the harsh light of the porch light, she saw Blaine.

Diana's eyes locked with her son's. She hadn't seen him in weeks, and now Blaine's young face looked weary.

"Come in," Mac invited the younger man, his eyes catching Diana's.

Blaine stepped inside the room, watching her almost warily. A younger image of his father, Blaine looked around the cozy room bearing Diana's neat touch.

She wanted to run to him and embrace him, but Blaine's accusing stare rooted her to the spot and caused her to lock her fingers tighter around the pillow.

"Hello, Mother. I've been waiting for you to come home," he said with Alex's you've-done-it-this-time tone.

"Hello, Blaine," she managed to say calmly. But

she really wanted to say, "I'm glad to see you—I love you. But why are you here now and like this?"

Mac moved quietly to her side. She found his warmth and substance reassuring. "You're welcome to stay here, Blaine," he said.

Remembering her manners, Diana introduced Mac. "Blaine, this is—" *My host? My lover?* "—Mac," she finished quietly.

Blaine stared at Mac. "You're nothing like Dad. You're exactly what I wouldn't think my mother would pick for a mid-life affair." The statement bore the stamp of Alex's elegant distaste.

Mac's head tilted a little, as though he'd just received a very small jab. "Blaine, that's enough," Diana said, plumping the pillow to still her shaking hands. Fighting layers of self-doubt, Diana faced her son's silent accusations. "Mac is—"

"You don't have to say anything, Diana." Mac crossed his arms over his chest. "You're welcome to stay, Blaine. But you will not insult your mother."

Blaine turned to Diana. "I know who he is—your boyfriend. He broke up you and Dad. Dad told me so. I just had to see it for myself. I didn't believe it, but now I know it's true."

Diana tossed the pillow to the couch. Her sons had never seen the full extent of her temper; she really did not intend to lose control now. "What did you say?" she asked carefully.

"Rick said it couldn't be true. That whatever was happening came after the divorce."

"That's enough, son," Mac said quietly.

Lifting her hand to silence Mac, Diana felt a cold chill sweeping across her flesh. Holding Blaine's eyes, she said, "It's all right, Mac. I wasn't unfaithful to your father, Blaine.'' She wanted to lace her fingers with Mac's, to use his strength.

Her sons' love was the cornerstone of her life; she had to fight to keep Rick and Blaine from slipping farther and farther away from her. But she needed time to think, and Blaine needed time to calm down and get some rest. ''Why don't you get some sleep, and we'll talk in the morning.''

Blaine glanced around the room. ''I've seen all I need to see. I'm taking off tonight—''

''There's plenty of room, Blaine,'' Mac interrupted, his dark eyes flowing over Diana's taut face.

''Let me handle this, Mac,'' she ordered quietly, facing her son fully. ''You're staying the night, Blaine.''

His rebellious stare locked with hers. Diana returned it evenly. ''It's a nice bed,'' she added, watching his indecision. ''Why don't you stay the whole weekend?''

''I drove nonstop from Missouri just to see you. I took off right after my last class.'' Blaine stated haughtily, glaring at Mac.

''Oh, shut up,'' Diana said as coolly as she could manage. Somewhere, somehow, her son had acquired an arrogance that grated on her nerves. She wondered briefly about the lovable little boy she had kissed good-night. ''So help me, Blaine. Your manners are inexcusable. You always were something of a pain—''

Blaine stepped back, shock written on his face. ''Mother!''

Diana thought she heard Mac chuckle, but when she turned blazing eyes to him, his face was positively too innocent. ''You shut up, too.''

"Yes, ma'am," Mac murmured contritely.

She glared up at him and then at Blaine. Men, the both of them. Men, with their possessiveness. The indignant son and the overprotective...friend. "Go get your things, Blaine. Mac can make a bed, and he'll show you where to sleep. I'm going to bed now, and I don't want to hear any...angry noises in the night. Or you can leave."

"Mother!"

Diana firmly turned her back and walked into her room. She closed the door with a soft but final click.

She paused, then jerked open the door. Her son stood uncertainly in the center of the room. "Blaine, Mac was not the cause of the divorce. And while you're in this house, you show some good manners."

She closed the door to lean back against it, shaking.

Diana watched the leafless branches sway in the winter wind, the silvery moon hiding behind a passing cloud. She tried to force the tension from her as she sat in the ancient cherry rocker.

Mac shouldn't have to put up with all of this, she thought. He deserved better than a woman's coming-out experience and an enraged son standing on his doorstep.

Diana pressed her hands against her thighs, hating the uncertainty. She knew her body's needs, felt the melting hot heat build in her. She massaged her temples, hoping to ease the ache. Lying in bed with Mac, she'd felt consumed...and it frightened her. "I'm old enough to be a grandmother," she whispered shakily.

She didn't want to care again at her age. She hadn't planned on Mac. But she had practically thrown herself into his arms. Mac was just too potent.

She wrapped her robe tighter around her, acknowledging the sensual tightness in her body. She wanted Mac. Wanted his hands on her, wanted his lips on hers, wanted the rough-tender way he touched her, as though she were his alone and he really cared. She shivered, fighting for control. Sex wasn't love, and she'd already had her chance.

Did love come courting a second time around? Or was Mac just part of her mid-life crisis?

Game time was over, she decided. She wanted to start thinking of Mac in terms longer than a few days. He'd become her necessary edge—the tender man. A man to endure the hardships and a man to stir up the excitement in her. She could trust him until the end of time, and that was worth fighting for. She cared for him, and it was time to define the terms of their relationship.

One fact stared her in the face—she had to come to terms with her son. For years she'd compromised her essence to her family. She'd played the generic mother who never regretted a moment.... She intended to stand on her own finally. She'd explain it all to Blaine and make sure he understood. She couldn't lose his love.

Diana's lids fluttered and she realized she was finally falling asleep. But she had barely nodded off when she became aware of Mac's woodsy scent. He was lifting her from the chair. "Come on, sleepy head," he said, "it's bed for you. We'll take care of all your problems tomorrow."

For the first time since childhood, Diana was tucked in and kissed good-night.

Sleepy, she encircled his neck with her arms and held him tight against her. She wanted Mac. The snuggly craggy warm feel of him next to her. "Hold me."

He chuckled, brushing a curl back from her face. "I do that and we'll both be in trouble. Your son isn't the understanding type right now. Go to sleep."

She turned her face toward the pillow, accepting the gentle touch of his hand on her cheek. She kissed the rough palm lightly. "You are really a nice man."

"Uh-huh. But it's costing me plenty, honey. I probably won't sleep a wink."

Diana had to tell him. "I never thanked you for taking me out tonight. I'd thought I was too old to start needing again."

Mac's big hand trembled as he caressed her forehead. "The last I heard, there were no age barriers on needing, honey. Nothing could be righter than what's between us."

He could always go back to playing bagpipes at midnight, Mac decided grimly, watching Diana's slender form shift beneath her robe as she cooked breakfast. When she turned to him, holding the platters of bacon and eggs, Mac knew he'd remember her forever.

A man doesn't easily forget a sleepy-eyed woman with tousled sunlit hair and sweet, sweet lips. When Diana made love to him, she forced out his loneliness, replacing it with her fire.

Blaine had come to claim his mother, and Mac fought the sour taste of losing Diana. Somehow, the trick on Benevolence had backfired.

She placed the eggs and bacon on the table, her teeth nibbling at her bottom lip as she checked the table settings for the third time. "Who called this morning, Mac? I heard the phone ring."

Mac scowled, avoiding her searching look. "Something about Old Bob's death. The sheriff found the same high-caliber rifle casings near an illegal elk kill.... You're going back, aren't you?"

"No."

Blaine entered the kitchen, stopping just inside the doorway. "Of course, she is."

Diana turned slowly to face her son. Mac noted the trembling of her hands, the tightening of her fingers on the salt and pepper shakers. "We need to talk about that, Blaine. Would you like to walk with me after breakfast?"

Mac felt the fear grow in him, felt it wrap tight around his heart. His life spread before him like an empty void, Diana's warmth already fading....

Why did he have to open his heart to her?

Wasn't losing one woman enough pain in a man's lifetime?

The noon wind was cold, tossing her hair against her face. Diana glanced at the stark mountains topped with snow and said quietly, "I like it here, Blaine. There's the peace I've needed for a long time."

Her son placed his hand against the barn, prodding a rock with his toe. "I can see something between you and Mac. You have a sort of glow now.... Do you really care for him, Mom?" he asked slowly.

"Yes, I do." She caressed his cheek, realizing how much he had gone through. "I love you and Rick, but there's another side of me, too. Mac is the gentlest man I know. He's made me happy. You want that, don't you?"

Blaine cleared his throat, frowning. "It's over between you and Dad, then? For real?"

She ruffled his hair as she had when he was small. Smiling gently, she answered, "It was over a long time ago. Meeting Mac, staying here, was an accident. But I'm so very glad he happened in my life, Blaine. I hope you'll understand."

Her son stared down at her for a long time before he took her hand. "I was pretty mean last night, wasn't I?"

Smiling, she hugged him. "Pretty awful. Come back to me, honey."

"I love you, Mom," he said simply, returning the hug. "Rick said you were out on a 'voyage of self-discovery.' He said to give you space. I should have had more faith—"

"Shh. You're here now and you understand. That's what counts."

"Blaine has talked with his father about Thanksgiving, Mac. Alex has already made plans, so Blaine is going to spend Thanksgiving with us. Is that all right?" Diana asked that evening after supper. Seated on the couch, Diana acted like the perfect hostess.

Mac fought his visions of loneliness, hiding behind the barricade of the local newspaper. He could feel panic rippling up his spine. He'd almost kept her, but now her son had arrived to claim her. Why hadn't he put his courting plans in high gear?

Mac could feel his teeth grind. A man couldn't bank on seduction, not when he wanted a woman like Diana to stay put.

Over the top of his newspaper, he glanced at her stealthily. Dressed in jeans and a bulky maroon sweater, she looked so beautiful. Mac shifted uncomfortably in his worn armchair, rereading the "Game Warden's Column" for the third time. He hadn't ever pulled out the stops when it came to wooing her, and the idea nettled him. He'd never played the part of a Romeo yet, but to keep Diana from leaving him and returning to that no-good ex-husband of hers, he just might....

"Mac, are you sleeping?" Diana asked, leaning forward to tug his paper lower. "I asked if Blaine could share Thanksgiving with us."

Mac allowed himself to drown in her brown velvet gaze, allowed it to sweep inside him, warming. He grinned slowly, watching the soft curve of her mouth return the gesture. "I'd really like that, Diana. In fact, why don't you invite Rick, too?"

"Really? You wouldn't mind having a houseful? Rick has a girlfriend who would die of loneliness if they were separated."

Blaine shifted, reaching down to pet Red's shaggy head. "Ah, Mom, I haven't had time to tell you about my girlfriend, Cindy. She's...ah..."

"She can come, too. This is lovely! A whole houseful of kids for the holidays, Mac. Isn't it great?" Diana clapped her hands, bouncing off the couch. She snatched Mac's head between her hands and gave him a short kiss on the lips. "Oh, thank you, Mac."

Both males stared, fascinated as she ran to a cabinet to extract a notepad and pen.

Dazed by the sudden happy flush washing Diana's cheeks, Mac murmured, "Fine. I'd like that."

Her son took a moment to recover, his expression thoughtful before it changed to excitement. "This is great!"

Uncertain whether either person would hear him, Mac offered quietly, "It's early in the season, but if they like to ski, there's a lift not far from here. I can borrow a couple of snowmobiles, too. There's already snow in the high country on the designated trails."

Both mother and son turned to Mac, watching him intently. Mac forced a swallow as Diana's small face softened and almost glowed. They gazed at each other. "Thank you so much, Mac," she murmured huskily, lowering her lashes over tear-bright eyes.

"It's nothing, honey," he returned in as deep and intimate a tone. Fascinated by the thick damp lashes, Mac reached out a finger to dry them. "Don't cry."

Diana's mouth trembled, her hand sliding into her son's larger one. "I'm just happy, Mac."

Blaine's astute eyes shifted from his mother to Mac, meeting the older man's mild stare. "She's the weepy sort. She's cried enough sad tears, maybe the happy ones will wash them away, huh?" he asked awkwardly, placing his arm around Diana's shoulders.

"Stop talking about me as though I weren't here, Blaine," Diana chided, sniffing delicately.

"Yes, Mother," Blaine answered too placidly, his gaze locking with Mac's quiet one. *Take it easy with her,* his stare warned. *Don't hurt her.*

Slowly, Mac extended his hand to the younger man, who gripped it. "I imagine we'd both better help your mother, before she spins herself into exhaustion, don't you think, Blaine?"

"Agreed."

Diana sniffed again and wiped her eyes. "Mac, I won't have you talking around me, either."

Watching her, Mac spoke to Blaine, "She's a soft one."

"And men talk about women chattering," Diana teased, her eyes sparkling. "Let's get busy!"

Thanksgiving arrived in a flurry of giggling girl-friends, happy sons, a beaming Mac and the scents of a roast turkey dinner. A layer of new snow blanketed the fields and weighted the tree branches. The sun decorated the landscape with a silvery glitter, which demanded a pre-Thanksgiving dinner snowball fight between the younger couples.

Diana couldn't resist drawing Mac into a corner of the porch. She grinned as he angled his tall body away from the threatening heap of skis. Hugging him tightly around his lean waist, she pressed her cheek to his chest. She nuzzled his well-washed sweatshirt with her cold nose. "This is so nice of you, Mac."

Mac glanced uncomfortably at the foursome fast approaching from the meadow.

"You can hug me too, you know," she offered happily. "Oh, Mac, I'm so happy. I feel like those kids—bursting with life, ready to meet new challenges. What's wrong?" she asked, looking up into his wary face.

"Look behind you."

Diana turned slowly, her arms still wrapped around Mac's waist. Watching her with unreadable faces were Rick and Blaine, snowballs poised in their gloves. The two girls looked anxiously from the brothers to Diana.

She turned to look at Mac's flushed face and grinned. "Are you embarrassed?" she asked, releasing him. "You'll have to hold your own with them, big guy. They have some idea you're after their mother.''

Even during dinner, Diana couldn't resist teasing Mac. She kept shooting him intimate glances over the food-laden table, just to torment him a little. He was so cute in his new cream-colored sweater, stammering now and then and appearing to wait for the ax to fall.

Just as Mac reached for his second helping of pumpkin pie, Diana couldn't resist saying, ''I have a little secret, guys. Want to share it?''

Blaine's filled mouth stopped chewing. Rick's fork stopped midway to his lips.

Struggling to keep his voice level, Rick said, ''Sure, Mom. What gives?''

Diana glanced at Mac, who looked as though he'd like to be dangling from a hundred-foot ski lift or rappelling down a rock cliff—anywhere but seated with her family. When Mac silently pleaded with her, Diana couldn't resist licking the dollop of whipped cream from her fork.

The come-hither gesture almost caused Mac to break out in a sweat. Just for extra spice, Diana trailed her fingertip across the back of his hand. To her delight, Mac's cheeks began to flush. ''Mac and I have been playing a little joke on Benevolence.''

''How so?'' Blaine asked cautiously, alert to Mac's uncomfortable expression.

''To win a championship chili contest, Mac announced our engagement.'' Diana winked at Mac. ''It's called 'influencing the judge.' Isn't that right?''

''Mother!'' Both Rick and Blaine looked as though they would go into permanent shock. Cindy and Alise giggled, as usual, and Diana found herself joining them. She laughed until the tears began to roll down her cheeks.

Rick recovered enough to say, "Mother, this isn't funny."

"Why not? I think it's hilarious."

Blaine emitted a noise that sounded suspiciously like a chuckle. "A whole town, Mom?"

"And surrounding homesteads. I rather like putting Mac on the spot, too."

Rick's expression began to shift, a grin toying with his mouth. "Having fun, Mom?"

"For the first time in eons. I really don't have a care in the world." Diana felt as though she'd shot through the walls of her box. The one that had kept her prisoner for so many years. The right and proper box that stripped her essence and demanded her soul.

Blaine lifted his water glass in a toast. "Here's to Mom. You deserve a little fun."

Diana looked at Mac's oh-my-gosh expression. "And now to cap off our first new-family holiday, Mac will play the bagpipes."

Later, when Mac decided to carry in the firewood for the night, both younger men donned their coats to follow him.

There, behind the house, standing before the wood-pile, Rick and Blaine faced Mac. The light snow drifted between them, covering their shoulders. "It's time to talk," Rick announced.

Blaine adjusted his knit cap and raised his collar higher against the winter wind. "Mom's having fun. Even an idiot could see how happy she is."

"Mom hasn't laughed like that for a long time. Especially when you offered to dance the Highland fling," Rick added.

"She did like showing me up when she did her own dance," Mac agreed, wondering why in Sam Hill he felt as though he was being interviewed.

Blaine propped a boot on a snow-covered log. "Mom even likes her job. I didn't know she knew anything about fishing or hunting. Seems like she knows some interesting hunting guides, too. She's stopped acting...so strained. It's like she's a kid again."

Both youths looked at Mac expectantly.

"If this little talk is going to take long, I vote we adjourn to the tack room in the barn," he offered warily.

Rick stood up, dusting the snow from him. "Suits me. Let's go."

The tack room was warm, scented of hay and animals and old leather. Mac lighted the kerosene lantern and fired the small potbellied stove. Rick carefully adjusted his length to a rickety wooden box. Blaine looked around, then settled into a chair next to a table. He shuffled the worn deck of cards he pulled out of his coat pocket. "Poker?"

"Count me in." Rick watched Mac. "How about you?"

On the third hand of stud poker, Rick leaned back on the wooden box. He shuffled the cards slowly. "What gives with you, Mac? Just what are your intentions toward Mom?"

"She's been hurt enough," Blaine asserted. "We understand now that Dad has a lot to answer for. We just got mixed up, somehow. It wasn't hard to do, considering the way she kept everything inside while Dad kept laying blame." He paused. "So what gives between you and her?"

Being interviewed by a woman's sons was a novel experience, Mac decided quickly. How could he say that he needed her like air?

Before he could answer, Blaine continued. "She likes this new independence thing. I think she should be encouraged to do what she wants. She deserves it, don't you think, Mac?"

"And what about this marriage thing, Mac?" Rick asked, frowning. "Just what are your intentions there? After all, a guy likes to think his mother is sacred, you know?"

"I want Diana to be happy," Mac answered with all the strength of his convictions.

Blaine toyed with a saddle buckle. "Oh, she's happy. We can see that. But what are you intending in the long run? I mean, the town is bound to get wise to the joke someday. You wouldn't leave her holding the bag, would you?"

"Diana will have to decide how to handle the matter. She's making her own decisions. For my part, I care deeply for her. If she stayed, I couldn't ask for much more out of life." Mac retrieved a bottle of red wine from beneath an Apache saddle blanket.

"You're not a boozer, are you?" Rick asked sharply, looking at the half-filled bottle. "Just how much do you drink?"

"Oh, lay off, Rick," Blaine interrupted. "The guy must be all of—" he looked at Mac appraisingly "—well, he's got a few years on him, but he seems to be in pretty good shape...for his age. If he drank heavily, we'd know it by now."

Mac couldn't resist grinning as he poured the wine into three tin cups. "Thanks. We old-timers need all the help we can get."

Holding his drink, Rick looked around the small room. "I suppose you own all this. I mean, Mom isn't going to get into any financial trouble here, is she?"

Rick shrugged. "It's over now. But somehow, Mom just didn't come up even when she and Dad split. There was no compensation for all that time she spent at home. It took a while for her to get on her feet, I guess. I remember looking at her one day and thinking, 'Mom looks like she's breaking in two.'"

Mac frowned, realizing how Diana had passed through so many difficult trials. No wonder she looked like a stray when she arrived on his doorstep. Why couldn't life have brought them together sooner? Why had she suffered alone? "I'm financially stable. She won't be responsible for any debts."

Rick nodded. "That's good. Now, ah, Mom is pretty, ah, righteous about marriage. I mean—" He swallowed a sip and glanced nervously at Blaine, then back at Mac. "She likes to tease you, like a girl, almost. And she touches you, like guys our age." He took a deep breath. "What I mean to say is, we don't want you taking advantage of her...innocence about the world. Do you have any problems with that?"

Mac met Rick's probing stare evenly. Diana had come to him, offering herself so sweetly to him. "Your mother and I are friends. I wouldn't do anything to hurt her."

Blaine pondered Mac's statement a moment. "I like that, Rick. Basically, I think the guy is okay."

"What about a real marriage?" Rick persisted. "There are lots of guys our ages turning up with baby brothers and sisters."

Mac closed his eyes. Making a child with Diana would be the sweetest thing in the world. But if he couldn't have that, he'd settle for any scrap of Diana possible. "I'd vote for marriage in a minute. I intend to try my damnedest to keep her any way I can."

"Whatever is happening is good for Mom. She's put on some pounds, and she's looking great.... Here's to her new life." Rick lifted the bottle.

The door squeaked open. "Here's to snowballs!" Diana yelled, pitching her snowball straight at Mac. It struck his cheek before he could duck.

"Here's to bull sessions!" Cindy lofted her missile straight toward Blaine while Alise plastered Rick's face.

"Women! You can't trust 'em," Blaine crowed, reforming the snow sliding down his face and running after the escaping females. "We'll teach you. Bull sessions are sacred to the American male!"

Mac slowly wiped his cheek, feeling his grin spread through him. "I believe Humpty can be put back together again. Once the house is quiet, she won't stand a chance. I am going to keep that woman. The question is how."

Eight

The huskies easily pulled Clancy's light sled over the powdery dry snow. Standing on the sled's back runners, her stomach braced against the seat, Diana finally felt as free as the golden eagle soaring through the sunlit morning.

With a fantastic Thanksgiving and Christmas behind her—her sons had obviously enjoyed spending their holiday vacations at Mac's—Diana expected the whole new year to follow suit. January was the perfect time to begin anew, to braid the past into the future.

Snow glistened on the San Juan Mountains; the fields and forests were draped with the heavy white blanket. The freezing wind ruffled the fur lining of her parka hood and stung her cheeks. But dark goggles protected her eyes.

She'd borrowed the sled for her day off, wanting—

no, burning—to make her private run, to explore without Mac's anxious eye or Clancy's cautions.

Red, acting as lead dog, knew the stretch well due to Clancy's frequent runs. Across the open meadows, swinging down a snow-covered lane and then to the higher country to a lone scraggy pine tree buffeted by wind and time.

The run was her baptism, her journey to freedom, wiping away the pain and insecurities. The strength was in her, growing.

Red picked up pace, and the huskies strained against the harnesses, running toward the wilderness. The snow from their feet sprayed across Diana's face, forcing her to tuck her chin deeper in the protective knit covering. She felt elated, ready to take on anything life threw at her.

Suddenly, there was a sound like that of a rifle shot. A dead tree cracked and fell near the trail.

In her mind's eye, she saw Mac. The gentle man with dark lighting eyes. He was a part of it all, the rebirth. Concentrating on him, Diana could feel the womanly essence tingle within her. She had been a girl when she'd married Alex, trusting him to form their lives. But with Mac, there was sharing.

She thought of Mac's behavior lately. Grumpy, wary, sidestepping any intimacy. She was certain that Mac watched her; she could feel him waiting. For what?

How could she let him know she wanted all of him now? How in the world did a woman pursue a man?

For just an instant, a sharp fear chilled her. She gripped the sled tighter. Mac was a born protector, a Colorado knight championing the wounded and the needy. Was she taking advantage of his tender heart?

The sled hit a hidden branch, bumping the runners beneath her boots. Diana controlled the sled, then called to Red, who had slowed his pace. "Hey, Red! Go for it!"

Go for it. It was her time. Her life was swinging in a new direction just as the sled coursed across the unmarked sunlit snow. She was a woman controlling her own destiny, finding confidence within.

But she needed Mac to complete her life.

In an alpine clearing, Diana noted Clancy's marker—a burned tree stump. She caught a sound, a chopping noise overhead, and saw the shadow of Mac's helicopter sweep across the blinding snow.

He hovered overhead, and beneath her knitted face covering, Diana smiled. "Let's go, Red," she called. "Gee!"

Leaving Clancy's trail, Diana slowed the dogs with the tug rope and brake, then leaped off the sled, running beside the team. The huskies, wanting to run, fought the slower pace, barking. Red turned his head to the pack and bared his teeth. Diana ran to him and patted his head. "Let's show him we know our stuff, boy!"

Loping beside Red, Diana ignored Mac's helicopter. She was light enough to run on top of the crust of the deep snow easily. She led the dogs in a circle, and after a few times around, they made a visible trail. Diana ran to the center of the giant circle. She threw out her arms, laughing up at Mac, then tramped on the snow, forming the eyes and mouth of a smiling face.

Mac's helicopter dipped and swayed in an answer, but when she thought he would land, the craft sailed toward the high mesas.

Frowning, she followed the helicopter into the blinding sun. "That's right, Mac. You've come just close enough, it's time to run away," she whispered, remembering how he backstepped every time she came near.

Since his lingering kiss beneath the Christmas mistletoe, Mac had acted like a man on a tight leash, and she didn't know why. But she intended to find out....

Diana walked to the dogs lying in the snow, their pink tongues hanging out. Six sets of huskies' eyes watched her as Red stood and stretched. She patted Red. "You're ready to run again, aren't you? Being free is quite a feeling—it makes you stronger, huh?"

Red licked her leather glove, his giant body taut. She smiled again, feeling very young and very certain of herself as a woman.

With a lingering glance at the helicopter, Diana began to run beside the back of the sled, waiting for the dogs to pick up pace. When they were running strong, she leaped onto the back runners to brace her body against the sled. Then she gave herself to the sheer freedom of the high country.

When Diana returned the team to Clancy late that afternoon, she had decided to call Alex at the first opportunity.

"Clancy is a fourteen-carat gold-plated idiot." Muttering to himself, Mac felt raw clear through as he opened the door to his house. Seeing Diana out in the wild, trusting a half-broken pack of running dogs with her life, was a nightmare. The new bullet hole through his helicopter windshield didn't help his nerves, either.

The lack of sleep nettled him. The sheriff had enlisted his aid to catch the elusive poachers. Between the long hours in the helicopter and the sleepless hours aching for Diana, Mac kept himself going on coffee and nerves. He wanted Diana down to his bones, but a man couldn't start courting seriously when he had pushed himself to his physical limits.

He had his sights set, but candlelight and roses took plenty of time to plan. Especially when there wasn't a French restaurant or a florist shop within miles. Mac had decided to put his strategy on hold until just the right moment. Diana deserved every ounce of magic he could muster.

He could wait…maybe.

Having the youngsters in the house had eased his tension, but maybe Benevolence had the last laugh. Could a hermit change his spots?

"In the middle of everything, she decides to become a full-fledged musher." He swept the snow from his boots with a broom, carefully stepping on a braided rug. He eyed Diana's small fur-lined moccasins and leggings—Eskimo mukluks—as he tugged off his snow-encrusted boots. "I should have put the copter down right there and made her hit the trail back, really laid down the law. Should have followed her every step of the way. Should have knocked Clancy into the next world when he suggested such a thing. She's not even up to one of those dogs' working weight."

Mac closed the door quietly as Red padded toward him. Taking off his heavy jacket and tossing it to the couch, Mac was determined to state his piece—dogsledding was just too dangerous for Diana.

Diana's low husky voice floated from the kitchen. "Yes, Alex. It was really nice talking to you, too."

"Alex," Mac repeated. Alex with the smooth voice and the country-club manners. Probably had a pedigree all the way up his...

Mac's heart stopped; his fingers trembled as he forced himself to sift through the day's mail. Alex probably knew all the right moves to win a woman's heart. Mac grimaced, feeling uncomfortable in comparison. He hadn't spent much time refining his courtship abilities. Unable to stand, he sank onto the sofa, holding the mail.

"I know, Alex," Diana continued. "It is hard.... Yes, I understand.... Okay.... You, too."

Mac winced, looking at a business envelope addressed to him. He'd had Diana for a time, seen her grow and mend and laugh. And now it was time for Alex.

Mac crushed the invitation to the church social and tossed it on the table. He'd given Diana the space she needed, tried to keep his senses from being filled with her scent, her warmth.

But playing buddy to a woman he craved like a bee craved blossoms wasn't exactly the easiest thing.

When she laughed, his heart turned flip-flops.

When she sat quietly in the evenings, he felt warmed clear through.

Diana. Feminine, gentle...delectable and saucy.

Mac heard her come in and say, "Hi."

A woman welcoming her man.

Mac found himself trembling. Because he fought the need to tug her to him, because he needed her down to his bones, Mac kept his gaze on the mail. "Hi, yourself."

"Are we crabby?" she asked lightly, settling herself beside him.

When he glared at her, Mac suddenly discovered that Diana was wearing a transparent negligee. His eyes widened, taking in the revealing garment that had just enough beige lace to conceal some parts of her. "What in Sam Hill are you wearing?"

"I've just showered, Mac," she explained after taking a sip of tea from the cup she held in her hand. "Ms. Simpson has invited us to dinner. If you want to go, I'll change."

She crossed her legs, and Mac found himself staring helplessly at a smooth length of her thigh. He forced his eyes to her face. "That meddling old—"

"Now, Mac, that doesn't sound like you." Concerned at once, she frowned. "What is wrong?"

"Plenty. Clancy ought to be shot for teaching you anything about mushing. Okay, it's fun, I know that. But a woman out on her own—anything could happen. What if you broke a leg? What if the dogs turned on you? Clancy's Nasty Boy weighs more than you do. What if those poachers decided to—"

"Poachers? You mean they still haven't been caught?"

Running his fingers through his hair, Mac took a deep breath. He hadn't meant to turn on her like that—it was just that he wanted her safe. She was so precious to him. "Listen, things can happen in the high country, and you wouldn't have a chance."

Diana's brown eyes darkened. "I suppose that's why you were checking up on me."

"I was checking up on a poacher sign. You just happened to be there."

"Really? Is that why you stirred up the snow with your helicopter? Hovering around like Papa Bear?"

Mac's frustration came to the boiling point quickly.

"Why can't you understand, woman, that it's dangerous for you? Especially a half-pint—"

Her eyes widened incredulously. "What?"

Mac lowered his face, scowling down at her, his chin jutting out. He felt as raw as a wounded bear, wanting to strike out at something. "What kind of a screwball antic was that—making a happy face in the snow? What if you fell into a crevasse or the dogs decided to run off? You can't just pick up and leave the house to run dogs the way Clancy does, lady."

Just a fraction of an inch away from his lips, Diana asked carefully, "Why can't I, Mac? Didn't I have your permission? Who are you, the lord of my life?"

Mac framed her face with his big hands. "This is why not." Placing his mouth on hers, Mac let his savage needs erupt. Roughly he deepened the ravenous kiss. He took her tongue into his mouth, caressed it with his own and felt his body throb with the need to enter her. Mac needed to claim his woman. To show her his heart, to bind her to him.

Forcing himself to end the kiss, Mac looked down at Diana's wide-eyed expression and her swollen lips. He'd kissed her with every ounce of his hot and insistent desire. He'd shocked her, he knew, looking into her darkening eyes.

"So I'm not smooth like Alex." He ground out each word.

"No, you're not," she agreed, watching him steadily. "You never were." Her tongue flicked out to moisten her bottom lip.

Mac felt the cut straight down his chest. He'd shown her the rough side of his passion. And scared her. There wasn't a reason in the world why she'd stay with him now. Where had all his good intentions gone?

Mac felt ill. He had to escape, to lick his wounds in private. "I'm taking a shower."

In the bathroom, Mac turned on the water full force. Stripping off his clothes, he stepped into the steaming hot shower. He closed his eyes and saw Diana's pale face. She was probably packing her bags now.

He scrubbed his flesh almost viciously, wishing he hadn't grabbed her with the debonair polish of a Borneo wild man. Hell, he was wild. Wild with fear of losing Diana. To Alex or a hungry mountain cat. Or a wayward bullet from a poacher's rifle.

Or maybe just his own clumsiness. He cursed at himself for mishandling her. He'd probably shocked her right down to her bones.

Mac lifted his face to the stream of hot water. He took a deep breath and wondered if she'd send him a postcard after she cooled down.

Maybe someday she'd accept his apology.

He heard a sound and turned to see Diana's small hand pressed flat against the shower door. "Get out of there, Mac."

"You get out of here and I will," he exploded, feeling caught by frustration and need of Diana. "Isn't anything private around here?"

"Okay." She tossed a towel over the glass door, and he heard the bathroom door click shut.

He turned off the water, toweling himself dry. "'Okay', she says. Just like that," he muttered, wrapping the towel around his waist. "How in the hell can you get a good fight stirred up with 'Okay'?"

When Mac jerked open the shower door, he found

Diana leaning against the counter, smiling patiently. "Do you always talk to yourself in the shower?"

He glared at her, feeling raw and happy to see her. Placing his hands on his hips, Mac narrowed his eyes. "Sometimes a man has to have some privacy. Why is it females feel as though they have to pry under a man's skin?"

Diana trailed a slender finger down his damp chest, then looked up at him, her eyes dark. "You've had your privacy long enough, MacLean. Tell me what you feel."

Mac glanced at the mirror behind her, which revealed the curves of Diana's trim back. The negligee swooped almost to her shapely bottom. He swallowed, forcing himself not to think of the fascinating little dimple just at the base of— In another moment he'd be grabbing her. "Not a chance."

Her fingertips circled his nipples; she watched as they hardened. Then she stroked his cheek. "Mac, I think you're afraid of me."

He jerked his head away from her touch.

"Mac, don't make me come after you," she threatened softly. "I can do it, you know."

"What in Sam Hill are you talking about, woman?" he asked sharply, aware of his body hardening, heating at her nearness.

When she unwrapped the towel that was around his hips, Mac trembled. "You're pushing your luck," he said unsteadily, feeling genuine panic as the towel fell to the floor. If she touched him again, he'd burn, he'd explode with the need to claim her....

Diana's skin was flushed, hot against his flesh as she brushed her cheek across his chest. Holding his eyes, she undressed and dropped the silken confection over his towel.

He closed his eyes. When they'd made love the very first time, he'd held back and she'd trusted him. Would he lose her now if he exposed his unrestrained passion?

When her lips nibbled his, he could feel her hunger, feel the potent beckoning. Stepping up to him, Diana let her softness curve into the damp hard planes of his body. "Take me," she whispered against his throat.

Mac fought his blatant desire, his flesh aching to join with hers. He knew he couldn't hold back the passion that kept him riveted to the floor. If ever a man wanted to possess a woman, he was that man. His throat dry, he whispered, "No."

Diana stilled, the small hardened tips of her breasts searing his chest. She leaned back to look up at him curiously. "No?"

Mac knew he had to escape or damn himself. He sidestepped her to walk to his bedroom bureau. He jerked open a drawer, taking out a pair of neatly folded briefs only to have Diana snatch them away from him.

In the faint light of the bedside lamp, he saw Diana toss his underclothing to the bed. She crossed her arms beneath her breasts, the motion raising them. His gaze followed the gentle swell of her hips and the lines of her slender legs—a seductive view that caused Mac to perspire. He tried to force his gaze away and found the task impossible.

Frowning, she tapped her toe on the braided rug. "I won't have it, Mac. You can be ill-tempered and nasty and act like a cornered old buck deer, but I won't have you keeping anything from me. I won't live like this—with everything tucked neatly away, words left unsaid.''

Her finger prodded his chest. ''You've been running away since New Year's. Just what is your problem, mister?''

Suddenly his bedroom seemed small. Diana, standing in her birthday suit, her eyes flashing angrily up at him, could drive a man to the limits. ''Leave me alone,'' he said between his teeth, glaring back at her.

Her eyebrows went up. ''Oh. You've reverted to the womanless hermit stage, then.''

''Watch it,'' he warned evenly, wanting to run his hands down her body, feel the racing of her heart against his. Lack of sleep and his desire for her had placed him on edge. He'd taken her cautiously the first time. But not now. He wouldn't be able to hold back if they made love now. And then she'd run.

Diana studied him coolly. ''I guess it's up to me, then.''

In the next instant, she pressed him against the wall, looping her arms around his neck. She smiled softly, and Mac's hands involuntarily fitted to her back and caressed its smoothness.

''There. I've got you.... Give in, Mac.''

When she stood on tiptoe to kiss him, Mac lost himself. Silken skin and tempting lips drove him to the limit and pushed him over. Mac could feel the primitive hunger beat through him as her lips parted, allowing his tongue entrance. Beneath his hands, her body moved, supple and willing to meet his demands. Her thighs pressed against his, increasing the ache.

Sweeping her up into his arms, Mac carried Diana to the bed.

"Oh, Mac," she whispered urgently. Holding him tightly, Diana's fingers tangled in his hair, bringing his mouth to hers, as though she, too, had hungers that raged out of control.

Mac's hands roamed over her feverishly, demanding as they stroked the length of her. He trembled, trying to bank the consuming fires momentarily.

Then Diana thrust against him, nibbling on his earlobe. "Don't hold back, Mac. Not now."

He breathed heavily, the desire rising. Diana opened to him, urged him into her fully, and they became one body, one driving force.

He'd waited too long, the tethers leashing him cut by the softness that was Diana. For a moment he stilled, absorbing the pleasure of Diana's warmth. She trembled, moving slightly beneath him. "Take me, Mac," she whispered huskily.

And then there was no waiting, only the wild beating hunger driving them on. He could feel the throbbing deep within him, his hands caressing her breasts.

His passion burned, the flames growing higher as Diana met his demands and issued her own. The bonding, sweet and furious, tasted of eternity and promises and sharing.

Each sound she made and the sweetness of her body enclosing him urged him on. Relentlessly, he tasted her tender body, savoring the taut buds of her breasts, relishing her satin-smooth skin.

Her soft arms and legs held him to her. Her head was thrown back against the first rippling tide of heat. Her fingers tensed up on his shoulders as she gave herself fully to the sensation.

Mac felt the surging ecstasy rise in her as she met his powerful rhythm. The tempest rose, swirling inside them as Mac showed her his primitive desperation, his need of her and more.

Later, as Diana's soft breath flowed across his chest, her head resting on his shoulder, Mac was overwhelmed with love and felt his eyes burn. Tears trailed down his temple as Diana's hand smoothed his chest, her palm catching the beat of his throbbing heart.

Diana turned and propped an elbow up on his chest. She kissed his hand when he tucked a damp strand behind her ear. "I love you like this, Mac. My own snuggly bear."

She nuzzled his chest, and he savored the intimate tangle of their limbs a moment longer. "I know you're tired," she said softly, blowing into his ear. "But tell me what's wrong?"

How could he tell her of his fears? "I'm just tired."

"Like hell."

He raised his eyebrows, feeling his mouth curve into a smile. "Clancy needs to watch his language."

Diana kissed the hard corners of his mouth, and Mac began to melt again. "You're the strongest person I know, Mac. Why are you frightened?" she whispered, tracing the contours of his lips with her tongue.

He breathed lightly beneath her sensual forays, bothered by the shattering driving way he'd taken her. "Did I hurt you?"

She laughed, the sound as soft as the mountain wind caressing the columbine flowers. "You freed me. I soared." Lifting herself, Diana lay on top of him. Her eyes, soft and drowsy and mysterious, looked down at him. "I've never felt like more of a woman."

She curled her arms around him, whispering against his neck, "Stop fighting me. I'm determined to have my way with you. I love this—the whispering, the sharing. Now tell me."

Diana could feel Mac's hard body tense, as though preparing to take a blow. Lifting her head, she placed her palm against his rough cheek. His black eyes flickered, looking away almost guiltily. "I have things to work out."

"Mmm. You heard me talking with Alex, didn't you?"

Mac turned to her slowly, his expression almost flat, evasive. It was then that Diana knew how he shielded himself, drawing back, aching.... Taking his hand, she linked her smaller fingers with his. His palm was warm and safe and rough with work. She'd seen those hands run over an ill calf, searching, helping.

"Let me tell you a story," she began softly, continuing to look at their joined hands. She could feel his breath fill his chest and linger before easing slowly out. As though he had taken a sharp blow and needed time to recover.

Against the white pillowcase, Mac's rugged dark face and black hair appeared as timeless as the mountains beyond the bedroom window. A man who would endure, she thought. Beneath her, his heart pounded hard and steady.

She held him, the strength of him leashed by her light touch. "I wish Alex the best. But he's caused trouble, and I called to correct him."

"I see." Mac's long hard body shuddered; his eyes

glittered beneath the long sweep of lashes. She saw the flash of pain, quickly concealed.

Diana smiled, knowing that she would pursue him if he withdrew. She'd never wanted to corner a man, but Mac was an altogether different story.

"Oh, God, I don't think I can take this," Mac muttered, watching her. "How considerate of you," he offered, easing her from him. "I don't think I've ever had such a discussion after...lovemaking."

Sensing him running away, Diana felt a cold wash of panic. Throwing caution to the wind, she reached for a pillow and plummeted him with it. "You hard-headed... I'm trying to have an intelligent conversation with you about emotions! I've had enough of your hiding, enough of being held at arm's length."

"Hey!" Catching her arms, Mac pulled her under him and pressed down on her full length.

The look she sent him back was pure sensuality, inviting. "I won't break," she whispered huskily, feeling the driving desire rising in him. "Oh, Mac..."

His mouth was warm, lingering, worshiping as he rubbed his lips across hers. "Are you telling me you need me, lady?" he asked roughly.

"Oh, Mac. I do need you so."

He brushed the pad of his thumb across her hot cheek, watching her eyes darken. "Why were you wearing that sexy slinky thing?"

She answered honestly, her heart fluttering as his lips hovered near her aching breast. "To seduce you, pure and simple."

"You've certainly accomplished the task."

"Beginner's luck, darling. Maybe we should see if my luck holds."

"Hallelujah."

Nine

Mac insisted on taking Diana to work the next morning, despite her objections. He treated her with endearing, old-fashioned, courtly manners. As though he were afraid to mishandle her, fearing she'd run away.

Watching him stand near the wood stove, talking to her boss and several other men as they sipped their coffee, Diana didn't think she could refuse him anything. Tilting her head, Diana considered Mac's easy long-legged stance. Looking very appealing in his thick cable-knit sweater and jeans, he periodically glanced toward her. Something blazed when their eyes met, a deep stirring heat that had nothing to do with the wood fire.

Diana felt her bones melt. For just the space of a breath, she felt Mac locked against her, hungry and demanding.

She felt rosy and cherished and very well loved. Mac was as rugged as the country and as open with his heart—and he was hers. Once Mac had determined she could hold her own with his passion, he wanted everything. Demanded everything. Was it possible the month was January and not spring? Was she eighteen again?

Wingman glanced her way. "Hey, Diana. How about more coffee?" he asked, raising his mug.

Mac's head turned toward her, causing her hand to tremble as she lifted the steaming pot from the brewer. Walking around the cheese barrel, Diana could feel the pull of his desire.

He was gazing at her so deeply, as though he could see through her maroon turtleneck sweater and worn jeans. She blushed right down to her toes. She liked being cherished and touched as though she were precious silk and satin. At the same time, she loved being his friend. A man like Mac was one to hold on to, and to make commitments to for forever.

Crossing to the group of standing men, Diana refilled their mugs. She wanted to turn to Mac and say, "Let's go home, darling. Show me again how much you need me...."

Instead she settled for a quiet smile up at him. The rest of the men, conversing in low rumbling voices, seemed outside their intimate loving circle. Mac took the coffeepot from her to place it on a table. Wrapping his arm around her, he drew her to his side.

It was a natural gesture to place her arm around his waist. Hooking her thumb over his leather belt, Diana leaned against him.

It was this, the sharing, that she had wanted so

desperately. The comfortable loving tenderness that a man like Mac could provide.

Neil chuckled. "By the looks of things, you two lovebirds had better get married soon. The whole town is dying to throw a big shindig."

"What do you mean?" Mac's fingers tightened on Diana's upper arm.

"Rayfield's been crowing he's going to be asked to be best man, once you get wise that he purposely sent you Diana. Thought he'd done you and her a favor. Said she looked like a stray, and you were the local stray collector. He had plenty of rooms that night she blew into town. Had her room key right in front of him when he got the idea."

Wingman's grin widened. "Benevolence finally put one over on Old Mac. We were just waiting to see the sparks fly."

"I didn't know." Mac grinned slowly. "But he's invited to the chili feed Diana and I will be throwing soon. So are the rest of you."

Henry Murphy's round face lighted up. "You're kidding. I thought we'd never be invited to the almighty MacLean estate. In fact, we've all been afraid you'd mess up and she'd light out as soon as she found you out. She's not wearing a ring yet."

Diana didn't need a ring to feel her commitment to Mac. She suddenly realized that in her heart, she had already decided to spend her life loving Mac. Life included making all sorts of decisions, and sometimes the heart knew a better direction than any bundle of sensible inhibitions. Besides, she didn't intend to have him bullied into marriage.

"The little woman needs a ring of some sort, Mac," another man offered. "If she were mine, I'd be wanting to put my mark on her. Other than those cute little marks on her neck, of course.''

When Mac didn't answer, Diana looked up to see him studying her closely. When his gaze ran down her throat, his expression changed sharply. He swallowed, easing his hand up her arm stealthily to tug up the neck of her sweater.

Wingman sipped his coffee, his eyes sparkling. ''Look at the two of them blushing just like kids. Cute, isn't it?''

''Okay, Neil, that's enough,'' Mac stated sharply.

''Whoa. Just teasing, boy.'' Wingman winked at Diana. ''Come on, men, I'll show you the new compound bows that just came in. Got some muzzle loader kits in at a fair price. When the primitive hunts come around, you'll have your muskets ready.''

As soon as the men left, Mac took Diana's hand and tugged her behind a fly rod display. He traced the tiny bruises on her throat with his forefinger.

She wrapped her fingers around his wrist, feeling the steady beat of his pulse. ''You only loved me, Mac.''

''That I did,'' he murmured huskily, the intimate tone causing her to quiver deep inside. ''What are we going to do about it, lady?''

Before she could answer, Wingman called over to them, ''By the way, Ms. Simpson said you two stood her up last night. She had the preacher over to dinner, too. Why didn't you show up, Mac?''

Mac looked down at Diana, humor and regret in his gaze. ''Looks like they're going to keep it up if I don't get out of here.''

He hesitated, seeming to want to say something else, when Wingman called, ''Oh, lover boy—''

"Don't lift anything heavy, honey," Mac instructed her after a brief hard kiss. "And if Clancy drops by today, tell him your sledding days are over, okay? You could get hurt."

He was gone without hearing her quiet firm answer. "No, I will not, Mac."

The early afternoon sun striking the snow-covered mountains caused Mac to squint behind his sunglasses. He kept the helicopter hovering over a snowmobile trail, following it and planning his keeping-Diana tactics.

The new trail led to a stand of trees, and Mac circled the aspens, searching for poacher signs. The snowmobiles weren't following the designated trails, and he'd already spotted a freshly killed doe.

"Okay, MacLean. You think you're up to trying again, huh? You know she could walk out at anytime, don't you?" he asked himself, swerving around a rocky butte. "She caught you flat-footed, you old goat. Got you stirred up until you forgot you were her friend. Came up on your backside. Now, what are you going to do?"

Mac checked his fuel level before continuing toward Smokey Mountain. "Okay," he continued, debating with himself as he followed the winding trails. "You haven't got a thing to hold her in Colorado. She could just be feeling gratitude."

Somehow Diana's lovemaking didn't feel like thank you's. It felt like…making love.

"I can design and build a modern house. I can even manage moving, if she wants to. It's just that somewhere in there, I feel as if I've taken advantage of her weakness. Women are delicate emotional creatures that way, especially Diana. Mac, you've just got to give her a little space, old boy. Keep cool while she's figuring out things.'' He shook his head and tightened his grip on the controls.

"Giving her space won't work,'' he argued with himself. "It's time to sweep her off her feet. Time to get her to say 'I do' and worry about whatever comes after, later. You're committed, son. Shoot, you know right now there will never be another woman for you. Try the champagne bit. Get down on one knee—get romantic. Tell her you love her, and you do, of course."

He caught the glint of metal and circled a thick stand of trees near an old avalanche. "Dogsledding and lifting heavy stuff is out, of course," he continued. "And walking by herself. I'll take care of her— What in Sam Hill?"

The sharp crack of a rifle shot sounded over the whirring rotor blades at the same instant that Mac spotted Terry Blakely's distinctive snowgear.

Diana pushed the huge antique dresser aside to scrub the hardwood floor beneath. She'd found Mac's note that he'd be late and thought it the perfect time to start making changes in the bedroom. She'd already done the living room yesterday.

Mac needed to make room for her in his life, she decided. Just as she had rearranged his closet to make room for her clothes, he needed to make internal adjustments, too. "Because I love the big lug doesn't mean he's setting up the rules of my life,'' she muttered.

Bending to tug a braided rug aside, Diana paused. "I suppose he'll do that backward slide, that sidestepping routine, when I tell him I love him. He's not an easy man to court. And I don't think I'll give him an ounce of space this time. Aggressive women may not be on his menu, but I think he can hold his own."

When Red whined, she sank to her knees and patted his head. "He's a heck of a guy, Red," she told the husky. "Caring, gentle... Okay, he's got a thing about leaving his chili seasonings alone. And he likes to play bagpipes—he could use lessons."

By the time she had scrubbed and rewaxed Mac's bedroom, Diana and Red had worked out Mac's entire problem: he was just too protective. She stood and rolled her cramped shoulders, then arranged her sons' pictures on the bureau, tracing the brass frames lovingly. She fussed over a basket of mauve silk roses and white baby's breath on a starched doily.

Diana studied the room she intended to share with Mac. The mauve curtains softened the rough-cut wall planks. A thick beige-and-dark-rose comforter covered the polished brass bed, and a light tan plush rug partially covered the beautiful hardwood floor. Before closing the door, Diana stated, "I'll leave his bagpipes and his chili alone...maybe. He might not like it, but I'm sledding to my heart's content. Clancy says I'm getting good enough to race, and I intend to."

Grinning, she bent to ruffle Red's fur. "I can't believe myself, Red. Diana Phillips—den mother, crosswalk monitor and bridge club chairman—loving a man so hard and seducing him."

Three hours later, Diana scanned the night beyond the house. When Mac worked evenings, helping the sheriff, he usually found time to circle the house. It was his way of checking on her, making sure that she hadn't slid into a snowdrift.

After another two hours, the grandfather clock clanged twelve times. Diana placed her teacup firmly on the saucer. "I'm calling the sheriff, Red."

Picking up Mac's radio handset, she pushed the button, copying his actions. "Ah, this is Diana. Could I please speak to the sheriff?"

The last of a man's rough curse shot through the radio's static before the sheriff answered. "This is 209. I'm the sheriff, kid. Get off the air quick. Just turn off the set and don't push any buttons, got it?"

Diana swallowed. She might not know radio code signals, but she had to know about Mac. She pushed the button again and spoke into the handset. "This is Diana Phillips," she enunciated clearly.

"This is Sheriff Sam Michaels. Get off the air, lady. We've got problems enough with Mac."

A cold wave of panic caused her to tremble. She clenched the hand monitor. Why hadn't she turned on the radio before? Why hadn't someone called her?

The sheriff's rough voice came over the static. "Look, just get off the air, Diana. Mac is working with the game warden and me. He's in a little trouble right now, and we're trying to get together a rescue team."

Diana's panic turned into sheer white-hot anger. "I'll get off the radio when you tell me where you're at."

"Do you know the penalty for waylaying the law, lady? Get off that thing so we men can get a team together."

Diana pushed the button grimly. "I want to know your location. I have a right to be there."

"It's snowing, there's a blizzard brewing up on Smokey now, and that's where Mac crashed, okay?"

the sheriff answered hotly. "We got the violators when they came down, and we've got some radio contact with Mac. He's okay, just a broken leg and a few bruises, he thinks. Now, I know you're upset, but will you get the blue blazes off that thing?"

If Diana knew anything, she knew she was not staying put while Mac was in danger. Eventually, the sheriff—apparently coached by others—told her their location.

The moment Diana stopped the pickup in front of the group of men, Wingman jerked open the door. "Diana, you ought to have better sense than this!"

Dressed in her warmest sledding outfit, Diana leaped out into the snow. She patted her thigh, motioning for Red to follow. "Where's Mac?"

Wingman shivered in the subzero arctic wind, the snow biting his face. "Come on into the makeshift tent. There's coffee—"

The sheriff marched up to Diana. "So you got here. I thought we might have two emergencies."

Taking her arm, he led her into the canvas tent. He shoved a Styrofoam cup of coffee into her hand. "Mac went down up on Old Smokey. From what we can figure out, a high-caliber rifle helped him."

"What are you doing to rescue him?" Diana stared at the game warden's expression and was frightened by what she saw. She took a deep breath, ordering herself to calm down.

The sheriff sipped his scalding coffee, studying the snow. "It's a touchy one, Diana. The copter went down in the high country. From what Mac says, any kind of noise at all could cause an avalanche that would take off the whole face of the mountain. If we run another copter up there, it could be dangerous."

"What about snowmobiles?" she asked as Red nudged her thigh, as though seeking comfort. She buried her fingers in his pelt.

"Same thing. They make noise. And at that distance, gas and the high altitude are serious problems. Other than that, Mac's leg won't take a lot of wrestling around. Add a blizzard expected to arrive in another twenty hours, and you've got bad news."

Red whined, looking up at her. "What about a sled?"

The game warden shook his head. "Dangerous. The only skilled musher around is old Clancy. He's out of shape. He wouldn't be worth a hoot. The rest of them haven't run the high country."

"But I have. Call Clancy—get his team up here. I can do it." Diana saw the hesitation in the men's faces. "I can do it," she repeated quietly.

The sheriff was the first to explode. "Hell, no! I'm not about to let you go up. He'd be all right if we left him there a while longer. The thing is, that mountain purely likes to avalanche. Ridiculous...a half-pint female—"

Diana smiled. She would show them what this half-pint could do. "I'm going up," she stated with quiet authority.

The sheriff resisted, uttering a stream of oaths that heated the canvas tent. But in the end, he sent a man after Clancy and his dogs.

In an hour, Clancy was squatting beside a light birch sled. He had been giving Diana plenty of instructions. He rubbed snow around the lashings to freeze and strengthen them. "She's a good one," he said with pride, referring to the sled. "Built to travel fast, runs on the snow like a leaf on the wind."

He glanced up at Diana. "Scared? For Mac or yourself?"

"Both," she admitted, trying to remember the nurse's instructions about the pain pills and the first-aid wrapping for Mac's leg.

"The dogs are wanting to run, girl. They can feel it deep inside. You can do it, the same as them. Just remember, if you come to a snowbridge, take it easy. Walk the dogs across, one at a time, if you have to—"

The sheriff stormed out of the tent. "Mac went down with two bottles of expensive Scotch. He's as drunk as a skunk and singing those damned Highland songs into the radio!"

He shot an embarrassed look at Diana. "Oh, hell, Mac made me promise to kiss you and tell you he loves you."

The sheriff—thought to be as hard as flint—bent down awkwardly to kiss her cheek. "Keep it to yourself, lady. But you're okay with me, too. Mac deserves the best."

"That she is," Clancy agreed. "Look here, me darlin'. You get up there in avalanche country, and you talk quiet to those dogs. They won't bark, then. Got it?"

The sheriff shifted uneasily, looking up at the mountain. "She's hell up there now. The only thing we've got going for us are those freak sun spots. Without them even radio transmission would be impossible."

The sheriff handed her a small radio transmitter/receiver. "Any questions on how to operate this thing? Mac's drunk, but he's giving us a chance to talk, now and then."

She nodded, then glanced up at the snow-covered mountain. It had always looked beautiful to her, but now it was only forbidding. Mac was up there, hurt, needing her. She hadn't even told him she loved him.

At the first light, Diana called to Red. The husky stood in his harness, shaking the snow from him. Clancy's malamutes copied him. "I'm ready," Diana told the men.

"I packed you a musher's special—sticks of butter, chocolate bars and a bunch of other stuff—to eat while you run," Clancy explained. "You can do it, darlin'. Old Clancy never taught a dummy yet." He hugged her awkwardly. "I'll pray to the good Lord for your safety."

Just past the timberline, Diana could feel the power rising in the dogs. The light sled coursed over the snow as though it were polished glass.

"Push them," Diana repeated Clancy's instructions beneath her knitted face mask. "And keep strong myself." After an hour, she reached into her provisions to extract a chocolate bar. "Mac, I'm coming."

Following the sheriff's orders, she repeatedly called the emergency base. Clancy talked her through the rest stop, reminding her to feed the dogs and check the traces. "Stop playing the lady with Nasty Boy," the old timer ordered through the radio static. "Let him run his heart out."

The shadowy pines gave way to rocky buttes and startling sweeps of deep snow. Coming onto a straight stretch, Diana called the base station. "The snow is different up here, Clancy. Like ice."

"Huh," he answered. "Stop the team and put on their booties. That ice could cut their pads. Lash 'em tight and knock Nasty Boy across the muzzle if he snarls. Check the booties every so often for wear—replace 'em if you have to. I packed plenty.''

Diana smiled beneath her face mask. The old man was with her every inch of the way. "I love you, Clancy.''

The radio crackled. "What the hell is going on?'' Mac demanded belligerently. "I thought I heard Diana's voice.''

Taking a deep breath, Diana answered, "I'm coming up, Mac. I'm running the dogs straight for you. Clancy and the sheriff are directing me. You'll have to talk to me now.''

"Huh?'' After a moment's silence, Mac growled. "Those idiots let you take a sled up here?''

When his blistering salty opinions of the men hiding behind women's skirts ended, Diana said simply, "I love you, Mac.''

The radio crackled, and Clancy singsonged, "I love you, too, Mac. The sheriff kissed your girl, and I hugged the daylights out of her. Kanoodled her nice and tight against me. What are you going to do about it?''

"Nothing,'' Mac responded, "but kill you. Wring your scrawny neck with my bare hands.''

When Mac finished raving, the nurse's voice came across Diana's receiver. "Diana, Clancy says Mac is drunk. You can't give him those pain pills now,'' she said urgently.

"What do I do, instead?'' Diana asked.

Mac's unsteady voice answered the question. "Easy. Let me drink whiskey until I'm blind.''

"Nurse?'' Diana asked.

"Okay, honey. Let him have his way.''

"It's good stuff, too," Mac added. "Not like Donaldson's rotgut."

Diana crossed a shadowy pass, the snowdrifts slanting precariously on the rocky bluffs. When she described the spot, the game warden answered, "Mac should be around there someplace."

Mac continued to grumble. "Hell of a thing, to let a sweet little woman save me. She should stay put where it's safe and let the lot of you freeze your—"

The radio crackled as Diana allowed the dogs to swerve around a fallen log. It was full light now, with threatening clouds looming around the mountains. Diana's face mask caught the freezing mist, and she quickly replaced it. Clancy asked about the dogs and decided they were strong enough not to rest. "Wait 'til you find Mac, then change their booties and boil 'em some blood broth out of the pack. Take a shot or two of the whiskey yourself. You'll need it. Mac's not happy with the lot of us over this. Okay, missy?"

"Damn it, Clancy," Mac roared. "Where is she?"

Diana pressed the radio button. Mac could fuss over her later to his heart's content, but right now he needed a firm hand. "Mac, shut up. Tell me where you are."

"You're bossy. Never did like bossy women. And you changed all the furniture around. I bumped my knee—of course that's the leg that's broken. Like it was hexed or something...."

"Oh, brother." The sheriff's rough voice entered the conversation. "Diana, follow that mouth."

"Mac, where are you?"

"I'm in a snow cave. Tucked in nice and tight.

Wish you were here with me, honey. Hey, you guys, get off the radio, okay? Some of this stuff is personal.''

Ten

After taking care of the dogs, Diana entered the cave.

Stretched out on a parachute covering the ground, Mac looked very pale. "Who are you? What the hell is going on?" he asked in a raw voice that was nearly a shout. "This isn't a Sunday school picnic up here, you know."

Diana straightened the blanket across the mouth of the cave, then patted the snow to secure the flap.

She turned to Mac, jerking off her parka hood and face mask. Pain etched his face, deepening the lines. His eyes flicked anxiously over her, and his hand shook as he set down a near empty whiskey bottle.

His gaze fastened on her face, then trailed across her mussed hair. "You're crazy, woman," he stated in a low raspy voice.

She saw the sheer fear in his expression before it was replaced by anger. She wanted to run to him. She was his friend and his lover; she intended to share his life.

But now wasn't the time to sort out their relationship, to end the game and make serious promises. She had to remember the nurse's instructions and follow them carefully. Mac didn't look pliant—if she had to bully him to make him take her directions, she would.

She opened a thermos of his chili, poured some into a cup and handed it to him with a spoon. "So how are you?" she asked casually.

He glared at her. "Just peachy. Getting ready for the ball. I hope you enjoyed yourself."

Seating herself on a corner of his parachute, Diana wondered how long she had loved him. It was a lasting love, fueled by passion and gentleness. Gazing at the dark stubble covering his jaw, Diana decided that Mac was more attractive than ever. "It was a nice run," she said, tilting her head to study him. She unwrapped a chocolate bar and munched on it as he glared at her. "You know, Mac, I think we'll have our pictures taken together. A nice brass frame—"

Mac stared at her. "This is no time to talk about decorating, woman! I've been worried sick about you." He paused, frowning as he chewed thoughtfully. "Something tastes different," he murmured ominously. "You've been messing with my recipe, on top of everything else."

"Mmm. Someone had to. What do you think?"

He probed the mixture with his spoon. "I think that's Donaldson's secret spice in there. What is it?"

She winked at him, grinning. Somehow, her resolution not to talk about their future together was just not going to work out. "It's my secret now. The only way I'll let you know, is if you'll share your life with me," she returned easily, looking around. "I didn't know it would be so light in here. I'd thought it would be very dark.''

Mac looked as if he had swallowed ten whole red-hot chili peppers. ''What are you saying?''

Diana licked her bottom lip clean of chocolate. She cautioned, ''Shh. Keep your voice down, sweetheart. There's a whole ton of snow over the cave that would just love to crush us. Now could you tell me about your leg, please?''

Mac cursed under his breath, gazing toward the snow ceiling as though he were asking for heavenly guidance. ''Women!''

She poured her chili into a paper cup. She reached for the whiskey, put in a measure, then stirred it in.

''What in Sam Hill are you doing now?'' Mac erupted as she sampled the mixture.

''Clancy told me to take a drink. I have to eat, so I'm saving a step.''

Mac's expression was undisguised disbelief. After a pause, he lifted the bottle and drank from it. Wiping the back of his hand across his mouth, he stared at her, challenging her. ''We're in a hell of a mess up here, lady. And in the middle of everything, you start talking about sharing lives.''

''Uh-huh. When are you going to tell me you love me, Mac?''

His face softened. ''I thought you knew. If you left, you'd take my life with you. Pure and simple.''

''That's nice.'' She turned to him fully, fierce long-ing blazing in her. ''Say it, Mac. You've told the world—now tell me. Face-to-face.''

''I love you,'' he said, then his expression changed to one of sadness. ''I didn't want to care. Feeling is like ripping parts of you away, throwing them into oblivion. Caring is risky.''

"I felt the same." She was suddenly shy. "I thought I was too old to feel this way. I really didn't want to, then along came this friend.... You listened and you cared, Mac. And then the other part came, too. It frightened me, wanting you so badly, the feeling of being all new."

After stripping his gloves off, Mac reached for her. He cradled her face and pulled her to him. "Come here...."

She held her lips from his—waiting for him to meet her on equal terms. "All or nothing, Mac," she whispered.

He rubbed his nose against hers, smiling. "You're quite a woman. My woman."

It was there in his expression—all the fierce loving pride she'd sought for a lifetime. The warmth and the tenderness just for her, just as she was.... Mac brushed her lips with his, and she felt the sensual pull of him draw her nearer. "Diana the huntress," he murmured softly, drawing her hand to his mouth. His lips pressed into her small palm as he closed his eyes.

He held her hand there, silently making his promises. Then he opened his eyes and looked longingly at her. "Does wonders for a man's ego—your coming after me."

"I always will," she returned, kissing him. "Count on it."

"We'll melt this cave if we keep this up," he whispered rawly a moment later.

Forcing herself away, Diana lifted the parachute material covering his legs. Mac had formed a rough splint using a branch and tied it to his broken leg. "It's okay," he muttered, running his fingers through her hair. He watched the strands fall from his fingers. "Do you know how I feel when we make love?"

Diana zipped up his parka, pulling it tightly around his ashen face, then eased him gently to his feet. His grimace of pain caused her stomach to knot. Wrapping her arm around his waist, she led him to the sled. "Tell me, Mac. Talk to me."

Mac grunted in pain as he lowered himself into the sled. "I love you, kid," he stated roughly. Then he glanced at the low threatening clouds. "If you don't mind, honey, I think we'd better make a run for it. Please?"

When she covered him with the heavy down sleeping bag, Mac groaned weakly. "Oh, God, I think I'm going to pass out.... What are we going to do now?"

Diana leaned down to kiss his cold lips. She kissed his closed lids and the top of his nose. "Why, honey, you're going to let me take care of you. You just settle down and enjoy the ride."

"Huh?" Mac asked, gazing at her blankly. "But I'm supposed to take care of you...." Then he fainted.

Mac stirred in the warmth of his own bed, finding Diana's small body curled around his back. When he moved slightly, her bare breasts rubbed against him enticingly. Her arm draped across his waist.

From downstairs came a voice as rough as nails scratching a blackboard; Clancy sang a musher's song at the top of his lungs.

Mac held his breath, fought his throbbing headache and forced open one eye. The early light of the cloudy dawn blinded him, searing through the ruffled curtains straight on a path to the back of his head. He clamped his lips closed, feeling the softness of Diana's thighs tangle with his. Her fingers stirred and played with the hair on his chest as she rubbed his back with her cheek.

"Sweetheart?" she asked in a tone husky with sleep. "How are you feeling?"

Clancy roared, "Boyo, boyo run your dogs till their tongues drag in the snow, and you still won't beat my merry crew!"

Ray, Ms. Simpson and Donaldson joined him for the next chorus, and Mac groaned. Halting her seeking fingers by covering them with his hand, he managed to say raggedly, "I'm fine. What's going on?"

She yawned, then propped herself up on his chest. She nuzzled his neck. "How's your leg?"

"Just great, considering it's broken." He felt himself growing heated as he looked straight into Diana's drowsy eyes—just as he did every time he looked at her. He brushed a strand of hair back from her cheek and kissed her waiting lips gently.

Diana sighed, resting her cheek upon his chest. She draped a slender arm around his neck and caressed him. "I like this—waking up as Mrs. Mac MacLean, honey," she whispered.

Her hand on him felt so good, Mac thought, stroking her hair. His hand slid down her smooth back. With his other hand, he rubbed his jaw—and was surprised. "It takes me two days to grow a beard like this. What day is it?"

"It's two days later," Diana answered, then kissed his shoulder.

Suddenly, Mac's brain registered what she'd said earlier, "Mrs. Mac MacLean?"

She nibbled his tanned shoulder. "Umm. You were absolutely horrible, threatening Clancy's life. It was the least I could do."

Closing his eyes, Mac remembered the explosion of happiness that had swept through him when Diana had whispered, "Of course, I'll marry you, honey.

Just let the doctor finish the cast. The sheriff can get us the license and fetch the minister. And we can take the blood test right here in the hospital.''

"Now," he had demanded roughly, catching her hand to press it to his lips.

"I pronounce you man and wife," the minister had proudly proclaimed later.

Now, Mac sat up in bed. "This is no good," he stated aloud. "You shouldn't have married me just because you felt sorry for me."

Diana sat up also, sunlight caressing the uncovered curves of her body. Frowning, she tilted her head a little to the side, a gesture he knew signified a challenge. She'd done that a lot lately, challenged him. And he'd liked it!

His gaze wandered downward to that tiny mole just to the right of her—he looked up, trying to keep from getting distracted. "Cover up. I can't think when you're—like that. You make me go all haywire. I can't think about anything but—" He tugged the sheet up, expecting her to hold it.

Diana let the sheet fall, and he forced himself to continue, "Besides, that crew downstairs could burst into this room anytime. Someone ought to scrub Clancy's mouth. Those songs aren't fit for a lady to hear."

"They're celebrating winning the game. By the way, Ray says I'm worth at least that antique musket, too. I've already told Rick and Blaine about the marriage, and they were very happy. They hinted at spending the whole summer with us," she said, grinning.

"We're supposed to be in our honeymoon suite, my darling husband. We have all the privacy we

want, with dinner awaiting us at the tug of that rope."
She nodded toward a cord tied to the bed.

Dazed, Mac looked around the newly decorated
room. He shook his head. "No. This won't do at all.
I had big plans—"

"It was the best we could do on such short notice.
What other plans did you have, Mac?" Diana asked
quietly.

Mac sighed. "I wanted to…"

"Yes?" Diana's sweet breath brushed his chest,
and Mac could feel himself melting.

"Well, I wanted to…sweep you off your feet. Anyway, I won't hold you to promises made under du-
ress." He had to look at her just once more before
she escaped.…

Diana brought his hand to her mouth, ran the tip
of her tongue across his callused palm. "Don't fight
me, darling. I'm holding the secret chili spice as my
edge." She placed his hand upon her breast, and her
inquisitive fingertips began tracing his ear, then
moved down his shoulder and lower. "From stray to
friend to loving wife," she whispered, her lips brushing his cheek. "It's true, then, Humpty can be put
together again."

Her lashes fluttered against his warm cheek playfully. "Is your leg hurting…too badly?"

Mac wriggled his toes, breathing in her sweet scent.
"I am…okay."

Seating herself on his lap, Diana gently tugged his
lobe with her teeth. "You're awake now, aren't you,
Mac? Fully awake?"

She felt so right in his arms. Stroking her thigh,
Mac agreed with a nod of his head. "You risked your
life for me. I was damned proud of you."

"I love you, Mac. It's as simple as that."

He looked into her clear brown eyes and saw his future, his happiness. With Diana there would be nothing but sunlight and roses.

"I wanted to marry you, Mac—I'd already decided before your accident. I just saw my opportunity then and reached out for it." She ran her fingers through his hair, watching the black strands catch the soft light. "I've been thinking about racing sleds and learning to fly your helicopter."

"Mmm?" Mac was too distracted by her mouth to hear her last sentence. He nibbled her lips, then trailed light kisses down to her throat.

"You didn't marry me just to get the secret spice, did you?" she murmured, caressing his cheeks.

Mac's head came up, and he saw Diana's seductive smile. It took his breath away. "I love you. I've waited a lifetime for you. Let me show you why I married you."

How could a woman say no? Diana asked herself when their lips met.

* * * * *

In August 2000, look for
TALLCHIEF: THE HOMECOMING,
Desire #1310
part of Cait London's irresistible miniseries
THE TALLCHIEFS,
and Desire's newest promotion Body & Soul.

Dear Reader,

The first man I ever fell in love with was a cowboy. He was twenty and I was five, and I followed him everywhere—apparently imprinting, like a duck. The second man I fell in love with was Jess Harper, the hotheaded, rough-and-tumble, vulnerable-at-the-core cowboy hero of the television series *Laramie*. The die was cast. Forever after I would love those hard-edged, softhearted men who are their own worst enemies and everyone else's best friends.

Tanner is one of them. I fell in love with him—even when I wanted to kick him in the, er, butt. I hope you'll fall in love with him, too.

Enjoy!

Anne McAllister

COWBOYS DON'T CRY
Anne McAllister

For Patricia Smith and Luigi Bonomi,
editors who make writers glad to write

For Walter C. Perkins.
1932–1993,
my first cowboy hero

One

Tanner could hear them arguing even as he came along the side of the barn.

"He can't."

"Can so."

"No way."

"Yessir."

"No disrespect, Ev," he heard Bates say earnestly in his polite, college-boy voice. "Tanner's the best at breaking broncs in these parts, no two ways about it. But I don't reckon even he could stay on this one."

As he rounded the corner, Tanner saw old Everett Warren spit in the dust, then aim a glare at the younger cowboy. "Shows what you know."

"Yeah," a third, much higher voice chipped in, and Billy, Ev's nine-year-old grandson, swung up on the corral fence. "Tanner can do anything."

Tanner grinned a little at the boy's confidence in

him. In fact, he hoped Billy was right. If he was, then everything would work out fine when he had to deal with his new boss this afternoon.

But before he had a chance to start thinking about that again, he saw Bates shake his head. "Not this mare," he said, nodding at the one whose bridle he held.

She was the sweetest-looking jet black beauty Tanner had ever seen. The upcoming interview faded from his mind at the sight of her. Talk about prime horseflesh.

Tanner stopped and simply admired the mare as she fidgeted, stamping, tossing her head and shimmying as Bates spoke.

"'Course he can. Can't you?" Ev added, when he turned and saw Tanner coming their way.

"You can ride her, can'tcha, Tanner?" Billy demanded.

Tanner didn't say anything, just stood considering her, tempted.

Ev grinned. "Sam Gallagher just brought her over. Says ain't no one can stay on her at his place."

"Plenty of guys have tried," Bates put in quickly. "Gibb got bucked off last week. Didn't last five seconds. Walker and Del Rio tried, too, and both of 'em bit the dust. Not surprising really, those two...but Gibb, he's dynamite."

"He ain't Tanner," Billy said stoutly.

"Ain't nobody better'n Tanner." Ev nodded emphatically, chewed and spat again. He looked at Tanner, his pale blue eyes clear and bright. "Show him."

Tanner cocked his head. "Just like that?"

"You've rid your share," Ev reminded him.

But that had been a while back. He was thirty-four

now and occasionally aware after a long day in the saddle of his thrice-broken ribs, a shattered ankle, a lumpy collarbone, a shoulder with a permanent tendency toward dislocation and the two pins still residing in his left knee.

Still, she *was* a beauty. And there was nothing in the world like pitting your strength against so much sheer energy, nothing that could compare with settling down onto a half a ton of twisting, surging animal. It felt as if you had the world by the tail.

Even so, Tanner hesitated. He looked with longing at the ebony mare, feeling the weight of his responsibilities pressing down on him as he did so.

"What good's a dead foreman, I'd like to know?" Abigail had scolded last spring when he'd hit the dust, concussed, after being thrown by a frisky bay. "I don't pay you to break horses or bones!"

"I'm fine," Tanner had assured her, swallowing the dirt in his mouth and wiping a streak of blood off his lip. "Don't fuss."

But Abigail Crumm had loved a good fuss. And when a woman got to be eighty-four, a woman did whatever a woman wanted to do. In this case it was to prevail upon Tanner to stop riding broncs.

"Is that an order?"

Abigail had given a tiny, dry laugh. "Of course not. I'm simply asking, Tanner." She'd slanted him a coy glance, adding in her best quavering old-lady voice, "I do so worry about you, you know."

Tanner had snorted. Abigail had smiled.

He hadn't ridden the bronc. A bad heart had made Abigail vulnerable and Tanner was damned if he was going to be the death of her. She'd had enough to worry about without him.

But now Abigail was gone.

The slight cold she'd brushed off in February had turned into pneumonia the first week in March.

He'd told her to go to the hospital. He'd told her orange juice and afternoon naps weren't enough. But Abigail had ignored him.

"You know horses, Tanner, I'll give you that," she'd said with as much briskness as she could muster. "You're a good cattleman, too. A wonderful foreman. But until you can show me a medical degree, I'll do my own doctoring."

"They got medical degrees in Casper. I'll drive you," he offered almost desperately.

But Abigail had simply smiled up at him from her rocking chair and taken another sip of juice. Outside the wind had rattled sleet against the windowpanes. "No."

"Damn it, you're not going to get well like this!"

"I've had a good life, Tanner. I'd rather die with my boots on like my daddy did than molder away in some hospital room."

"You're not gonna molder, Abigail!"

"No," she said firmly. "I'm not."

She hadn't. But she hadn't survived, either.

Two weeks ago, almost late because he'd had to ride halfway to Hole-in-the-Wall to fix a fence, Tanner had sat slumped in the back pew at her funeral to listen to Reverend Dailey remind everyone what an inspiration Abigail Crumm had always been.

"She went her own way. She did her own thing. At one time or another, she had the cattlemen, the oil men, the sheep men, and the townspeople all mad at her. But there wasn't a more caring person in the whole of Wyoming than Abigail Crumm."

Reverend Dailey's eyes scanned the packed church, looking at all the people whose lives Abigail Crumm had touched. Then he smiled. "Or," he added, "a more surprising one."

At the time Tanner hadn't realized the full import of that statement.

Now he did.

And in a little less than an hour he'd be meeting the biggest one.

He'd been prepared to have Abigail leave the ranch to one of her causes. The good Lord knew she'd had plenty of 'em—all the way from stray cats to homeless children. And Tanner had figured he could handle that. Being foreman with an absentee landlord was the best of all possible worlds. Besides, who else would she leave it to? Ab had no living relatives. As highly as she thought of her old friend Ev, he didn't have the stamina to manage a spread this big, and Tanner knew she wouldn't leave it to him.

In fact, he'd made damned sure she didn't.

"The hell you say," he'd sputtered when she'd told him she was thinking of naming him her beneficiary. "What would you go and do a stupid thing like that for?"

"I trust you, Tanner. You know the ranch better than anyone."

"I know what a load of work it is. You ever see a happy rancher, Abby? 'Course not. They got too many worries to be happy. No thanks. I'm a cowboy, not a rancher. And cowboys don't stay. We're free. No strings attached. I came with my saddle. I'll go with my saddle. That's the way I like it."

"You've been here four years," Abigail reminded him.

"And I can leave tomorrow."

"Do you want to?"

He shrugged, feeling uncomfortable under her speculative blue gaze. "'Course not," he said after a moment. "Not now anyhow. You need me."

She smiled gently. "Yes."

"So—" he shrugged "—I'll hang around awhile. Because I want to. Not because I have to. Don't you go tyin' me down."

Abigail just looked at him for a long moment, so long that Tanner wondered whether she was really seeing him or something else entirely. Finally, she'd nodded. "Whatever you say, Tanner."

When Ev came home and told him over supper what the will said, he found that she'd left him a horse trailer and her two best saddle horses. "Portable assets," she'd called them.

She left the ranch to Maggie MacLeod.

"What the hell's a Maggie MacLeod?" Tanner had asked, taking the cup of coffee Ev handed him. He hadn't had time to go to the reading himself. Cows didn't stop calving just for wills to be read. "Never heard of it."

It sure as hell didn't sound like stray cats. But Tanner didn't really care. One cause was as good as another as far as he was concerned, as long as whoever was in charge stayed out of his way and let him do his job.

"Not a committee," Ev had said. "A woman."

A woman. *One* woman? Tanner frowned. "Just a regular...person, you mean?" Not a cause at all?

"Uh-huh." Ev nodded, grinning.

"What sort of woman?"

"Schoolmarm."

Tanner couldn't believe it. Visions of starchy, desiccated old prunes fogged his mind. Heaven knew he'd had his share of them. All those years and all those classrooms had seemed like some particularly enduring form of torture to Tanner. He couldn't wait to get out.

And now Abby had left the ranch to one?

"Hell and damnation!" He leapt to his feet and stalked around the room.

Ev's grin vanished and he glanced at Billy, then gave Tanner a reproving look. Tanner didn't apologize. He was too busy envisioning what a mess a schoolteacher could make out of the Three Bar C.

"She teaches down in Casper," Billy volunteered. "Third grade. Like Ms. Farragut."

"That's a hell of a recommendation," Tanner muttered. Old Battle-ax Farragut looked like she could freeze a herd of cattle in July, and Tanner knew from what Billy and Ev said that there was only one way to do things as far as she was concerned: Farragut's way. His jaw tightened.

"Ab met her at some soup kitchen," Ev added. "Ladlin' out for the homeless."

"The homeless?" Tanner echoed. He couldn't quite see Farragut doing that. But a do-gooder wasn't much better.

"Swell," Tanner grumbled. "She'll probably want to knit caps for the cattle."

Billy giggled.

"How come Ab never brought her out here?" he muttered, kicking out a chair and dropping into it, scowling.

"She did once or twice. You were gone. Riding fence or feeding cattle. What you were supposed to be doin'," Ev said. "Ab didn't need you to vet her visitors."

"You met her then? What's she like? She live in Casper?" If she had a house and was settled in, that wouldn't be so bad. She could be a landlady from there. Not quite as good as a cause, but...

Ev shook his head. "Nope. And she ain't never been on a ranch before. 'Cept to visit Ab."

Tanner's mouth opened and shut twice before he could say, "You mean Ab went and saddled us with a city slicker?"

Ev shrugged. "She seemed nice enough. Real pleasant, I thought. And, of course, Ab liked her."

"Ab liked more folks than Will Rogers did!"

"Even sour-faced old skunks like you," Ev said easily. He clapped his hand on Tanner's shoulder. "Where's your faith in human nature, boy? Ab wasn't no fool. If she liked this Maggie well enough to leave her the ranch, well, that's good enough for me. I reckon she knew what she was doin'."

Tanner didn't reckon anything of the sort, but he wasn't going to win an argument with Ev about it. Ev had always believed the sun rose and set on Abigail Crumm, and there wasn't any arguing with him. Anyway, a more cheerful thought had just occurred to Tanner.

"She'll probably stay in Casper, then," he said. "City lady like that won't want to be stuck out here. Besides, there aren't many homeless this far out."

But yesterday's mail had brought a letter from Clyde Bridges, Abigail's lawyer, that squelched that hope.

"Miss Maggie MacLeod is looking forward to seeing the Three Bar C." Not even Ms., Tanner had noted grimly. Worse and worse. "She'll be coming on Wednesday. Would you please be available to meet with her at four to discuss her move to the ranch?"

Move to the ranch?

Tanner had stared at the words, willing them to vanish. They hadn't.

He'd shut his eyes and tried once more to imagine the sort of fanatic schoolmarm whom Abigail would've appreciated enough to do something as harebrained as this. Then he tried to imagine such a woman living on the Three Bar C. It didn't bear thinking about.

His only hope was that she'd see it that way, too.

The Three Bar C was not your *House and Garden*–variety ranch. It was damned near a nineteenth-century relic, miles from town in foothills of the Big Horn Mountains. The two-story house was built of pine logs that Abigail's father had cut himself and dragged with his team to the site. It had four walls, a stone fireplace and character, but not much else. Even running water and indoor plumbing had arrived within recent memory.

It was no place for a woman.

Abigail had been born here, of course. But that meant she'd grown up to it, knew it like the back of her hand. She'd never had another home.

Miss Maggie MacLeod, whoever she was, had. She wouldn't belong.

And at four o'clock today, in less than an hour, Tanner was going to have to convince her of that.

"I dare you," Ev said now.

Tanner blinked, startled back to the present. "What?"

"To ride her."

"Maybe he's got too much sense to risk it," Bates suggested.

Ev shook his head. "Not Tanner."

Tanner gave him a baleful look. "Thanks a lot."

"Just meant you ain't afraid of risks." Ev lifted a brow. "Are you?"

It was crazy. It was insane. He hadn't ridden an unbroken horse like this mare in over a year. His doctor would be furious. Ab would be spinning in her grave.

He reached for the reins. He needed the challenge. He needed the thrill, the physical release that he knew would come from trying to bring chaos under control. He would do it; and then he would sort out Miss Maggie MacLeod.

"Awwright!" Billy shouted as Tanner swung up into the saddle.

In an instant the horse had gathered herself together. Beneath him, Tanner felt her bunch and thrust, exploding as she tried to throw this unfamiliar burden from her back.

Flung high and hanging tight, Tanner laughed. He thrust his arm into the air, exulting in her blowup, savoring the surge of powerful energy, the challenge of controlling it, of controlling and taming this little black beauty of a horse.

The landscape blurred around him. Ev and Bates and Billy faded, the fence and the barn evaporated, the car coming over the snow-covered rise disappeared into a haze of winter white and dusty blue.

The world became a swirl of color. All that mattered lay beneath the saddle leather between his legs, in the gleaming sweaty hide of the ebony mare, in the challenge of bringing her under control.

She jumped and snapped, hopped and twisted. Tanner hung on. She raced and shimmied, arched and bucked. Tanner clung.

And then he began to get the rhythm of her. He caught her beat and moved with it. His spine twisted, his knee pained, his head snapped back and his hat flew off.

He stayed on. He anticipated. He compensated. He leaned, arched, dug.

The mare ducked her head, lunging forward, then all of a sudden, jerked back, whipping him upward, unseating him.

He flew. Flipped. Hit.

Hard.

He was in heaven.

Had to be.

Why else, when at last he opened his eyes, would there be an angel with the greenest eyes, the most kissable mouth and the most gorgeous mane of wavy auburn hair he'd ever seen staring down into his face?

He smiled. So there were eternal rewards after all. And hell, he hadn't even had to be a complete saint to get one! Fuzzy-minded and light-headed, Tanner reached out tentatively to touch her.

"Don't move!"

The sound of her voice was so unexpected that he jerked. It hurt—but no more than reaching out had.

He shut his eyes carefully, trying to get his bearings. Was he in heaven or wasn't he? He didn't think you were supposed to hurt in heaven, but his Sunday-school teachers had never been the best.

Slowly he opened his eyes again, expecting the vision to have vanished.

She was still there, bending even closer now. Her skin looked soft as the petals of Ab's summer roses and there was a faint rosy flush on her cheeks. And God, that mouth! How long had it been since he'd kissed a woman? Tanner swallowed and started to struggle up.

She put out a hand to stop him. "I said hold still. Don't try to get up yet."

She even sounded sort of angelic, her voice was gentle on his ears, caressing almost. Did angels caress? He wanted to ask her, but he couldn't. He still hadn't caught his breath.

All he could do was lie back, give her a muzzy smile and shut his eyes again. His head buzzed.

"He ain't fainted, has he?" This voice was gruff and distinctly non-angelic. *Ev.*

Hell.

Tanner forced his eyes open again. There were other faces crowding into his line of vision now— Ev's, grizzled and worried; Billy's, dismayed: Bates's, resigned.

So much for heaven.

But—he gave his head a small painful shake and tried to focus his gaze—then who was she? Because she still hadn't gone away, this redheaded angel of his.

Tanner levered himself up on his elbows in the mixture of mud and slush and barnyard muck to squint at the woman who was apparently neither a figment of his imagination nor a result of his having fallen on his head.

"Be very careful," she said to him. "You might've broken something."

"Prob'ly did," he said with a gasp, grateful at least that he could finally speak. "Serve me right."

"I told him so," Bates murmured.

"He done better'n Gibb," Billy said stoutly.

"Did," the auburn-haired vision corrected absently.

And hearing her, Tanner moaned.

"What's wrong?" she asked him quickly.

"*You're* the schoolteacher?" He couldn't believe it and knew at the very same moment it was dead-certain true.

His former angel smiled. "That's right. I'm Maggie MacLeod." She held out her hand to him.

He didn't take it. He'd probably have pulled her right down into the muck if he had. Besides, his own were jammed deep in muddy gloves and he wasn't taking them off for the sake of politeness.

Anyway, he didn't want to shake hands with her.

Not just for one reason now, but for a multitude.

This was his new boss? The proper lady schoolteacher? The boot-faced drill sergeant he'd been expecting?

They sure as hell weren't making schoolteachers the way they used to. So much for battle-axes like old Farragut.

But in her way, this one was far worse. She was the prettiest damned woman he'd seen in a month of Sundays. And he was lying flat on his back in the mud in front of her! Suddenly Tanner was burning with embarrassment.

Gritting his teeth, he got to his feet. He would have

fallen flat again if Ev and Bates hadn't grabbed him and hauled him up unceremoniously between them.

Being vertical wasn't as much of an advantage as he'd hoped. Maggie MacLeod was almost as tall as he was. The top of that beautiful head of hair was exactly at his eye level. He shook Ev and Bates off and planted his feet squarely.

"You're early," he accused.

"A little." She didn't apologize. But she did smile. And he couldn't help it—it still looked like an angel's smile. There was even a very tiny, very kissable dimple just to the side of her mouth. "I didn't know how long it would take to get here," she was saying when he jerked his attention back to her words. "Some of the gravel roads aren't the best this time of year, you know. I did better than I expected."

And worse than he had hoped.

Tanner grunted. He reached up, intending to jerk his hat down and scowl at her from beneath the brim in the fierce, intimidating look he used whenever he wanted to exert his authority.

His head was bare. He could see his hat lying in the mud clear on the other side of the corral. He swallowed a curse. His hair tangled damply across his forehead and he couldn't even shove it back without making himself a bigger mess than he already was. His fingers flexed and tightened in frustration.

Maggie MacLeod was still smiling, but was also looking at him a little doubtfully. "I have an appointment with Miss Crumm's foreman. Someone called—" she hesitated "—Tanner?"

"That's him," Billy said brightly, poking Tanner in a very sore rib just in case she hadn't already guessed his identity.

Her smile faded momentarily and Tanner felt a split second's hope that she'd take off running in the other direction. Or that maybe, if she wasn't a part of his dream, he was a part of hers and any minute they'd both wake up.

But, Maggie MacLeod said briskly "So it is." She started to offer him her hand again, took a look at the mud and stuffed her fingers into the pocket of her trousers. "Well, it's nice to meet you at last." She waited, expecting a response, apparently.

"Yeah, you, too," Tanner managed after a moment.

"You didn't come to the lawyer's office, I don't believe?"

"Had work to do. Ranch doesn't run itself."

"Yes, that's what Mr. Warren said. Is it—" she hesitated again "—*Mr.* Tanner or..."

"Just Tanner," he said flatly. He glanced at Ev almost desperately. "What time is it?"

"Almost 3:15."

"Our appointment was for four," he said to Maggie.

"Yes, but—"

Tanner jerked his head in the direction of the ranch house. "You can wait in there. I'll be up at four." Surely he could get his act together in half an hour.

Turning on his heel and thanking God his knee didn't go right out from under him, he stalked across the corral, snagged his hat and continued on toward the ebony mare.

"Come on, sweetheart," he said, reaching for the reins again. "You an' I got some work to do."

She didn't wait "in there." She stayed right where she was. She went only so far as to scramble up onto the top rung of the corral fence and settle herself next to Billy. And there she stayed, watching his every move.

He ignored her.

He climbed back into the saddle and put her right out of his head. He didn't even notice her gasp when the mare shot up into the air and twisted so that he nearly fell off. He didn't pay a bit of attention to her rapt gaze or the way her head moved to watch as he and the mare plunged from one end of the corral to the other. He hardly saw the way she flipped her long red hair back out of her face when the wind whipped it around, or the way she winced and sucked in her breath when he got thrown to the ground.

He got thrown three more times.

He could've got thrown a hundred and he wouldn't have given up. Hell, it wouldn't have mattered if the mare had broken every damned bone in his body and killed him in the process.

He wasn't quitting in front of Maggie MacLeod.

Still, each time he hauled himself out of the mud, his shoulder seemed a little less stable and his leg was worse. His ribs began to feel as if the mare had done a tango on them. And the last time he landed, he bit his tongue so hard that he could still taste the blood. Gritting his teeth, Tanner staggered to his feet and headed over to where Ev held the horse.

"You don't have to do this," Bates said quickly.

Tanner took the reins. "Yes, I do."

"Not 'cause of what I said," Ev said quickly. "I didn't mean for you to kill yourself."

"I'm fine."

"'Course you are. That's why you're limping an' spittin' blood."

Tanner ignored him, still not glancing at the woman on the fence, yet feeling her eyes on him anyway as he swung once more into the saddle.

Blessedly, the mare was as tired as he was. And this time when he got on her back, she did nothing more than give a couple of half-hearted bucks and a shimmy, then she tossed her head and trotted easily around the corral.

"I tol' you so," Billy crowed. Ev grinned, and Bates looked downright impressed.

Tanner couldn't tell what Miss Maggie MacLeod thought. She didn't say a word and he didn't glance her way. It was all he could do to keep from grimacing at every step the mare took. But he rode her around twice more before he urged her over to the far side of the corral and slid carefully out of the saddle.

Leaning against her, he talked to her, soothing her. She needed that, but so did he, in order to give his trembling, aching leg time to adjust once more to solid ground. Even so it damn near buckled when he took his first step.

"You okay?" Ev asked him.

"Swell." He winced, then walked gingerly, masking his limp with as much nonchalance as he could muster as he led the mare toward the barn.

He waited until he got there and could support himself with his hand against the doorframe before he turned and faced Maggie MacLeod.

He glanced at his watch. It was quarter to four. "I'll be up to the house as soon as I've got her settled. Put on the coffee and we'll talk."

* * *

Tanner had never played football, but he didn't have to be a quarterback to know that there was truth in the cliché about the best defense being a good offense. He also knew he needed one. Bad.

"She's really beautiful, ain't she?" Billy asked him, skipping along ahead of Tanner, but glancing back at Maggie, who was walking toward the house.

Tanner didn't have to glance back. Imprinted on his mind from a mere few seconds of watching her was the way she moved. He could shut his eyes right now and still see the feminine sway of her hips in those soft, elegant trousers. He swallowed and brushed past Billy into the bunkhouse. "She's all right," he allowed.

Bates, following along after him, snorted. "All right? She's a fox."

"You don't have to drool," Tanner snapped.

"Hey—" Bates lifted his hands and stepped back "—I was only saying. I'm not poaching." He looked Tanner up and down. "You want her, you can have her."

"What the hell would I want her for?" Tanner grumbled. He pulled off his shirt, wincing as his shoulder popped.

Bates grinned. "What would you want her for? You don't know? Hell, Tanner, I knew you were a little slow sometimes, but I thought even you knew what to do with a woman!"

"Shut up, Bates," Tanner said with a geniality he didn't feel. He stripped off his shirt and yanked a clean one out of the closet. Most of his clothes were up at the house, since he'd moved up there last year. Now he was glad he kept a few things down here. He padded into the bathroom and turned on the shower, then paused to consider his face in the mirror.

He was grimy and sweaty and filthy. Under the dirt he could see the beginnings of a bruise on his cheekbone where one of the stirrups had caught him when he was flying through the air. And there was a cut over his left eye, but the blood had pretty much dried. The cut inside his mouth wasn't worth worrying about.

He turned his head, looking at his face dispassionately. He wasn't what any woman would call really handsome, though they didn't exactly run in the other direction. He had a lean face, weathered. His eyes were blue and deep set beneath dark brows. He needed a shave. He scowled at his reflection.

He frowned too much, Abby told him. "Smile, Tanner," she was always telling him. He made himself smile. It could have been worse.

Once he got the mud off and the whiskers, he'd clean up pretty good.

Of course, he needed a haircut. He rarely bothered to get his thick, shaggy hair trimmed. There were always more important things to do whenever he got to town. Maybe he could yell for Ev and see if the old man wanted to take a few whacks. And then Maggie wouldn't think—

Whoa!

He stopped dead, staring at himself in the mirror, making himself run that thought through his head again. *Maybe Maggie wouldn't think—*

Again he stopped.

Finish it, he commanded himself.

Maybe Maggie wouldn't think he was such a bum.

Damn it, what did he care what Maggie MacLeod thought of him?

He flipped the shower off again, instead simply ducking his head under the tap of the sink, scrubbing his face and hair until most of the grime was gone.

He took an old razor out of the medicine chest, studied his whiskery cheeks, then put the razor back again.

There was no reason to spruce himself up for Maggie MacLeod. He was working for her, not courting her, for God's sake.

Tanner hadn't courted anyone in years. Wasn't ever going to again!

The very notion that he might, even in his subconscious, have considered it, infuriated him. Scowling, he stalked back into the other room.

"Hand me that shirt," he said to Billy.

"I thought you were going to— Aren't you going to—?" Bates glanced toward the shower, then back at Tanner's still-sweaty torso. He shut his mouth.

Tanner buttoned the shirt and jammed it down into his jeans. If the faint odor of horse and mud clung to him, that was too damn bad. If Maggie MacLeod thought she was going to like ranch living, she'd better get used to the smell.

He shoved away the thought that Abigail would have had his hide if he'd ever dared show up at the house like this. The Three Bar C might not be the center of the civilized world, but Abigail had been a hat-and-gloves-type lady.

Tanner had known better than to take his sweat-and-mud-stained body anywhere near her. She'd demanded civilization even from the likes of him.

But Maggie MacLeod wasn't Abigail.

She was a thorn in his side and he was going to do his damnedest to get rid of her.

He was glad he'd stayed awake all last night preparing a series of rational arguments that would convince a dried-up, prune-faced schoolmarm that the Three Bar C was no place for a lady. He prayed to God the same arguments would work as well on Miss Maggie MacLeod.

As he strode across the yard and climbed the stairs to the porch, the wind shifted and he caught a good whiff of the corral smell he was bringing in with him.

Maybe he wouldn't need rational arguments at all, he thought with a grin. Maybe just one look and one deep breath would be enough to send her packing.

A guy could hope.

Two

With his hand on the doorknob, Tanner hesitated, wondering if she'd expect him to knock. Did she know that he and Ev and Billy had been sharing the house with Abigail since last summer?

But before he could decide what to do, he heard her call out, "Come in."

She was sitting in Abigail's rocking chair near the fireplace, and while he'd been concentrating on walking without a limp, now he stopped dead, jolted at the sight.

No one ever sat in that chair except Abby.

He opened his mouth to protest, then realized that it didn't matter anymore. Abby wouldn't care.

Abby had wanted it this way, he reminded himself grimly.

And the worst thing about it was Maggie MacLeod looked comfortable there, as if she belonged.

She looked warm and cozy. Settled. His jaw tightened.

Someone—her probably, for Tanner couldn't imagine anyone else having done it—had laid another log on the fire, and now it burned cheerfully, crackling and snapping, just the way Abby had always liked it. On the end table next to her she had a tray with a coffeepot, mugs and cookies.

Where'd she get cookies? Tanner wondered irritably.

He took off his hat, rolling the brim between his palms, and stood scowling at her. Maggie got to her feet and came toward him, smiling. Without her coat on, he could see that her figure was as every bit as angelic as her face. Those elegant trousers that had swayed when she walked were a dark green, soft wool. She wore an off-white sweater with a sort of loose rolled collar that offered glimpses of the lightly freckled creamy skin of her neck. And below that her breasts lifted the soft angora of the sweater—

"—glad you survived your encounter with the bronc."

He blinked, jerking his gaze away from her breasts, swallowing hard and discovering that she was once more offering him her hand and waiting expectantly.

A tide of hot blood coursed up his neck. She must think he was an idiot! He loosed his fingers from the brim of his hat and took the hand she offered him.

Her grasp was firm and warm and soft. *Womanly skin.* He couldn't remember the last time he'd felt skin that silky. It made him more aware than ever of the rough calluses on his own. He drew his hand away quickly and stuffed it in his pocket.

"Just part of the job," he said gruffly.

The skeptical look she gave him made him shift from one foot to the other uncomfortably. But then she smiled and shrugged. "I'm sorry you felt you had to hurry."

Her gaze flicked from his stubbled cheeks to his dirty jeans and he saw immediately the interpretation she had put on his lack of grooming.

"I didn't hurry! I mean I—" Damn it, he might've known she'd miss the point!

Showing up unshaven and reeking of a barnyard didn't mean he was dying to be at her beck and call, but he could hardly say that. His scowl deepened. He crushed the brim of his hat with his hands.

"In any case, I appreciate your taking the time for me, Mr...."

"It's not Mr., ma'am. I told you, just Tanner."

"Is that your first name, then?"

"No."

She smiled and he saw that damned dimple again. "What's your first name?"

He frowned. "Robert."

It sounded odd to say it, to hear it said aloud. He'd been Tanner for so many years that he could hardly remember being anyone else. Even his brothers called him Tanner. His father hadn't, of course. But Bob Tanner, Sr., when he'd called his eldest boy anything, had simply called him "Son." Certainly no one had called him Robert for years—not even...

Deliberately he shut off the thought. No one had called him Robert since his mother, in fact, and she'd died when he was seven.

Maggie MacLeod smiled at him now and took his arm. "Come and sit down, Robert."

He might've known.

"Everyone calls me Tanner, ma'am," he corrected her firmly, but he had the feeling she didn't hear him.

He sat down, not on the sofa as she indicated, but on the hearth, leaning back against the rough stone and watching her warily while she poured two cups of coffee. His arm still tingled where she'd touched him. Surreptitiously he rubbed it against his side.

Maggie looked up. "Is something wrong?"

He colored furiously and sat up ramrod straight. "No, ma'am."

She nodded easily. "If you're not comfortable there, you might prefer the sofa," she suggested.

"Here's fine." It was as far away from her as he could get.

"Suit yourself."

Hell, if he could do that, he wouldn't be here at all. He twisted the brim of his hat harder.

"Do you take milk or sugar?"

"Black. Please," he added when the one word sounded too abrupt.

Maggie got up and handed him one of the mugs, then added a dollop of milk to her own, stirring it in. She settled back into Abigail's chair and lifted the mug to her lips. She sipped, swallowed, then smiled at him. He tried not to notice.

"I'm so glad to talk to you at last. I know we haven't met, but I feel like we have. Abby told me so much about you."

"She did?" Swell. He wished Abby had told him anything at all about her. Then maybe he wouldn't be feeling quite so much as if he was walking on quicksand right now.

He wanted to be able to plunge right into his arguments for her staying in Casper. But while he could envision saying them firmly and forcefully to a battle-ax like old Farragut, somehow with Maggie his mouth felt dry and the words wouldn't form.

He took a swallow of coffee and studied Maggie MacLeod the way he sized up an unknown, untried horse.

But the ebony mare was a lot easier to figure out than Maggie was.

She wasn't what he'd expected. Some ancient, do-gooding loony wouldn't have surprised him. Hell, it was what he'd hoped for. Maybe Maggie was a do-gooding loony. He'd just never met one who looked quite like her before.

He wondered for the first time just what Abigail had had in mind when she left Maggie the ranch. The old lady had always been a doer, a manipulator, a campaigner with a million causes.

Just because she was only one woman didn't mean Maggie wasn't one of them, Tanner realized. What sort of cause was Maggie MacLeod?

But studying her more closely didn't provide any answers. All it did was make him aware of how damned attractive she was and how, even now, his body responded to her.

For years Tanner had been able to take women or leave them. Mostly he did the first, then the second.

Except if they looked like gentle, love-you-forever types like Maggie MacLeod—then he took off running and never looked back.

Which is what he ought to be doing right now, he thought grimly. Except he couldn't. He'd promised Abby he'd stay for awhile and help the new owner make the transition.

He hadn't thought anything of it when he'd made

the promise. And if it made Abby rest easier, what was the problem?

Trust Abby.

"What'd she say about me?" he asked at last. He didn't know where else to start, and it might help if he knew what sort of nonsense Abby had filled her head with.

"How much she depended on you," Maggie replied. She leaned back in the rocker and set it in motion gently, still smiling at him. "She said you were the reason she was able to keep the ranch going, that if you hadn't been here over the last few years, she would have had to move to town. She said you worked day and night, that you helped Mr. Warren keep the house repaired, the truck running and the cattle fed. She said you were a good horseman." Her smiled widened slightly. "She said you were a wonderful influence on Billy. The kindest, most thoughtful, most responsible man she'd ever known."

Tanner ducked his head, discomfited by the praise. "Yeah, well, I guess I'm a regular paragon, aren't I?" he muttered gruffly.

Maggie laughed. "Abigail certainly seemed to think so."

"She was prejudiced," Tanner said flatly. "Any good hand would do what I do."

"Including almost getting yourself killed on a horse this afternoon?"

"I survived."

"You're still limping."

So he hadn't managed to hide it from her. "No big deal."

"Maybe not. But your survival is a big deal. You die and this place falls apart. I don't know a thing about ranching. Without you, the Three Bar C would be chaos.''

"You could find somebody."

"But Abby promised me you."

The simple words hit like a fist in the gut. Maggie herself seemed to realize they might be taken another way, too, for her cheeks took on a deeper hue, and she looked down at her coffee cup. God, she was even more gorgeous when she was embarrassed.

And God help him if he didn't stop thinking that way! "I'm a hired man, not a slave. I can leave whenever I want."

His terseness seemed to take her aback. She looked at him warily. "Is that a threat?"

A promise, he wanted to say. "It's got nothing to do with you. It's me. I don't like bein' tied down."

Auburn brows lifted. "Really? Why not?"

He shrugged, surprised at the directness of her question, unwilling to answer it. "I like my freedom," he said after a moment. "And I'll take it when I'm ready. Meantime I promised Abby I'd hang around for a while to make sure things are running smooth."

"Thank you," she said gravely.

He nodded. "They will, you know. You don't have to supervise. I mean," he went on pressing his point, "you don't have to hang around here, move in. Ev says you've got a place in Casper. Feel free to stay there."

"I don't want to stay there. I like it here. No," she corrected herself, "I love it here."

Tanner stared at her. "It's bleak and cold and lonely as hell."

"It's an hour from Casper."

"The hub of the western cultural world."

"It's a nice town. I've lived in plenty of worse places, believe me."

"You have?" That surprised him.

"My parents are missionaries."

It figured. He groaned inwardly.

"We spent a lot of time living in huts in the middle of nowhere."

"Well, then, you probably want a bit of civilization."

"I want a home."

Her words rocked him. It was as if some long ago bell echoed in his mind. And at the very moment he heard it, he tuned it out.

"You got a home in Casper."

"I have an *apartment* in Casper. I can make the Three Bar C a home. It was Abigail's home," she went on. "That's why she left it to me."

"Huh?" Tanner wasn't following and he was sure he needed to. Things were happening that he didn't like.

"Abigail knew I wanted a home. I've never had one. I've moved all my life."

"So've I," Tanner said. "Nothin' wrong with moving."

"No. Not for some people. But I've done all I want. Now I want someplace to put down roots. To stay. To have a family."

"Casper," Tanner muttered desperately.

Maggie gave him a patient smile. "No. Here. My parents are still abroad, but I have two brothers, one in Colorado and one in Nebraska, and I want to make a home—for myself and for them. Abigail said you had brothers. You must know what I mean.'' She was looking at him intently.

He knew what she meant, all right. ''You don't always get what you want,'' he said.

''No. But it's no excuse for not trying, is it?'' She bit off a piece of cookie and looked right at him.

Tanner's gaze slid away. He shrugged. Stalemate.

''Why do I get the feeling you're trying to get rid of me?''

Because he was, of course. ''I'm only trying to do you a favor. The Three Bar C isn't all warm and cheery and fireplaces and stuff. It's muddy and windy and wild and cold, and most times there's not a soul for miles around. There's no people here. Nobody to talk to.''

''There's you. And Mr. Warren and Billy.''

''We don't count. We're not—not...'' he groped for the word ''...conversationalists.''

''I don't mind.''

I do, Tanner wanted to shout at her. He gulped his coffee, scalded his throat and began coughing. He jumped up and limped around the room. Maggie got up to come after him and pat him on the back.

He brushed her away. ''People will talk,'' he said finally, desperately, when he could speak at last.

''Talk? About what?''

''*Us.* You. Me.'' Even saying it made hot blood course into his face, and the amused look on her face when she realized what he meant made it ten times worse. ''A single woman doesn't live with a bunch of bachelors! It isn't done.''

''Well, Abigail certainly didn't tell me everything about you,'' Maggie said, grinning. ''She never once mentioned you were a puritan.''

"I'm not a puritan, damn it!"

"Chivalrous, then?"

"I'm not being chivalrous, either! It's common sense. You're a schoolteacher! Schoolteachers got to set a good example, don't they?"

"Yes."

"Well, then—" he took a deep breath "—you'll set a lot better example staying in Casper."

"But I'm not staying in Casper. I believe there's a bunkhouse." She glanced pointedly out the window toward the log building just this side of the barn.

"So? You want us to move out there?"

"Not necessarily. I will."

"You can't do that!"

"Why not? Is that likely to create a scandal, too? Or is someone already living there? A tall, dark, handsome, single ravisher of young women, perhaps?"

Tanner felt as if he was losing his grip. The ebony filly had been a piece of cake compared to Maggie MacLeod. "Of course not. It isn't used now except during roundups."

"Then what's the problem?"

"You can't let us live here while you move into the bunkhouse! You're the boss, damn it."

"For all the good it seems to be doing me." Maggie laughed, then shrugged. "Well, then, I'll leave where I stay up to you, since you know how things are done in these parts. But try to figure out what to do with me soon, will you, Robert? I'll be moving in on Saturday."

So Tanner moved out.

What the hell else could he do?

He didn't move off the ranch. He didn't hand in

his resignation and take off for another state, which is what he'd have preferred. He still had his promise to Abby to consider.

But the very night Maggie announced her intention of moving in, he spent his time, between checks on the cattle, moving into the godforsaken bunkhouse.

It leaked. It was drafty. Ev and Billy thought he was nuts.

"You'll die of pneumonia," Ev told him.

"You'll drown," Billy said.

But Tanner knew better than they did what the dangers in his life were. And he was in greater risk from constant exposure to Maggie MacLeod.

Ev told him he was overreacting. But Ev didn't understand, and Tanner wasn't explaining or even admitting what the problem was.

It was hard enough even admitting the problem to himself.

Maggie reminded him of Clare.

Well, not of Clare herself, really, for Clare had been small and blond and fragile-looking. But of the way he'd felt about Clare.

He'd thought it was a once-in-a-lifetime thing, a product of adolescent hormones, that bolt of instant attraction that could come along and knock a guy on his butt. He wished to God it had been.

There was no way he was going to go through that again.

But if he'd said as much, Ev wouldn't know what he meant. Ev had never heard of Clare. Nor had Bates. Nor Billy. Nor anyone else hereabouts. Not even Abby.

Clare was the part of Tanner's past he tried not to think about. His biggest risk. His greatest failure.

His ex-wife.

Ex-wife. They'd been married such a short time it was hard to even think of her as his wife, let alone his ex. Especially since, for the last fourteen years, he'd tried not to think of her at all.

But for ten months, when she was nineteen and he was barely twenty, he'd been married to her.

And he'd failed her.

She'd been nice about it. She hadn't even blamed him, though God knew she should have. If he'd had a dollar's worth of sense, none of it ever would have happened. It wasn't the dollar's worth of sense he'd needed, he reflected not for the first time, it was a condom.

If he hadn't been such a green kid, if he hadn't been in such an almighty hurry to satisfy his carnal urges, Clare would never have become pregnant. He could remember with absolute clarity the feelings that had hit him the day she told him.

"Pregnant?" He'd almost choked on his disbelief.

Clare nodded, huddled against the door of his pickup. Ordinarily she was pert and pretty, always smiling. Now she looked small and cold and scared.

No colder or more scared than he.

He wanted to ask if she was sure it was his, but one look at her and he knew he couldn't do it. Besides, he thought savagely, if there was the remotest possibility that he wasn't the father, surely Clare would have grasped at it. Damn near anyone would be a better catch than him!

God knew he had enough responsibilities without even thinking about taking on another one. Or two!

His mother had died when he was seven. His father had kept them together just barely, but he'd been killed in a riding accident a year and a half ago. At eighteen, Tanner had gone to work full-time, cowboying on a medium-sized southern Colorado spread while at the same time trying to keep his two hotheaded younger brothers, Luke and Noah, on the straight and narrow.

He wondered for a moment what they'd say when they found out he'd fallen off the straight and narrow himself.

He glanced over at Clare and saw that she was crying now. He felt like crying himself. But cowboys didn't cry. He hadn't, not even at his father's funeral. "Hey," he said softly. "Clare. Hey, don't. Don't. It'll be all right."

She'd looked up, her blue eyes still brimming as they met his. "What do you mean, all right?"

"We'll—" he cast about desperately for an answer, one that would make her tears dry up, that would make things okay, that would make her smile "—get married," he said.

Clare swiped a hand across her eyes. "Do you mean it?" She sniffled and rubbed her nose against her jacket.

"Sure. Why not?" He tried to sound more confident than he felt.

"But I thought—since you've got Luke and Noah—I mean—"

"Luke and Noah will like it," he said. "Somebody littler to tell what to do. They'll be uncles." *And he was going to be a father?* The thought still rocked him. It didn't seem real.

"You're sure?" Clare was blinking now, looking brighter.

"Of course." It might actually be the best thing

that could happen, he told himself. Luke and Noah needed more stability than he'd been able to give them. Maybe he and Clare together... "We'll be fine. All of us. We'll have a home."

It was like a dream, airy and insubstantial, but it was all all he had to hang his hopes on. *A home.* Sometime, back before his mother had died, he'd had a home. Warmth. Comfort. Love. A place to come back to, to look forward to.

He smiled at Clare suddenly and leaned over and kissed her. "Yeah. A home."

So they'd married. He'd scraped together enough money to buy a five-times-used old trailer, which his boss let him put out on the land. But there wasn't room enough for the four of them, so he and Clare lived there while Luke and Noah stayed in the bunkhouse up the road, another kindness on McGillvray's part, since both of the boys were in school all day and he didn't need to give them room and board at all.

Tanner had been grateful. He'd actually been glad to have Clare to himself. He'd been smitten with her the first moment he'd seen her, pert and pretty, smiling at customers in Harrison's Hardware Store. She had dreams, plans, hopes, and she shared them all with him. She wanted to go to college, wanted to be a nurse, wanted to see the ocean, to fly in a plane. He'd listened, nodded, smiled, kissed her, kissed her again.

Now that they were married, he wondered if she wanted to be a mother.

The Clare whom Tanner ended up married to wasn't the Clare he'd lusted after since the day they'd met. That one had smiled shyly and clung to his arm when he'd taken her out. That one had kissed him and told him he was her man. This one was sick every morning, cried at the drop of a hat, woke him nightly with her restless turning and insomnia and screamed at him that he was never there when she needed him. He knew a woman's body changed during pregnancy. He knew her moods swung and her desires did, too. But knowing that in theory and understanding in practice were two different things.

He'd tried. God knew he'd tried. But he couldn't be there all the time, could he? He had a job. Money was tight. McGillvray had let several men go. He'd sympathized with Tanner's plight, had praised him for his willingness to accept his responsibilities. He'd kept Tanner on, and now he was depending on him. Hours were long and those sure weren't the days when a cowboy could carry a cellular phone.

As if Tanner's job didn't put enough pressure on his fledgling marriage, Noah was cutting classes to ride broncs. He was only a sophomore, too young by far to drop out of school, and the principal was calling Tanner, the closest thing to a parent Noah had, to convince his brother to shape up.

He could hardly have called on Luke. Luke, who'd always been the closest to their father, was taking Bob Tanner's death hard. "Who gives a damn!" he'd shout whenever Tanner tried to talk to him. He spent most of his nights drinking and fighting and pulling boneheaded stunts on a dare. Five times in their brief marriage Tanner had had to get up in the middle of the night and drive into town to bail Luke out of jail.

No, he wasn't there when Clare needed him.

He wasn't there the day the baby was born.

He couldn't recall now exactly where he'd been.

All he could remember was coming back late one April evening, having missed supper by several hours and dreading the tongue-lashing he knew he was going to get the minute he opened the trailer door. Clare wasn't there.

Nor was there any supper waiting, hot or cold. Just silence.

Blessed silence, Tanner had thought at the time.

He remembered guiltily now how he'd basked in it, albeit briefly, before wondering where she'd gone. After a time he'd looked around outside, called her name, then shrugged and put her absence down to the vagaries of pregnancy. Maybe she'd gone for a walk or up to the ranch house to talk to McGillvray's cook.

Tanner went back inside and helped himself to some pork and beans cold, right out of the can. He was just finishing them when there'd come a pounding on the door.

It was Ned Carter, the foreman. Clare had taken sick, he said. McGillvray had driven her to the hospital.

Even then Tanner hadn't thought about her losing the baby. All he'd thought was he hoped she was good and sick if she was bothering McGillvray about it. He owed his boss enough without his wife crying wolf over the least little thing. But he didn't want McGillvray to have to haul her back, too, so he'd borrowed Ned's pickup and driven the thirty miles to the closest hospital.

McGillvray had met him at the door, looking worried and relieved and sad at the same time.

He clapped a hand on Tanner's young shoulder. "I'm glad you're here at last." And before Tanner could apologize to him for whatever inconvenience

Clare had put him through, McGillvray said to him, "I'm sorry as hell about the baby."

Tanner said he was sorry, too. What he was was numb. Lost. Dazed.

The baby was dead. His son. McGillvray told him it was a boy. Tanner never saw him. Never even saw Clare that evening. She'd had a hard time, they told him. She'd been sedated, and she was sleeping at last. He didn't wake her.

He went home alone, his mind curiously blank. He woke up in the night and reached for Clare. She wasn't there. He remembered. His son was dead. He tried to summon emotion, pain, hurt. He felt empty. Light, almost. As if he'd escaped a close brush with disaster. It horrified him so much he went into the bathroom and was violently sick.

He never told that to anyone. Certainly he could never tell Clare. He could never explain to her how he felt. He didn't understand it completely himself.

Nor did he understand her.

She cried a little when she got home. Then she just got very remote and quiet and barely spoke to him at all.

She was coping in her own way, he told himself. And he was grateful, because he couldn't help her. Hell, he could barely cope himself.

All he could do was work and ride. He spent more hours than ever before out on the range. He didn't feel good. He didn't feel happy. But he felt better there than facing Clare in the confines of their trailer night after night.

It was sometime in late summer when she told him she'd been talking to Dr. Moberly, the doctor who'd delivered the baby. "He's worried about me," she said. "He says I need to get out of the house, get busy, do something."

He was probably right, Tanner thought, but he didn't know what to suggest. Where the hell was she going to go, stuck out there in the middle of the ranch by herself?

"He thinks I ought to go back to school," she went on.

For the first time since she'd lost the baby, Tanner noticed that there was a little color in her cheeks.

"Swell," he said, feeling the pressure more than ever. "And did he say how we were supposed to afford it? And how you're going to get there? We're thirty miles from the damned school. And tell me, did he suggest what you might study?" He knew he was being sarcastic. He knew he was wrong, that he was hurting her and that he had no right to. He couldn't help it. He'd have liked to go back to school, too. He'd have liked someone to suggest the answer to all his problems.

"He said I could work as a receptionist for him," Clare told him quietly. "And you know I've always wanted to be a nurse."

For a moment Tanner had just stared at her. His questions had been rhetorical. Her answers were not.

"How're you going to work for him," he'd asked finally, "livin' clear out here?"

"I thought," Clare said slowly, carefully, "that I might move to town."

You could have heard a slot machine whir in Las Vegas two full states away. Tanner felt something hard and heavy as lead settle somewhere in his midsection.

He looked at Clare, really looked at her, for the

first time in months. She was still beautiful with her porcelain complexion and her fine-boned face. He could still lust after her without even trying. But he hadn't been able to make a home with her. He hadn't been able to give her what she needed. And whatever he might have needed from her, he hadn't found it, either.

"Is that what you want?"

"I want to study nursing, Tanner."

"And...us? What about us?"

Helplessly, Clare shrugged.

"Do you want a divorce?"

She twisted her hands. "I...think it might be best. I mean, it's not as if we were in... I mean, I know you only married me because...because of the baby." She swallowed and looked up at him with watery blue eyes and he thought she might start crying again. "I'm tying you down."

He didn't know how long he stood there looking at her, weighing her words and his thoughts.

Maybe he should have argued with her. He didn't. He remembered all those hopes and dreams she'd shared with him, the ones she'd shelved after he'd got her pregnant. He remembered her the way she'd been when he first knew her, happy, smiling. He saw how much she'd changed, how much being married to him had changed her.

"Yeah," he'd said at last.

And no one had come close to tying him down again. Clare had done exactly as she'd said. She'd worked for Russ Moberly as his receptionist. She'd got her nursing degree. And last summer, Noah, who'd spent a night in the town as he traveled between rodeos, reported that she'd married her doctor.

"Got two rug rats already," Noah had said with his customary cheerful insensitivity. "Looks happy. This time I think marriage agrees with her."

Probably it did, Tanner thought. This time she had the right husband. A husband who had it in him to be the sort of man a woman needed, the sort she could depend on.

Not him.

Never him. He wasn't going through that again. Not ever. He'd learned his lesson. And he'd never even been tempted by another marriageable woman.

Until Maggie.

Three

On Saturday morning Tanner stood in the doorway to the barn and watched as Maggie drove up in her little white Ford, pulling a trailer behind.

She was wearing jeans today, and a bright yellow jacket that stopped just before it would have done him the favor of covering the curve of her slender hips. Then she spotted him, smiled and waved, and his gut clenched and his whole body came to attention.

So much for any vague hope that his attraction to her might have been a one-time thing or a result of falling on his head. Tanner lifted his hand, then dropped it abruptly, sucked in his breath and turned away.

Billy and Ev, of course, trooped right out to meet her, beaming and smiling, happy as a couple of cattle in corn. Bates probably would have been there, too, Tanner thought grimly, if he hadn't sent the younger man out at sunup to check on the cattle they were expecting to calve.

He glanced out the door again as Maggie crossed the yard, smiling at Ev and Billy. He heard Billy's high-pitched voice and then Maggie's laugh. The morning breeze whipped through her long red hair.

He wanted to run his fingers through it. He grabbed his saddle and heaved it onto Gambler's back, then drew the cinch up tight, put on the bridle, swung into the saddle and headed out. Billy came running to intercept him. "Maggie's here, Tanner! Ain'tcha gonna help her move in?"

"Nope."

"How come?"

"It's not what she pays me for."

She was standing with Ev on the porch, watching as he approached.

"'Morning," she called.

He gave her a curt nod in greeting and rode on past.

"What'sa matter with him?" Billy asked.

Ev chuckled. "It's spring. The sap is risin'."

"Huh?" said Billy, but Tanner, flushing as he dug his heels into Gambler, knew precisely what Ev meant.

He was a grown man. A foreman, for God's sake. A responsible, wage-earning adult.

He was also so hungry his stomach thought his throat had been cut. He lay on his bunk, listening to it growl, and reminded himself that he'd missed meals before.

A guy didn't need to eat lunch or dinner every day, he reminded himself for the hundredth time. There wasn't a cowboy alive couldn't stand to shed a few pounds.

That was why he hadn't gone up to the house for dinner, not because he didn't want to run into Miss Maggie MacLeod.

"Yeah, right," Tanner muttered. And if he believed that, next thing you knew he'd be believing that nonsense about lemonade springs and big rock-candy mountains.

All right, so he was avoiding her, had been avoiding her all week. There was nothing wrong with that. He was doing his job the way he was paid to do it, the way he'd always done it. And he didn't need to check with any angel-faced schoolteacher every few minutes for directions. He wouldn't have gone up to see Abby.

Of course, he would have seen Abby every evening at supper, anyway.

All week long he'd managed to avoid Maggie.

"Dietin'?" Ev had asked him, cornering him in the kitchen late one evening when he was ferreting through the cupboards in search of food.

"Calves don't know when it's suppertime," Tanner replied gruffly.

"Reckon not," Ev said. "Maggie's thinkin' you work too hard. Is that what it is?"

"Of course," Tanner said shortly.

"I wondered." But if he looked on speculatively as Tanner carried his sandwiches back to the bunkhouse, at least he didn't say what he was thinking.

But tonight, another Saturday, an entire week from when Maggie'd arrived, Tanner was starving. It was because he hadn't even gotten breakfast, let alone lunch and dinner.

He'd been headed up to the house for breakfast when he'd seen her sitting in the kitchen. Normally on days she drove off to school, he was in and out before she even came downstairs. But this morning, damn it, there she was, puttering around the stove. Ev was nowhere in sight.

She was wearing jeans and a long-sleeved, dark green shirt, and as she moved, Tanner was struck by how long her legs were. They were damned shapely legs, too. He wondered how it would feel to have her legs wrapped around him.

And that was when he knew he couldn't go in for breakfast. He'd taken off for the hills as fast as he could.

Now, fifteen hours later, he was starving. Muttering under his breath, Tanner hauled himself up off the bed and stalked over to the cupboard, jerking it open and ransacking it once more. There had to be a can of beans, a packet of crackers, some beef jerky—any-thing!—that some long-departed hand had left behind.

He didn't find a crumb.

He hadn't had time all week to go to town and stock up on rations. During calving season, free time wasn't something he had a lot of, and he hadn't dared ask Ev. Ev would've wanted to know why he needed food when they had a kitchen full.

Sighing, he turned on the radio and grabbed the latest *Stockman's Journal*, then dropped down again onto the narrow bunk. He'd read until the lights went out in the house and everybody'd gone to bed.

Then he could sneak up to the house and fix him-self a sandwich. Or four.

His stomach growled. "Wait," he told it.

The unexpected knock at the door made him jump.

Please God it would be Ev, feeling sorry for him and bearing supper.

It was Maggie.

In one lithe movement he swung his feet to the floor and sat up. "What do you want?"

"I missed you at dinner. Seems I've been missing you all week."

"I wasn't hungry. Besides I've got work to do. Doesn't always fit in with mealtimes."

"Maybe we should change the mealtimes," she suggested. She was wearing her hair piled up on top of her head. Tanner could see the pins. He wanted to remove them.

"What do you want?" he repeated sharply. He got to his feet and strode over to the farthest window before turning around to face her.

"I'd like to go out with you tomorrow."

"Go out with me?" He almost choked on the words.

Maggie's cheeks reddened. "Not on a date," she said quickly. "I just meant... Ev says you check the mother cows every morning and I'd like to come."

"No."

His vehemence made her blink. "What do you mean, no?"

"Just what I said. I'm workin' when I'm out there, not guidin' pleasure tours. I don't have time to baby-sit." He folded his arms across his chest and stared at her. His stomach growled.

"It wouldn't be baby-sitting," she said mildly after a moment.

"No? What would you call it?"

"Boss-sitting?"

His teeth came together with a snap and he knew he was trapped. "So you're pullin' rank?"

"Well, saying pretty please didn't seem to be doing me any good," she said with gentle irony. "What time do we start?"

He considered her, took in the heightened color in her cheeks, the sparkle in her big green eyes, the soft thrust of her breasts and the lush curve of her hips that her jeans outlined. *How about right now?* his body suggested to him. Mother cows were the furthest thing from his mind.

"Robert?"

"Damn it! I told you my name is—"

"Tanner. Yes, I know. Very well, *Mis-ter* Tanner, I will be accompanying you in the morning. What time do we start?"

"I'm leaving at sunup."

"I'll be ready." She started toward the door, then stopped and looked back at him. "Abby never said you were surly and hard to get along with, either. Or is it just me?"

Tanner raked his fingers through his hair. "Sorry," he muttered. "It's just there's...I've..." But there was no way he could explain. "It's a busy time of year," he muttered at last.

"Well, I don't want to make it worse for you. I just want to know what's going on, to learn all I can about ranching so I won't mess up." She smiled. "Ev says you're afraid I'll try to run the ranch when I don't know what I'm doing. He says you're afraid I'll make a mess of things and cause trouble in your life."

Good old Ev. Tanner's mouth twisted. "Ev talks a hell of a lot."

"He just wanted me to know," Maggie said simply. "He thought it might make things easier between us."

What would make things easier, Tanner wanted to tell her, was if she'd hightail it back to Casper and stay the hell away from him.

"He say anything else?" Tanner asked dryly after a moment.

A smile flickered across her face. "He said you needed a woman in your life."

Tanner gaped at her.

She laughed. "Do you think he's matchmaking?"

"The hell he is!" Tanner slammed his hand against the dresser, furious, hoping she couldn't see the hot blood that had rushed to his face. "I'll kill that nosy old coot. I'll—"

"I get the point," Maggie said lightly. "You have nothing to fear from me."

Oh, didn't he? Tanner wanted to say. He didn't say anything, just folded his arms against his chest once more and prayed she'd leave.

She turned back to the door again, then paused once more and glanced over her shoulder. "Too bad you weren't hungry. We had the most wonderful savory stew with peas and dumplings. It was scrumptious. But perhaps you'll feel more like eating by breakfast time. See you then." He could hear her footsteps on the plank stairs and then she was gone.

Tanner picked up the *Stockman's Journal* and tossed it on the table, flicked off the light and flung himself down on the bed.

His stomach growled.

Tanner got to the house before dawn. He was earlier than usual, but there was a lot to be done. And if he missed Maggie, well, that was just too bad. She'd have to understand.

He looked in the window first, steeling himself in case she was already there. She wasn't. So he breathed easier and opened the door as quietly as he could, hoping not to make noise and wake her. He expected he'd have to fix his own breakfast. Even Ev wouldn't be looking for him this early.

But he found bacon, still crisp and hot, in a covered dish on the back of the stove. In another there were scrambled eggs, and in a third, a pile of warm pancakes. There were hash browns and applesauce, too, as well as the usual pot of strong black coffee.

Tanner breathed it all in, his knees weak from hunger. God bless the old man. He'd really outdone himself, Tanner thought, sitting down and putting it away with relish. "I take back every evil thought I've ever had about you," Tanner said to Ev's absent spirit.

But he apparently didn't want any thanks. He was nowhere around. Just as well, actually, Tanner thought, though it showed a bit more circumspection than was usual for Ev. Tanner had fully expected knowing looks and a blatant wink or two.

He finished off the bacon, eggs and hotcakes. He took a second helping of applesauce and downed another cup of coffee, glancing over his shoulder once or twice toward the stairs, afraid that at any moment Maggie would be coming down them.

She never came.

Probably slept in, Tanner thought with a ghost of a grin. All that business about getting up and coming with him had been no more than mere talk. He shouldn't have spent the night tossing and turning after all.

He carried his dishes to the sink and rinsed them off, then left them on the drainboard for Ev to wash up later. Still no sound of footsteps on the stairs. He felt easier with every passing minute.

He wondered what she'd do if he tiptoed up the steps, stuck his head in her room and woke her. And there was the way to disaster, he told himself sharply. Thinking about Maggie in bed was no way to solve his problem.

He flicked off the light and headed out the door, stuffed his feet into his boots and zipped up his jacket. Then, drawing a deep breath of clean frosty air, he made his way to the barn.

Maggie was already there.

Tanner muffled a curse under his breath and glanced around to check the possibility of getting out without her seeing him. There wasn't one. He sighed, then leaned against the doorjamb and watched.

She had a saddle on Sunny, the ten-year-old sorrel gelding that Abby used to ride, and she held a bridle in her hand, trying to slip the bit into the horse's mouth.

"It won't hurt you," she was saying to the horse. "It's a very humane bit. I checked. Honest. I read up on them just last night."

Tanner shook his head, half amused, half amazed. Maggie approached the horse again, holding the bridle up, grinning widely at him, showing him her teeth, then opening her mouth and clacking her teeth together. "Open up," she said. "Like this."

Sunny pulled back his big horsey lips at her.

"That's it, Sunny," she cooed. "Just like that. And now I'll…" She tried to slip the bit between his teeth.

He jerked his head away and clamped down hard. Maggie muttered under her breath.

Tanner tucked his fingers into the front pockets of his jeans. "Why don't you try 'pretty please' on him?"

Maggie spun around to face him, her eyes wide, her cheeks flushed. This morning she had her hair back in what he supposed was meant to be a utilitarian ponytail. But tendrils escaped around her ears and made him want to reach out and touch them. God, it was worse than with Clare. He'd never had to keep his hands in his pockets every minute around Clare.

"I tried that, too, I'm afraid," Maggie said, smiling. "He's as immune as you are. What does work?"

He dragged his mind back from its preoccupation with the physical Maggie MacLeod. "Knowing what you're doing," he said with as much flatness as he could muster.

"I'm sure it would. But Plato once said that we had to do things first without knowing how in order to know how after we've done them."

Tanner heard the faint hint of hurt in her voice and cursed his abruptness. But hell, it was only self-preserva-tion. "You reckon Plato knew a lot about ridin' horses?"

"I don't know. I only know it's all I've got to go on unless you'll show me." She looked at him expectantly in the dim light of the one overhead bulb.

Tanner's jaw tightened. He wanted to say no. He wanted to tell her to take her saddle and her bridle and her whole damn ranch and get out of his life. Or at least he wanted to get out of hers. Why the hell had he made such a promise to Abby anyway?

Finally he strode toward her. "Give it here." He

took the bridle out of her hands, careful not to touch her as he did so. Then, quickly and deftly, he slipped the brow band into place, slid the bit between the horse's jaws, adjusted the throat latch and handed her the reins. "There." Then he turned toward his own horse and, with what he hoped was casual indifference, began saddling Gambler.

"Thank you," she said quietly.

"You're welcome." She wasn't, but what was he supposed to say? A glance out of the corner of his eye showed him that Maggie was taking the bridle off Sunny even as she spoke.

"What the hell are you doing?"

"Taking the bridle off so I can practice."

"What?"

"I saw *you* do it. I can't learn unless *I* do it." She got the bridle off again, dropped it, turned it upside down, then right side up, and started again. All the while he stared at her, torn between outrage and bafflement.

This time she got the brow band on all right, but the gelding pulled his head away when she approached him with the bit.

Instinctively Tanner moved to catch the horse's head.

"Don't," Maggie said. He saw the set of her chin, the determination in her eyes, and his arm dropped to his side.

"Fine. Do it yourself."

She tried. She fumbled.

He clenched his fists so as not to reach out and help. "Talk to him, firm like," he told her. "And don't hesitate like that. If you do, he can see you're scared of him.''

"I'm not scared of him."

He grinned. "Tell him that, not me."

"I'm trying." Maggie shot Tanner a hard glance, but seeing his grin, she grinned, too. He looked away.

"Come along now, Sunny," she coaxed. "We're in this together, and Robert is laughing at us."

Tanner sucked in his breath.

Maggie grinned at him again, then turned back to the horse. "You don't want to spend the whole morning here, do you? And we will until we get it right."

Then she stuck the bit right between Sunny's teeth. Half triumphant, half amazed, she beamed delightedly. "Oh, you smart horse. I did it!" She turned her face to Tanner's, her cheeks glowing.

She was so radiant he took a step backward. "Like I said," he told her gruffly, "you just gotta be firm. Show him who's boss."

Maggie laughed. "Just you remember that."

Damned right, Tanner thought. As much as he didn't want to think about her being his boss, maybe it was the best thing to think about. Maybe that would keep him from making a fool of himself. Deliberately he turned away and finished saddling Gambler, working swiftly and mechanically, pulling up the strap and tightening the cinch. He put on Gambler's bridle and led him toward the door of the barn. "Come on. Time's wastin'. Can you ride or are you planning to learn that today, too?"

"I can ride."

Tanner gave her a doubtful look, but when she simply lifted her chin and said, "Unless, of course, you'd like to teach me,'' he got on Gambler and headed west.

"Why aren't you feeding the cattle today?"

"They can manage on their own. There's grass. It's not all snow cover now. See?"

"Do you feed them most days?"

"If there's snow cover."

"How much do you feed them?"

"Too much."

She smiled at him and he felt unaccountably as if he'd said something clever. She'd been plying him with questions since they'd started out. At first his answers had been terse. But at her persistence, he'd expanded on them. And she'd dogged his every step, braving a brisk west wind to peer over his shoulder, poke her nose in everything he did, wanting to know about things he reckoned kindergartners knew the answers to.

But it didn't take him long to see that she didn't.

"How?" she asked curiously. "Why? If she's in labor, why are we leaving her? What are we leaving her for?"

"We'll check on her on the way back," Tanner promised. The cow was just beginning to look like she might deliver. It could be quick; she was a first-time mother. He'd have plenty of time to show Maggie around and come back later and deal with her.

"You're sure she's going to be all right?"

"She'll be fine," he promised.

"When do you plant hay?" she wanted to know.

He was amazed that she listened to his answers. Hung on his every word, damned near, he thought wryly as the morning passed. And he couldn't help feeling flattered, even when he didn't want to be. He explained about the haying, even admitting he'd rather be anywhere else than on the seat of a tractor.

Hell, he thought, disgusted with himself, he hadn't talked that much in years.

He suggested she return to the house when he was done. He wanted to get back to the cow he'd left in the pasture. But Maggie insisted on coming along. They were longer getting back than he'd figured, mostly because he'd been running off at the mouth. And one look told him the cow was going to be the one to pay for it. He dismounted hurriedly, cursing his stupidity under his breath.

"What's wrong?" Maggie climbed down, too.

"I shoulda been here." He hunkered down behind the cow, who was now lying on the snowy ground, exhausted and laboring.

Maggie came to stand behind him. "I thought you said she was all right on her own."

"Was," he muttered. "No longer."

"Can I help?" She knelt down beside him.

"Get out of my way. Go stand over there by the horses." The contraction was passing. He needed to check her now, to see the position of the calf, to see if there was a live calf he might still save. He should've checked her more closely earlier. But he hadn't wanted to make a production of it then. There was something very physical and very basic about labor.

He hadn't wanted to deal with it in front of Maggie. Now he had no choice.

He stripped off his gloves and checked the position of the calf, afraid of what he was going to find and not surprised when he did.

In the best of deliveries the calf's head and front feet were in perfect position for entry into the world. But if this had been one of those, the calf would have already appeared. All Tanner could feel when he tried was a tangle of legs. He muttered under his breath.

"What's wrong?" Maggie was back again, standing right behind his shoulder.

He considered his options. There was a very good chance that, no matter what he tried, neither the cow nor her calf would make it.

She'd been in labor longer than he'd thought. All the natural lubricant he could count on to help ease the calf around and on its way had long since dried up. She wasn't a big cow, either. With some it was easy to turn the calf for delivery. It wouldn't be easy with this one.

A calf leg kicked weakly against his fingers and, as long as there was hope of getting it out alive, he knew he had to try. He straightened up and went to get his rope. Maggie watched him, but she didn't speak. He made a slipknot in the rope and waited until the contraction ended. The cow made a weak, painful sound.

"That must hurt her." Maggie looked at Tanner with huge, stricken eyes as he slipped the rope in.

"It'll be worse if I can't bring the damned calf around." The next contraction was already upon her, squeezing his arm like a vise. The tiny foot kicked his hand again, hard.

The cow tossed her head, struggling.

Maggie knelt in the snow and grass and mud, stroking the cow's neck. "It's all right, Susie," she crooned softly. "It'll be all right. You'll see."

"Susie?" Tanner's eyes jerked up to meet hers.

Her gaze met his. Her face flushed almost defiantly. "Why not? I don't suppose she has another name?"

He shook his head.

"Then we'll call her Susie. It's more personal that way. Then she'll know we care and that we're trying to help her."

Tanner wasn't sure cows had any idea when you were trying to help them. Sometimes he thought they might. He'd never named one, though. It was hard to name one when you figured it was going to end up on a dinner plate.

"Suit yourself," he muttered. The contraction was lessening. He fumbled with the rope, trying to slip it over the two front feet and bring them around before the next contraction hit.

Getting the feet together was only the beginning of his trouble. Then he had to turn the calf, all the while praying its head would come forward, not lay back.

With each contraction he was forced to wait, to grit his teeth against the fierce pressure on his arm, to hope that he didn't lose the little progress he'd made.

And at each passing he tried to get a grip on the calf's head or shoulder, tried to bring them forward in line with the feet as he pulled on the rope with his other hand.

He was only barely conscious of Maggie. She knelt in the muck, soothing the cow, murmuring to her, with reddened hands rubbing her coarse hide slowly and rhythmically in time with the contractions.

Tanner felt the rope begin to slip and cursed as he lost his grip on the end of it.

"I'll pull."

"You can't..."

Maggie pushed a lock of hair out of her face,

smudging her cheek with a bit of mud. "She's my cow, isn't she? A fine rancher I'd be if I sat back and let her die."

"All right. Pull slow and steady, just like I was doing, and stop if I tell you."

Maggie nodded. She got to her feet and steadied herself, then started to pull. He could see her new boots, mucky and bloody now, braced in the muddy field just inches from his arm. The next contraction passed. He wriggled his hand behind the calf's neck, applying pressure to bring it in line with the front feet. He felt the movement.

"Yes..." The word hissed from between his clenched teeth. His arm trembled. A contraction built once more, the pressure cutting off his circulation again. "Stop!"

Maggie stopped. They waited, motionless, breathing hard, until once more Tanner said, "Now," and started to push slowly and steadily while Maggie pulled.

And this time the calf came free.

The head and forelimbs, along with Tanner's hand, slipped into view. The rest of the calf came quickly after and he caught it, then lay it on the muddy ground.

Maggie dropped the roped and knelt down beside it. "Is it..." Her voice was hollow, her face ashen.

Tanner didn't answer. He hunkered down over it and cleared its mouth, then waited. Nothing. He bent and blew into it, forced air down into its lungs once, then again. Again.

It gagged, then choked. All four legs twitched. One eye opened, then the other.

"It's alive!" Maggie exulted. She laughed. She

crowed. She crouched down and planted a kiss on its messy head. Then she looked at Tanner, her green eyes sparkling. "You did it! Oh, Robert! You did it!"

And then she launched herself at him and kissed him, too.

The force knocked Tanner flat on his back. His arms came up and went around her all of their own accord. All the breath went right out of him.

The warmth and the weight of her robbed him of whatever coherence the sheer impact hadn't. Only his body responded, and his lips. Hers were warm and wet. His were starving. He couldn't help himself. Desperation could only protect him so far. Common sense simply fled.

When her lips touched his, he kissed her.

It had been years since he'd kissed a woman like that. Fourteen long, hungry, lonely years. There had been women in his life since his divorce from Clare. But they had been few, and none of them had promised more than a night's satisfaction.

Maggie did—as he'd known she would.

The notion terrified him. He jerked his head aside, then grasped her arms and tried to shove her away.

Maggie pulled back, her face flaming. But still she straddled him, and he could feel the press of the juncture of her legs against him. He shoved himself up, but that only made matters worse.

"Oh!" She scrambled off him and he got to his feet, turned his back, adjusted his jeans. "I'm... sorry," Maggie said in a tiny voice.

"It's all right." It wasn't. It was awful. It had felt so good having her on top of him, her breasts pressing against his chest, her lips on his. He reached over and snagged his hat out of the muck and jammed it on his head.

He hoped to God she hadn't noticed the way his hands had gripped her waist, hadn't felt the instinctive masculine response of his body to her touch.

He got to his knees and ducked his head, reaching for the calf and hauled it up next to the cow's head.

She put out her tongue and gave it a tentative lick. The calf made a noise and nuzzled against her. Her eyes, rheumy and lackluster, brightened. She licked again, nosed her child, licked some more.

"Mother love," Maggie said softly. Her voice sounded just a little bit hoarse.

Tanner nodded. He didn't answer because he knew his would have been a whole lot hoarser. He didn't look at her, either, just gathered up his rope, tugged his hat down harder, then got to his feet and moved toward his horse. Maggie started to follow him, then turned back.

"Look, Robert. Just look at them," Maggie said. "Isn't it wonderful?"

And the joy in her voice brought his gaze around, first to the cow and calf, then, because he couldn't help himself, to her. She was dirty and slightly disheveled, and with just a hint of embarrassment still in her cheeks, she looked positively radiant—the most beautiful woman he'd seen in his entire life, Clare included.

"Wonderful," Tanner croaked, and turned desperately back to his horse.

Four

"**S**he's got a lot of try, that gal," Ev said as he helped Tanner put some new shingles over a leak in the bunkhouse roof. He was perched on the ridgepole watching as Maggie learned how to trim hooves from Bates.

Tanner grunted, but he didn't spare her a glance.

"I reckon Abby'd be right proud of the way she's come along."

Tanner kept hammering.

"You'd think she'd have plenty to do, just teaching all them little kids all day. But she's right here pitchin' in every time I turn around. Hell, she's up at dawn fixing breakfast every morning. She's—"

"What d'you mean, she's fixing breakfast? You're dishing up when I come in. She's still upstairs."

"That's 'cause she comes down first, puts on the coffee and makes the pancake batter and gets the bacon goin' while I'm shavin'. Then she goes up and takes a shower and I dish up."

"She's doin' your job." Tanner scowled.

"I know that. I told her so. She said she likes to."

"Last weekend...the day I took her out with me... did she cook then?"

"Yep. Let me sleep in."

"You shouldn't let her." Tanner was outraged.

Ev grinned. "Tell her that. I tried. She said she's the boss."

Tanner placed a shingle and whacked in a nail with one blow.

He didn't know why it should matter that Maggie was cooking breakfast in the morning. It was still food. What difference did it make who cooked it? Logically, there was no difference at all. Deep down, though, it did matter. It was like she was cooking for him.

He didn't want her doing for him. It made him nervous.

"Reckon she'll want to brand calves next," Ev said with a chuckle. "She and Den Baker were talking yesterday about when the roundup should be."

"That's my job!"

"But it's her ranch," Ev reminded him. "She wasn't making decisions, Tanner. She only wanted to know. Said she was hopin' her brothers would be here. They get off around Easter."

More grief. "The last thing we need is a couple of greenhorns gettin' in the way."

"Maggie ain't getting in the way."

Ain't she? Tanner wanted to ask. He hammered on another shingle.

"Reckon you'd've asked her out by now," Ev said, shooting him a glance out of the corner of his eye.

"Why the hell would I do that?"

"You been vaccinated against pretty women then?"

"She's my boss."

"That don't mean you ain't noticed." Ev grinned slyly. "I reckon she wouldn't care."

"What the hell are you talking about?"

"Her bein' the boss. Reckon she's got an eye for you, too."

"Ouch! Hell!" Tanner popped his hammered thumb into his mouth.

Ev cackled like a crazy man. "Got you goin', don't she? You ain't no steer, Tanner, even if you're tryin' to act like it right now. Maggie's a hell of a fine-lookin' woman, and she likes ranchin'. Just about the best combination there is. So...what're you waitin' for?"

Tanner's hammer hit the roof with a resounding smack. "Mind your own goddamn business!"

Ev just grinned.

"I'm not interested in gettin' tied down," Tanner said in a more modulated tone after a moment. "Not with her. Not with anyone. Besides," he added recklessly, because he knew Ev thought the world of Abby Crumm, "if Ab thought I'd be makin' eyes at her heir, she'd have fired me, not made me promise to stay on."

"You think so, do you?" Ev regarded him over the tops of his spectacles. "Well, she wasn't no fool, our Ab. But just go right on foolin' yourself if you want."

Tanner snorted, not dignifying that remark with a

reply. Any answer he made would play right into whatever trap Ev was laying next.

But Ev didn't say anything else, just began to whistle softly, looking up every once in a while to watch Maggie as she bent over the horse's hoof.

Tanner watched, too. He couldn't help it. There was something about a trim female in jeans that caught a man's attention. Bates didn't have to bend so damned close to her, for God's sake. He was practically hugging her!

Tanner shifted irritably, adjusting his jeans, and, with his heel, knocked the hammer to the ground.

"Hell!"

Ev laughed at him.

It wasn't funny. Not a bit. He didn't want this, didn't want the temptation, the distraction that Maggie brought into his life. But even when he tried to avoid her, it didn't work. She was everywhere he went.

Like Ev, he'd assumed that a full-time teaching job would leave her little time to intrude in his life.

He hadn't counted on riding in one afternoon to find Maggie and four third graders crouched in a stall in the barn. "What the hell—I mean, heck—are you doing?"

Maggie looked up and smiled at him. Even now, every time she did it, it felt like a kick in the gut. "Would you believe that some of my children have never seen a cow up close, even in Wyoming? I wanted to show them Grace."

Tanner stifled a groan. Grace—God help him—was a calf. An orphan calf he'd found bawling next to its dead mother in last Sunday's snowstorm. He tried to get another mother cow to take it, but none had lost a calf and he didn't have a prayer. So he'd brought it in slung over the front of the saddle.

Maggie had taken it over—and named it Grace.

"Because it was through the grace of God that you found her and brought her home," she told Tanner quite seriously, her wide green eyes luminous as she'd looked up at him from where she knelt on the floor of the barn, feeding the calf.

She was looking like an angel again. "Suit yourself," he muttered, beating a hasty retreat.

It seemed like every time he went into the barn after that, Maggie was there feeding Grace. And now she had a circle of eight-year-olds sitting there with her, with Billy showing them the bucket with the nipple, demonstrating how the feeding was done. Ev was always telling him that Billy's teachers couldn't get a word out of him. They should see him now, Tanner thought.

He was unsaddling Gambler when Maggie appeared at his side. He stepped back, her nearness still capable of unnerving him.

"Grace is a big hit." She smiled at him, then looked over to where Billy was helping one of the girls give Grace the bottle. "They love her."

"They don't have to feed her day and night."

"My, aren't you grumpy this afternoon," she teased. "Get up on the wrong side of bed?"

"Lucky when I can get to bed." For the last four nights he'd been out with calving cows.

"Should we hire someone to help you?"

"Waste of money. I can do it myself. Anyway, looks like no one's ready to calve tonight, so I'll have a break."

"Good. You can take the children back to Casper with me."

"*What*? I can't do that!"

"Why not? I'd like the chance to sit down and talk to you uninterrupted."

"No, I—"

"We haven't really had a chance since I moved in. You've been busy and so have I. But tonight—"

"I can't!" Tanner said desperately. "I've got to— got to—to muck out the barn."

"I'll help you muck out the barn when we come back."

"No!"

Maggie cocked her head. "You know, Robert," she said, one corner of her mouth lifting as she looked straight at him, "the way you're constantly trying to avoid me, I could get the impression that you're afraid of me."

"I am not afraid of you!"

"Really? Then prove it."

He ought to know better than to take a dare. Damn it, his brother Luke was the one who took dares, not him.

But what was he supposed to do when Maggie lifted her chin and grinned knowingly at him like that? He sure as hell wasn't going to let her think he was running scared.

Probably it was a good thing, he told himself, being forced. Maybe what he needed was a few hours of nonstop company with Maggie MacLeod. Maybe then whatever itch she was inspiring in him would be scratched. In any case, he didn't see that he had much choice.

They took the utility truck, which had plenty of room for all the kids when he put the seat back in. It also gave him plenty of elbow room in the front seat—as long as Maggie didn't do anything stupid like slide over and sit next to him.

The moment the thought occurred to him, he glanced in her direction. But she was turned and talking to the children in the back, asking them what they thought about feeding Grace, and he began to relax a little.

He liked listening to her talk to the kids. She wasn't patronizing like a lot of his teachers had been. And she didn't bark out orders to them, either. She seemed genuinely interested in them. And they were equally interested in her. They knew all about her life, it seemed to Tanner. About her parents and her brothers and the places she'd lived growing up.

"Do you like it better here or in the jungle?" one of the little boys asked her.

"Oh, here," Maggie said. "But the jungle was interesting. You should go sometime."

The boy's eyes widened. "You really think I could?"

"If you want to bad enough," Maggie told him.

"Like you wanted your home?" one of the girls asked her.

"Just like that, Dena," Maggie said. "I was extremely blessed by Miss Crumm's generosity, of course. But I would have made a home wherever I settled. She just made it possible for me to be here."

"How long you gonna stay?" the boy asked.

"For the rest of my life, I hope."

"You stayin', too, Mr. Tanner?" he asked.

"Not me," Tanner said.

"How come?" The boy bounced forward on the seat to peer over into Tanner's face. "Don'tcha like Miz MacLeod?"

"Sure I like her," Tanner said, flexing his fingers on the steering wheel. The truck seemed suddenly to be getting smaller.

"Then how come you're gonna leave?"

"Because it's what *I* want to do." Need to do, his mind raged silently.

"You know what I think?" Dena said. "I think you should marry her."

Tanner's head whipped around so fast he almost drove right off the road. Maggie pressed her fist to her mouth to stop a smile, then turned to Dena and said gently, "I think that's a decision best left up to Mr. Tanner and me, Dena."

The girl kicked her foot against the back of the seat in front of her. "I was only sayin'. Don't you want to get married?"

"Yes," Maggie said.

"No," said Tanner.

Maggie looked at him for a second before turning back to Dena. "There. You see?" she said lightly. "It would never work. Come on now, look where the sun is setting. Who can tell me what direction we're going?"

She kept them talking until they were all dropped off and she and Tanner were sitting alone in the truck together.

"Sorry about that," she said, folding her hands in her lap. "I didn't imagine they were going to try their hand at matchmaking."

He shrugged. "Doesn't matter." He hoped she didn't notice the high line of color that he was sure still tinged his cheekbones. He put the truck in gear. "You need to do some shopping before we head back?"

"A little," Maggie said. "And then I'm taking you to dinner."

He protested. She pulled rank. He grumbled.

She laughed. "I think I'm beginning to like this 'boss' business. Come on into the grocery store with me."

He didn't argue this time. He didn't remember much Shakespeare from high school, but he did remember the bit about protesting too much. Besides, he didn't see what harm he could come to with her in the grocery store. Which just went to show how shortsighted he was.

It was like being married to her. Maybe it was just that he had marriage on the brain after what Dena had said. But he couldn't help it.

Married people went grocery shopping together.

He remembered doing it with Clare—walking down the aisles side by side, him pushing the cart, her picking things off the shelves, looking to him now and then for approval. Maggie did it now, seeking wordless approval for some package of beans and rice she was considering. It tore at his gut.

He shoved the cart at her. "Think I'll just get some air," he said, and headed rapidly for the exit.

He was pacing around outside, feeling like an idiot, when Maggie came out ten minutes later and apologized to him. "Sorry about taking so long. But I'll make it up to you. I know a great place to go for dinner."

Once more he tried to convince her they didn't need to go out to dinner. Once more she won.

"We need to talk. If we're going to work together, we need to get to know each other."

Tanner thought he knew her better than he wanted to already, but he couldn't tell her that. "So, fine. Let's go. Got any ideas?"

She did. Her choice surprised him. She directed him back out of Casper and north on the highway to Kaycee. "It's fabulous. They have the best smothered green chile burritos in the world," she told him.

"I know."

His response made her blink, then laugh. "Of course you do. Why do I think I'm the first one to discover these places?"

In fact, he'd eaten there plenty of times. And Maggie was right: they did have the best smothered green chile burritos he'd ever eaten. But somehow tonight they tasted even better.

It was because of Maggie. Tanner knew it. He knew, too, that he shouldn't enjoy it, that it was dangerous as hell to let down his guard with her even for an evening. But he couldn't seem to help it. Her enthusiasm made him smile in spite of himself. Everybody knew her. Everybody greeted her with a comment and a grin. They grinned at him, too.

"Got yourself a looker, eh, Tanner?" one of the waitresses said to him.

He opened his mouth to deny it, then couldn't. After all, it was true. He shrugged, glancing down at Maggie by his side. Just for the moment, why not just go along for the ride? It was a little like the way his brother described bronc riding. "If I can't control it, hey, I just try to hang in there and enjoy the trip," Noah had said with a grin. "Sometimes that's enough to keep me from getting my butt kicked."

Tanner prayed that the same would apply to a dinner with Maggie. He looked at her as the waitress left after taking their order.

"You come here a lot?"

"One of the waitresses is the mother of one of my kids. She can't make it to conferences very often because she has so far to drive, so I stop in on my way home and she feeds me and we talk." Her brow wrinkled. "You don't think that's a conflict of interest, do you?"

"I don't know," Tanner said, deadpan. "Depends on if the kid's grades are improving."

Maggie laughed. "I only wish they were." She sipped at the beer the waitress set in front of her. "Were you a good student, Robert?"

"Tanner," he corrected. "No, I wasn't."

"Me, neither. We moved around too much. And then, when I had to come back to the States for high school, I missed my parents and brothers dreadfully. I wrote letters all the time. I never studied."

That surprised him. He'd had her pegged for a straight-*A* student, a Little Miss Perfect, and he'd never imagined her lonely. He didn't like to think about her needing someone and not having them. "You must've done all right," he said after a moment. "You're a teacher now."

"Because I worked hard and because I wanted to be."

"You're lucky to have gone to college."

"You didn't?"

"No." He wasn't going to say anything else, but she didn't comment, just looked at him expectantly, so he went on. "It wasn't that I wouldn't have liked to. There wasn't enough money when I got out of high school. I was saving what I could out of the little I made, thought maybe I'd go the next year. But then my father died.''

''And he didn't leave you any legacy?''

''Oh yeah, there was a legacy. He left me my brothers. They were seventeen and fifteen.''

Maggie whistled under her breath. ''It must have been so hard on you. How did you manage?''

''Badly.'' And he didn't care how long she waited, he wasn't expanding on that.

Maggie smiled. ''I doubt that. You strike me as a very capable man. Very responsible.''

''I tried,'' Tanner muttered. She didn't have to know how he'd failed.

''What are they doing now?''

''Luke—he's the older one—is in California. He's the stunt double for Keith Mallory.''

''Keith Mallory?'' Maggie's eyes bugged at the mention of one of Hollywood's most popular young actors.

''Luke got all the looks,'' Tanner said wryly, ''and none of the common sense. You know the sort of pictures Mallory does?''

Maggie nodded. They were almost all action-and-reac-tion, bar-fights-and-bedlam, horse-and-car-chase flicks.

''Well, he and Luke are a match made in heaven 'cause Luke never met a stunt he wouldn't try.''

The job, which had come by the fluke of Lucas's simply being in the right place at the right time, had been his brother's salvation, as far as Tanner could see. Doing most of Keith's stunts had provided a channel for his recklessness, a positive use for energy that all too often threatened to spin out of control.

The waitress brought their burritos and two glasses of beer. Maggie took a bite before asking, "What about the other one? I suppose he's a rocket scientist."

"Noah? Hardly. He's a rodeo bronc rider. A damned good one. He's gone to the NFR the last five years in a row."

"NFR?"

"National Finals Rodeo. They have it every December in Vegas. Only the top fifteen money winners in each event get to go. Like I said, he's good."

"You must be very proud of both of them."

"They turned out okay, I guess." There was no need to tell her that it had been far from smooth sailing for any of them.

"Will I get to meet them?"

"I don't see much of 'em, but they call sometimes. Feel sorry for me stuck out in the back of the beyond, I guess." He gave an awkward shrug and bent his head, concentrating on his burrito again. He wasn't used to talking this much. Maybe it was the beer. Or maybe it was just that Maggie was easy to talk to. *Too* easy to talk to.

He changed the subject. "What about your brothers?"

So she told him about her brothers—about Duncan, the elder, who was working on an advanced degree in geography at the University of Colorado, and about Andy, who was an undergraduate at Wyoming.

"He doesn't know what he wants to do," she told Tanner finally, after having described a few of Andy's more daring scrapes. "He's at loose ends academically. I think he'll like the ranch. He keeps telling me he wants to be a cowboy.''

Tanner drained his beer. ''A right-thinking man.''

''I'm sure he'll be delighted when you tell him so. He's coming this weekend.''

Tanner had forgotten that. It was a measure of how much he was mellowing under the influence of good food and beer that he didn't feel his customary protest welling up inside. He finished his burrito and pushed his plate away. The waitress poured him some coffee and he lifted the cup to his mouth, settling back in the booth and sipping it.

Surely it wouldn't hurt just to look at her. He wasn't buying; he knew that. But just this once, for a few stolen moments...

Maggie looked up and saw him watching her. ''Are you in a hurry?''

He shook his head. ''Tell me about this jungle you grew up in.''

She did, talking easily and with fondness about her growing-up years. Listening to her, Tanner could imagine her as a child, all knobby knees and eager grins, and then as a teenager coming to the States, her enthusiasm more cautious, her eyes more wary. He could see all those things and more in the woman she'd become.

Maggie took a swallow of coffee. ''I'm talking too much.''

''No.'' He could have listened all night.

''But we have the barn to muck out, remember?'' She grinned at him.

''Forget the barn. I'll get Bates to help in the morning.''

"Well, we probably ought to go anyway. We have to get up early."

He knew she didn't mean it the way he took it. He knew it was only his imagination that had them getting up together. The waitress brought their bill. Maggie reached for it. Tanner got it first.

"I invited you," Maggie protested.

"Tough." It was like looking at her for just a moment had been—wishing. Indulging himself in just the smallest bit of pretence, the fantasy that he'd really had a date with Maggie MacLeod.

Of course, he knew he hadn't. But damn it, if a guy couldn't have reality, if he had to make do with dreams, was it such a crime if he based those dreams on what little he could muster from real life?

It was dark as they walked to the truck. The wind was cold and there was still frost in the air, and if he'd dared, he'd have slipped his arm around her as they walked. He did open the door for her. Another little bit of fantasy. She thanked him. Her voice was soft. He almost had to strain to hear it. He got in the driver's side and started up the engine. For just a moment he wished she'd slide over next to him, let her hip press against his.

But there was only so much reality that a fantasy could stand. That would be carrying things too far.

He flicked on the radio as they drove. Neither of them spoke. Just as well. Anything they said would spoil it, tip the balance, kill his dream.

He wasn't so dreamy that he forgot to do his job. He stopped to check on the cattle on the way to the house. "You can drive home if you want," he said as he got out of the truck. "It's not that far. I can walk."

"I'll wait," Maggie said, and she smiled at him in the moonlight. His heart kicked over.

Careful, he warned himself. *It isn't going to happen.*

It couldn't happen. He wouldn't let it.

He only wanted the dream. The cattle cooperated. He was back in the truck within twenty minutes. "All's well," he said, rubbing his hands together, then started up the engine.

He helped her carry the groceries into the house. There were only two bags. She could have managed alone, but he couldn't seem to let go. After they'd put the groceries away and he'd asked for and received a glass of water, he had no other choice.

He slanted her a smile and backed toward the door. "I'll, er, see you tomorrow."

Maggie followed him onto the porch. "Yes. Thank you for dinner. I didn't intend for you to pay for it."

"I wanted to."

They looked at each other for a long moment. He wanted to kiss her. He remembered the time she'd kissed him, when their lips had touched, when his body had burned. Maggie ran her tongue over her lips. He shut his eyes.

He knew his limits. Kissing her was beyond them. He hurried down the steps.

"Robert?"

He glared at her. She grinned. "I just wanted to say how much I enjoyed the evening, the company."

"Me, too," he said, then strode quickly across the yard. It was no more than the truth. He had enjoyed it. Far too much.

Five

Maggie's brothers showed up exactly as predicted, the week before Easter. Duncan, the elder, was tall and dark-haired and serious. "The Professor," Ev called him, half teasing, half respectful. He called the younger brother, Andy, "The Pest." Tanner called him "City Slicker" or "Slicker" for short. Andy didn't mind.

A freckle-faced, bright-eyed redhead who was even more irrepressible than his sister, Andy MacLeod wanted to do everything, see everything, learn everything at once. And most of all he wanted to emulate Tanner.

Somehow or other—whether from Maggie or Ev, Tanner never knew—Andy had determined that he was the font of all ranching knowledge. He followed him like a puppy.

At first Tanner grumbled about it. "It isn't like I

don't have enough to do," he complained to Ev. "Now I've got a shadow wherever I go."

But Andy's willingness to admit ignorance and his determination to learn the ropes won even Tanner's grudging admiration before long.

He was a better rider than his sister and an instinctively good roper. He even did dirty work like digging postholes, but what cemented him in Tanner's high regard was that he didn't bat an eye when Tanner suggested that he muck out the barn.

"It's part of the job, isn't it?" Andy said.

"Bates doesn't seem to think so."

Andy grinned. "My dad always says that if you're going to run things you've got to know how to do everything from the ground up."

"You planning on running things, are you, Slicker?"

Andy colored fiercely. "I didn't mean that," he said quickly. "I'm not after your job, Tanner. I swear I'm not."

"It's okay," he said easily. "I know that."

In spite of himself, he liked Andy. If he told Andy to try something, Andy tried it. "You got to learn by doing," Tanner told him, the way Tanner's father had taught him in turn. So Andy did. The boy's persistence impressed him. Although he supposed he shouldn't have been surprised. Not after Maggie.

Maggie.

Always there was Maggie. It had been a mistake going out with her. It had been hard enough to control his attraction before he'd fed his fantasies. Now he was a wreck. He daydreamed constantly. His nights were worse. He had a prayer of controlling his thoughts during the daylight hours. At night he was at the mercy of his desires. And his desire was for Maggie. It didn't matter that he told himself she was off-limits, that she wasn't a one-night-stand woman, that she'd want forever while he wanted anything but.

It didn't matter because wherever he went, there she was. She had a week's vacation for spring break while her brothers were home and she spent it with them. And that meant she spent it with him.

Oh, every once in a while she would stay in the house and go over some book work with Duncan. But mostly she rode out with Andy—and Tanner.

"You don't need to," Tanner told her time and again. "That's what you have a foreman for."

"I need to," Maggie said. "I want to."

There was no arguing with her.

So he'd hoped to get a little respite in the evenings when he could retreat to the bunkhouse. He reckoned without Andy.

"Why sit down there by yourself," Andy asked him, "when you can be up here with us? Maggie and I are makin' doughnuts tonight. Why don't you come?"

Reluctantly, Tanner came. Maggie tied an apron around his waist and set him to work mixing flour and baking powder and stuff.

"Might've known you'd put me to work," he complained. But he had a good time.

The next night Andy followed him back down to the bunkhouse after supper and kept talking to him, assuming that Tanner would be coming up with him when he returned. Tanner couldn't think of a good reason not to, so he went. It had begun to sleet and there was a cold wind coming down out of the mountains.

Duncan had laid a fire in the fireplace, and a Bob Marley CD played on Maggie's stereo. Ev was teaching Billy and Duncan how to play cribbage. Maggie was sitting on the sofa with one of the scrapbooks of the history of the ranch that Abigail had left.

"Show me," Andy commanded, and Maggie made room for him on the couch.

"Come join us," she invited Tanner.

He shook his head. "I'm fine right here."

He sat in the old wing chair stretching out his sock-clad feet in front of the fire, listened to the patter of sleet against the window and watched them all.

It was the sort of evening he'd once dreamed about having when he was married to Clare—the sort he remembered from when he was a very little boy.

Only instead of Ev bent over the dining room table, his bald head between Duncan's dark and Billy's fair one, Tanner remembered days when his father had taught him and his brothers how to play cribbage. He listened to Andy and Maggie murmur and laugh over the scrapbooks and remembered when he and Luke used to go through the Christmas scrapbooks their mother had made for them. He wondered for the first time in ages what had become of them.

Thinking about his mother, remembering her and the warmth of his childhood years, made him restless. He got to his feet and wandered toward the window.

"Bored?" Maggie materialized at his elbow while he was staring out into the darkness, still feeling that indefinable longing.

He looked at her, felt another kind of longing, shook his head quickly and moved away.

Maggie frowned. "How about joining Andy and me for a game of Scrabble?"

"I'm not much for games," Tanner said gruffly, and then cursed himself silently when she looked even more unhappy.

He didn't want her to think he didn't like her, didn't like being invited to join them. He did like it! He liked it too damned much! If she knew the way he really felt about being around her... If she knew the sorts of dreams he had, both awake and sleeping...

He rubbed the back of his neck, the combined tension and arousal he always felt around her getting worse, not better. "I ought to check the cattle one more time anyhow, then turn in. Gotta roll out early."

"We'll go with you."

"No!"

She looked at him, startled, her frown deepening further.

"I mean—" he moderated his tone "—there's no use you coming. I'll be fine on my own. Besides—" he said, giving her a faint grin, "—only fools or cowboys voluntarily go out in weather like this."

Maggie smiled gently. "Maybe I'm a fool—" she began, and at the look in her eyes, Tanner quailed.

He shook his head abruptly. "You're not."

And he was out the door and down the steps before she could follow him. He didn't look back until he was almost to the barn. She was still standing in the door, watching him.

He noticed the strange truck the minute he rode into the yard. He thought he knew most of the trucks within fifty miles. There weren't that many. But he didn't know anyone with a new Dodge 250 with an extended cab. He rode past it slowly, allowing his curiosity to dictate Gambler's pace. It had Wyoming plates starting with a 5. Laramie or thereabouts. He frowned, wondering who they knew from Laramie.

"Whose truck?" he asked Billy when the boy appeared on the porch.

"His name's John," Billy said.

"John who?"

"Dunno. He's a friend of Maggie's."

Tanner took off his hat and shoved his fingers through his hair, then continued on his way to the barn, shooting one last glance over his shoulder toward the house, curious about this friend of Maggie's. He told himself he shouldn't be. It was none of his business who her friends were.

Andy was in the barn when he led Gambler to his stall. Tanner was surprised to see him.

"You're in early."

"I ran into Maggie and John up near Teller's Point. They helped me finish checking the fence and I came down with them."

Tanner frowned, not at all sure he wanted anybody else checking the fences. But then, it was Maggie's ranch. If she wanted to do it, it shouldn't matter to him. "Who's John?" he asked Andy.

"Haven't you met him yet? I know Maggie wants you to. He's a friend of hers from college. Now he's getting his Ph.D. in agricultural economics or something at UW. Sharp guy. You'll like him."

Tanner grunted. He unsaddled Gambler. Andy finished with his horse. "I did Sunny and Randy, too," he told Tanner. "Maggie and John rode 'em up on the range. But I told Maggie I'd brush 'em down so she'd have time to show John the books."

Tanner's brows drew down as he bent over Gambler's hoof with the pick. What the hell was she showing John the books for? The Three Bar C's finances weren't any business of his. Tanner flipped extra hard at a piece of hardened mud, hit the frog and got kicked for his trouble.

"Damn! Sorry," he muttered to the horse. Gambler edged sideways uneasily. Tanner murmured soothingly, trying to concentrate on what he was doing.

"Well, I'm off!" Andy said cheerfully. "I'll see you in the house for supper." He paused at the door to the barn. "Sure will miss this place."

Tanner looked up. "When're you leaving?" Their holiday was almost over. Duncan had left last night for Boulder.

"I'm riding back with John tonight."

"Oh. Good."

"Good?" Andy yelped.

"I didn't mean that. I meant..." But he could hardly say he felt unaccountably relieved at this reason for the mysterious John's arrival. "I just meant it's good you've got a ride. And you'll be back before you know it."

"Four weeks," Andy said. "Not quite actually. Twenty-seven days till my last final's over." He grinned sheepishly. "I counted. Promise you won't have the roundup till I get here."

"Well..." Tanner drew the word out, enjoying the look of dismay growing on Andy's face by the second. "No, Slicker, we'll wait for you."

Andy grinned. "Thanks, Tanner. See you at supper."

They were eating in the dining room. They ate in the dining room at Thanksgiving, Christmas and Easter. They were using Ab's good family china, the stuff her grandmother had brought out from Maryland in a covered wagon or some damned thing. Tanner wondered if he should've worn a suit and said so.

"Don't be ridiculous," Maggie laughed. She reached out and took his hand, drawing him toward the living room. "Come and meet John. He's a very old and dear friend of mine."

Tanner allowed himself to be towed. In the living room, sitting in the wing chair, was a lean, bespectacled, dark-haired man dressed in jeans and a sweater. He had the sort of features that had never been rearranged by a bronc. Women probably liked him. A lot. Tanner figured he was in his late twenties. He had one of the ranch ledgers on his lap, but he set it aside and stood up when Maggie came in.

"John, this is my foreman and the man who keeps things going around here, Robert Tanner. Robert, this is John Merritt. We went to boarding school out east together, then we went to college together. For years John was all the family I had. He's in Laramie now working on his doctorate. Land use and reform is his specialty, so I've been talking to him about the Three Bar C."

John Merritt held out his hand, smiling and studying Tanner with about as much curiosity as Tanner felt about him. "Pleased to meet you, Robert. Or do you prefer Bob?"

"Tanner," Tanner said through his teeth. "Everyone calls me Tanner."

Merritt grinned. "Except Maggie." He gave her a fond look and tugged at her hair, which she had pulled back in a leather thong against the nape of her neck. "I know Maggie. She's a law unto herself, isn't she?"

Tanner felt his jaw tighten at the familiarity between them. He had to consciously will himself to relax before he nodded his head.

"Do you want something to drink before dinner?" Maggie asked him. "Ev says it will be another fifteen minutes or so before it's ready."

Tanner hesitated, noticed the glass of wine by the chair where John had been sitting and shrugged. "I'll have a whiskey."

Maggie looked momentarily taken aback, then she smiled. "Of course. Ev, where's the—" she raised her voice to call.

But Tanner cut in. "I'll get it."

It was another gut feeling that Bates could have put a name to—probably something to do with a deep-seated male need to defend his territory. Tanner didn't care what anyone called it as long as John Merritt acknowledged that he was the trespasser at the Three Bar C, that this was Tanner's domain, not his.

He strode over to the buffet and opened the door, took out the bottle of whiskey that he and Ev and Abby had last opened when they'd toasted the New Year, and poured himself a generous dollop, then added a bit more for good measure. He turned, his eyes flicking over Maggie, John, Ev, Billy and Andy who were all looking at him.

"Want any?"

Ev, Maggie and John declined.

"I might—" Andy began. But Maggie said, "Don't even think it." And when John added, "Not if you plan on doing any driving tonight," Andy subsided with a rueful shrug.

"I'll have one for you," Tanner told him, swallowing the liquid in one fiery gulp, then pouring himself another.

"I reckon it's just about time we ate," Ev said hurriedly. "Come on, young man," he said, chivying Billy ahead of him toward the kitchen. "You can help me bring out the food. You might want to lend me a hand, too," he said to Tanner, giving him an arch look.

Tanner followed him into the kitchen. "What do you need me for?"

Ev snorted and muttered something that sounded very much like "I don't," before he thrust the handle of a carving knife at Tanner and said, "Carve the roast, while I make the gravy."

"Why me?"

"Because if you're going to do any carving, I'd just as soon it was on the meat and not the company." He handed Billy the bowl of mashed potatoes and steered him toward the dining room.

"What the hell's that supposed to mean?" Tanner demanded.

"It means settle down. It means stop knockin' back the whiskey like the state's goin' dry tomorrow. It means stop bristlin' like a mad dog about to attack."

"I wasn't going to attack," Tanner protested.

"Coulda fooled me," Ev muttered. "Carve the roast."

Tanner carved. It was just that sometimes you met a guy who set your teeth on edge. Nothing personal. Just bad vibes. He couldn't help it. It was like that with him and Merritt from the moment he'd laid eyes on the other man.

He made quick work of the roast, more aware of the muted sounds in the living room—of Andy's eager voice, Maggie's soft tones and Merritt's deeper, scholarly ones—than of the meat he was cutting.

"Hell, you don't have to cut it in bite-sized pieces," Ev grumbled. "G'wan in to supper." He paused. "And behave yourself."

Muttering under his breath, Tanner went. He sat. He dished food onto his plate. He ate with stolid determination. He didn't say a word. He listened while John and Maggie reminisced about their boarding-school days. About the time John had done something dreadful to a hated Latin teacher, and about the time Maggie had done something even worse, the details of which were lost in gales of laughter that set Tanner's teeth on edge. He listened while Andy told John all the things he'd learned about cowboying during his week at the ranch, and listened with increasing irritation while John encouraged him.

"There's a lot to learn, isn't there, Tanner?" he said, lifting his gaze to meet Tanner's.

"Mmph," Tanner said through a mouthful of mashed potatoes.

"It's good to learn from someone who can give you hands-on experience," John went on. "You're lucky," he told Andy.

"I know it," Andy said. "Tanner's the best."

"He certainly seems to be doing the best with what's here," John said. "I told Maggie that when she took me out to see the ranch today." He and Maggie shared a smile.

Tanner stabbed a piece of roast with considerable force.

"But it's hard to make a ranch break even these days," John went on. "Unless you diversify."

Tanner stopped chewing. His eyes narrowed.

Encouraged by what must have appeared to be avid interest, Merritt went on. "There is a place, though, near—what's it called? Teller's Point—that is a little too steep for cattle. To make the best use of the land there, I was telling Maggie she ought to consider sheep."

"*Sheep?*" Tanner's fork hit the plate with a clatter. His fists clenched. He stared bug-eyed at the man across the table from him.

John laughed. "I know, I know. The old animosities die hard. But it's prime sheep land, Tanner. Rockier than the rest of your range. Not as good grass. Sheep can handle it. Cattle can't. I know Miss Crumm's ancestors are most probably spinning in their graves at the very notion of sheep at the Three Bar C, but Maggie agrees that—"

Maggie agrees?

"Ab's ancestors be damned! *I'm* spinnin' right here," Tanner came close to yelling. "Sheep!" He fairly spat the word. He fixed a glare on Maggie. "What the hell are you doing, bringing some highfalutin' expert in? Don't you think I know a damned thing? I may not have the booklearning he does, but I've been around a damned sight longer. But I forgot, this is your *home* now, isn't it? You can do what you want! Well, fine, do it. I'll bet Ab's real pleased!"

He tossed his napkin on his plate, shoved back his chair, stood up. He almost broke a pane of glass in the door when he slammed it on his way out.

"Well, it's about time."

Tanner stopped dead on the steps of the bunkhouse as Maggie's voice came to him out of the darkness.

"What do you want?" He tried to make out where she was.

Then he heard the chair squeak on the narrow porch and saw a dark form rise. He took a deep breath and brushed past her, opening the door and flicking on the light.

"To talk to you," Maggie said, following him in.

"Hope you haven't been waiting long...Boss." He shed his jacket and tossed his hat onto the dresser, only then glancing over his shoulder.

She was wearing the slacks and angora sweater she'd worn the first time he'd seen her. Her cheeks were red and he wondered guiltily how long she'd been sitting out there, then told himself that it was her problem if she wanted to lurk around in the cold waiting for him. He was just doing his job.

Tanner kicked out a chair. "Talk away."

She sat. He stayed standing with his elbows braced against the wall behind him.

"You were rude tonight."

He shifted uncomfortably. "So?"

"I was embarrassed."

"I'm not your kid! You don't have to be embarrassed on account of me."

"I do if you act like a jerk in my house."

He scuffed the toe of his boot on the plank floor. "Sorry." His tone was truculent. He couldn't help it. It had been five hours and he was still mad. Bad enough she had to drag home her smart friends, but when they started telling him how to run the ranch—!

"I'm sorry, too," Maggie said quietly. "I wasn't trying to undermine your authority tonight. And John didn't mean to imply that you didn't know what you were doing.''

''No kiddin'?'' Tanner said with just a hint of sarcasm. He breathed a little more easily. At least she thought his reaction had to do with the sheep. He strode over to the window and stared out into the blackness.

''No, he didn't,'' Maggie said firmly. ''And you know it, too.''

''I do? How?''

''Because you suggested sheep to Abby yourself!''

Tanner's head whipped around and he stared at her. ''How the hell do you know?''

''Because Ev told me.''

Tanner cursed under his breath. He clenched his fists.

''He told me it was a long-standing battle between you and Abby,'' Maggie went on implacably. ''He said you used to argue about it daily.''

''I mighta mentioned it once or twice,'' Tanner said to the wall. ''I'm no damned *agricultural economist,*'' he gave the words a bitter twist, ''so you can imagine how much attention Ab paid to what I said.''

It was Maggie's turn to say a rude word. Tanner looked at her, shocked.

''If you can swear, so can I.'' She stood up abruptly and faced him head-on. ''So what I want to know is, if you weren't mad about the sheep, just exactly why did you slam out of the house?''

Tanner jammed his hands into the pockets of his jeans. ''Never mind.'' He stared away from her resolutely.

She reached for his arm and tried to turn him to face her. Her touch scorched him. He jumped as if he were burned, looked for an escape, but he was backed into a corner. Maggie stood between him and the door.

"No, I want to mind. I want to talk about it. And I want to know why it is that every time I come near you, you run off like some spooked stallion."

Because that was exactly what he felt like! "If it bothers you, stop comin' near me," Tanner snapped, still trying to edge away.

Maggie didn't move. "It is sexual." She said the words in wonderment, as if the revelation had just dawned on her.

"What the hell's that supposed to mean? What's sexual?" He felt as if his face was on fire. He almost couldn't say the word in front of her.

"Why you're running." Her expression changed. A smile replaced the wonderment.

"I'm not running!"

Maggie shook her head, still smiling, looking at him. "Yes," she said softly, "You are."

Hell. He gritted his teeth and looked away.

Suddenly her expression grew serious. "Don't you...like women, Robert?"

His gaze whipped back to meet hers. "Damn! Of course I like women!" The tips of his ears were burning.

Maggie's smile returned. She sighed with obvious relief. "Well, I'm glad to hear it." Then she sobered. "So is it me?"

"Is what you?" He felt as if he were strangling.

"Do you think I'm going to attack you?"

God, didn't he wish! "No, damn it, of course I don't think you're going to attack me!"

"Perhaps you're afraid of sexual harassment."

"What?"

"Well, I am your employer. And it just occurred to me that you might be afraid of us having more than, um, a working relationship...that I might start to expect you to..." For the first time, Maggie faltered. Her cheeks reddened.

Tanner drew his tongue across his upper lip, unsure whether or not to be glad she seemed to be getting as flustered as he was. "I don't think you're going to jump my bones," he said gruffly.

"I won't," Maggie promised solemnly. Then she cocked her head. "But not because I haven't been tempted."

Tanner's eyes widened. He hadn't thought it was possible to feel any more uncomfortable. He was wrong. He swallowed. Hard. He scowled at her, expecting her to blush and look away.

But she was looking at him with frank appreciation and he was the one who ended up with the blush suffusing his face.

"Don't be ridiculous," he muttered, turning away from her.

"I'm not. You're a very handsome man. A strong man. A capable man. I'd have to be blind not to be attracted."

"You're not attracted," Tanner said hoarsely.

"Do you think if you keep telling yourself that, it will be true?"

"It better be true."

"Why?"

"Because," Tanner muttered. "Just because." God, why was she doing this to him? Did she enjoy watching him squirm?

"Because you're attracted, too?" He heard her

move, heard her footsteps approach on the smooth plank floor. And then she was so close he could swear he felt her breath against his back.

He wheeled around to face her, breathing fire. "I am not attracted to you!"

Their gazes met, locked. They stood frozen in time for so long that Tanner thought they might stay that way forever.

Finally Maggie spoke. "Ah, Robert," she said softly. "Ab said it, but I didn't believe it."

"What are you talking about?" he rasped.

"She said you were always trying not to care. She said that you didn't want to. She said someday she hoped you'd stop lying to yourself."

"I've had enough of your meddling," Tanner told Abby. He stood, bareheaded, and kicked at the fresh-mown grass in the little hillside cemetery where lay the last earthly remains of Abigail Crumm. He was glad there was no one else around to hear him.

He felt sure Abby did.

"First you sic this city-slicker girl on me. Then you start tellin' her how I think. Hell, woman, when'd you ever know how I thought?" He paused, recollecting. "Well, besides the times you knew I was looking for a fight and you wouldn't let me find one." He scuffed his toe in the grass again.

"This isn't like that. This is different. You got no business meddlin' here. You had no business makin' me promise to stay. None."

He stared hard at her headstone, as if it might channel some sort of response.

"It was like you were matchmaking." He fixed the headstone with a hard glare. "Were you?"

This time he didn't need an answer. He could see Ab's enigmatic smile in his mind's eye, could see the teasing glint she'd have had in her pale green ones.

He shrugged. "It's part my fault, I suppose. You didn't know. I should've told you…about…about Clare. But you know now. I'm sure you know now. If you got to heaven, Ab, damn it, you've got to know! So you got to know it won't work!" He looked at the headstone pleadingly.

He sighed and bent his head. "Anyway, I can't do it any longer. I can't."

If he'd expected a voice from on high to liberate him from his promise, he was waiting in vain.

And even as he said the words, he saw Ab the way she'd been the day he'd made the promise. It had been only two days before her death. She was getting progressively weaker, but Tanner hadn't wanted to admit it at the time. Abby had known the truth. She, unlike Tanner, had never lied to herself.

"So, you're a better man than I am, Abby Crumm," Tanner said hoarsely now.

But even admitting it, he knew he owed her.

She'd given him a chance to show what he knew, to take all those years of working for some other boss and prove what he'd learned. She'd even given him the chance to own his own ranch, but he'd been afraid to take it. She hadn't reproached him. She'd been quiet, but gentle. She'd understood.

And now he was standing here trying to break the one promise he'd made to her.

Why?

Because he was afraid. Afraid of his own emotions. Afraid of getting too close to Maggie MacLeod.

If he fell in love with Maggie, he'd want to marry

her. And he didn't want to fail again. Not the way he'd failed Clare.

So go, he told himself. Maggie would let him leave. She wouldn't hold him to the promise he'd made Abby. She'd find someone else to run the Three Bar C until Andy was ready for the job.

Hell, she could probably ask Merritt to find her the best man in Wyoming.

And did he want that? Tanner asked himself.

He rubbed a palm across his face. God, he didn't know what he wanted anymore. He blinked rapidly, then stared out over the land. It was stark land, not very forgiving. It asked a lot of a man.

But it gave something back, too. It gave a man courage. It gave him self-respect. It gave him the guts to carry on year after year.

Or it crushed him.

The land hadn't crushed Tanner.

His promise to Abby might. Did he dare risk it? Could he manage his feelings long enough to show that same kind of courage where his promise to Abby was concerned?

He stared at Ab's headstone. It was granite. Gray and enduring. He knew it would outlast him, that it would reproach him every day of this life and the next if he didn't at least try.

The best thing about spring roundup, and something Tanner had never really appreciated until this year, was that when you were thinking about rounding up several hundred head of cattle, you didn't have time to think about anything else.

He didn't have time to brush his teeth or change his socks, much less moon about Maggie MacLeod.

He blessed Abby, considering the rigorous schedule divine intervention of a sort.

Instead of lying awake at night thinking about how Maggie looked in jeans or what it would be like to take her to bed, he worried about which cowboys would be available, which horses they would bring, how he ought to pair them up and send them out, and what sort of devilment the cattle would get into this time.

The advantage to this being his fourth roundup on the Three Bar C was that he was beginning to get a pretty good idea of just what sort of problems he could expect.

For the most part Abigail's herd was an easygoing lot. They didn't take one look at you and head off eighty miles an hour in the other direction. Most of the year, at least. Spring fever, though, seemed to take its toll on them as well.

As docile as they might be when there was just one or two cowboys lurking about, it was as if they had a sixth sense when it came to roundup. They seemed to know just when they were expected to cooperate—and then they did the opposite.

It was Tanner's job to outthink, outsmart and outmaneuver them.

He did this by lying awake at night plotting his strategy, figuring the number of cattle, the number of men, the savvy of their horses, the lay of the land. He threw in variables like temperature, wind, weather and who might not be able to make it at the last minute and whose horse might pull up lame.

And then he tried to think of alternative plans.

He knew as well as the next guy that there was just so far he could get with all the plans and alternatives in the world. But they were consuming, they were necessary and they did keep him from thinking about Maggie MacLeod.

Most of the time.

There was the odd moment, however, that fleeting instant when the sight or sound of her would catch him unawares. It was like being blindsided, knocked flat. One minute he'd be clearheaded and coherent, and the next he'd be fumbling for what he was supposed to be doing or saying or thinking.

"Reckon you might need training wheels for that horse?" Ev asked him finally, the night before the roundup. In the middle of explaining who was coming in the morning, Tanner had caught a glimpse of Maggie in the doorway and had turned so far that he almost fell off when Gambler stepped sideways.

He could feel the hot blood course into his face. "Just, uh, thought I saw something."

"You did," Ev agreed solemnly. Then he grinned and gave Tanner a knowing wink.

Tanner scowled, tugged his hat down, then looked away. He'd been keeping out of Maggie's way ever since he'd made up his mind to stay. It hadn't been too hard, given the amount of work he had to do. But still there were times he couldn't help but run into her. And at those times he did his best to appear as disinterested as possible.

If Maggie thought it was amusing, she didn't let on. Ev did, because Ev saw more than any old man had a right to. But Ev, after Tanner had chewed him out about telling Maggie about the sheep, was a bit more circumspect. Still, it didn't stop him smirking.

The morning of the roundup dawned clear and cool. Tanner was up well ahead of it. It was still dark when he went to the house to eat. The lights were on and he expected to find Ev already cooking breakfast for the hands as they showed up. He found Maggie.

"Where's Ev?"

"He's got the flu." She filled a plate, and when she turned to hand it to him, he saw dark smudges under her eyes, as if she hadn't slept.

He wanted to ask if she was up to all this, Ev's work as well as her own, but he didn't want to sound concerned. Not about her, anyway. She'd take it wrong.

He took the plate she handed him and set it on the table, then turned and climbed the stairs to the bedrooms. It was the first time he'd been up here since he'd moved out. He walked quietly along the hallway and tapped on the door to Ev's room, then opened it a crack.

Ev was lying huddled in his bed. He moaned, then opened one eye. "Checkin' to make sure I ain't faking it?"

"Of course not," Tanner said, ignoring a twinge of guilt at the accuracy of the remark.

"Hell of a thing to happen," Ev grumbled. "Poor Maggie." He fixed Tanner with a hard look. "I was gonna do most of the cookin' and she was gonna help outside. Reckon we'll be one person short now."

"Somebody'll show up."

"Well, if they don't, don't you go gripin' at her."

"Me?"

Ev snorted. "Don't go soundin' so blessed innocent. You ain't. You ain't hardly had a cheerful word to say to her in weeks."

"I haven't hardly talked to her in weeks!"

"That's exactly what I mean. Well, you talk to her now. You tell her everything's gonna be fine."

Tanner pressed his lips into a thin line.

"Tell her," Ev insisted. He moaned again, grimacing and holding his stomach.

Tanner sighed, tugged on his hat brim and backed out the door.

There were four cowboys packing away breakfast by the time he came back down. He sat at the table and began eating, too. When he'd finished, he took the coffee mug Maggie handed him and met her gaze.

"Thanks for the breakfast. It was good." His eyes flickered to the dishes filled with ham and bacon, eggs and sausage, pancakes and potatoes. "You're doin' fine," he told her, the way Ev had instructed him to.

He wasn't prepared for the smile that lit her face. It was like being socked in the gut. "Thank you," she said. She touched his hand.

For an instant his fingers closed over hers. Then he pulled his hand away, nodded his head, then raised his voice. "I'll be waitin' outside so we can get started."

The day was a blur of activity. By sunup eight crews were fanning out in various directions to round up and bring in the cattle. Only one bunch ran in the wrong direction and had to be regathered. Tanner, watching, felt lucky that that was all they'd screwed up. But he couldn't breathe a sigh of relief. With more than a hundred bawling babies being separated from their mothers, and more than a hundred mooing mother cows looking desperately for their mislaid children, there was plenty of work to be done.

The Three Bar C had always branded in what some

people now thought of as "the old-fashioned way,"
using
a regular iron, not a calf table and electric brands as
some did now. The calves were all branded, their ears
notched, their horns removed with hot lye paste. The
bull calves were castrated. All the calves received a
seven-way vaccine. It was hot, sweaty, dirty work.

And Maggie was right in the middle of it whenever
Tanner looked around.

He'd expected that she'd be in the house fixing the
huge meal that would follow the branding. And from
what he heard, she'd done her fair share of that. But
she was in the thick of things outside, too. Once when
he looked over she was sitting on a calf, holding it
down for Bates who was using the dehorning paste.
Another time when he glanced around she was in-
jecting vaccine into a calf. Still another time he saw
her taking a turn with the branding iron.

That was when she looked up and their gazes met.
Her auburn hair was coming loose from the band
she'd pulled it back in. Tendrils of it stuck to her
cheek. She had a dirt smudge on her forehead and
nameless muck on the front of her shirt. She looked
about as far from a prim schoolteacher as he could
imagine. She grinned at him.

In spite of himself, Tanner grinned back. Then,
abruptly, he remembered how dangerous his feelings
about Maggie were, how easy it would be to pursue
her, to want her. He turned back to the corral and
yelled at Andy to start bringing in another bunch of
calves.

It wasn't until they were almost finished that Tanner noticed John Merritt was there as well. He was

on horseback moving the mother cows and their calves back up toward the foothill pastureland.

Tanner stopped next to Andy as he let the last calves run back to their mothers. "What's he doing here?"

"Helping out."

"All the way from Laramie?" Tanner said sarcastically.

Andy glanced at him, surprised. "Maggie called him when Ev got sick in the middle of the night. Wanted to know if he knew anyone else who could help. He said he'd come."

"She didn't ask me. There are plenty of people hereabouts."

"Well—" Andy shifted uncomfortably "—I think maybe Maggie needs to, um, not be turning to you for every little thing."

"I'm the foreman, damn it!"

Andy gave an awkward shrug. "I guess it's just that…she's the boss."

Tanner's teeth came together hard. "Fine," he muttered. "She can get whoever she wants." He gave Gambler a nudge with his heels and set off toward the south pasture, as far away from Merritt as he could manage.

The barbecue was in full swing by the time the cattle were settled to Tanner's satisfaction. The hands and the neighbors and their families were all sitting at tables and on rugs under the cottonwoods, eating, talking and laughing. Even Ev was among them.

"Quick recovery," Tanner said as he came up beside him.

Ev looked faintly sheepish. "Reckon it was somethin' I ate."

"Probably," Tanner said dryly. "Looks like Maggie found you a replacement."

"Sure was nice of him to come all the way up to help out. That's a long drive."

Which was something of an understatement, Tanner thought. His gaze scanned the tables and rugs until he found Merritt. He was, naturally, sitting with Maggie and Andy on a rug near the old shed. They were laughing. Maggie had her head tipped back and Tanner's eyes lingered on the graceful line of her throat. He felt the awareness beginning to pool within him. He shut his eyes, turning away, then grabbed a plate and began to load it with chicken and ribs.

In the old days someone would have had a fiddle and someone else would have brought a guitar, and after the food had been eaten and the talking had slowed, someone would have begun to play, to tempt tired, wornout cowboys to look again at the women in their lives, to tease them into maybe just one dance.

Tonight someone brought out a boom box, someone else turned up the volume and another generation of cowboys started looking around. Some were eager, some were shy. But before long, four couples were dancing in the dirt clearing between the house and the barn. Tanner leaned back against a cottonwood and watched.

One of them was Bates, his head bent close to Amy Lesser's, his arms holding her tight against his angular body. Amy didn't seem to mind. Tanner watched as Andy sidled up to Mary Jean, Bates's sister. She was no proof against Andy's eager grin.

Tanner's gaze slipped toward Maggie. She and

Merritt were sitting close together on the blanket, but whether they were actually touching or not, Tanner couldn't tell. His gaze met Maggie's for an instant. Then he looked away.

A moment later a shadow fell across him and he looked up to see her standing there. "We did it," she said. She was smiling.

He knew what she meant. They'd completed the roundup; things had gone well. They should be pleased. He nodded. "Yep."

"Come celebrate with me."

He looked up at her.

She was holding out her hand. "Dance with me."

He swallowed, let his gaze drop slowly, considered the invitation, the desperation with which he wanted to accept it, the probable outcome if he did. He raised his eyes again and met hers and shook his head slowly. "I don't think that would be a good idea."

Maggie's smile faded. Her hand fell. "Whatever you say, Robert," she said after a moment, her voice absolutely toneless. She turned on her heel and walked away.

Tanner looked down at the ground where he sat, plucked at a weed, yanked it out by the roots. "Damn," he muttered under his breath. "Damn it to hell."

Six

He had to drive more than an hour, clear to Casper, before he found what he was looking for.

When he'd left the barbecue, fuming, he hadn't even known what he wanted except to leave, to put as much space as possible between himself and Maggie MacLeod.

Maggie had made the mistake of asking where he was going.

"Leaving," he'd growled as he'd stalked past her. "Or don't you think I've worked hard enough today?"

"Of course you have," she said a little uncertainly, her hand still resting on John Merritt's shoulder.

"Then I'm taking a little well-deserved time off. And that's all you need to know." He didn't care that Maggie, John, Andy, Ev and half of the inhabitants east of the Big Horns stared after him in astonishment.

He took off in a spray of gravel, driving fast and furious, not realizing until he hit the outskirts of Casper exactly what it was he was looking for: an escape—a little nightlife, a little joy, a big opportunity to meet a willing member of the fairer sex.

Another night Tanner might have had enough maturity to walk away from a wet-T-shirt contest.

Tonight it seemed like a good place to start.

The Wildcatter was, as its name indicated, as often frequented by oil-company men as by homegrown Wyoming cowboys. The music was loud, the enthusiasm louder and it was late enough that the highlight of the evening, the wet-T-shirt contest, had begun by the time Tanner got there.

The first contestant was already up on the makeshift platform at the end of the room when the bartender shoved a beer in Tanner's direction. He took a long swallow, then leaned back against the bar to watch.

There were half-a-dozen contestants. All of them better endowed than Maggie MacLeod. He studied them closely—the two blondes, the redhead, the three brunettes—and wondered what it would be like to dance with them, kiss them, run his hands over them.

The frustration that had been growing for weeks—no, months—rampaged in him. He watched as the women came forward in response to the whistles and hand claps. He studied their assets as the official "wetter" used a spray bottle to reveal them. He tried to imagine taking any one of them to a motel and doing what Maggie and John Merritt were probably doing at this very moment.

His jaw clamped shut.

Suddenly his line of vision was obscured. A leggy blonde brushed up against his arm. "Hi, honey." She smiled at him, her voice sultry, attractive and definitely inviting.

"Evenin'." He glanced at her. She didn't have the obvious attributes of the contestants on the platform at the end of the room, but even she probably had more to show off than Maggie had.

"Buy me a beer, cowboy?" she suggested.

He signaled to the bartender. The blonde edged closer to him. "I'm Carrie. Who're you?"

"Tanner." He finished his beer. The bartender poured him another. Carrie rubbed her cheek against the denim of his jacket. He remembered how he flinched away from the desire that shot through him every time Maggie touched him. He tried to find that desire here. He tried to imagine taking Carrie to a motel, easing off her skintight pink shirt and the rest of her clothes, laying her down and making love to her.

He'd never had any trouble imagining doing that to Maggie—even when he didn't want to.

He felt more than disinterest now. He gulped his beer and looked desperately back at the girls on the platform, trying to muster up interest in one of them. From the stamping and shouting and whistling going on around him, it was pretty clear that the other men weren't having any trouble relating to their considerable charms.

Carrie pouted. "They may have more than me," she said when she noticed where his gaze had focused, "but boobs aren't everything, are they, sugar?'' She gave Tanner a coy smile and brushed against him again.

He cleared his throat and shifted his weight. ''Er, no. I...reckon not.''

She reached for his hand, toying with his fingers. ''Why don't you let me show you what else I've got.''

He couldn't.

God help him, even faced with an outright invitation, he couldn't say yes.

Damned if he knew why.

His hormones thought he'd lost his senses. His body clamored at his betrayal. The frustrating pressure in his loins told him he'd lost his mind. But for all that certain parts of him frantically craved the release he was sure this woman could provide, he couldn't take her arm and walk out with her. He couldn't contemplate going to a motel room with her. He couldn't think about having sex with her.

Because he couldn't stop thinking about Maggie.

He tipped his head back and drained his glass, then looked at Carrie and shook his head. ''Can't,'' he said. ''Thanks, but no.''

Carrie looked at him, taken aback. ''No?''

Tanner gave a rueful shrug. ''Not tonight,'' he said. ''I...gotta get going.'' Shoving some bills toward the bartender, he gave Carrie a quick nod and strode out of the bar without looking back.

The spring night had cooled considerably and served as a temporary balm to his overheated body, but it did nothing for the frustration that had been tormenting him for weeks.

There was only one thing that would really ease it. One woman.

And he hadn't a snowball's chance in hell of making love with Maggie MacLeod and walking away. It was more than his life was worth to even think about it.

He flung himself into the truck, flicked on the engine and jammed it into gear. In his mind's eye he could see Carrie's smiling come-on, could feel the pressing need even now against the fabric of his jeans. He remembered the sight of Maggie as she laughed at Merritt's words, her hand on Merritt's arm as they danced, the possessive curve of Merritt's arm around her.

If Maggie felt any frustrations tonight, Tanner was sure John Merritt was solving them for her.

He headed up the highway, furious.

It was past two by the time he turned onto the gravel road that led into the Three Bar C. His fury hadn't abated, nor had his frustration. But he slowed down anyway because he didn't want to announce his return with any more noise than he had to. He even turned off his headlights as he came into the ranch yard. He looked for Merritt's car.

He didn't see it, but that didn't mean he wasn't still here. Maggie might have had him pull it into the shed. Or—and this thought made his stomach hurt even worse—she might have even left with him.

There was still a light on in the kitchen and another on the back porch—as if she'd left it on to light up her return.

He got out of the truck and started toward the bunkhouse. Habit alone made him stop at the barn. In his hurry to be gone this evening, he hadn't taken the time to check the two cows that still hadn't calved. He wanted at least to look in on the horses.

He did it quickly and casually, until he came to the last stall.

Sunny wasn't there.

Tanner stared at the empty stall, then shook his head, trying to clear it of the two beers he'd had in Casper, trying to figure out where he'd gone. Sunny's saddle and bridle were gone, too.

No one rode Sunny. Except Maggie.

She couldn't have. Wouldn't have, he assured himself. She had no reason.

He rejected the notion even as his mind was beginning to grapple with the unpleasant truth: she very well might have. Especially if she knew he hadn't checked the cattle.

Maybe the cattle had nothing to do with it. Maybe she'd gone off for a moonlight ride with Merritt.

He sure as hell didn't want to go looking for her if that was what she was doing.

But what if she hadn't?

It was the middle of the night. She ought to have returned by now. Unless...

Quick as he could, Tanner saddled Gambler and led him out.

He headed toward the pasture just east of the ridge, the one where he'd put the two remaining pregnant heifers. He had no way of knowing if that was where she'd headed. He had no way of knowing if she was with Merritt. He'd feel like a complete fool if she was.

He couldn't stop himself.

There was precious little moonlight to see by. He opened the gate and pulled out his flashlight and scanned the countryside, searching for any sign of Maggie or the horse.

Nothing.

Nowhere.

Not until he came over a rise and played the light along the edge of a stand of trees. For an instant its arc caught Sunny in its beam.

Before he could call out, he heard a voice. "Robert! Over here." She sounded frantic.

Tanner gritted his teeth. He played the flashlight over the area, looking for her. At least there was only one horse. But what if she was hurt? He spurred Gambler across the field toward the sound of her voice.

"What in the hell are you doing?" he began, swinging out of the saddle.

"Help me."

There was a thread of panic in her voice that squelched his anger. With the help of the flashlight he found her crouched on the ground, her arm in the business end of a laboring heifer.

"Thank God you're here! She's having a lot of trouble with this calf. It's coming out all wrong. Or rather, it isn't coming out at all." Her voice quavered slightly. She sounded exhausted, but determined.

Tanner crouched beside her. "Let me see." He cursed himself for his selfish desertion of duty. He was the one who should have been out here tonight, not Maggie.

She shifted aside to make room for him, moving to soothe the cow as she had done the last time. "Shh now, sweetie," she crooned. "Everything will be fine. Robert's here."

As if he was going to make things all right. Tanner's jaw clenched. He checked the position of the heifer.

"Don't get your hopes up," he muttered, tossing

off his jacket. He hadn't brought his rope, so he pulled his belt out of the loops, then braced himself.

He supposed he was lucky. This calf was smaller than the last one he'd had trouble with, and the cow hadn't been in labor as long. But it took some work to get its head forward and in position and the belt around its feet. Then he settled his own feet against the heifer and pulled on the belt while the cow strained to deliver her burden.

"Here she comes!" Maggie cried.

And the next moment he had a messy, bloody, squirming calf in his lap.

"Oh, Robert! Oh, heavens!" Maggie exclaimed. She was laughing, exulting as the calf wriggled in his arms and he lifted it to place it in front of the mother.

"Thank God," he muttered.

"Thank *you*. I knew you could do it," Maggie said, her voice warm and approving. "It's fantastic."

Tanner grunted. "It was luck." By rights he should've lost the calf and the heifer. He sure as hell didn't deserve any praise.

"I'm so relieved you came when you did," Maggie said now, crouching next to him, watching as the cow licked her calf.

"I should never have left," Tanner muttered. He finished with the afterbirth and hauled himself to his feet. "I should've been here when she started."

"It was your time off."

"I shouldn't have taken it."

"You deserved some time off. I agreed to it," she reminded him.

"It was my job," Tanner said doggedly. He shook his head. "I'm sorry. You better get yourself a new foreman."

Maggie looked up at him, shocked. She scrambled to her feet. "Don't be ridiculous. What sort of nonsense is that?"

"It's not nonsense. It's called fulfilling your responsibilities. I didn't fulfill mine. I'd fire anyone who let me down like this." He met her gaze, grateful the darkness covered at least some of the shame he felt.

It was the same guilt all over again, the same guilt that had assailed him when Clare had lost their child and he'd been nowhere around. The calf hadn't been quite so unlucky—no thanks to him.

"Well, it's a good thing you're not me, then," Maggie said at last. "Isn't it?"

He didn't answer.

"Robert, really. It's okay. You were here." She laid a hand on his arm. He tried not to flinch away. Her touch could undo him and he knew it. He wasn't up to fighting her right now.

"I might not have been. I showed lousy judgment and you know it."

Maggie just looked at him. "This isn't just about the calf, is it?"

"Leave it, Maggie."

She sighed. "If you say so. But I say you're allowed a lapse."

"I don't—"

"I don't care what you say," Maggie went on firmly. "You came when it mattered."

"But—"

"That's enough, Robert. Come on. You're a mess. You need to get cleaned up."

"Not now." He couldn't ride back with her now. "I'll be along."

"I'll wait for you."

He shook his head. "No. You've done your share. And mine," he added heavily.

"I don't mind wait—"

"No." His voice was flat, brooking no argument, and Maggie must have realized he wasn't going to be talked around.

"You're an ornery, stubborn, pigheaded cowboy," she told him.

He nodded. "Thank you, ma'am."

She dimpled and gave the brim of his hat a tug. "Hurry home," she said softly, then mounted her horse and started toward the road that led to the house.

Tanner watched her go. She was perhaps thirty yards from him when he called after her, "How come Merritt didn't come with you?"

He could have kicked himself the moment the words were out of his mouth even though he knew he couldn't have stopped them. Nor could he help the surge of elation he felt when Maggie turned in the saddle and called back to him, "He left before midnight."

It was a cool night for skinny-dipping. The water running down from the mountains was almost pure melted snow. The shower back in the bunkhouse sounded a lot more tempting. But the drumming of the water in the shower stall would wake Andy, asleep on the other side of the thin-walled partition.

Anyway, Tanner thought as he tied Gambler to a cottonwood and headed toward the creek, a little cold creek water might just possibly shock some sense into him. God knew he needed some.

The swiftly moving creek was almost twenty feet wide and perhaps three feet deep. There was a swimming hole farther south, but he didn't have time to ride there.

Besides, he wasn't here for swimming. He was here to wash off the remains of the calf's birth and to dampen, literally, his sexual frustration.

Tanner tugged off his boots and socks, his jacket and shirt and jeans. If Maggie had stayed he'd have kept his shorts on.

If Maggie had stayed...! There was a laugh.

He wouldn't be anywhere near this creek in his underwear if Maggie had stayed with him. That would have been asking for trouble.

He stripped off his shorts and T-shirt and dropped them by his jacket. Then he picked up the clothes the calf had mucked up and carried them to the creek.

The cool night breeze made him shiver. The icy water shocked him. He bent, scrubbing his clothes against the rocks, swishing them in the water, scrubbing them some more and finally rinsing them. Wringing them in his hands, he carried them back to the bank and spread them on the grass. If there was any desire left in him after he plunged back in the icy creek, those clothes would take care of it on the way home.

He turned and headed back into the creek, ducking under, shuddering as the frigid water enveloped him, yet grateful for the ache it shot through him. It was an ache that would blot out his desire for Maggie MacLeod. His body might not enjoy it as much as it would have enjoyed a tumble in the sheets with the girl from the bar, but his mind and his emotions would be happier.

He didn't know how long he stayed in the creek. Long enough so that all those surging feelings of desire were well and truly cooled, long enough so that his skin felt numb and his fingers shriveled.

He wasn't cold now so much as anesthetized. But when at last he stood and made his way carefully across the slick rocks to the bank, the cold breeze smote him.

He grabbed his jacket and blotted himself dry. Then he picked up his T-shirt and pulled it over his head and stepped into his shorts. Then he reached for his soggy jeans.

"I've brought you some dry ones."

He jumped a foot, two feet—damn, he didn't know how high.

"M-Maggie?" he croaked, glancing around wildly.

There was a rustling from a thicket and Maggie stepped into the moonlight, holding out a pair of jeans.

"I saw you head for the creek. I thought you might be going to wash off. So when I got back to the house I went down to the bunkhouse and got you some dry things." She stopped, still holding the jeans, standing perhaps five feet from him.

The cold water had done no good at all.

One word in Maggie's soft tones, one look from Maggie's green eyes, and all Tanner's hormones were standing at attention again. Literally.

He muttered something desperate under his breath.

"What?" Maggie's own voice had a faint, breathless quality. She stepped closer. Her hand, still holding the jeans, dropped to her side. She ran her tongue lightly over her lips. Her wide eyes caught him as surely as he'd ever caught a deer in the sight of his gun.

Tanner's breath lodged in his throat.

She took another step. And another.

And then, when she stopped so close that their breath mingled and her breasts and his chest nearly touched, he couldn't help himself.

He bent his head and, trembling, touched his lips to hers. He drank of her sweetness, tasted her, urged her mouth to open for him, to let him in. He didn't stop to think. God knew he'd been thinking far too much. For weeks all he'd been able to do was think. And it hadn't done him one bit of good. He'd certainly never been able to forget.

From the moment he'd lain in the corral dirt and opened his eyes to see her standing over him, he'd wanted her.

He wanted her still.

And though he knew with just that one tiny shred of rational common sense that was left to him that what he wanted was wrong for both of them, right this instant he couldn't help himself.

He needed to hold her, to touch her, to taste her. He needed it with every fiber of his being, with every singing nerve, and every clamoring cell.

And Maggie didn't resist. On the contrary, she dropped the jeans and wrapped her arms around him, ran her hands up under the damp T-shirt against his back, stroking his shivering, burning flesh, making him shudder, making him need. He thrust himself against her, knowing it was all too obvious how much he desired her. There was no hope of denying it now.

Her fingers threaded through his hair, her lips melded with his. Her tongue slipped inside his mouth and sent him soaring with desire. He held her to him in the cradle of his thighs, reveled in the brush of her worn denim jeans against his bare legs. Her hands skimmed down his back again, toyed with the waistband of his shorts. He arched forward, pressing his arousal against her, moving, throbbing, needing.

"Yes," Maggie whispered. "Oh, yes." She feathered little kisses all over his face while he did the same to her, then their mouths met again with hungry desperation. "I love you, Robert. I love you."

The words cracked like a bullwhip against his conscience, jerking him back to reality, to a time larger than now, to a world that would go on after his hunger had been sated.

With every bit of resolve that he could muster, Tanner wrenched himself back, snatched his mouth from hers, held her body away from his. He gulped in great lungfuls of air, tried to calm the stampede of his heart, the thrum of the blood in his veins.

"Stop," he said hoarsely. "Got to stop."

Maggie stared back at him, dazed, as hungry as he, hurt etching her face, confusion filling her eyes. Her lips were parted in a tiny O so tempting that he wanted to kiss her again—and again—and never let her go.

But it couldn't happen. He couldn't *let* it happen.

"It's all right," Maggie assured him.

"It *isn't!*"

"But I do, you know, Robert," she said softly.

He gave his head a little shake, confused. "Do?"

"Love you."

He shook his head fiercely. "No. You don't. You can't! You don't know..." he said, his voice tight with anguish. He turned away from her, snagged the dry jeans off the ground and, stumbling, tugged them on, wincing as he zipped them up.

"You don't know," he repeated.

"So tell me." She looked at him with gentleness, with warmth, with all the care he'd craved for so long.

He shut his eyes, felt the cold air heaving in and out of his lungs, tried to get a grip on himself, didn't have much luck.

So tell me.

It sounded so simple. It was so damn hard.

He pulled on the shirt she'd brought him, too. His fingers fumbled with the buttons, buying himself time. But he knew he owed her some explanation, at least.

"You want a home," he began at last. "You said that from the first." His voice was ragged. He cleared his throat.

"Yes."

"I can't...do that."

"Why not?"

"I don't know!" he said, anguished. "Maybe it's a genetic failing. No, probably not. My old man seemed to have managed. Hell, maybe it's just me!"

"But how do you know you can't?" Maggie persisted.

"Because...because I've tried."

She looked at him, waiting, not speaking.

"I've been married."

There. He'd said it. Told her what he hadn't told anyone since he'd left Colorado. "And you can ask her," he went on bitterly. "She'll tell you I was lousy at it. She'll tell you I was never there when she needed me! Hell—" he took an angry swipe at his eyes "—you think I was negligent with this calf tonight. Clare was pregnant. She was having our baby. And I wasn't even there when she lost him!''

He heard the sharp intake of Maggie's breath, then felt her move close, put her arms around him. He should have shoved her away. God knew he didn't deserve her comfort. But he couldn't do it. He just stood there, trembling, aching, suddenly hurting more now for the loss of his son than he'd hurt fourteen years before.

"Can you tell me?" she asked softly.

And so he told her about coming home that night, about being relieved when Clare wasn't there. He told her everything about that day. It didn't come out at once. It came out in harsh, aching chunks. But he managed it all—until he got to the baby.

"I never—" his voice sounded harsh and strange even to him "—I never even saw him!"

It was the cry he'd never been able to share with Clare. He'd tried to be strong for her, to be tough and silent and forbearing, not saying a word lest she think he blamed her when he'd blamed only himself.

"If only," he'd said to himself a million times as he fixed fences, herded cattle, doctored pink eye, cut hay. *If only.*

But all the if onlys in the world couldn't bring back the son he'd never known, the home he'd hoped to make.

For years he'd pretended it didn't matter. Cowboying was enough. Moving on was fine with him.

Because he'd never given himself another choice. Meeting Maggie had forced him to face what he'd told himself he had no right to, forced him to confront the dreams he'd thought were dead.

He pressed his face against her shoulder, felt a

shudder shake him. Her arms tightened around him, held him fast and made him wish—*Oh, God, how they made him wish*—that he could risk a second chance.

Finally he pulled back, scrubbing at the dampness around his eyes with his hand, embarrassed. "Sorry," he muttered. He jammed his fists into the pockets of his jeans, ducked his head. "I shouldn't have done that."

"On the contrary," Maggie said softly, her hand still on his arm, not letting him go. "I think it's high time you did."

Tanner cleared his throat. "Maybe. But it... shouldn't have been you."

"No," Maggie said. "It probably should have been...your wife. You never told her, did you?"

"I couldn't. We didn't talk. We just..." He flushed, remembering what Clare's primary attraction was. "We were kids. Being married at that age, for us at least, was a joke. On us. We didn't know what we were doing. I had great hopes." He gave an ironic laugh at the young naive fool he had been. "But when—" his voice caught in his throat "—when the baby was born early, when he died...everything just...fell apart. I couldn't stop it."

"I know you, Robert. I'm sure you tried."

"Did I?" How many years had he wondered about that? He gave a harsh half sob, half laugh. "Sometimes I think I was just glad to get out, glad that he died!" He looked at her, expecting to see mirrored in her face all the self-loathing he'd lived with for so many years. His own anguish was unbearable. "Do you have any idea what it's like, thinking you're the kind of person who's glad his own kid died?"

And then she was holding him again and he really was crying this time. There was no way he could hide it or pretend he'd gotten something in his eye or anything else. He felt like the world's biggest jerk, but he couldn't help it.

Maggie didn't try to stop him. She just held him, rubbed her hands over his back, kissed his cheek, his ear, his hair. Then she fished in her pocket and handed him a handkerchief, as if it was a perfectly normal thing that he'd just done.

"Lots of guys break down and bawl in your arms?" Tanner said after he'd cleared his throat and could talk again. She might not be embarrassed for him, but he was embarrassed as hell.

"John did."

Tanner stiffened at her mention of Merritt. "When his marriage fell apart?" he asked gruffly.

"No. When we were in college his mother died."

"Oh." He felt like an even bigger fool. "I'm sorry. I didn't mean—"

Maggie laid a hand on his arm. "John and I are friends, Robert. We have been for a long time."

"You don't have to explain. It's none of my business."

"Yes, it is," Maggie told him, "because I love you."

"Don't say things like that." He turned away and, grabbing his wet clothes and pulling on his jacket, headed for his horse. Doggedly, Maggie followed him. "It's true. I think I fell in love with you the day I came. I watched you ride that black mare, watched her buck you off over and over—"

"Swell," Tanner muttered.

"—And I watched you get right back on. I admired

you tremendously. You had guts, stamina, commitment.''

He swung into the saddle. ''Yeah, where horses are concerned, I'm a regular marvel.''

''You sell yourself short.''

His teeth clenched. ''I see myself realistically. Horses are one thing, love is something else. I tried. It doesn't work. *I* don't work.''

''You were scarcely more than a child!''

''Just the same,'' he insisted stubbornly, ''I failed.''

''And you won't try again?'' She stood there looking up at him, offering him her heart. He could hear it in her voice, see it in her eyes. She offered him dreams and hopes, the promise of a future that he didn't dare contemplate no matter how much he wanted to.

He shook his head. ''I...can't,'' he whispered.

Her chin jutted. ''Can't? Or won't? Don't you want to, Robert? Or are you afraid?''

He met her gaze defiantly. Then, seeing the love in hers, he looked away.

''Don't push me, Maggie,'' he said, then touched his heels to the horse and rode off.

Seven

So now she knew.

It wasn't something he'd ever wanted to talk about. Certainly not to Maggie. But maybe it was just as well.

Now she wouldn't be thinking she loved him. Maggie MacLeod was no fool. It wouldn't take her long to realize she'd had a close call, that a relationship with a man like him would be the biggest mistake she could ever make.

Tanner knew he ought to be glad it had happened. But sometimes—just sometimes—when he saw her watching him from a distance, looking at him sadly, it hurt. He tried not to think about it. He tried to do his job, to teach Andy, to stay out of Maggie's way.

Why not? They had nothing to talk about except the ranch, and if he managed things right, he didn't have to say much to her about that. If she thought he was avoiding her, well, he was.

And now she ought to understand why.

But she looked at him so unhappily. Damn, did she think he wanted to be this sort of man?

He was grateful when the time came for him and Andy to take the cattle up to the summer pasture. It would require several days, days when he wouldn't have to see her watching him from a distance, days that his gut wouldn't clench at the sight of her, and his heart wouldn't ache because now she knew the worst.

Ordinarily this trip was made during one of Tanner's favorite times of the year. He looked forward to being out on the range, to the wilderness, to the solitude, to the genial companionship of the one or two men who came with him.

But going with Andy made it hard. The boy had learned a lot. He was quick and eager and determined, always asking questions, always trying to help.

Like his sister. Too damned much like his sister. It was bad enough having Maggie constantly in the back of his mind. It was worse having Andy along to remind him even more of her.

Tanner knew he was being curt with him, that Andy didn't know why, that he thought it was something he'd done that was making Tanner stay away from him as much as he could.

Tanner couldn't help it. He excused it by telling himself it was better for the kid to learn how to handle things on his own.

"Remember," he said, sending Andy in the other direction. "You learn by doing. I can't do it for you."

And if Andy sometimes looked at him a little warily and a little sadly, too, well, that was just too bad.

The kid was learning. He was like his sister that way, too. Tanner knew that Maggie would have made Abby proud of her. She'd be proud of Andy, too. He didn't stop to consider what she'd think of him.

Watching the kid now, as they herded the last cow across the track and up through the forest into the high, verdant meadow, Tanner thought he'd done all right.

Andy shut the last gate, then leaned back in the saddle and took off his hat, surveying with proprietary pride the settling herd. He rubbed the sweat from his forehead with one grimy hand and grinned, then glanced over at Tanner. His gaze was still a little wary, as if he was unsure of Tanner's approval.

"That's it?" he asked.

"That's it."

"So we did it?"

"We did it." Tanner rode over to the creek and slipped out of the saddle to dip his neck scarf in the water and wipe his face. The icy water trickled down his neck.

Andy joined him and did the same, then he clapped his hat back on his head and whooped loud and long.

"What was that for?"

"'Cause I'm finally a cowboy." Andy grinned, tasting the word, savoring it on his tongue. Then he stopped and glanced hesitantly at Tanner. "Aren't I?"

Tanner nodded. "You could say that."

"Would you say it?"

Tanner looked at the young, freckled face, at the green eyes so like Maggie's. In them he saw hope and faith in the future, purity, innocence and self-esteem. All the things he'd once had. He hoped to hell Andy got to keep them. "Yeah, Andy, I would."

"It's 'cause of you, Tanner. Learn by doing. I do everything you do."

"Don't, for God's sake, do everything I do," Tanner said gruffly, swinging back into the saddle.

Which was good advice, because moments later, he fell off his horse.

"Tanner what?" Ev's eyes bugged. He stared, stupefied, first at Andy, then at Tanner riding into the yard slowly, his face white and pained, his left arm wrapped tightly against his chest and held in place with Andy's shirt.

"The cinch broke," Tanner muttered, embarrassed beyond belief.

He saw Maggie come out on the porch, take one look at him and start running. He cursed under his breath.

"Hold his horse," she instructed Billy, then she looked at Tanner. "I'll help you down,"

"I don't need help." He clenched his teeth, clutched the saddle horn for balance and swung down. White-hot pain shot through his arm and shoulder as his foot hit the ground. He couldn't stop the expletive that passed his lips as Maggie's arm slipped around him.

"Easy," she soothed. "Give me a hand, Ev. We'll get him to the truck."

Tanner made a feeble effort to shake them both off. But he was light-headed, almost groggy with pain. He winced as Ev helped him into the pickup.

"Where to?" Maggie asked Ev.

"Casper. He's prob'ly broke something."

"I dislocated my shoulder."

"Again?" Ev grumbled.

"Does he do it often?" Maggie asked.

"Usually I can pop it back in. This time I... couldn't."

Maggie turned to Ev. "Call ahead and tell them we're coming."

"Ev can—" Tanner began.

But Maggie just slid behind the wheel. "Let's go."

In terms of sheer pain, the trip to Casper was less awful than riding down the mountain. But sitting next to Maggie for an hour, trying desperately not to disgrace himself by puking or fainting, was sheer hell.

He was just congratulating himself on having made it when Maggie opened the door of the truck in front of the emergency entrance and he put his feet on the ground. The world begin to shift. From a long way off he saw Maggie move toward him and heard her say, "Wait a sec—"

The world didn't wait. It came up to meet his face.

There was apparently no end to the ways he could make an ass of himself in front of Maggie. But why, he wondered, if he was going to faint, didn't he have the good sense to stay out for the duration?

Why did he have to come around as nurses and orderlies were picking him up, as Maggie was saying, "Mind his shoulder," as some helpful busybody was unbuttoning his shirt and undoing the snap of his jeans to help him breathe?

He struggled against them, but the pain stopped him dead. He sagged and shut his eyes as they lay him on the cart.

"Has he fainted again?" Maggie asked.

He wished to God he had.

"Take him into the examining room," he heard one of the nurses command. "And if you'll just come with me, I need some information...."

And that, Tanner thought, got rid of Maggie. He breathed easier for the first time since she'd come out of the house.

He felt himself being rolled into one of the examining rooms. The door shut. Through his closed lids he could sense the glare of the overhead lights.

Nurses bustled, muttered and clanked things. Drawers opened and shut. Then the door creaked again. Heavy footsteps approached.

"Well, hell, Tanner," said a jovial masculine voice. "You again. Thought I told you I'd seen enough of you this year."

"Hullo, Brent." He didn't bother to open his eyes. "I tried to put it back myself."

Brent Walker had done his share of stitching and patching Tanner during the past three years. He'd put the shoulder back before, too.

"Roll this way." Brent patted the side away from Tanner's damaged shoulder, and carefully Tanner did as he was told, until he was lying on his face. He still hadn't opened his eyes. He didn't need to. He knew what was going to happen.

Brent took hold of his arm. "Just a little shot to make it hurt less. Marybeth?" More footsteps; a stool moved. Then the cool swab touched his back. A needle pricked and stung.

After a few moments Brent said, "Okay, Tanner. Ready? Hang loose now."

Two pairs of hands held him steady. He knew exactly what would happen next and braced himself. He dug his face into the starched pillowcase and wished for purchase for the toes of his boots. Cool fingers touched his right hand. He gripped them fiercely, felt Brent move his arm, pull and—

"Hell!"

Involuntary tears sprang to his eyes. He crushed the hand he held in his.

"All done," Brent said cheerfully. "You can open your eyes now."

Tanner did.

Maggie was sitting on a stool just inches from him, her fingers locked tight in the grip of his hand.

He muttered an oath under his breath. "S-sorry." He tried to loosen his fingers. They barely worked.

She chafed them lightly with hers. "It's all right. Are you okay now?"

"I'm fine." He shifted around and started to sit up. The world was still unsteady.

"Take it easy," Brent said, catching him by his good arm. "You don't want to go fainting again."

"I'm not going to faint," Tanner said irritably. "I was just a little light-headed earlier. It'd been awhile since I ate."

"Right." Brent handed him a sling. "Wear it for a week. And sit still. You're not finished yet. While we've got you here, we might as well let these lovely ladies clean you up."

Tanner didn't know what he meant until one of the nurses eased his shirt clear off and two others started dabbing at his face and his neck and a spot on his head. Then he realized that when the cinch gave he'd suffered a bit more damage than just his shoulder. He was scraped from his neck to his ribs. He tried to sit stoically under their ministrations. Maggie watched avidly.

"You don't have to stay," he said.

"I don't mind."

"I thought you were filling out forms."

"I don't know much of your personal history."

She knew more than anyone else, Tanner thought.

"Anyway, they said you could do it after." She didn't move an inch. She waited until they were finished cleaning him up, until they had rebuttoned his shirt, trussed him up in the sling and, to his chagrin, had even refastened his jeans for him. Then, after he'd filled out the forms and swallowed two of the pain pills Brent gave him, she pocketed the rest and followed him out, like a herd dog with a balky steer.

"He'll be sore for a few days," Brent told her just as if Tanner were her child. "Looks like he whacked his head, too. Have someone keep an eye on him for the next day or so."

"See I don't fall off my horse again?" Tanner growled.

"You won't be on a horse for a few days," Brent said firmly. He turned back to Maggie. "Make him sleep, but wake him up every few hours. You got to keep an eye on this guy. Last spring it was his knee. This is the third or fourth time with the shoulder. Don't know if he's accident prone or what."

Tanner shot him a dirty look.

"He's a pretty good horseman usually. But, well—" Brent grinned "—I think every now and then he figures he needs a little TLC."

"The hell I do!"

"And with such a pretty new boss—"

"I still got one good arm. I can break your nose for you, Walker!"

"He gets a mite nasty when you call him on it, though," Brent said without missing a beat. "Humor him a bit. He won't malinger long."

"I've never—!"

"Shh, Robert." Maggie took his good arm and drew him along toward the exit. She was smiling at him, amusement lighting her eyes. "He's just teasing."

Tanner didn't think it was funny.

"Robert?" he heard Brent say behind him.

Maggie glance over her shoulder. "That's his name."

Brent cocked his head. "Well, I'll be damned."

The pain pills made him groggy. He caught his eyes closing and his head slipping sideways half a dozen times at least. He jerked upright again, wincing, damned if he was going to fall asleep and wake up to find his head on Maggie's shoulder. Or worse, and probably more likely, her lap.

"You ought to rest," Maggie said.

"I'll rest when I get back."

"Ev will make up the bed in Abigail's room. It won't take long."

"I'm not sleeping there! I live in the bunkhouse."

"You're supposed to have someone to watch you."

"Andy can watch me. He lives there, too." There was no way he was staying in the house with her. It was bad enough seeing her at a distance.

"Don't be ridiculous."

"I'm staying in the bunkhouse. If you don't like it

fire me. If you won't fire me, I'll quit." He glared at her, defying her to argue with him.

For a minute he thought she was going to. But finally she sighed. "Fine. Be muleheaded. Stay in the bunkhouse."

"I will."

"Robert?"

"Uh?"

"Robert?" A hand touched his arm.

"Wha—"

"Robert, can you open your eyes?"

He blinked, dazed, into the darkness. Where the hell was he? "Who?"

"It's me," the voice said. "Maggie."

Maggie? Agitated, he started to sit up, then the soreness stabbed him again and he sagged back against the pillows, blinking up at the woman who bent over him in the darkness. "Wha' the hell are you doing here?"

"Checking on you."

"Andy—"

"Andy has to get up earlier than I do. He's doing your work now, too, remember?"

Tanner scowled. "Thanks for reminding me."

"Sorry. Are you all right? Do you need more pain pills?"

"No." Which was a lie.

"Doesn't it hurt?"

"Like hell."

"Well, then—"

"I don't want 'em. They make me stupid."

"Oh, is that what's causing it?"

He frowned. "I don't like the way they make me feel."

"But can you sleep without them?"

"I could if people didn't keep wakin' me up. Go away."

She didn't say anything, nor did she move. His shoulder was throbbing. His head ached. And he knew damned well she wasn't going to leave without stuffing the pills down his throat.

"Oh, hell. Give 'em to me then."

At least she didn't say "I told you so." She got a glass of water, then held it to his lips while he took the pills.

"If you need anything else, just call."

"I won't bother Andy." He would have rolled over and turned his back on her, but his shoulder hurt too much.

She woke him one more time before sunup. This time he was quicker coming around and he knew right away who it was.

"Damn, you're taking this serious, aren't you?" He glowered at her in the predawn dimness.

"Just checking." She smiled. She looked like an angel again. He shut his eyes.

"Wakin' Andy, too, probably," he muttered.

"Andy's getting plenty of sleep."

"So can you. Leave me alone." This time he did roll over, even though it hurt like hell.

So he was rude. So he shouldn't have been so abrupt with her when she was only trying to help. But damn it, he didn't need her help! He needed her to stay away.

"G'way," he muttered.

"What?"

"Are you still here?"

She leaned over him again. "What's wrong?"

"You, damn it. Hovering. Go away and let me sleep."

She touched his hair lightly. A shiver ran through him. "Go to sleep then, Robert."

"Tanner," he muttered. "Tanner, damm it."

"Whatever you say, darling," Maggie whispered.

Oh God, were those her lips touching his hair?

The sun was up the next time he opened his eyes. This time Maggie didn't wake him. She was asleep herself. In Andy's bed.

Tanner blinked, disbelieving. He shook his head, felt it pound, a result of the fall and the painkillers. But even through the fog that was his brain, the image didn't change.

Maggie was there.

He eased over onto his right side and lay shoved up against the pillows, just looking at her. He knew she shouldn't be here. A part of him was furious that she was. And another part of him, the part that had for so long ached after her, simply wanted to look his fill.

The temptation was too much for him. She lay curled on her side facing him, one hand gripping the blanket, hugging it against her breasts, the other tucked under her cheek. Her gorgeous hair was loose and tousled, dark auburn against the white pillowcase. Her lips were slightly parted, curving in a tiny smile. Tanner's tongue touched his own lips, which felt suddenly dry.

There were dark circles under her eyes, as if she hadn't had enough sleep. No surprise there. She'd been bouncing up like a jackrabbit all night to see if he was all right.

And he hadn't even known she was there.

Ev and Andy had helped him to the bunkhouse. Ev had helped him get undressed. Andy had gone up to get some supper, offering to bring him some. But Tanner had said he just wanted to sleep—and he had, not even remembering when Andy came back.

Obviously, Andy hadn't come back. Maggie had.

And had slept less than three feet away from him all night. Nursemaiding him. And unless he got up and got himself dressed before she awoke, she'd probably insist on dressing him, too.

He eased his aching body around so that he sat on the side of the bed. His head felt as if some blacksmith had set up shop inside and was working three shifts. He would've liked to sit there and get his bearings, but he knew she'd wake up and find him if he did.

He hauled himself to his feet, grimacing when the bedsprings creaked, expecting any moment to see Maggie's wide green eyes flick open. Thank heaven she merely sighed and shifted slightly, then puckered her lips as if she were giving someone a kiss.

Tanner averted his gaze. Then, with his arm against his chest, he walked carefully toward the bathroom.

He would have liked to take a shower, but he was sure the noise of the spraying water against the shower stall would wake Maggie. So he contented himself with brushing his teeth and slopping water on a cloth and scrubbing his face and torso, all the while trying not to do more than he had to with his sore shoulder.

When he'd finally dried off, he crept quietly back into the bunk room and reached for his jeans.

"I hope that doesn't mean you're planning on getting dressed."

He jerked around, swearing from the pain in his shoulder. Maggie was still lying on her side, but those wide green eyes were open now and fastened right on him. He grabbed his jeans from off the chair.

"What the— Of course it does!" He bent over, lifting one foot, trying to stick it into his pant leg, a difficult business since he could hold the jeans with only one hand. He lost his balance.

Maggie leapt out of bed wearing an oversize T-shirt and nothing else. "Sit down!" She grabbed him by his right arm and hauled him down onto the bed next to her, so close their bare thighs touched.

Out of the corner of his eye he could see the rise and fall of her breasts beneath the thin cotton. It wasn't something he should have noticed. Not if he wanted to keep his sanity. Both of them were breathing too damn hard.

"Go back to bed, Robert," she said after a moment. "You need the rest."

"Hell of a lot of rest I'm going to get with you waltzing around the bunkhouse half naked!"

Color flamed in her cheeks. "I was not waltzing! I was trying to take care of you."

"I don't need taking care of."

"Right. You're so tough and so capable and so perfectly fine on your own, aren't you?"

"I try," he grated.

"And you're determined to be that way forever."

"I have to be, and you know it."

"I don't." She touched his knee and his whole body stirred in response.

"Stop it," he said through his teeth.

"I don't want to stop it. I love you."

"What are you trying to do to me?"

"Get inside those walls you've built up around you. Break them down. Set you free." There it was again, her heart right there in her eyes, ripe for the taking.

"Damn it, Maggie!" He raked trembling fingers through his hair. "How the hell long do you think I'm going to be able to go on resisting?"

"I don't know," she said softly. "How long are you?" A faint line of color touched her cheekbones, but she didn't look away. And then she leaned toward him slowly and, keeping her eyes wide open, watching him every instant, she touched her lips to his.

Her mouth was sweet and warm, beckoning him, drawing him in, assuaging his desperate hunger, yet deepening it at the same time.

And Tanner was powerless to resist.

He'd fought too long, too hard. There was no fight left in him. He could only taste and touch and savor, could only open his mouth and press his lips even harder against hers, surrendering and conquering at the same time.

But even that wasn't enough, just as he'd known it wouldn't be. He wanted more. And more. He bore her back onto the bed, his mouth still locked with hers, his body clamoring for equal time. His shoulder ached, limiting what he could do, bludgeoning him with reality, and for an instant he pulled back.

But Maggie still looked at him, still beckoned him. She lifted a hand and lay it against his cheek, stroking his two-day-old beard softly. Her thumb ran lightly across his lips. "Robert, stop fighting it. Come to me."

Some needs were too great, some aches too deep. If she was willing—if even knowing the worst of him, she still wanted him—he couldn't say no.

Her small nipple erect beneath the cotton begged to be tasted. He touched it with his lips.

She shivered. "Yes, Robert. Yes!" Then, instead of holding herself still and compliant, she lifted her hands and slid them down to skim along his sides, to trace the line of his ribs, to brush lightly across his chest. The feel of her fingers on his bare skin was like fire, burning and arousing.

He slid callused fingers under the hem of her shirt, drawing it up so he could see her breasts, so he could watch them peak and see the way they trembled as he touched them gently, as he bent his head and laved them with his tongue. He wished his shoulder didn't hurt so much. He wished he had full use of both his arms and hands to give her all the pleasure he'd dreamed of giving her.

But he didn't have a long time to wish or to concentrate on his hurts. Maggie was sitting up now, pressing kisses against his chest, touching him lightly with her nails, then with her tongue. She set off tremors that centered his passion, his need for her.

"Maggie! Don't! You're going to—"

She stopped, her hands still against his chest as she looked up into his eyes. "You don't like it?"

"God, yes, I like it. It's going to... I'm going to..." He gave a shaky half laugh, half sob. "I like it way too much. We gotta slow down."

She smiled, a catlike, enigmatic smile. "So we'll slow down."

She leaned forward and pressed a kiss against first one of his flat nipples, then the other, then she splayed her hands against his chest and he fell back, at the same time reaching for her with his right arm to draw her on top of him so that she straddled his thighs.

The shirt had slipped down again and he pushed it up. Maggie grasped it by the hem and pulled it over her head in one sensuous movement, then tossed it aside. Then she settled against him again, still smiling, her breasts bare to his gaze.

He couldn't stop looking, couldn't stop touching. There was a fine tremor in his fingers as he grazed the peaks of her breasts, as he made her shiver, as he made her smile.

He remembered the first time he had seen her: she had been looking down at him like this. She hadn't been smiling then; she'd been worried, concerned. Caring.

He saw that care in her eyes now, along with the smile. It made his heart lodge in his throat. No woman, not even Clare, had looked at him quite that way before—as if he were everything she'd ever hoped for.

He wasn't. He knew that. So did she.

She had to know. But just now, he needed to pretend. Just for the space of a few moments, a few hours, he wanted to be that man for her.

Again his fingers lifted to touch her, to trail lightly across her breasts, to draw a line down the center of her, slowly and deliberately, rough calluses against silken soft skin. Down, down, until at last, well below her navel, they reached the thin bit of material that were her panties.

His mouth crooked in a grin. He'd never known schoolteachers wore such scandalous panties.

Whenever he'd imagined undressing Maggie MacLeod, and despite his best intentions he'd done his share of it—why else would he have so many scars from mending fences this year?—he'd always stripped away her sweaters and jeans, her blouses and skirts to find serviceable, no-nonsense, white cotton underwear. Schoolteacher underwear.

Not underwear like this.

Never in a million years would he have imagined Maggie in panties that were no more than this scrap of peach-colored lace.

He swallowed, contemplating them and the woman who wore them, this woman who had tempted him beyond his endurance, who was more mysterious and more desirable than all the other women he'd ever met. She sat very still, watching him, waiting for him to make another move.

He couldn't wait. He slipped his fingers beneath the elastic. The back of them brushed lightly against the smooth, warm skin of her belly. The tips touched the soft curls at the apex of her thighs. His fingers gripped the lace and drew it down. Maggie moved to accommodate him, to let him draw the panties down her legs, wriggling free of them. Then coming back to straddle him again, she slid her own fingers down his chest to feather across his abdomen, to slip beneath the confines of his briefs.

She touched him. One simple touch and he almost lost control. He'd waited so long, daydreamed so much. He'd felt it in his mind a thousand times before—and a thousand times he'd never come close to imagining the reality of her hand on him. It was soft, gentle, feather light. It teased, it tantalized, it tormented. And then it grew bolder, firmer.

"Mag-gie!" Her name was a hoarse exhalation of breath, strangling him. His fingers sought her warmth, her moisture. He saw her bite her lip as he teased her, opened her. She grasped his briefs and tugged them down and he lifted his hips to make it easier for her.

And then he was free, the cool morning air touching his heated flesh as it ached for her to touch him, to stroke him again, to let him into the warmth of her body.

She was ready for him. He was sure of it, could see it, could feel it. He needed to do one thing, though, first.

"Maggie! In my jeans. My wallet."

She frowned, then seemed to realize what he was asking for. She reached down and snagged his jeans off the floor, got out his wallet and gave it to him.

With fumbling fingers Tanner took out the foil package he'd bought in anticipation of the wet-T-shirt contest.

"Show me how," Maggie whispered.

He sucked in his breath. "Like this." Then he shut his eyes as she did it, struggling desperately for control. He was right on the brink, and she'd barely finished when he muttered, "Now! Let me in! Please, Maggie. I can't wait any longer."

Maggie eased herself up. Her hair fell forward, obscuring her face, as with both hands this time, she drew him toward her, guiding him. He nudged against the very center of her, felt her warmth, her welcome. He bit his lip.

"There," he muttered. "No. Yes. Yes. There."

"Help me," Maggie whispered, and Tanner's hand came to meet hers, seeking, finding, easing him in.

"Yes." It was a hiss through his teeth. Sweat beaded his forehead as her tightness began to close around him. He drew her down, thrusting upward as he did so, needing to be inside her—a part of her at last. She tensed. He felt a sudden barrier, stopped, and then couldn't stop any longer.

His hips surged up to connect them completely. With one hand he touched her breasts and teased her nipples, while with the other he began a gentle exploration of the petal softness at the juncture of her thighs. He smiled as his touch made her writhe and squirm. He gloried in the heightened pink of her cheeks, in her lips, full with the passion of arousal.

She moved more quickly now, and Tanner moved with her, caught in a storm of longing he'd never before experienced, captured by a woman he didn't understand, sensing a completeness he'd never known before, but wanted to know again and again.

He felt Maggie's body contracting around him, felt her shudder and tremble and grip him for all she was worth. "Oh! Oh, Robert!"

And he surged into her one last time, spending his passion within her, then sank back onto the mattress, shattered, and gathered her against his chest.

He didn't know how long they lay like that. He felt her heart thundering against his, stroked her back with still-trembling hands. Maggie nestled her head in the curve of his neck and shoulder. Then, as her breathing slowed, she lifted her head and raised her body slightly away from Tanner's chest to look down at him and smile.

She brushed his hair off his forehead.

She traced the line of his brows, trailed a finger down his cheek, tickled the corner of his mouth, making his lips curve into a smile.

She kissed his nose.

"I love you," she said.

And Tanner closed his eyes and hung on to the moment, knowing all too soon it would be gone. He couldn't pretend any longer.

His time had run out.

Eight

It was a long time since he'd gone down the road. Too long. He should've left the Three Bar C sooner. Four years was too long to stay in one place. It made a man lazy, soft.

It was wide open spaces a man really needed. A pickup, a trailer, horses, a saddle. Those were the things that mattered. Nothing else.

Better not even to bother saying goodbye. Who knew? Maybe he'd see them all again someday. Or maybe not.

Tanner drew a deep breath, then let it out slowly, felt the cool night breeze on his arm as it rested on the door of his truck. He was doing the right thing. The only thing.

He'd let Maggie breach his final defense. He had nothing left.

With luck she wouldn't realize he was gone until

morning. He could be a couple of states away by then. Not that he expected she'd send out an APB on him. Hell, when she thought about it, she'd be thanking her lucky stars she'd made such a narrow escape.

And it wasn't as if anybody else would care. Ev and Billy were a pair. They'd be fine without him. And Andy—Andy for whom he'd left a note saying, "You've got what it takes to be foreman"—Andy would be thrilled.

There was Abby, of course. But he'd stopped at the cemetery as he'd driven past. It was almost pitch-black, only a sliver of moon hanging in the canopy of stars, but Tanner had made his way unerringly until he came to stand by the granite marker at Abby's grave.

"I tried," he said after a moment. "I did the best I could. And if it isn't good enough for you, I'm sorry. The way I see it, I had a choice: I could fail you now or fail Maggie later."

He didn't wait around to see if Abby might say something from on high. He got back in his truck and headed south.

It didn't take him long to realize that going down the road was different this time. The anticipation was gone, the eagerness to see new places, try new things.

It would come back, he told himself. It had been four years since he'd taken more than a few days off; he would need a little while to adjust.

He wasn't in any hurry to find another job. There was money enough to get by until more work was available in the fall, so he just drifted around. He visited some old friends in LaJunta; he dropped in on an old rodeo traveling partner who had a little spread near Farmington. He left his horses and the trailer there, figuring to pick them up in early fall. Then he headed back north as far as Cheyenne for Frontier Days to watch his brother, Noah, ride.

"Son of a gun!" Noah exclaimed when Tanner knocked on his motel-room door. He reached out and dragged his brother into the room, where five other cowboys lounged in chairs and on the beds. "You remember Tanner, don'tcha? What're you doin' here? I stopped in at your place to see you on my way down. They said you'd quit." Noah looked as if he didn't quite believe it.

"I did."

"Come on. Let's walk down by the pool." He steered Tanner back out of the room and toward the swimming pool. "What the hell'd you leave for? Thought you loved that damned ranch? Couldn't even pry you loose to come down to Cheyenne last year."

"I had work to do last year."

Noah lifted a dark brow. "Ranch learn how to run itself in the meantime?"

"I got fed up. You heard Abby died…"

Noah nodded. "Yeah, I meant to call and tell you I was sorry. But, hey—" he grinned "—she gave you a hell of a replacement. That Maggie's a good-lookin' gal."

"You talked to her?" The words were out of Tanner's mouth before he could stop them.

"Sure. Had dinner with her as a matter of fact. We went to that good little place down in Kaycee."

"You took her out?"

"Sure. Why not?" Noah gave his best imitation of a leer. "When have I ever passed up a pretty woman?"

"As long as having dinner with her is all you did!" Tanner said tightly.

"Ah, like that, is it?" Noah flopped down in one of the lounges and grinned up at his brother. "Open your mouth."

"What?"

"I want to see the hook."

Tanner gritted his teeth. "It's not like that. I just know what you're like—and I don't want you messing around with Maggie. She's a lady."

"Reckon you messed around with her."

Tanner reached down and grabbed his brother by the front of his shirt, dragging him to a sitting position. "We were not 'messing around!'"

Noah looked at him, shaken, then gave him a faint grin. "Whatever you say, big brother." He eased Tanner's fingers away from his shirtfront and swung his feet around so he sat with his forearms resting on his knees. He looked up at Tanner, his expression serious. "I don't get it. She looks stricken every time she talks about you. You practically punch me when I even mention you gettin' together with her. What's goin' on?"

"Nothing."

"Look me straight in the eye and tell me that again," Noah said. It was what their father always used to say to them when he suspected a less-than-truthful reply. Tanner had never been able to lie to his father. He didn't find it much easier to lie to Noah.

"She thinks she loves me," he muttered.

Noah gave a low whistle. "Heavy stuff."

"Yeah."

"Do you think you love her?"

"I try not to think about it!"

"Ah. Yeah, I know how that works." Noah grimaced, and Tanner remembered that for plenty of years his brother had fancied himself in love with Lisa Pickney, a tawny-haired barrel racer who hadn't been interested in him. In the end, all Noah had been able to do was try not to think about it.

"Anyway, it doesn't matter if I do or not," Tanner said finally. "I'm not getting married again."

"Why not?"

"You remember what happened with Clare."

"Yeah, so? Maggie's not Clare."

"But I'm me."

Noah scratched his head. "Whatever that means. It's too deep for me, big brother. Still, I think you're nuts. I sure as hell wouldn't be runnin' the other way if I had a looker like that thinkin' she loved me."

"You'd get married?"

"If it was a girl like Maggie."

There was nothing Tanner could say to that. He shrugged. Noah regarded him curiously, as if he might be able to understand what drove his brother if only he looked long enough. Tanner could have told him not to bother.

"I just need a change," he said finally. "I thought I might go out and see Luke after you win Cheyenne." He managed a grin.

Noah grinned back. "Yeah...when I win Cheyenne. Well, a guy can hope. Be a good idea, you goin' out to see Luke. I saw him a while back. He drove up to Santa Maria when I was there for a rodeo. He, Keith and Keith's girl. But you better go quick. They're leavin' for location in mid-August, I think."

"Location where?"

"Don't know. It's a western, he said. One of those

gutsy hell-bent-for-leather types that are making a comeback. Or at least Mallory hopes they are. Might be New Mexico or Texas. Hell, it might be Spain for all I know. Luke gets around.''

"Maybe I'll go with him.'' Spain might be far enough away to get red hair and green eyes out of his mind, Tanner thought as he stretched out on one of the lounges.

"You oughta go see Clare.''

Tanner sat bolt upright. "Why the hell should I do that?''

Noah shrugged. "So's you can get on with your life. Hell, the way I see it, brother, you're still married to her.''

"I am not still married to her! In many respects,'' Tanner added in a low voice, "I don't think I ever was.''

"Maybe. Maybe not. But I'll tell you one thing, you're a damned fool to throw away a chance with a woman like your Maggie.''

"When did you start givin' marital advice?''

"About the time you stopped having the sense God gave a goose.''

"Well, if you're going to spend the rest of the week giving me advice like that, I think I'll skip staying around to see you ride.''

Noah smiled and stretched his arms above his head, wincing as his muscles complained. "I've said my piece. Now it's your turn. You got to think about what I said.''

Tanner thought about it more than he would have liked. Though Noah never brought up Maggie again, it was as if she was right there with them for the rest of the week. There were pauses in the conversation, occasional periods of silence that were somehow filled with memories of her, visions of her. Tanner was glad when the week was over.

"I tried to win for you," Noah said. He was nursing a black eye, courtesy of his own flying fist. But he was standing in the pay line.

"You didn't do so bad." Tanner said. "Made the short round. Finished third. Pretty respectable, I'd say."

"I do what I can," Noah said modestly. "You leavin' now?"

"Uh-huh." Tanner shook his brother's hand. "Reckon I'll see you sometime. Where you gettin' your mail?"

"Durango." He gave Tanner the box number.

"I'll drop you a line, let you know where I end up."

"Do that." Noah hung onto Tanner's hand a bit longer. "Tell you what I'd rather have you send me."

"What's that?"

"A wedding invitation."

Fortunately, Luke didn't know about Maggie. And if he was surprised to see his brother turn up on his Southern- California doorstep early one August morning, he gave no sign.

"I'm not...interrupting anything?" Tanner asked as Luke, looking bleary-eyed and wearing only a pair of shorts, stepped back to let him in.

One corner of Luke Tanner's mouth lifted. "Think I've got a bedroom full of starlets, do you?"

"Maybe I was hoping." Tanner tossed his duffel bag on the floor and looked around.

Luke's house, a Spanish-style two-story stucco

only feet from the wide white sand of the South Bay, was a far cry from the sort of place Tanner was used to. And if the house wasn't enough, the silver Porsche in the driveway and the customized Harley next to the back door attested to his brother's affluence and fast-lane life-style.

"Well, I'm sure I can find you someone suitable," Luke said after a moment. "Just let me know what you have in mind."

But the only thing Tanner had in his mind was Maggie. Everywhere he went, there was Maggie. Before he'd spent the week with Noah, he hadn't been able to forget her. Noah, having seen her and formed his own opinions, made it impossible to forget her. But even the sights and sounds of Southern California didn't seem to be able to blot her out of his head.

"I need some sleep," he told Luke, who obligingly pointed him in the direction of a bedroom.

But sleep brought dreams here just as it had everywhere else. And the dreams brought Maggie.

Luke didn't ask him any questions. He took Tanner to the set with him, to parties with him, to the beach and even down to Mexico for a few days of deep-sea fishing. He introduced Tanner to a bevy of beautiful women, most of whom stared and simpered and were fascinated with the notion that he was "a real cowboy."

Tanner threw himself into everything Luke thought up, hoping that it would occupy his mind, but somehow there was always a part of that mind wondering at every moment what was happening back on the Three Bar C, whether Andy was coping, whether Ev and Billy were well, whether Maggie was remembering him the way he remembered her.

Finally, after three weeks and no improvement, Tanner decided it was time to move on.

"You don't have to go," Luke told him. "I'm off for Utah on Monday for the new movie, but you can stay in the house as long as you want."

But staying in one place, even such a single man's paradise as Luke's version of Southern California, wasn't going to solve Tanner's problem. Apparently play of any kind wasn't going to solve it. He needed to get back to work.

Haying wasn't any cowboy's idea of a dream job. It was a measure of Tanner's desperation that when his friend Gil, the rancher near Farmington, said, "Don't suppose you'd like to help with the haying, would you?" that he practically jumped at the chance.

Gil looked at him, taken aback. "Should I call the doctor?" he asked his wife.

Jenn shook her head. "Not for this kind of sickness."

"I'm not sick," Tanner said flatly.

"No," Jenn agreed complacently. "You're in love."

"Why the hell would you say a thing like that?"

Jenn smiled. "I know the signs. Moody, depressed, can't eat or sleep. If California couldn't snap you out of it, you're in pretty bad shape, Tanner. And when you actually agreed to help with the haying, well—" she shrugged "—there isn't any doubt."

"I just want to help out an old friend," he muttered. "Even if the old friend has a nosy, interfering wife."

Jenn laughed. "Whatever you say, Tanner. Whatever you say."

But haying, however tedious, hard, hot and monotonous it was, didn't help either. After a week and a half, he was no closer to forgetting Maggie than he'd ever been. It was because it didn't sufficiently occupy his mind, Tanner decided. He needed a challenge.

"I'm goin' up to Durango next week and ride a bronc," he told Gil.

"Are you nuts? You haven't rodeoed in years. You'll wreck your knee. Or dislocate your shoulder again. Or break your neck. Then again—" and here Gil, who had come to believe all Jenn's preposterous speculations, looked at Tanner closely "—maybe that's what you want?"

"Don't be an ass," Tanner grumbled. "I signed up a couple of weeks ago. Figured if I didn't want to, I could turn him out. Are you coming?"

"To watch you get bloody and broken? No, thanks."

So Tanner went by himself.

"You're coming back after, aren't you?" Jenn asked him.

"If Noah's there, I'll probably go down the road with him a spell—"

"Check out a few hospitals," Gil put in dryly.

"Thanks for your confidence," Tanner said in a sour tone. He got into his truck. "You don't mind keeping the horses and trailer awhile longer?"

"We'll put it on your tab." Gil grinned.

Tanner gave him an answering grin. "I reckon you owe me for all that haying."

"That was therapy," Gil said. "I oughta have charged you. Would have, 'cept it didn't do much good, did it?"

"Not yet," Tanner said heavily. "See you around."

Noah was in Durango. He rode and won. Tanner rode respectably. He got sore, but not bloody. His shoulder stayed in place. His knee didn't cave in.

"Not too bad for an old man," Noah told him afterward over a beer. "You serious about traveling with me for a spell?"

"Yeah." He was. Because riding took total concentration. For eight seconds he hadn't thought of Maggie at all. It was a start.

Going down the road with Noah was serious business. They traveled the length and breadth of all the western states, hopped a plane to someplace in Alberta one Thursday night, flew back to Albuquerque the following evening, got in the truck and drove again after the rodeo. Tanner did them all, praying that his knee would endure, that his shoulder wouldn't slip. It was insane. Unlike Noah, he had no possibility of contending for the NFR. It was just another form of therapy, another way of trying to fill his life, to forget the Three Bar C and Ev and Billy and, most of all, Maggie. It was just a little more drastic than anything he'd attempted yet.

He tried not to moan when he got up in the morning. He tried not to groan when he got out of the truck after hours on the road. The only time he balked was when Noah said they were going to Bluff Springs.

"It's not a big deal," Tanner argued. "You can miss it."

"I'll be damned if I'll miss it. I drew Haverell's Hotshot."

Tanner understood. Hotshot was an NFR bronc. Any cowboy who drew him would be a fool to turn him out and lose a chance at an almost-sure win, especially a man who was currently eleventh in the standings like Noah. It was a long time till November. A lot of horses. A lot of miles. A lot of rides. And you never knew from one day to the next what would happen.

Most of the time you were fine. Sometimes, as Tanner knew all too well, you weren't. So you hoped. You drove. You flew. You rode. And you took every day as it came.

They went to Bluff Springs.

And Tanner hoped he wouldn't run into Clare.

His own horse in Bluff Springs was called Deal's Rampage. "A twister," Noah told him. Tanner's shoulder had survived so far—just barely. It didn't survive his encounter with Rampage. In fact, he felt it pop almost as soon as the chute opened. The horse twisted hard to the right, ducking his head, spinning, and Tanner, as he hung tight, couldn't stand the strain.

Clutching his arm against his stomach, he made his way out of the arena.

"Want me to call the doc?" Noah asked him. He'd already ridden, had scored an 87, and they didn't have to be in Salida until tomorrow. He was more than willing to look up a doctor. The Emergency Medical Technicians, too, were standing around looking hopeful.

Tanner shook his head. He gritted his teeth and tried popping his shoulder back in. The pain almost blinded him. A curse escaped his lips.

"Let's find a doc," Noah said.

"You can put it back in," Tanner said. He led the way to the truck, had Noah drop the tailgate, then he lay down on it and let his arm dangle. "Pull it," he commanded.

Noah shuddered.

"Pull it," Tanner said again.

Noah pulled.

Tanner fainted.

"Hello, Tanner." The voice was soft and had just a hint of a southwestern lilt to it.

Tanner blinked again, staring up at tall trees, white clouds, blue sky—and Clare. He frowned, tried to lift his arm to rub a hand across his eyes, felt the pain, remembered what had happened and winced. Carefully he looked around. He was still lying on the tailgate of the pickup, though he was on his back now. He could see Noah over by the fence, working studiously on his rigging, ignoring them. Mostly he could see Clare.

"Russ fixed your shoulder," Clare told him.

Russ. The doctor who'd delivered their baby. The man who had encouraged Clare out of her depression, who'd gotten her interested in something again, who'd helped her achieve it. The man who'd believed in her, supported her. Married her.

Tanner didn't say anything. He couldn't have if his life depended on it.

"We'd brought the boys to the rodeo," Clare went on rather quickly. "I had no idea you were...I mean, I never thought..." She colored slightly and looked away, then back at him again. "Anyway, when you fainted, Noah made them call for a doctor."

"The EMTs?" Tanner asked hoarsely.

"They were busy with a barrel racer. Russ is with

them now. He left me to watch you. Can I—can I get you something to drink?"

Tanner shook his head and swung his legs around, trying to sit up. He felt dizzy and disoriented. He didn't want to see Clare at the best of times. He sure as hell didn't want to see her now.

He glanced again at Noah, remembering what his brother had said he ought to do, wondering if Noah had somehow engineered it. At the same moment Noah glanced over at him. Their eyes met, Tanner's bleak, Noah's challenging.

Tanner turned his head.

"It's...been a long time," Clare said finally.

"Yeah."

"You're looking good. Other than the bruises, I mean." She colored again. "It's awkward, isn't it?"

"Uh-huh."

"It always was," Clare said after a moment. "We never much talked."

"No." Tanner stared at the toes of his boots. "My fault, not yours. You talked. I was too young and too dumb," he said finally. "I thought it would all work out without us having to say anything."

It was as much as he had ever admitted to her, and it had come well past the time when it would do any good. But he knew that, no matter what, he had to say it, had to clear the slate between them.

"I was as bad as you," Clare said ruefully. "We had unrealistic expectations. And you had enormous responsibilities, far too many for someone barely twenty. I wanted to help you, but I just became another one. I'm sorry."

"Don't apologize," Tanner said hoarsely. "For God's sake, don't do that! If anybody should be apologizing, it's me. I was...I was never there for you. Or—'' he swallowed painfully and looked up to meet her eyes ''—for the baby. I'm sorry.''

Tentatively, Clare reached out and touched the back of his hand. He saw that hers was strong and capable, callused now. A working woman's hand. She had matured just as he had. More, probably. She had moved on, married, had children. He turned her hand and clasped it in his. His eyes blurred. He blinked, waiting until his vision cleared before he dared look at her again.

"So you're a nurse?"

She nodded. "I held you while Russ popped your shoulder back in. I didn't even flinch." She smiled at him.

"Why would you?" he said with a small smile. "I was the one who was hurting."

"You didn't even know it," she reminded him.

They looked at each other for a long moment. He remembered what a lovely girl she'd been. She was still attractive, but somehow what he'd felt for her didn't compare with what he'd come to feel for Maggie. Was it a matter of adolescent hormones versus adult attraction? he wondered.

He hesitated, then had to ask, "Are you happy?"

Clare's gaze flickered toward where the ambulance was parked and then toward a pair of boys now talking to Noah. Then she turned back to Tanner. "Yes."

"Are those your boys?"

"Yes. Dan's nine. Kevin's five."

They were fair like their mother, tall like their father. Tanner wondered what his child with Clare would have looked like. He felt his throat grow tight.

He had to swallow twice before he could say, "Good-lookin' kids."

"Thank you." She paused. "Do you have any?"

He shook his head.

"Are you married?"

"No."

"Never? Haven't you ever married, Tanner?" She cocked her head, looking at him with concern.

He looked away. "No."

"Is it…" she hesitated "because of us?"

He wanted to lie to her. He couldn't. He shrugged. "I don't think I'm cut out for marriage. I didn't do a very good job of it."

"Neither of us did," Clare said.

"You made a success of this one."

"And you haven't tried." She said it softly, but Tanner could hear the gentle accusation. "That's the one thing I never thought about you, Tanner."

"What's that?"

"That you were a quitter."

"I thought," Tanner said casually to Noah the next morning, "I might head north, see about gettin' a job again. It's almost time for roundup and I sure as hell can't ride broncs."

Clare's husband, Russ, had made that plain yesterday afternoon. He'd been cordial and very professional. He'd asked Tanner about the shoulder, heard how many times it had slipped out and told him he was crazy to think about riding anymore. He'd mentioned surgery and stress exercises, and personal responsibility and adult behavior. Tanner had gotten the point.

But worse than the threat of surgery was the mem-

ory of Clare's words. *I hadn't thought you were a
quitter.*

He hadn't thought he was a quitter, either. A non-
starter, maybe, where Maggie was concerned, but
he'd only been protecting her. Hadn't he?

Or had he been protecting himself?

The question was enough to have kept him awake
all night, tossing and turning, cursing the pain and
then the painkillers that Noah insisted he take.

"Sounds like a good idea," Noah said now.
"Where you thinking on goin'?"

Tanner shrugged. "Reckon I'll see what opens
up."

If Noah suspected what he really had in mind, he
was tactful enough not to talk about it. "We're
headin' toward Durango again Monday," he said.
"You can pick up your truck."

He stopped in Kaycee for gas and a little recon-
noitering. He wouldn't just drive into the Three Bar
C without scouting out the lay of the land. Hell, he'd
told himself half a hundred times on the drive north
that for all he knew Maggie had gotten fed up and
packed it in. Maybe she wasn't even on the ranch
now.

"Well, how do you like that? Tanner's back!"
Rufe at the gas station said. "Where you been, you
ol' son of a buck?"

"Here and there," Tanner said, pumping the gas.
"Just goin' down the road."

"Back to stay now?"

"Hard to tell. When's the roundup at the Three Bar
C?"

Rufe blinked. "You mean you don't even know?"

"Told you, I've been gone. Why? Is somethin' wrong?" Tanner felt anxiety come boiling up.

"Naw, not now. Kid had a rough time for a while, but he said the other day he figured it was the best thing you coulda done for him—tossing him in an' hopin' he'd swim." Rufe grinned.

"Andy, you mean? Slicker?"

Rufe spat on the ground. "That's the one. You don't need to call him that anymore though. Reckon he's earned a new name."

Tanner smiled and finished filling the tank. Well, at least the place hadn't crumbled. And Andy seemed to have earned the locals' respect.

"They started rounding up this week," Rufe said. "Sure they'll be glad to see you, 'specially Maggie. She was always sweet on you."

"Was she?" Tanner wondered and dared to hope.

It looked the same as he drove in. It looked warm and welcoming. It looked like home. And in a few moments he would see Maggie. His heart pounded. His palms felt damp and his mouth drier than the high-plains desert. He parked the truck alongside the house and went up the back steps.

He put his fingers around the doorknob, then stopped. He remembered the first time he'd come to see Maggie here, when he'd belonged and she hadn't. He licked dry lips, then lifted his hand and knocked.

It was a full minute before he heard footsteps. The door opened. Maggie stood in front of him with her glorious red hair and her beautiful ivory skin, with her scattered freckles and her kissable lips. But there was no smile on those lips, no welcome at all. And in her eyes there was none of the joy he'd seen so often, that he'd actually come to expect to see whenever she saw him.

She looked stunned.

It was nothing compared to how he felt himself. Even though he hadn't been able to forget her for almost three months, he still wasn't prepared for the intensity of the longing he felt the moment he saw her again. It was magnetic, the pull he felt toward her. And only the coldness in her eyes and the sight of John Merritt at the kitchen table kept him right where he was.

"Maggie." His voice sounded a little rusty.

"What do you want?" Hers sounded like cold steel.

To hold you, he thought desperately. *To kiss you and love you. To start over and try again.*

"A job," he said. It was all he could think of. He couldn't say what he wanted to say—not now, not when she was looking at him like that, not when Merritt was sitting there looking at him.

"Just drifting through?" she said, her tone hard.

No, damn it, he wanted to yell at her. *I'm back forever! I'm back to stay.*

But he couldn't get the words past his lips. He clenched his fists at his sides and gave a little shrug and a half smile. "More or less." It was wrong, all wrong, and he knew it. He should never have come. He should have known better.

When was he ever going to learn that he didn't know heads from tails in a relationship? Maggie didn't want him there, not after what had happened between them.

He tucked his hands into his pockets and turned

away. "Never mind," he said and started down the steps.

"Wait."

He stopped halfway down and turned to look up at her.

"All right. You're on. We ship on the eighth. I'll pay you for two weeks, starting tomorrow. You know where the bunkhouse is."

Nine

There were three other guys staying in the bunk-house. Andy wasn't there. He'd moved back to the house a couple of months ago, according to Maggie. It was the one bit of information she'd volunteered. Otherwise she'd been as cold and impersonal as a cigar-store Indian.

She didn't seem to feel anything for him. It was as if what had happened between them had happened between two other people completely. She'd turned back to talk to Merritt. There was nothing left.

At least in Maggie there wasn't.

Tanner wished the same was true for him. But if he'd spent half the way back hoping he wouldn't feel a thing and the other half afraid that he wouldn't, he now knew beyond a doubt that he loved Maggie MacLeod.

And he couldn't tell her so. Not when she looked

as if she would shoot him between the eyes if he tried. No, that wasn't true. She looked as if she would stare at him as if he were speaking a foreign language, then walk away.

It was just as well Andy wasn't in the bunkhouse when he came in, he thought. He didn't know how Andy would feel about him being back. He didn't know what Maggie had told him about the circumstances under which he'd gone.

The note he'd left had been as noncommunicative as he could manage. He'd written something about wanderlust and moving on, about being sure Andy could handle things.

He'd tried to write a note to Maggie as well, but no words had come. There had been no way to tell her what he felt. And in the end, he'd convinced himself she'd know why he had gone. She knew better than anyone except Clare how bad he was at relationships.

Had she told anyone else? he wondered. Had she told Merritt?

But if Maggie didn't care at all, Andy was delighted to see him. The boy's face broke into a wide grin when he rode up to the barn that evening and spotted Tanner.

"Hey, Tanner! You're back! Fantastic! Have you seen Maggie? Did she tell you about the mare? Did she show you how Grace has grown? Did you see the sheep?"

Tanner let the questions flow over him, basking in Andy's welcome, wishing his sister had given him a tenth of the enthusiasm. But then, he reminded himself, he'd never hurt Andy the way he'd hurt Maggie. He had no right to expect more from her.

"I just got here, Slicker," he said, then grinned. "I hear you don't deserve the nickname anymore."

Andy beamed. "Who told you that?"

"Rufe."

"I hope it's true."

"Rufe wouldn't have said it if it wasn't."

"Well, then, I owe it all to you. You taught me and then let me do it on my own. Not many people would have had that kind of confidence."

Tanner ran a hand against the back of his neck, discomfited by Andy's endorsement of what had been no more than desperation on his part. "I didn't know," he said roughly. "You might have blown it."

"I might have," Andy said. "But so far I haven't. And with you back to help with the round-up, I reckon I won't. You are stayin', aren't you?"

"For the roundup."

"That's all?"

"We'll see," Tanner said.

Andy flung an arm over his shoulders. "Well, come on, we'll go up to the house and have something to eat."

Billy's enthusiasm equaled Andy's. He launched himself at Tanner from the top of the porch. Catching him against his still-sore shoulder, Tanner winced.

"What's wrong?" Andy asked.

"Pulled my shoulder out again a week or so ago." His gaze strayed to Maggie, who was sitting on the porch peeling and dicing apples for sauce. He was remembering the last time he'd hurt his shoulder and how she had spent the night with him. He remembered what had happened after that night, too.

Maggie's face was carefully blank. She kept right on peeling and dicing and didn't even look at him.

"Is it okay now?" Andy asked.

Tanner nodded. "I'll be able to put in a full day's work if that's what you're worried about."

"It's not," Andy protested. "We don't care if you work or not. We're just glad you're back, aren't we?"

"You bet," Billy said.

Maggie didn't say a word.

Tanner wasn't sure whether anyone else noticed that she didn't talk to him all evening or not. There were enough other people around that the conversation never lagged. Stoney and Wes, two of the hands who were sharing the bunkhouse with him, were there for dinner, and Maggie talked at length with them. She talked to Andy about the sheep and to Ev about who would cook what meals. She helped Billy with his math after dinner, and spoke at length on the phone with someone. Tanner didn't know who. Merritt probably, because he wasn't there.

But she never spoke to him. Never even looked at him.

Not until he was leaving. As he was going out the door to head back to the bunkhouse, he spoke to her directly. "You got anything special you want me to do tomorrow?"

Then she looked at him. "Ask Andy. He's the foreman."

As it happened, Andy asked him. The boy had learned a lot over the summer, but he'd never directed a roundup before. And as the days passed and the cattle needed to be rounded up and brought down, he spent a lot of time conferring with Tanner.

"I know it's a lot to ask," he apologized. "I mean, me bein' called foreman, and asking you to tell me what to do, but—"

"I don't mind," Tanner assured him. He was happy to help. It gave him the illusion that he was contributing something, that he wasn't completely wasting his time. He'd never have gotten that feeling if he'd had to depend on just the few encounters he had with Maggie.

Maggie acted as if she didn't know he was alive.

He tried to get Ev to talk, but Ev wasn't talking much, either.

"How've things been while I was gone?" he said the first time he could actually nail Ev down, which wasn't until the evening of the third day he was there.

Ev was putting up tomatoes for winter and he clattered his jars and lids and tongs for a considerable time before answering. He eyed Tanner at length over the tops of his wire-rimmed glasses. "If you'd cared," he said finally, "you wouldn'ta left."

Tanner, who'd been hoping for a casual conversation that he could lead around to finding out a little more about Maggie's attitude toward him, had a pretty good idea of what Maggie's attitude was just from that.

"You're sore I left."

"Oh, hell, no," Ev said, banging the lid on the canning kettle. "Why should I be sore? I figured you was undependable all along. Never could understand why Ab trusted you."

"That isn't true," Tanner said quietly. "You trusted me as much as she did."

Ev turned and glowered at him, hands on his hips,

chin jutting over the top of his tomato-stained white apron. "So I'm a fool, too."

"I couldn't stay," Tanner said finally. He traced a line on the linoleum with the toe of his boot.

"Yeah, I know. 'Cause you were yellow."

The stark words speared him. Tanner opened his mouth to deny it, but knew he couldn't. "Maybe," he admitted. He rubbed his hand against the back of his neck, trying to ease the tension in his muscles. "Maybe I was."

"So what're you back for now?" Ev demanded.

"Maybe I found some courage."

Ev snorted. "Did you?" He didn't sound as if he believed it for a minute. "And you expect Maggie'll welcome you with open arms?"

"She already didn't," Tanner said tightly.

"Yeah, well, unlike some of us, Maggie ain't no fool."

"No," Tanner said heavily. "She's not."

But he was. He had to be, to keep hoping this way. She certainly gave him no encouragement. He worked long and hard every day, bringing cattle down, sorting them out, teaching Andy how to separate them and shape up the herd for market.

The only reward was the work itself. It gave him a sense of accomplishment that he'd forgotten in the months he'd been gone. He'd missed that, too.

He'd missed the ranching, the planning, the labor, the sense of feeling tired but fulfilled at the end of a hardworking day.

He'd missed taking Gambler into the high country and just looking over the land, watching the colors shift, the shadows shrink, then lengthen. There was no place on earth he'd ever loved the way he loved this land. He'd never realized how tied he'd become to the Three Bar C until he didn't have it anymore. For the last three months he'd been lost. He'd gone down the road with never a thought to what he'd left behind. Now he realized that he'd missed the ranch almost as much as he'd missed Maggie.

And having it now was a bittersweet pleasure at best, for in little more than a week the roundup would be over, he thought as he cooled down Gambler Friday evening before supper. If Maggie hadn't softened toward him by then, he would be no better off than he had been before he came.

In fact, he'd be worse.

"Supper will be in half an hour," Andy told him when he came out of the barn. "Mag's running late tonight. Duncan just got here. He's come to help out."

"Duncan?" That surprised Tanner.

Andy grinned. "It's catching. Ranch fever, Ev says we've got. Dunc came back a couple of times after you left in the summer. He's turning into a pretty good hand."

Tanner's mouth quirked into a grin at Andy passing judgment on anyone's ability as a hand. "I'll take a look at him tomorrow," he promised.

"Do that. You want to play Scrabble with us after supper?" Andy asked eagerly, then his expression took on a downcast turn and he shook his head. "I suppose you're goin' into town with Wes and Stoney and Jim?"

As a matter of fact, Wes had invited him to come along that morning. All three of the younger men were looking forward to a Friday night in Casper.

Tanner told himself he'd probably be better off if he took them up on it. He'd certainly get a warmer welcome at any bar in Casper than he would in Maggie's living room.

"I'll play Scrabble," he said. It was what amounted to a last-ditch effort. Maybe she would talk to him, give him an opening, and after the game he could suggest that they take a walk.

The first part of his hoped for scenario actually came to pass. Maggie did speak to him.

"I thought you didn't like games," she said, fixing him with a hard stare as he came in the door and approached the table where she and Andy and Ev were sitting, the Scrabble tiles spread out before them.

"A man has the right to change his mind," Tanner said. He smiled at her, hoping for an answering one. She looked down at her tiles. He took the seat opposite her, stretched out his legs and collided with hers. Hastily Maggie pulled back.

"Hey, Tanner," Billy said from where he was sitting with Duncan on the floor. "Duncan's teachin' me about gravity and magnets and stuff. You wanna see?"

"After, okay, sport? Andy tells me you're helping out this weekend," he said to Duncan.

"Doing what I can," Duncan replied. He seemed to bear Tanner no ill will. Obviously Maggie hadn't talked to him either. He turned back to Billy and began drawing something on the pad in his lap.

"Well, let's get on with it. Never thought I'd see the day I'd be playin' Scrabble." Ev said it as if it were a dirty word. "Ab an' me used to play poker. Well, I looked up some words today so's I'd have a chance against all you smart folks. Let's play."

The "smart folks," Tanner figured out pretty quickly, didn't include him. He wasn't verbal at the best of times, and this wasn't one of those.

But it would have helped if he'd had some notion of what he was doing. As it was, he might have fared just as well if the tiles were in Greek.

He just watched Maggie. He remembered the way she'd looked the night he'd come upon her in the field delivering the calf. He remembered the way she'd felt when she'd surprised him as he came out of the creek. He remembered the way she'd welcomed him into her arms, into her body when—

"Damn it, Tanner," Andy said. "I said it's your turn."

"Huh? Oh, er, right." He stared blindly down at the tiles before him, his body tight, his mind shattered. Desperately he shoved some tiles onto the board.

"There."

Andy frowned. Ev scratched his head. "What's that?"

"*Guppy*," Tanner said. "It's a fish." At least he thought it was.

"*Guppy* has two *p*'s in it," Maggie said.

He blinked at her, busy contemplating her lips, remembering their taste.

"You misspelled *guppy*," she said sharply.

"Oh." Hot blood rushed up his neck into his face. He retrieved his tiles and tried again. All he could think of then was *puck*, but he didn't have a *k*, so that was out. He shoved the tiles around this way and that.

"Ain't there a time limit?" Ev complained. "You're takin' forever."

"Fine," Tanner snapped. He shoved a pair of tiles

into place, settling for *up*, which netted him a whole four points. But given his current state of mind, he knew he ought to be glad he'd thought of that.

He tried to catch Maggie's eye whenever she looked up. She never looked his way. He tried to make small talk.

"So, how're the sheep doin'?" he asked.

"I need to concentrate," she said.

Tanner sighed, fidgeted, adjusted his jeans. "You're doing a lot better than the rest of us without concentrating," he said gruffly.

She didn't answer him, just laid her tiles out neatly, then shoved her hair out of her face and leaned her chin in her hand, waiting. Tanner stared at her, fascinated.

"Tanner! Damn it, it's your turn again!" Andy almost shouted at him.

One time, by chance, while he was fumbling with his tiles, he glanced up and caught her looking his way. Their eyes met for only an instant, but it was still there—the connection he'd felt from the first moment he saw her. "Maggie." He breathed her name.

Abruptly Maggie pushed back her chair. "This game has gone on forever. I quit. I'm tired," she announced. "I'm going to turn in."

Andy stared at her. "You can't quit. It's the middle of the game. And anyhow, it's only nine o'clock!"

"If you don't want to play Scrabble we can do something else!" Tanner said desperately.

But it didn't do any good. Maggie was already up the stairs.

It was torture. Pure and simple torture. Being with Maggie and not having her, not sharing a smile with her, a few words, the touch of a hand. He should have left.

He couldn't. She was as necessary to him as the air he breathed. He waited every day for some sign that she still felt the love she'd once claimed to feel for him. And every day his fears and his disappointment grew. He'd never worked harder or suffered more in his life. Not even after his son had died and his marriage had failed.

He couldn't count the number of times he watched her from afar and thought, *Please, Maggie. One look. One smile.*

He never got another chance.

He saw her every day, but never alone. She was halfway across a pasture from him or she was coming out of the barn as he was going in. She was at the other side of the kitchen or the other end of the dinner table. And the night before the trucks came to pick up the cattle, when he volunteered to dry the dishes she was washing, she shook her head.

"No, thank you. It's not your job."

"I know that. I don't mind. I like doing dishes!" he lied.

She didn't laugh at the absurdity of his statement. She just took a towel, dried her hands, waved her arm in the direction of the sink and gave him a little bow and smile. "By all means, then, be my guest. I'll call John and discuss what I should be doing for the sale with him."

And she left him with a sinkful of dirty dishes while she went into the living room and talked to John Merritt on the phone.

He didn't think anything could hurt as much as that had.

This is my herd, he wanted to yell at her. *I bred them, I raised them, I took care of them.*

But he knew what she would say in turn. *You left them. You left me. You had no right to come back.*

So he washed the dishes and wound up breaking a glass in the dishwater. He was twisting a rag in the glass so hard that he cut his hand open and watched the blood turn the water red.

It hurt, but not as much as listening to the soft sound of Maggie's voice talking about the herd, the ranch, the future with Merritt.

And then it was over.

Two weeks gone in the blink of an eye. The last of the cattle loaded. The last of the trucks gone.

Tanner stood in the yard and watched until he couldn't see them anymore. Wes took off right after the trucks did, got his pay, grabbed his gear, shook hands all around and headed west.

"We're goin' to a movie," Billy told Tanner. "Me and Maggie and Granpa. Down in Casper." They got in Maggie's little white car. She didn't even look at him as she walked past.

Stoney and Jim and Duncan left next. "We're goin' out an' hang one on with The Perfesser," Jim said, clapping Duncan on the shoulder.

"You want to come?" Stoney asked Tanner.

He probably should—to deaden the pain a little. He shook his head. "Not this time."

"I'll go," Andy said hopefully.

"And sit on the curb all night if they're checkin' IDs?" Duncan said.

Andy sighed and watched their truck as it bounced down the road toward town. "One more year," he muttered, then brightened. "Actually only five more months."

Tanner, looking at him, couldn't ever remember being that young.

They stood together in the waning sun until there was nothing but silence left. "You want to play a game of Scrabble?" he asked Andy.

Andy looked at him, startled, then blushed. "Well, actually I've, uh, got a date. You know Jack Bates's sister..."

"Mary Jean."

Andy grinned. "Yeah. She's pretty cool. She, er, rented a couple of videos and invited me over." He hesitated. "You can...can come if you want."

Tanner smiled ruefully. "Thanks, but I don't think I've quite got to the third-wheel stage yet." But it seemed he was getting close. He turned and started toward the bunkhouse.

"Tanner? What happened between you and Maggie?"

The question stopped him in his tracks. It was the first time Andy had even suggested he knew there was anything wrong. The youth shrugged awkwardly and came toward Tanner.

"I'm not blind, you know. She was hurt bad when you left. Real bad."

Tanner swallowed. "She might've been hurt worse if I'd stayed."

"How? What do you mean?"

Tanner shook his head. "It's none of your business."

"Maybe not." Andy chewed on the inside of his cheek. "Is it hers?"

Tanner nodded.

"So have you told her?"

"Haven't had a chance."

"You've been here two weeks!"

"She won't talk to me."

Andy made an exasperated sound. "Have you tried?"

Tanner, feeling cornered, shifted from one foot to the other, then rubbed the back of his neck. "Aren't you late for your date?"

"Maybe I am," Andy said. He gave Tanner a pointed stare. "And I wouldn't want to hurt Mary Jean's feelings. Not the way you hurt Maggie's." He turned and started toward the house.

"It isn't the same damned thing," Tanner called after him in the growing darkness.

It wasn't. It was a thousand times worse.

She paid them off in the morning. She sat at the kitchen table and wrote out checks, handing them to each of the hands in turn, always with a smile, a kind word and her thanks.

"You did a wonderful job," she told Stoney. "I'll see you next fall, I hope."

"I appreciate your help," she said to Bates. "You've really come through for us all year."

"I can't tell you how happy I was that you were here to help out. Come back next year," she said to Jim.

One by one they thanked her, too, tipped the brims of their hats and went out.

Until only Tanner was left.

Maggie bent her head, ignoring him standing there two feet from her. All her attention was focused on filling out his check. She finished writing her signature with a flourish, tore the check off and held it out to him. Her bright green eyes met his squarely for the first time since he'd arrived two weeks ago.

Tanner ran his tongue over his lips, a million words inside him screaming to get out, a million things he had to tell her, a million feelings he had to share.

"Maggie." His voice was barely a croak.

She pushed back her chair and stood up, her eyes now nearly level with his. She shoved the check toward him again, her impatience obvious. "Your check."

He didn't know what else to do; with nerveless fingers, he took it.

"Thank you, Tanner," Maggie said, her voice flat. "Now goodbye."

Ten

Until he loved, no man was ever lonely.

He'd never understood that until now. Solitude was one thing, Tanner thought, leaning his arm on the open window of the pickup and driving south. Loneliness was something else.

Loneliness was having a damned crater where the pit of your stomach used to be. It was having a constant ache at the back of your eyes, a soreness in your throat, a wild and desperate longing that wouldn't go away.

She'd dismissed him with five words. But two had said it all.

She'd called him Tanner. And she'd said goodbye.

She'd never called him Tanner before, not in all the months he'd known her. Right from the first she'd smiled and called him Robert. Even when he'd protested, had insisted that everyone called him Tanner, still he'd been Robert to her.

He wasn't now.

And it hurt.

God, he'd never realized how much love could hurt. He thought he'd hurt after his divorce from Clare. He didn't know the half of it. Clare had been under his skin. Maggie was a part of his heart.

But he wasn't a part of hers. Not any longer. He'd killed whatever love she'd felt for him. She'd practically shoved the check into his hand. And then, while he stood, rooted, staring at her, she'd flipped her checkbook shut and said, "Excuse me, please. I'm late. I have an appointment for a haircut in town."

And she'd gone.

She brushed right past him out the door, went straight to her car, got in and drove away. Tanner stood in the doorway, stunned.

And what could he do then but leave as well?

He'd packed his gear, hitched his trailer, loaded his horse and headed out. Going over the ridge toward the highway, he'd run into Andy taking some of the cattle back to the north pasture. His riding was easy now, his movements sure. He'd come a long way in the last few months. He'd do fine.

They'd all do fine.

Except him.

Andy stopped him, looked at the trailer, at Gambler's nose poking through the slats, then at Tanner leaning on the steering wheel. "Does this mean what I think it means?" he'd asked.

"Roundup's over," Tanner said with as much nonchalance as he could muster.

"So you're going?" Andy's voice was heavy.

Tanner gave an infinitesimal nod of his head.

Andy just looked at him. "You're a fool."

Tanner didn't have to be told.

He made it to LaJunta by nightfall. He had friends there. He could stop, rest, eat, sleep. He drove on. If he kept going he could be in Texas before the sun came up.

And what was in Texas?

Nothing.

Everything he loved was behind him. Texas—and the future—stretched out ahead of him, bleak and cold.

Ahead of him there wasn't a town for miles. He couldn't see a ranch, nor a windmill, nor a cow. As far as he could see ahead of him, he was alone.

He'd been alone before. After Clare he'd thought it was what he wanted—to be free, not to care.

But, damn it, he did care. He cared so much it was tearing him apart. He'd never been able to tell Clare how he felt about anything—their marriage, their child, their divorce. He'd always hoped she'd tell him.

And this time when he'd come back, when he'd seen Maggie there with Merritt, all the things he'd wanted to say to her had fled. He hadn't been able to tell her anything, either. He didn't have enough confidence in himself.

And so he'd worked, and bided his time and suffered in silence. And then, because he'd gotten no encouragement, no warmth, no declaration from her, he'd given up, left without talking.

Just the way he had with Clare.

Was he really going to make the same mistake again?

* * *

It was dawn when he pulled into the yard of the Three Bar C. There was a light on in the kitchen. Ev, probably. Maybe Andy.

At least Tanner hoped so, because all of a sudden his mouth was dry and his stomach roiled. Having great resolutions for spilling his guts had been fine in the middle of nowhere, but the thought of actually having to go through with them was scary as hell.

He gripped the steering wheel until his knuckles showed white, took a couple of deep breaths that he hoped would steady his frazzled nerves, then got out of the truck.

The kitchen curtains twitched, but he couldn't see who was behind them. He shut his eyes, gathered his courage, opened them again and knocked on the door.

It jerked open almost at once and Maggie, in her robe, her hair now short and shaggy, stared out at him. Her lips tightened. A muscle in her jaw twitched. "Now what?"

"I want a job."

She blinked. "Roundup's over," she said shortly and started to shut the door.

Tanner stuck his boot in to hold it open. She glared at him. He went on, "I know that. I want more than that."

Her eyes widened, then her chin tilted stubbornly. "Andy's my foreman. I told you that."

"Fair enough." He was getting his bearings now, settling in.

"I can't afford to hire any other cowboys except seasonally."

"I don't want seasonal work. I want full-time."

"I have Bates. He's dependable."

"No more dependable than I am."

"I can't—"

"I want you. I love you. Marry me." This last came out in a rush. He didn't mean to simply blurt it out that way. He would have liked a little more finesse, a little more of a percentage that she wouldn't throw him out on his ear. He should have known he'd blow it. He'd never be a talker, not even to save his life.

Maggie stared at him. "What did you say?" Her voice was hollow. Her face was white.

Tanner's was red, and he knew it. And Maggie could see it this time. There was no darkness to hide behind.

There was nothing left at all anymore. He'd laid it all on the line. His body. His soul. His heart.

Over the hill he could hear the faint sounds of cattle. Down by the barn birds were singing. The coffeepot perked and the old mantel clock gave its quarter-hour chime.

Tanner couldn't look at her, could only wait. He shifted his weight, stared at the toes of his boots, at the worn boards of the porch. Then, finally, he lifted his eyes to meet hers, terrified of what he would see.

Her own eyes were downcast. She gave her head a little shake. Then, slowly, she reached out a hand and drew him inside. Her fingers were as cold as the room was warm. He could feel them shaking. Or, he wondered, was the tremor in his own?

He pushed the door shut behind him and stood facing her, their hands still joined. Then she loosed her grip on him and he felt immediately bereft, abandoned. But then her hands came up and skimmed over his sides, brushed across his shoulders and down his arms. She seemed to need to touch him, to be sure he was solid and real.

Then, "You love me?" she whispered. She sounded dazed when at last she looked at him.

He nodded wordlessly, swallowing hard, holding himself still under the brush of her hands.

Her gaze became more intense. "You want to come back to stay. Permanently?"

God, yes. Forever. He nodded again. "If you'll have me," he said, his voice little more than a croak.

"And you want to marry me? Th-that's the job you wanted?" Her voice broke on a half sob, half laugh.

"I want to marry you." He said it again, slowly this time, looking straight at her, offering her his heart with his eyes, offering her all he had been and, with her help, all he hoped ever to become.

And then he saw it. There! In her eyes he saw glowing once more the love she'd given him time and again. The love he'd spurned and scorned and rejected, the love that had scared him and freed him and, finally, brought him home. The love that until now he had always pushed away.

This time he didn't. This time he reached for it, reached for Maggie and pulled her close, bowing his head, feeling the tears sting against his lids as he crushed her hard and fast in his arms. And her arms came equally hard and fierce around him, locking him in so tight that he wondered if he would ever break loose and hoped he wouldn't.

"I never knew..." he whispered raggedly. "I never understood—"

"I know. I know."

"I was too much of a fool!"

"You're not."

"Not now, maybe. I was. And I will be again if I don't have you. Please, Maggie. There's so much I want to say, but it's so hard. I want to try. I want to succeed this time. I can't do it without your help. Please, say yes."

And Maggie said, "Yes."

Cowboys don't stay in bed till noon. They don't scandalize old men and young children and their future brothers-in-law. Unless, of course, they're too far gone in love to think straight and redheaded women have enticed them beyond all their power to resist.

But Tanner had driven all night, he'd laid his heart on the line, and when Maggie had taken his hand and drawn him with her up the stairs, he didn't know about all the other cowboys in the world, but he was damned if he was going to say no.

He did manage to protest a little. "What's Ev gonna think?" he whispered worriedly as they crept up the stairs and passed the old man's closed door.

"That you've finally come to your senses," Maggie said and pulled him into her room.

"And Billy?"

"He's too young to care."

"And Andy?"

"Andy's already out with the herd. He'll never know." She halted just outside her door and turned to look at him. "But we'll stop right here if you want to."

Tanner could hardly wait to wipe that impish grin off her face. He pushed her gently through the door and shut it behind them.

Maggie stepped back and lifted her face. She raised

her hands and laid them on his chest, then looked into his eyes, her own green ones wide and expectant.

Tanner smiled and bent his head. He was much better at nonverbal communication.

Their loving was by turns gentle and desperate, eager and tentative. They kissed and stroked, gazed and worshipped, touched and teased. And Tanner began to appreciate once more the joy of Maggie's body. But while an appreciation of the physical Maggie MacLeod was where he'd started all those months ago, he found that what he really valued was Maggie's spirit, her soul, her boundless capacity to love.

He wanted to lose himself in her, to know her as intimately as he had once so briefly known her. But, because he really was trying, first Tanner talked.

They were curled together in the quilt on Maggie's bed, her head resting on his chest, his fingers stroking her ear and hair to let their passions cool a bit, let their rampaging hearts slow down.

Finally Tanner lifted his head enough to press a kiss onto the top of hers, then he lay back again and swallowed, trying to decide where to begin.

"I can't believe I'm really here," he said at last, because that more than anything was really what he felt in his heart.

Maggie raised her head and their eyes met. Hers were a warm jade now, with nothing left of the coldness he'd seen in them over the past two weeks. "I can't, either," she said softly. "I never believed you'd come back."

"I had to. Besides, I did come back before," he reminded her.

"But you didn't say anything."

"Merritt was here."

Maggie looked at him horrified. "You mean you would have said you loved me then? Why didn't you? I told you John was a friend."

"I know. But you were looking like you wished I was dead. It seemed like a big mistake."

"You stayed anyway."

"I couldn't leave," he said simply.

Maggie drew her finger down his cheek wonderingly. "Then later, after John left...why didn't you tell me?"

"Every time I saw you, you glared at me. If looks could've killed I'd have been six feet under."

"I was afraid...of what I felt for you."

Tanner stared. He hadn't thought it had happened to her, too. "Then you know how I felt."

Maggie nodded. "I was afraid I'd betray myself before you left again. I almost did when I gave you that check."

"I wish to God you had."

"But...what happened? You did leave. And then you came back. What changed your mind?"

Tanner lifted one shoulder in an awkward shrug. How could he explain what he didn't know for sure himself?

"It was Texas, I guess," he said at last.

"Texas?" Maggie rolled over to lie looking at him, her chin resting on her arms, which were folded across Tanner's chest.

He stared up at the ceiling, remembering how he'd felt out there in the middle of nowhere, when the vastness of a world without Maggie had really hit him.

"It's where I headed when I left. I don't know

why, really. I guess because it was there. But the closer I got, the bigger it got—and every bit of it was lonely. It scared me to death.'' He raised himself up on his elbow and looked at her. ''I know how to be alone. Over the years, well, you know I've been alone a lot. After the mess I'd made of marriage to Clare, I thought it was better that way. But the closer I got to Texas, the closer I got to bein' empty, to seeing the rest of my life as nothing but empty. And…I've been empty for so damn long, Maggie. Too damn long.'' His voice broke, his throat closed. ''I just never knew it until I met you.''

It was more than he'd said in one breath in years, maybe in his entire life. It might be more than he could ever say again, unless Maggie helped him change. But for what it was worth, it was what he felt.

And Maggie understood. She edged up and kissed him tenderly. It was a long kiss, a slow, thorough, leisurely kiss that began to heat once more his barely cooled blood. But then she stopped kissing him and lay her smooth cheek next to his stubbled one, nuzzling him briefly.

''I thought I'd die when you left after we'd made love,'' she confided. Her voice had an ache in it that he'd never heard before, and he turned his head to try to see if her expression was as hurt as her words. It was. ''I wanted to.''

''No,'' Tanner protested.

''I did. It was awful. The ultimate rejection.''

''I didn't mean— I thought I was protecting you!'' he said with anguish. ''I didn't know what else to do. I sure as hell couldn't resist you. I'd just proved that. And you said you loved me—''

"I did!"

"Though God knows why you should have," he said grimly. "I was a jerk to you. I didn't want you here right from the start. I tried to get rid of you."

Maggie cocked her head, smiling slightly. "Did you?"

Tanner blinked, confused. "Didn't I?" Sometimes now he wondered just what he'd been doing. A corner of his mouth lifted, too. "Is that what Bates would call an approach-avoidance conflict?"

Maggie's smile widened and he noted the tiny dimple at the side of her mouth. "I think that's it."

"Well, whatever you call it, it was a hell of a mess," Tanner said. "I wanted you. Desperately. And I was pushing you away at the same time. I had to. It was pretty damned clear you weren't into one-night stands, and as far as I was concerned, a relationship had no future."

"And now it has." Maggie said the words simply, starkly and with absolute faith.

Tanner shut his eyes and considered the idea. A future. A marriage. He and Maggie together. Forever. And he believed it—perhaps for the very first time.

"It isn't going to be easy," he said.

"I think you've already proved that," Maggie replied dryly.

He grinned. "But you reckon you can bully me into making a tolerable husband anyway?"

"I think you're going to make yourself into a wonderful husband," Maggie told him.

Her confidence startled him. It was so much greater than his own. All the way back home during those hundreds of miles and hours of driving, he'd thought about his hopes, about his fears, about what a marriage would ask of him, about whether he would have the courage to open up, to trust, to try.

And then he thought about Maggie, about her love for him, as deep and abiding as any he could imagine. He thought about his love for her, which seemed new and fragile and untried.

He thought about telling Andy some months ago that the only way to learn something was by doing it.

The same, he supposed, went for loving. And for being a good husband. Maybe even, someday, being a father.

"What about kids?" he asked her suddenly. "Do you want any?"

"Of course I do. Lots of little Tanners. Half a dozen at least."

"Half a dozen?" He looked at her, horrified.

Maggie laughed. "Well, maybe two or three." Then she hesitated. "You want some, don't you?" she asked, as if it had just occurred to her that, given his earlier experience, he might not.

"I do. Very much. I never realized how much until just recently. Until I told you about—about the baby... I'd never talked about him at all. I'd never let myself think about all the things I've missed, that I wanted and was afraid to want. I'd never really grieved."

Maggie slipped her arms around him then, holding him close, kissing him. And the passion he'd kept banked for so long burst into flame. He kissed her back, hungrily, eagerly, fervently.

And then he loved her, fully and completely. He showed her with his hands and his lips and his body the things that he still couldn't find the words to say. And he gloried in her response, in her desire as she met him move for move, in the glow of love that shone in her eyes when together they shattered and at the same time became one.

"Maybe we could try for half a dozen," he said as soon as he could get his breath.

Maggie giggled and slipped her arms around him, hugging him close. "We'll try for a hundred if you want. I love you, Tanner."

He drew back, looking down at her, questioning, worried. "Tanner?" he echoed.

She gazed at him, touched his cheek, smiled. "Robert," she amended, touching her lips to his. "I love you, Robert."

He never corrected her again.

* * * * *

Also available in July 2000, look for
BLOOD BROTHERS, Desire #1307,
a unique two-in-one collection featuring Anne
McAllister and Lucy Gordon.

And in November 2000, don't miss A
COWBOY'S GIFT, Desire #1329, part of
Anne McAllister's popular
CODE OF THE WEST series.

Silhouette ROMANCE™

Escape to a place where a kiss is still a kiss...

Feel the breathless connection...

Fall in love as though it were the very first time...

Experience the power of love!

Come to where favorite authors—such as Diana Palmer, Stella Bagwell, Marie Ferrarella *and many more— deliver heart-warming romance and genuine emotion, time after time after time....*

Silhouette Romance— stories straight from the heart!

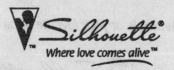

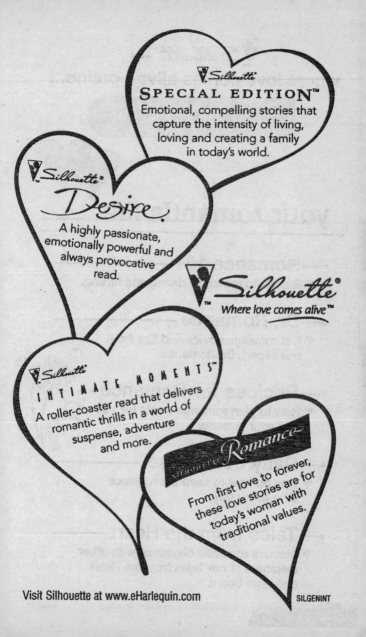

SPECIAL EDITION™

Emotional, compelling stories that capture the intensity of living, loving and creating a family in today's world.

Silhouette® *Desire*,

A highly passionate, emotionally powerful and always provocative read.

Silhouette®

Where love comes alive™

INTIMATE MOMENTS™

A roller-coaster read that delivers romantic thrills in a world of suspense, adventure and more.

Silhouette *Romance*—

From first love to forever, these love stories are for today's woman with traditional values.

Silhouette

where love comes alive—online...

eHARLEQUIN.com

your romantic life

Romance 101
♥ Guides to romance, dating and flirting.

Dr. Romance
♥ Get romance advice and tips from our expert, Dr. Romance.

Recipes for Romance
♥ How to plan romantic meals for you and your sweetie.

Daily Love Dose
♥ Tips on how to keep the romance alive every day.

Tales from the Heart
♥ Discuss romantic dilemmas with other members in our Tales from the Heart message board.